51%

51%

MATT WITTEN

To our children's children's children

Praise for 51%

"Matt Witten's 51% is a thrilling and adventurous glimpse into an all-too-possible, terrifying future, with characters full of heart who fight for justice against the cruelty of corporate-led AI. I couldn't put this book down—read it now!"—**Lee Matthew Goldberg**, author of *The Mentor* and *The Great Gimmelmans*

"Sharp, urgent, and impossible to put down. 51% is the dystopian thriller America needs right now. A premise so good I wish I had thought of it."—**Daniel G. Miller**, *USA Today* bestselling author of *The Orphanage By The Lake*

"Matt Witten takes us on a hallucinatory trip into a dystopian near-future in which fire and police departments, once-public hospitals, and even streets have been ruthlessly privatized, services go to the highest bidder, and the indebted sell themselves to profit-making syndicates. Witten's noir thriller moves at propulsive speed, intertwining beleaguered cops, corporate predators, underground rebels, and AI-driven supercomputers. It is a world whose seeds, Witten suggests, have already been planted."—**Fergus M. Bordewich**, award-winning author of *Klan War*

"Part cop-drama, part dystopian-nightmare, and completely unputdownable, 51% draws us into a near-future society where everything is privatized and monitored. When a young girl owned by a syndicate is murdered, an officer in the for-profit NYPD, Inc., takes on the case—against the urging of his colleagues, as this investigation is not likely to pay out. A thought-provoking and propulsive look at greed, autonomy, and resilience in a world gone wrong."—**Allison Buccola**, author of *The Ascent*

I

PART ONE

FREEDOM STREET

Chapter One

4:32 am

Haylee and Juke

In her tiny one-bedroom speck on 20th Street, Haylee Navarro tossed and turned. Finally she got out of bed, threw cold water on her face, and made coffee and oatmeal to fortify herself. She'd been eating this exact same breakfast for weeks and was stupefyingly sick of it, but her income had been pathetic lately—her last murder paid less than twenty dollars!—and oatmeal was all she could afford.

Especially with her syndicate taking so much off the top.

She glugged down the coffee, pushed her short, no-nonsense brown hair off her forehead, and banged her fist on the kitchen table. "You are tough and you are ready," she said out loud. She ripped open the kit she'd bought last night off the interdrone, taking out a Q-tip and a shiny green sheet of chemical paper.

All she had to do was swab the Q-tip inside her cheek, roll it on the paper, and within seconds she'd know. Either the paper would stay green, or it would turn *holy-shit-I'm-pregnant* red.

Or to be precise, she thought, *holy-shit-I'm-pregnant-broke-and-single* red. A picture of Harrison came into her mind, and she bit her lip to keep from crying. She raised the Q-tip toward her mouth, closed her eyes, opened wide—

—and her *I!* buzzed.

She thought about ignoring the call, but if that paper did turn red she'd need every dollar she could scrounge up. So she put down the Q-tip and double-tapped her phone. "Hello," she said.

As she waited for the bot at the other end to tap in, she told herself: *hey, cheer up. Maybe this will be the murder I've been waiting for.*

That was the crazy thing about the crime marketing biz: you'd bumble along for weeks, even months, living on oatmeal—and then suddenly, boom! You catch a homicide that pays you fifty Reagans.

* * *

Two miles away, at his studio speck in Brooklyn, Juke O'Keefe didn't hear his I! at first. His snoring and his hangover swallowed up the buzzing. But then it got louder, and at last he groaned awake.

He grabbed the phone to shut it up and read the text: "Dead woman on Freedom, corner of Canal." *Great*, he thought with a sigh. *No shortage of bizness in this city.*

He got out of bed—just a mattress on the floor—and headed for the kitchen. At thirty-three, Juke was tall with a bumpy nose and a two-day stubble. His deep-set gray eyes always seemed to be searching for something. He wasn't exactly handsome, but sometimes when he smiled, his whole face seemed to crinkle up. When that happened, women would give him a longer look.

But most nights for the past three years, ever since his personal life fell apart, Juke came home from his homicide detective gig with the NYPD, Incorporated, or as everyone called it the NYPDinc, and wound down alone. After a day of confronting unspeakable evil—and even worse, office politics—he generally felt unfit for human consumption.

He often wondered what it had been like working homicide back in his father's day, before the NYPD got privatized and bought up by a syndicate, before detectives had to raise money themselves to solve their murders. It must have been a hell of a lot easier.

Well scruck it, no use complaining. The pizza box on the kitchen table had a couple leftover crusts. Juke opened a creaky window to the icy pre-dawn air and set the crusts on the fire escape. He whistled to the wounded pigeon with ragged wing feathers and just two toes on his right foot, who he had nicknamed Fuck Y'all, that lived on the roof across the street. The bird flew off the roof, dodged the holographic signs littering the sky, and landed on Juke's fire escape, where he ate his breakfast.

Then Juke found a bottle of bourbon and poured himself a shot. This would be his last drink until after he solved the murder. It was the promise he made himself at the beginning of every case, and it was a promise he always kept.

* * *

Thirty minutes later a grimy gray dawn broke over the South Village. The pollution meters atop the light poles were on red, and many of the people hurrying through the cold to their early-morning gigs wore stylish, brightly colored masks.

Juke rode toward the crime scene on Houston Street, which had a special this morning: only two dollars per mile. He was in his beat-up old black Zan, the Department's standard unmarked, driver-free car. It was a Sri Lankan piece of crap, and the self-driving digitals were always giving out.

As the Zan turned left on Freedom, Juke opened the NYPDinc feed on his phone and read the scant available details of the case: the victim's body lay on the street. Apparent hit and run. She was found by a passing driver who called it in at 4:05 a.m.

Juke told his car to park several blocks from the crime scene. He always liked to walk to the scene instead of driving, so he could look around and get some context for what happened. Also, it gave him a little time to adjust to the fact he was about to see a dead body.

Home-brewed coffee in hand, he stepped past a vintage Starbucks that shimmered in the smog, flowing from green to purple and back again. Next door, a giant chirping holographic cricket advertised "Manhattan's Best

Bugburgers."

Up ahead, a line of droopy yellow tape read: "CRIME SCENE DO NOT CROSS—NEW YORK POLICE DEPARTMENT, INCORPORATED." But Juke didn't see any other cops at the scene. He couldn't see the body either, because a bunch of civilians had gone over the tape and were crowding around it, screwing up the evidence. Juke's hangover began hammering away, and he cursed silently to himself. It was way too early in the morning for this bugshit.

He guzzled the rest of his coffee, stepped to the civilians, and waved his badge at them. "NYPDinc. Get back over the tape. All of you, *now.*"

The two homefree men in the bunch were no problem, shuffling off quietly. But a stolid-looking woman in her fifties, a teacher or nurse maybe, stood there with arms folded, eyeing Juke up and down.

"You gonna find her killer?" she asked belligerently.

He shut his eyes for a moment. "Gonna try," he said as politely as he could. "Now step over the tape, please."

"You won't do a damn thing, you fucking Dinc," the woman sneered. "Except maybe look in her wallet."

The other civilians tittered, watching Juke to see how he'd handle it. He gritted his teeth. "Get over the tape—unless you have information for the NYPDinc. Who wants to be interviewed first?"

That did the trick. They all took off in a flash.

Now that they weren't obstructing his view anymore, he got his first good look at the body. The woman lay face up on the street three feet from the curb. She was young and wore silver high heels and a shiny metallic dress that was too short for the freezing November night. Her figure was lush, and she would have been beautiful except her face was bloodied and battered. Black tire tracks ran along her legs and the hem of her dress.

Juke could see his partner Haylee now too, kneeling by the dead woman's legs taking pictures. He was a little chunked at Haylee for not getting rid of the civilians herself, though he knew that wasn't technically her job. She was a Crime Marketing Consultant, not a full-on cop like him.

"Where the hell is our backup?" he asked.

Haylee stood up. "And good morning to you too. They've been here and gone."

"Oh for God's sake."

"A rich plastic surgeon got zapped on the Upper East Side. They all went up there."

"What a bunch of dicks." Sometimes Juke hated his fellow cops like so many civilians did.

"Can't say I blame 'em," said Haylee. "This case is a pretty obvious loser. Random hit and run, with a classic low-return victim."

Juke had been working with Haylee for a month, and he could tell she was good at her gig—even if they hadn't had much marketing success yet. So when she annoyed him like right now, he reminded himself she was only twenty-six and had been through hell lately, and cut her some slack. He bent down and examined the tire tracks on the dead girl's legs.

He said, "Somebody hit and ran, alright, but that's not what killed her. There's no bruising on her legs, which means she was already dead." He forced himself to look at the girl's bloodied eye, at the dark purple cheek that had been split open in two places. "Somebody beat her to death."

"They killed her, then ran her over?" Haylee said, dubious. "Why would they do that?"

Good question. Juke was guessing the killer drove here with the dead girl in his trunk, then dumped her on the street. But if he hoped to make her death look like a car accident, he did a piss-poor job. "Make sure you get good pictures of the tracks. Did we recover her phone?"

"It was gone when I got here."

So the killer could be a guy who knew her and wanted to hide her text and snap history.

Or else some rando stole the phone so they could sell it.

Except when a woman was killed in an up-close, vicious way like this, it was almost always a boyfriend, ex-boyfriend, or wannabe boyfriend. He touched her neck, gently pressing his fingers down. It felt cool but not cold yet, and there was still some give. He guessed she had been dead for less than three hours. He began studying the damage to her face—

And in seconds, without him even noticing, his hangover was gone. He didn't have time for it. With no M.E. on the scene, he needed to figure this out himself. More civilians gathered at the tape, and traffic noises picked up all around, but he barely noticed. As he knelt to check the girl for clues, he got the sensation he often had at times like these: he was entering another world, where time slowed and his father, who died when Juke was ten, stood ghostlike beside him, looking down at the body too.

When Juke was a kid, his Dad's bedtime stories were always about the killers he'd brought to justice when nobody else at the Department seemed to give a damn. Even back then, before privatization, there was pressure to focus on glam murders and slough off the homicides of the poor and unconnected. But his Dad's motto, said jokingly but meant seriously, was: "No victim too small."

Juke had always lived by this mantra—except once, three years ago. He'd never forgiven himself, and he thought he never would.

So now, as he leaned down and counted the dead girl's bruises, he softly whispered his Dad's words.

Meanwhile, Haylee stood beside him watching with growing alarm. *Please, not this again.* She needed to stop Juke from getting all emo stuck on this piece-of-crap murder, like he did two weeks ago with the Fernandez homicide. She couldn't afford another total money pit like that case.

Especially because her shiny green paper had in fact—God help her— turned red.

Juke was thinking out loud. "Looks like the killer used his fist, not an object."

Haylee raised her voice to distract him. "I linked this girl up. She immigrated from Crimea five years ago. She has no family, no boyfriend according to her profile, and nothing in her bank account."

But Juke was lost in his own world, his fingers brushing the girl's black hair off her cheeks. "She was hit at least five times, probably more…"

Haylee held her I! in front of Juke's face to show him the key stats proving the vic's poverty. "So in case you didn't hear me? Nobody will ever pay us actual money to solve this murder."

Juke looked up at her without speaking. Encouraged, she continued: "If we wrap quick enough and get her off to the morgue, maybe we can still get a piece of the doctor murder uptown. Get paid for a change."

But Juke kept eyeing her silently, like he was judging her. She stiffened. Sometimes he made her feel like such a bitch. She never used to be so cynical, but dammit, she told herself, nobody benefited—not the victims, not their families, *nobody*—when you wasted time on murders that, let's face it, would never get solved. Closing a case required a lot more than just hard work and dedication, you needed the ka-ching to hire forensics people, buy search warrants—

Juke said, "So no known boyfriend?"

"Right. No nothing."

Juke looked at the girl's short dress. "You think she was partying or working last night?"

"There's no record of any job on networld."

Juke figured either the girl didn't have a gig or she had one she didn't want to talk about. Or maybe like a lot of Gen Deltas, the generation that came of age around 2040, she kept her links minimal, trying to maintain a zone of privacy. "What's her name?"

Haylee didn't want to say it out loud, didn't want to make this dead girl any more real, but she had no choice. "Don't ask me how to pronounce it," she said, then read the name off her screen. "'Talia Qirimoglu.'"

He held out his hand for her I*!* "Let me see."

She gave it to him. But instead of reading the financial stats like she wanted, he stared at Talia's picture.

The girl had been twenty-four, with long straight hair and high cheeks. She was smiling, but her dark eyes seemed to hold a trace of sadness. Juke sensed those eyes had seen way too much darkness in their short time on earth. He couldn't stop looking at them.

"Oh man," he said.

"What?"

"Her eyes. They remind me of a girl I used to know."

"Oh tutti," Haylee groaned, "that's just tutti frutti. I guess now we can kiss all objectivity goodbye."

Juke knew he could get too intense for people. Most Crime Marketing Specialists only lasted a few months with him before requesting a transfer. So he tried to lighten up. "Doob, don't be such a pessimist. Maybe Talia has some ka-ching secretly stashed inside her digital toothbrush that we can get ahold of."

"Yeah, dream on. Her shoes say she's got nothing."

While far from an expert on women's footwear, he had to agree: those frayed plastic straps said Amazon Special at best. Then he noticed something on Talia's left ankle. He leaned closer.

"She was a fifty-one percenter," he said.

Haylee looked. "I don't see the scar."

Juke pointed. "Right here." Sure enough, right above the top strap was the telltale brown scar. It marked the spot where her syndicate had inserted a GPS biochip.

Haylee felt a twinge of discomfort, as she often did around fifty-one percenters. Like a lot of people, she wanted to believe fifty-one percenters were different: lazy, drug addicted, mentally ill...

But there was always the dark, submerged fear you could end up like them one day.

It would start so innocently. Maybe you make a deal with a syndie where they pay for your high school and college education in return for twenty percent of your income for ten years. Common enough; Haylee had made that exact deal herself. She didn't regret it. It had opened the door to her whole career. People had been making this kind of deal ever since the second decade of the century, when the student loan crisis got out of hand. Colleges and computer programming boot camps began offering their students "income share agreements," as they were called. Other schools soon followed. ISAs were heralded as a way to help low and middle-income students go to college.

But then private investors got involved and the syndicates moved in, and the pandemics and Eight-Year Depression hit. People started using the new investment system for all kinds of other purposes besides education.

Maybe you need a little money to do an unpaid internship, so you give up one percent. You need a car, and you give up another three P.

And then…

Then comes the killer blow out of nowhere, that you have no control over: you get in an accident and need a back operation, and can't work for six months, and before you know it: boom. You owe fifty-one percent of your income to the syndicate. Now they own you. They put a biochip inside you so they always know exactly where you are. They can make decisions about your life: where you live, what job you take. Ever since the Syndicate Job Creation Act got passed, they can order you to take mood-altering drugs to become a more productive worker. You basically belong to them until you finally get under fifty P again—but a lot of people never do.

Haylee shivered. The oatmeal rumbled in her belly. With her syndicate taking twenty percent of her income for the next seven years, she was already living on the edge. What if she had a difficult pregnancy, or her baby had genetic problems that needed fixing, and she had to give up another ten or fifteen P? That would push her way up into the danger zone. She and her kid could end up homefree, hunted by the predators that roamed the dark streets—

No, don't go there. Just do your gig and get through the day.

As she tried to refocus, she heard somebody behind them say, "Who cares if she's dead, I'd still do her."

Haylee and Juke turned and saw three teenage boys by the crime scene tape, laughing.

Juke stood and stepped toward them. All at once, the three boys saw the rage in his eyes. They stopped in mid-laugh. Then, without saying a single word to him or each other, they all turned and ran like hell.

As Juke and Haylee watched the boys tear off, Juke said, "See, this is what happens when we just bag 'em and tag 'em. People lose respect for human life."

"Quit being so damn high and mighty," Haylee snapped. Juke's eyes narrowed, and she was afraid she was going too far, but she couldn't stop herself. "Look, I feel bad for Talia. I lost a loved one too. But you gotta leave the Marvel bugshit for networld. Let's go find a murder where we can actually do some good."

What she really wanted to do was grab Juke by the shoulders and scream: *Look, I'm pregnant, okay? I need fucking ka-ching!*

Juke looked at her for a long moment, then down at the body.

"You're right," he said. "This case is a total loser. There's no way we should take it."

Haylee expelled a huge sigh of relief. "Okay, good—"

"But we're taking it anyway," Juke said.

Chapter Two

4:54 am

Safiya, Rey, and the Red Queen

In her drafty Lower East Side speck, Safiya Bassani-Jones' eyes opened. Immediately she sprang wide awake. *It's happening,* her brain shouted, *it's really happening. Tonight. In less than twenty hours!*

Safiya was thirty-one, with light brown skin and long, curly black hair that spilled onto the pillow. Her partner Rey's lean, pajama-clad body spooned her, his breathing calm and easy—sleep meds, Safiya suspected. Reaching her arm out carefully so as not to wake him, she took her computer off the night side table. She unrolled it and started writing a blast.

She wanted to get it written now, so she could send it out to networld the second they completed tonight's operation. If this op was successful, millions of people—hell, hundreds of millions!—would be eager to read her words.

She wrote, "My friends, tonight we are kickstarting the next American revolution—"

Suddenly her burner I! buzzed. *Who could be calling me at 4:56 a.m.—on my burner?*

She disentangled herself from Rey and slipped out of the bedroom, stepping around the two kittens, Tubby and Tubman, that ran up and rubbed against her feet. Shutting the door behind her, she double-tapped her burner and said quietly, "Whoever you are, this better be good."

A panicky voice gasped over the phone, "Oh God—she's dead! Somebody killed her. She's dead!"

What the hell? It was Diego, she realized. Despite the voice-altering app Rey had installed in Diego's I*!*, she still recognized his slight accent. "Who's dead? What are you talking about?"

"Talia!"

Safiya was too shocked to speak.

"I was supposed to meet her at one. She didn't show up!" Diego was breathing fast, talking in spurts. "I couldn't sleep. I had the news feed on. They showed a body, on Freedom Street. It was her!"

Safiya said, "Okay, listen: stay right where you are."

"No. I need to go there—"

"Bad idea. You're in no condition. We can't have them questioning you."

"But she's lying there. She's all alone!"

"No she's not. I'm on my way there right now."

"Oh God," Diego said. Safiya could picture his frightened eyes and the long, thick scar running down his cheek. She had never totally trusted Diego—he seemed a little volatile and high strung—but Talia had vouched for him.

He gulped and asked, "Is it our fault?"

She was wondering the same thing but said, "No, of course not."

He wailed, "But what if they know about us? What if the syndicates found out we're de-chipping?"

Safiya's pulse pounded. Diego was talking way too much, even if this was burner-to-burner. "It'll be okay. I'll call you," she said, and tapped off.

What a disaster.

* * *

Down in the basement of the old New York Public Library building at 42nd and 5th, the Red Queen was hard at work analyzing communications data. She'd been going at it all night long but wasn't tired yet, because above all else the Red Queen was relentless. Right now she was listening to a convo between two unknown parties using burners. When the man said, "What if the syndicates found out we're de-chipping?", she knew she had a major problem.

The Red Queen basically ran the New York division of the Syndicate Agency for Public Safety, descended from the old CIA. Her primary responsibility was coordinating the Anthill, a network of agentic AIs that gathered intel on the general population. The Anthill fed its mountains of data to regional Supers—or superintelligences—like the Red Queen. Along with her sisters in the other divisions , she constantly evaluated the incoming datastreams to stay one step ahead of the Resistance.

The Red Queen herself was imposing, weighing over forty tons including her massive cooling system. At five thousand square feet and painted fire engine red, her server racks occupied the entire main room of the basement.

Recently she'd grown even more powerful. Every I! sold in the country for the past five years contained secret, encrypted spyware that automatically uplinked the contents of all I! communications—call, texts, emails, and snaps—to the Anthill. This wasn't just about knowing who contacted whom, a power the Agency had held for decades and that the general population had come to accept. Now the Agency could actually see and hear every single thing gen pop did or said on their I!'s.

The Big Six syndicates that funded the Agency made sure the Red Queen was judicious with this potent new tool. She didn't use it to solve irrelevant crimes like murders or rapes. Instead, she searched for any communications that indicated somebody was cheating—or even *thinking* of cheating—the syndicates. Overheard phrases like "black market," "dark networld," or the surprisingly common "don't tell my syndicate" would instigate closer surveillance.

Even more crucial, the Red Queen raced into action whenever she encountered any hint of possible Resistance activity. The word "de-chipping" was an instant trigger for investigation, especially if it seemed connected to an actual plan. That was why, at 4:57 a.m., the Anthill had linked this burner convo to the Red Queen. She was working the case within a millisecond of hearing the magic word.

Within eight more milliseconds, she discovered both burners were GPS-protected—extremely suspicious—and both voices were digitally altered—even more suspicious.

No question: this whole scenario screamed Resistance.

These two carbon units needed to be ID'd, arrested, and severely neurointerrogated.

Fortunately, despite the suspects' efforts at secrecy, there were plenty of other ways to extract datascoop from their conversation. Their voices were immediately analyzed in depth for accents and regionalisms. Their word choices and vocal patterns were compared to every other I! communication in New York in the past year, in search of a match.

The Anthill began crawling with digital data.

The Red Queen was on the alert.

* * *

Safiya and Rey hurried a mile on foot to the crime scene. But they didn't want to get too close, in case the cops started questioning or videotaping bystanders. They watched through their I! cams from a street corner a block away, with anti-pollution masks hiding their faces.

Rey lifted his cam to focus on the crime scene, taking a deep mindlessness breath to calm his fears. Rey's full name was Reiji Matoshi. Twenty-six and tough-looking, he was lean and chiseled from the gym, with a military-style buzzcut and leather jacket. But he was born bougie, a professor's kid from the burbs, and sometimes felt way out of his depth fighting for the Resistance. Now was for sure one of those times. He'd gone to bed last night dreaming of being a Rez hero, but this morning Safiya shook him awake and told him Talia was dead—murdered!—and the syndicates might be onto them. If he and Safiya got jacked, they'd be thrown in prison for years, maybe decades.

He took another breath, trying to double his mindlessness like he'd learned in college psych, and looked through his cam.

Next to him, Safiya zoomed in for a better view—and saw the blood and tire tracks on Talia's face and body. She gasped. *Oh God, poor Talia.* Who could have done a thing like this to her?

She tried to remember if Talia ever mentioned any jealous exes or stalkers or anybody like that. But mainly when she talked about herself, it was about how she wanted to escape to Canada.

Safiya went through their history together, looking for clues to what happened last night. She thought back to the morning she first met Talia, at an espressaccino joint in midtown. Talia was sitting at a corner table, drawing a picture of snow-capped mountains beneath a starlit sky in the Canadian Rockies. Safiya fell in love with the picture, and with hopeful, sad-eyed Talia, instantly.

If Talia could somehow make it to the border she'd be free, because the Canadians rejected syndicate control. Where the US had gone one way, Canada had gone the other, especially since the trade wars. They would let her in, just like they admitted escaped slaves and war resisters in the past.

But the problem was, how could a fifty-one percenter like Talia possibly reach the border without getting caught? Her biochip revealed her exact GPS locay. If she ever came within a hundred miles of Canada, the syndie border cops would instantly track her and jack her.

Simply ripping the chip out of her body wouldn't help. That would set off a bio-alarm inside her blood which lasted thirty-six hours, emitting radio signals that went straight to the Anthill. She'd be a sitting duck. Rumor had it if you were a woman, the border cops took turns assaulting you before they locked you up. Then you got charged with ripping out your chip and damaging syndicate property.

But despite these obstacles, Talia never stopped dreaming of one day being free. And Safiya dreamed right along with her. For almost four years, Safiya's Resistance cell had been hunting for a strategy to help fifty-one percenters escape. They recruited biologists, chemists, and hackers to try and jam or disable the biochips' GPS signals. They failed again and again, but Safiya wouldn't allow them to give up.

Then, three months ago, a miracle happened: a friend of Safiya's, a doctor at Merck Hathaway General, discovered a way to beat the biochips at last.

Safiya and her cellmates—their affectionate name for each other—barely slept for a week as they debated excitedly what to do next. At last they agreed on a plan: they would invite a small, select group of pioneers, the "New York Nineteen," to de-chip and escape to Canada together. Then they'd blast out their triumph to the world and show everyone how to beat the biochips just like they did. Hopefully they'd inspire a tsunami of desperate fifty-one percenters all over the country to escape too.

Talia was a member of the Nineteen. But now, on the very day she was about to make her mad dash to freedom, she'd been murdered. Why? Was there a connection?

As Safiya tried to figure that out, Rey turned to her. He looked relieved, even buoyant. "There's only two Dincs at the crime scene and no M.E.," he said. "Looks like nobody's knocking themselves out to solve the murder. We should be okay."

"So you're glad Talia's killer won't get caught?" Safiya said, irritated.

"Hey, I hope they find the guy—but not if it means they find out about *us*."

Rey was right, of course. If the cops learned about their connection to Talia, they were screwed. Safiya shouldn't have gone off on him.

She shifted her cam to the left and saw one of the two cops: a good-looking brunette, on the tall side. A hologram advertising Hodu rollup computers hung low in the air, blocking her view of the other cop. But when the holo shimmered off and the cop stepped closer to Talia's body, she was able to see him—

Holy shit. Her heart started thumping.

Rey said confidently, "Those Dincs'll be gone in five minutes. They'll ship Talia off to the morgue and that'll be the end of it."

Safiya put her hand to her chest. "No, it won't."

"Sure it will. Why wouldn't it be?"

"'Cause that cop won't give a rat's ass if this murder is worth zero dollars or a million." She turned her face away in case Juke happened to look in her direction. "He'll investigate it as long as it takes."

Rey eyed her, puzzled. "Do you know him?"

"Yeah," said Safiya. "Way too well. We gotta get out of here."

Chapter Three

5:51 am

Juke and Haylee

Juke was examining the street near Talia's body for blood when he looked up and saw two people wearing masks—a tall, slender guy and a woman with long, dark, curly hair—hurrying away down the sidewalk.

Juke stood up, startled. The woman looked just like Safiya! From the back at least. Straining to see her better, he caught a glimpse of cinnamon skin under the side of her mask.

He was tempted to chase after her—but then caught himself. *Doob, get a grip. Three years later and you still imagine it's her every time you see some girl with dark curly hair.*

Besides, whoever this girl was, she had a guy with her. Safiya didn't want to be with Juke anymore. He had thought she was the love of his life, but she made very clear on that rainy morning three years ago, the day after Christmas, that she felt differently. Juke bit his lip hard and went back to work.

Meanwhile Haylee stood beside Juke, unaware of his turmoil. She was mentally running through her options, which didn't take long since she had none. It was exasperating. As Homicide Detective, Juke was the team leader with total say about which cases they took on—even though in Haylee's opinion, her job as Crime Marketing Consultant was just as important. Maybe even more so.

Her only hope now was that somehow they'd solve this case quickly and get it over with. She followed Juke to the sidewalk, where he looked up at a holographic sign: "THIS ROAD OWNED BY TCG SYNDICATE—3 DOLLARS PER MILE." Then he walked over to the nearest vehicle sensor. The syndicates used these sensors, which looked like old-school parking meters, to automatically debit the account of anyone whose car drove on their roads.

The syndies had owned these streets for fifteen years now, along with most of the other roads and highways in the country. It was part of the privatization trend that began early in the century, as proponents of small government gained power. First Medicare and Social Security went private, then the post office and national parks, then the schools… Now the syndies had taken over pretty much everything the government once ran.

Haylee basically thought the system worked okay. Sure, there were drawbacks; she'd read the Big Six owned eighty percent of the economy now, swallowing up small businesses too. And the government's safety net was gone. But on the positive side, having less government meant a lot less regulations, and taxes were just a fraction of what they used to be—the IRS was dead and gone. Now that was something to celebrate!

And best of all, Haylee knew: syndicates create jobs.

The electric eye on the vehicle sensor was blinking red. "The sensor's down," Juke said.

Haylee nodded. "Yeah, they've been down on this whole street since ten last night. Which means we can't ID the vehicles that drove through here." She couldn't resist a little dig: "Yet another reason this case dogs it."

Juke didn't respond to her last remark. "So that explains why the killer dumped her here," he said, looking up and down the block. "I'm not seeing any other cams, are you?"

"No."

"I should probably up the drone footage."

"I doubt it's worth the fee."

Juke growled his frustration as he walked back toward the body. He was always bitching to her about the NYPDinc farming out so much work—drones, forensics, autopsies—to outside contractors. He said, "Drone footage only costs two hundred—"

"Two fifty."

"Whatever. At the very least, the Department will give us five hundred seed money to solve this case."

"Which I'd prefer to spend on my own salary, thank you very much." Then, so she wouldn't sound overly selfish, she added: "The smog was at eight point five last night, and the nearest streetlight is way over there. The drone footage won't be worth anything."

Juke sighed, which she took as an acknowledgment that she was right. Down the block, a small traffic jam had formed where cars were getting stopped by the crime scene tape. Haylee got distracted as they began honking their horns in all kinds of different ways: screaming, heehawing like donkeys, cursing in foreign languages… Government deregulation gave people a lot of small freedoms, like programming their horns any way they wanted.

But Juke, unlike Haylee, had a gift for ignoring the clamor. He saw something on Talia's left arm, just above her elbow: four small bruises. His pulse quickened as he understood what these bruises meant.

He said, "The killer grabbed her arm. Squeezed hard enough to leave marks."

Haylee looked. The four bruises were so faint, they hadn't even registered on her. She had to hand it to Juke, he was stellar at investigating murders.

Too bad he did such a lousy job of picking them.

Juke placed his fingers on top of the bruises. "Killer was right-handed," he said.

"Well, that sure narrows it down." But then Haylee checked the bruises more closely. She needed to quit acting petulant and accept she was stuck with this case. If she couldn't bank off it, she might as well at least learn something.

Haylee had been a crime marketer for four years, ever since college. Her gig was basically sales: convincing people to donate money to the NYPDinc to solve crimes. She made pitches to the victims' relatives and friends, spoke at neighborhood churches, and put together crowdfunding videos. Her crowning achievement thus far was back in May, when a promising young cyberathlete was murdered and she gave a fundraising speech at a tournament in Nestlé's Square Garden. The homicide investigation netted twenty-eight thousand dollars in donations that very same night. Haylee had never even raised twenty-eight Reagans in a week before. She and Harrison drank some serious Chilean champagne that night.

But recently, after the NYPDinc cut back on investigative personnel, Haylee had begun doing a way bigger share of the actual crime solving. The more she learned about the nitty-gritty of detective work, and the more diverse her skill set, the better positioned she'd be for the new, even more streamlined NYPDinc.

Juke touched the back of Talia's right hand. "Looks like she fought back. Her hands are pretty scratched up."

Haylee nodded. "So if we had dollars for testing, we might find the killer's DNA under her nails."

Juke looked up at her. "Maybe Talia's syndicate will pay us to find her killer."

Haylee gave a short incredulous laugh.

"It's worth a shot," Juke said. He felt a little defensive now that he was treading on Haylee's area of expertise. "And if that doesn't work, we can always crowdfund the investigation."

Haylee folded her arms skeptically. "What's our hook?"

"Come on, she's a beautiful girl who was brutally beaten and murdered."

"Dime a dozen. Now if the guy was a serial killer, then we'd be in bizness."

"Doob, you're the marketing expert. I know you can turn this girl into a few bucks."

Haylee looked down at Talia. She had gorgeous legs, it was true, and a sexy if cheap dress; but her bloody, messed-up face ruined the whole effect. "Crime Marketing 101: dead body shots only help you ka-ching if the face is recognizable."

"So vidshop the blood away," Juke said. "We'll raise five thousand easy from do-gooders, hit the Crimean churches for more, and then solve the case snap-quick with DNA. After the Department takes their fifty P, you and me'll clear at least a Reagan apiece." He raised his hands triumphantly, like it was a done deal.

"Right, just like we did on the Fernandez case," Haylee said. "Fifteen bucks for two weeks' work."

"It was seventeen. Listen, kid, our luck is about to change."

"Good, 'cause I'm getting awful tired of having to wash my clothes in the sink."

Juke shook his head, frustrated. He wanted to explain to Haylee why he *had* to work this case, no matter how poorly it paid. He wanted to tell her what happened the one and only time he didn't follow his father's code.

But he had never told anybody about that, except Safiya, so he didn't say anything now. He looked up. A tiny spot of blue was trying to poke its way through the smoggy sky. "The light is perfect right now," he said, with way more optimism than that blue pinprick warranted. He stood next to the body. "Let's do this. Where do you want me? By her head?"

Haylee sighed, giving in. "Yeah, fine. Start out standing up, then we'll go to a squat shot."

As Juke finger-combed his hair, Haylee smoothed Talia's dress, making sure the tire tracks on the silver hem showed clearly. After all, that was the best visual selling point of this whole murder. Haylee always tried not to mess too much with criminal evidence, but you had to balance that against the need to raise dollars.

She stood back up and regarded Talia. She decided she'd shoot Talia's face first, then pan down her body and zoom in on the tire tracks...

Soon Haylee was visualizing the entire video in her mind. This was the part of the gig she loved best. Sometimes she dreamed of going to film school, then to Vancouver with all the other wannabes and trying to make it as a movie director.

Yeah right, she thought, *like I have the ka-ching for that—*

"How do I look?" Juke said, straightening his collar.

"Hungover."

"You mean incredibly handsome?"

Haylee wasn't having it. The honking had stopped for now, and they should start rolling before that changed. She raised her *I!* and zoomed in on Juke's face.

"Okay. One, two, three…"

She was about to say "Go!", but then heard chanting behind her, getting louder. She turned.

Oh no.

Six or seven pathetic fools in baldheaded pigtails and bright orange robes were dancing up to the tape, chanting "Hare rama, hare Krishna" and shaking tambourines. The Krishnas made it their special mission to show up at murder scenes and chant loudly, and recently they'd disrupted several of Haylee's videos.

She lowered her *I!* and snapped, "We're doing a video, cut the damn screeching—"

Suddenly she noticed one of the Krishnas was a young boy, about twelve. From underneath his bald pigtail, he stared straight at her with what looked like hatred.

Haylee's eyes locked on his—

In a flash she went back six weeks in time, and she and Harrison were at the front door of a speck in Brooklyn, and a young boy with a mohawk was pulling something out of his jacket—*shit, it's a gun!*—and pointing it at Harrison…

As Haylee stood at the crime scene, staring back at the young Krishna boy, the roar of that six-week-old gunshot exploded in her ears.

Without even thinking, she grabbed for her holster, yanked out her .38 Heston, and aimed it straight at the boy.

Everything went quiet and dark. She looked at the boy through a long hollow tunnel.

Juke moved carefully toward her, his palms opened wide in a gesture of peace. "Easy, partner."

His voice echoed. Haylee looked at her gun. She didn't remember pulling it. *Oh God, I didn't shoot anybody, did I?* She felt like she'd heard a gunshot.

"Haylee. Put it down."

No, I couldn't have. The boy with the pigtail is still standing there.

Everybody was staring at her: Juke, the Krishnas, the boy. A dark wet spot formed on his robe, at the crotch.

Haylee said, "I'm sorry."

She started to put her Heston back in its holster, but Juke said, "Why don't you give me that?"

She handed it to him, shamefaced.

Juke put her gun away in his jacket pocket and finally allowed himself to breathe again. He was almost as relieved as Haylee that she hadn't shot anybody. Then he turned to the Krishnas and said, "Okay, guys, take off, okay?"

The boy was more than ready to leave. But the Krishnas' leader said, "No."

Juke looked at the man in surprise. He was in his forties with tired grayish skin but piercing green eyes. "We need to honor the victims of violence," he said. "It's necessary for the karma of the city."

Then he started up with the Hares again. Almost immediately his people joined in, even the scared, piss-stained kid. "Hare rama, hare Krishna..."

Three teenage girls with Starbucks green-and-purple hair, "Starpunks," came across the street and joined the chanting, clapping their hands. An elderly woman carrying two large plastic bags began dancing ecstatically.

Too bad Juke never drank on the gig; a little slug of bourbon would go down real smooth right about now. This was getting out of control fast. Any moment, drummers would come and people would jump the tape and start whirling in a circle around the body. You could totally forget about preserving the evidence then. Meanwhile his partner just stood there, her face blank. Juke didn't think she'd go off again, but he wasn't a hundred P sure.

He turned back to the head Krishna. "Doob, you just had a gun pointed at you. I'd consider that a karmic sign to get the hell outta here."

But the man just smiled. "People are always pointing guns at us. We're used to it."

Juke kind of liked this guy. He empathized with religious people, no matter how nutty their beliefs. Ever since Juke's dad died in a random car accident, he had been agnostic himself, just a shade from atheist, but there was something about their searching he appreciated. He said, "Brother, we're honoring this girl too, okay? You need to quiet down so we can do our gig."

But the Krishnas and company responded by chanting even louder, while their leader said, "You don't honor a person by trying to make dollars off her."

Haylee stepped to the man before Juke could stop her. He hoped she didn't have a second gun. An inch from the leader's face, she snarled, "You baldheaded fuckers better move your funky karma elsewhere before we throw your orange asses in prison for obstructing a murder investigation. That's how we'll make our ka-ching—off your fines."

"All we're doing is chanting," protested the one woman in the bunch— maybe the twelve-year-old's mom, if this group believed in moms.

But their leader had had enough; maybe he was afraid of a second gun too. He backed away from Haylee and said, "We'll pray for your chi."

Then they all danced off down the street, the Starpunks and the elderly woman too, shaking their tambourines and Hare Krishna-ing as they went.

As the chanting faded in the distance, Juke eyed Haylee narrowly. "So glad to see you've gotten over your PTSD," he said.

Haylee froze. *He better not report me to the Captain.* She couldn't afford to be suspended—not now, of all times.

"I wasn't really gonna shoot him," she said, but it sounded hollow even to her. Her stomach churned.

"Coulda fooled me. Did you have a flashback?"

"Not really," she lied. But she felt like Juke was seeing right through her, so she added, "I mean maybe for a second, but that's just 'cause he had the same kind of pigtail as the kid that..." She broke off.

Juke frowned, watching her. "Are you getting any help?"

She forced a laugh. "Sure, 'cause I have so much money for a therapist.

I'm fine. Really."

"Get a psych-bot. They cost less than a cup of coffee." Not that he'd ever asked for help from an AI therapist himself.

"Who's got dollars for coffee?" Haylee said, and took out her I! "Look, are we gonna do this crowdfunding video or not?"

"You sure you're up for it?"

"Yeah, I'm sure. Let's go!"

Juke rubbed the back of his neck. "I don't know. Maybe you should go home for the day."

She panicked. What if Juke thought it over and decided he needed a different, more stable partner? "Please, Juke. Work is the best therapy for me. I'm okay, really I am."

Haylee waited for a few agonizing moments while Juke studied her.

He was thinking he really should send her home—hell, he should probably report her. But he couldn't bring himself to do that to her, not after everything this young woman had been through. And besides, he needed her help today. So finally he said, "We'll deal with this later. For now I'm holding your gun."

This was as good an outcome as Haylee could have hoped for. She was so relieved she couldn't speak. She just nodded.

Juke got back into position next to Talia's head and said, "Ready when you are, Vancouver."

He'd given her that nickname a month ago, when they shot their first video together. She was glad to hear his bantering tone come back. Looking at Juke through her I! cam, she had to admit he did look handsome right now—

Stop it. Whatever nonsense her pregnancy hormones were up to, she needed to shut them down. "Okay, hit it, Humphrey."

"Who?"

"Humphrey Bogart. From *Casablanca.*"

Juke looked blank, like he'd never heard of what was still, in her opinion, the best movie ever. She said, "One two three... Go!"

Juke cleared his throat and began, "Hi, I'm NYPDinc homicide detective

Juke O'Keefe. I'm here on the Lower East Side with a beautiful young woman named Talia—"

Haylee pointed downward, and Juke obediently squatted next to the body without missing a beat: "…who was brutally assaulted and murdered last night, then dumped in the street—where somebody ran her over."

Haylee panned to the tire treads on Talia's legs and zoomed. *Perfect.* She began to relax into her work, as Juke continued: "Talia was a sweet girl. But she was a long way from home, and her whole family is dead. Who will pay for justice for this girl?"

Way to hit the orphan button, Haylee thought, as Juke stood back up and gazed straight at the cam. "Folks, it has to be you. You can be heroes. Please—help us catch the monster who killed this girl before he kills again! Testing under Talia's fingernails for DNA will cost five thousand dollars."

Haylee smiled. Actually it would cost two thousand, but a little exaggeration never hurt. Her partner was in prime selling form this morning. Maybe he was right and this case would catch fire after all.

Juke pointed at the cuts on Talia's face and said, "Testing all this blood will cost even more. Anything you can give—fifty dollars, twenty dollars, even *one* dollar—will help make our city a safer place. Please, click on the red button at the upper right corner of your screen."

He put his hands in front of him and tented his fingers together, as if praying. "Talia will be eternally grateful. God bless you."

He held his pose as Haylee panned down to the body, then faded out.

"How'd I do?" he asked.

"Always fishing for compliments," she teased. "You did good, Humphrey. Let's do it again. This time say the words 'mystery' and 'rape.'"

"We don't know yet if she was raped."

"So? She doesn't have any family who'd be upset, and we'll get extra bucks."

Juke thought about it for a moment, then nodded. "You're right. It won't hurt the investigation any. I'll do it."

"And you should say it was a serial killer."

"No," Juke said firmly.

"Oh come on, be a sport."

Juke hated using serial killers as a marketing tool; that crossed a line for him. But all he said was, "It wouldn't work, people would know we're full of shit. The Department has cried serial K so many times, it's gone meme."

Haylee decided not to push it and risk getting Juke out of his rhythm—not when he was doing so well. She bent down over Talia's body and undid a button on her dress, showing a little extra cleavage.

"You don't think that makes her look too slutty?" Juke said.

"Trust me, that little flash of boob is worth a hundred dollars, easy."

Juke shook his head. "We're such whores."

As he took up his position beside Talia, Haylee held up her I! and asked, "Ready for take two?"

"More than ready." Juke was eager to get this video finished with so he could do some actual homicide investigating. The first hours after you found the body were always the most important. He needed to hurry up and get his ass over to Talia's speck.

Haylee said, "Okay: one, two, three… Boom!"

Juke closed his eyes briefly. Whenever he did one of these videos, he took a moment to channel his father's spirit.

Then he opened his eyes and gazed at Haylee's cam.

"Hi," he said. "I'm Juke O'Keefe. I'm here with a young woman who was brutally raped and murdered. And I won't rest til I find her killer."

Chapter Four

6:14 am

Safiya, Rey, and the Red Queen

Safiya and Rey hurried away from the crime scene, careful not to run so they wouldn't draw attention. An underground app showed them the best routes for avoiding syndicate street cameras, some of which had been disabled by hackers and Resistance members. They went past a gray concrete bunker that housed a Berkshire Vanguard Syndicate elementary school, BVS-22, and turned left. Safiya looked back to make sure Juke wasn't following them.

"I don't see him," she said.

Rey threw her a sidelong glance. This whole Dinc ex-boyfriend thing had come as a rude surprise. He'd known she had a serious boyfriend once, but she never talked about him. Rey was under the impression the guy had moved out of town.

Rey had met Safiya two years ago when he was living in Little Chile, working as an AI wrangler for a syndie and feeling aimless. One night, walking to a bar near Washington Square, he happened to see Safiya speaking at a "Break the Chains" flare.

Instant crush.

He spent the next year chasing her. First he joined the above-ground, more or less law-abiding arm of the Resistance and helped her organize flares. Then, because his comp sci background gave him major hacking skills, he helped her on some illegal ops. Finally Safiya trusted him enough to invite him to join her cell. Eleven months ago, the two of them succeeded in hijacking TikTagram and Foxbook for a whole day and blasting their newsfeeds with Rez propaganda. In the flush of that glorious escapade, they became a couple. They had shared more heady victories in the months since, and Rey loved thinking of himself and Safiya as romantic outlaws.

But sometimes, in his dark moments, he was afraid they wouldn't last. He'd never had a girl half as cool as Safiya in his whole life.

As they stepped around a big pothole in the sidewalk, he asked, "Are you still friends with this doob?"

Safiya shut her eyes for a moment, and a pained look flitted across her face. Rey figured she was annoyed at him for being jealous.

But Safiya was thinking about Juke. "I haven't seen him in three years," she said, as she pictured him at the crime scene, bent down over Talia's body.

God, he hadn't changed a bit. Seeing him with Talia reminded her of all the forgotten souls Juke was so taken with, doing his white-knight thing. She had been so in love with him once—

"What would this guy do if he found out you and Talia were connected?" Rey asked. "Would he protect you?"

"I don't know," said Safiya. "I broke up with him. He probably hates me."

Rey frowned, upset. "That's a scary thought. Maybe it's not a coincidence your ex-boyfriend is the guy investigating this murder."

"What do you mean?"

"What if he took the case 'cause he found you in Talia's digitals? He knows you and Talia were involved in seditious acts, and he wants to jack you—or at least scare the shit out of you."

Safiya shook her head. "No. Juke wouldn't go out of his way to hurt me."

Sure, their relationship got seriously chunked toward the end. After the terrible case that tore Juke apart, he started pushing everyone away— including her. Then, one Sunday night coming home from a murder in Queens, he drove off a bridge. He would have been killed if a couple of tree branches hadn't miraculously broken his fall. He claimed his car's digitals malfunctioned, but she always believed it was a suicide attempt.

She asked him to try neurostim or at least see a therapist, but he refused. He also refused to consider quitting his job or joining the Resistance, even though in her opinion working for the NYPDinc was killing him. Instead he started drinking heavily and got even more obsessed with his work. The more she tried to help him, the more he yelled at her and pulled away, until she couldn't take it anymore.

So yeah, the end had been pretty awful. But still… "He's not like that," Safiya said. "He's a good guy."

"He's a Dinc. He could've changed in the last three years."

She had to admit she didn't really know what Juke was like now.

"You think he still has a thing for you?" Rey asked.

She caught the plaintive tone in his voice and finally became aware of his jealousy. She truly didn't have time for that now. "I have no idea. Quiet for a sec," she said, as she buzzed Diego on her burner *I!*

Diego answered immediately, like he'd been waiting for her call. "Yeah," he said.

Safiya said, "Listen, we gotta figure out some stuff. Were your *I!* communications with Talia secure?"

She could hear Diego taking a breath, trying to stay calm. "Yeah, she always called my burner. From *her* burner."

"Any shared links?"

"No."

"Networld videos?"

"No."

Rey, listening in, asked, "What about Talia's computer?"

Safiya repeated the question into her phone. "What about Talia's Hodu? Did she keep it clean?"

"I think so," Diego said uncertainly.

"You think so?" she probed.

"Well, she might've been writing a graphic," Diego admitted.

"A graphic novel? About what?"

"About our escape. She wanted to blast it out as soon as we got to Canada."

Safiya and Rey exchanged a disturbed look. This was potentially terrible. She said into the phone, "How specific was Talia about—no, don't answer that."

She needed to know exactly what was in that graphic, and if Talia had put anything else on her Hodu about tonight's op. But it was too dangerous to ask that on the phone, even if they were using burners.

Safiya's mind raced, filling up with horrible scenarios. *What if Juke gets hold of Talia's Hodu?* It would take the NYPDinc tech guys about half a minute to hack in. If they found anything on there about the op, the NYPDinc would come after Safiya and Rey fast and hard—and so would the Agency.

Would Juke try to protect me? But he couldn't, not on something huge like this. Besides, he owed her nothing. Maybe he wouldn't pursue the case himself, but he'd give it to someone else, he'd have to. His Crime Marketing Specialist—probably that other cop at the crime scene—would realize she could get a fat reward from the Agency for reporting a de-chipping conspiracy, and she'd go for it. So would the tech guys. Safiya and Rey would be dead meat, along with everybody in the New York Nineteen.

Everybody who had trusted Safiya with their lives.

She didn't recall seeing Talia's computer at the crime scene. *What if Juke already took it?!* She composed herself and asked, "Do you know if Talia had her Hodu with her when she died?"

"Probably not, she was working last night. She always left it at home."

Safiya sighed with relief—but only for a second. She knew Juke's M.O. He would head for Talia's speck as soon as possible to search for clues. She needed to beat him there and grab the computer before he did.

"Where did she live?"

Diego gave her Talia's address in the Bronx, then asked tremulously, "Do you want me to go there and get it?"

It hit Safiya like a shot: *maybe Diego killed Talia.*

That was def the first thing Juke would suspect. And if he went after Diego, he'd likely find out about tonight's op. "No, you stay out of sight.

Don't go home and don't go to work. Don't even tell *me* where you are."

Diego's voice turned frantic. "What are the Dincs thinking? Who killed Talia?!"

"I don't know. Soon as I find out anything, I'll call you."

"Her getting killed right before we go on the run—it's gotta be connected."

Yes, Safiya thought, *but how?* "I promise I'll call you."

"Are we still on for midnight?" Diego asked.

"We're still on. Don't worry, I'll take care of this."

With that, Safiya double-tapped her burner. Then she and Rey headed for the subway to the Bronx.

They needed to move fast.

* * *

Down in the basement of Agency headquarters, the Red Queen listened intently to this second phone convo between the man with the slight Mexican accent and the woman who acted like his boss or supervisor.

Based on the tens of thousands of cases the Red Queen had worked on, she knew there was one thing that induced Agency-wide paranoia: the threat that some day the Resistance would discover a way to de-chip people. This was especially true now, with the Big Six planning a huge new expansion of the biochip program. They had an ambitious goal: to insert chips not just into fifty-one percenters, but into everybody who made any kind of deal with a syndicate—even for as little as one percent. Soon Congress, bought and paid for by the Big Six, would be passing a law making this legal. By a year from now, the vast majority of Americans would have chips. In twenty years, gen pop would forget there had ever been a time when they weren't chipped. It would all seem as normal and natural as a flu shot.

The syndicates used the latest biotech to prevent de-chipping, and so far it had worked brilliantly: in seven years, there had been virtually zero successful escapes. But with the Resistance constantly searching for new ways to beat the system, the Agency needed to stay vigilant.

Since the Red Queen didn't care about murder, the phrase "Who killed

Talia?" from this new I*!* convo didn't particularly interest her. However, "escape," "go on the run," and "Are we still on for midnight?"—combined with "What if the syndicates found out we're de-chipping?" from the same two parties' earlier convo—were deeply troubling.

Even more disturbing was the Red Queen's psycholinguistic analysis of the female party in these convos. She appeared relatively young, in her twenties or early thirties. Yet her clear, firm tone; emphatic word choice; steady speed of speech; use of repetition; and brief, focused sentence construction all indicated extremely strong leadership qualities. In fact she registered a 9.8 on that scale—almost unheard of.

This was a yellow-flag situation, at the very least. The Red Queen had already alerted all Anthill AI agents in the New York area to watch for any I*!* or networld chatter that might possibly be related to an attempt to de-chip tonight. Now she alerted her human handlers at the Agency as well. They needed to ID the two parties to these convos immediately and bring them in before they did any damage.

Especially the young woman—the leader.

She was dangerous.

Chapter Five

6:35 pm

Jeannie Bardach and the New York (Nineteen) Eighteen

Jeannie Bardach had been awake since dawn, totally wired. D-Chip Day was here at last!

She decided to get all packed up, even though she wouldn't be leaving til tonight. Safiya had said to put everything she wanted to take to Canada inside a small backpack. So now she rummaged through the bedroom closet in her sixth-floor midtown walkup, trying to figure out what to bring with her.

But how do you fit a whole life into something so tiny? she wondered. She debated whether to stuff a third pair of socks and underwear into her pack. But then she wouldn't have room for the green frog puppet that her son Nicholas had loved so much when he was a baby.

At age sixty-two, Jeannie was the oldest member of the New York Nineteen. The Walmart Lifestyle Syndicate took a fifty-one percent stake in her two years ago. That was when Nicholas, just out of ninth grade, hacked into the syndicate's financial system so he could go to high school for free. But he got caught and sentenced to seven years in a syndicate prison. It would have been longer, except Jeannie sold a large share of herself to pay off his hundred-thousand-dollar fine. Now Jeannie was hoping that when Nicholas got out of prison in five years, he would come join her in Canada and they'd start over together.

Jeannie finally took her socks and underwear and threw them decisively across the room. She pushed Nicholas's frog puppet into the tiny space in her backpack that was left. One day he would see that frog again and know how much his Mom loved him and had always loved him, no matter what he'd done.

All across the city, the eighteen surviving members of the New York Nineteen woke up on their final morning in the city feeling charged up as never before. Their years of indentured servitude were almost over at last. They were about to be free!

The eighteen were organized into six small cells that had no contact with each other. So most of them knew nothing about Talia's murder.

And they didn't have a clue that both the NYPDinc and the Red Queen were hot on their trail—and getting hotter.

Chapter Six

6:58 am

Haylee and Juke

The Battery was flooding again, and a slimy seaweed-crustacean odor hung in the air. Haylee shut the car windows as she and Juke rode back to headquarters. She wondered if being pregnant made it smell even worse.

Oh God. *Pregnant.*

The Zan pulled up at One Police Plaza, and Juke and Haylee got out. They walked up the front steps, passing a blue holo that read: "NEW YORK POLICE DEPARTMENT, INCORPORATED." Headquarters was a giant concrete behemoth, just as imposing now as it had been way back in the 1970s when it was built. But it was showing major signs of decrepitude, with chipped concrete and cracked glass. Ten-foot-high graffiti—one huge word, "RESIST!"—defaced the front wall.

Haylee said, "I hope the Captain's in a good mood."

"Could happen," said Juke. "I think I saw him smiling once five years ago."

* * *

The homicide squad room was looking a little seedy too these days. The stringy gray carpet had been there for two decades, and the cubicle walls, once white, had faded to beige. The bulletin boards were so pockmarked, you could barely find a place to stick in a thumbtack where it wouldn't immediately fall out.

But the squad room did have tutti digitals. An interactive map of the city with colored dots marking unsolved homicides dominated one wall. The most lucrative murders were lit up in bright red. These were the cases where the victim's family, friends, or crowdfunders had promised to pay at least one hundred thousand dollars if the NYPDinc caught the killer. Murders worth fifty thousand dollars lit up in blue, while yellow meant twenty-five K; pink was ten K; and anything under ten Reagans got a tiny gray dot that was barely visible.

About a year ago, a new digital display—**"HOMICIDE TEAM OF THE MONTH"**—premiered on the opposite wall. It honored whichever team raised the most ka-ching. This month's winners were Detective DeAndrey Jackson, a big, bald, arrogant guy in his forties with a loud gold necklace that Juke always wondered if he'd stolen from a murder victim; and his partner, Crime Marketing Specialist Neil Campbell, a skinny, shifty-eyed guy in his thirties. Underneath their smiling pictures was a caption: "CONGRATULATIONS TO DEANDREY AND NEIL **RAISED $227,800!"** The two of them had won the prize for three months straight and represented everything Juke hated about the NYPDinc.

Juke and Haylee walked past the display with their Captain, Gary Burgess. Fifty years old with greasy brown hair, pasty white skin, and a paunch, he looked more like an accountant than a cop. But this was his fifth year running the Homicide Squad.

Burgess was watching Juke and Haylee's raw, unedited, crime-scene video on his rollup. Hopefully he'd give their video a thumbs up and feature it prominently on the Homicide Squad link. Then it would have a much better shot at bringing in donations.

On the rollup screen, Juke squatted next to Talia's body, imploring, "Please—help us catch the monster who killed this girl!"

Burgess double-tapped his rollup and the screen went blank. He said, "I'm just not feeling it. Where's the boo hoo? Where's the grieving relatives?"

"She's an orphan," Juke said. "She has nobody to grieve for her. That's the whole point."

"But there's nothing in this video that'll make gen pop cry. No tears, no ka-ching."

Haylee frowned. Now that she was watching the video through Burgess's eyes, she had to admit she agreed with him. Her first instinct—*loser case*—had been right all along.

But she felt like she had to back up her partner, so she said, "This is a tragic story. She was a beautiful girl with her whole life ahead of her."

Burgess snorted dismissively. "She's not a ten—or even a nine. Seven point five at best."

Haylee could see Juke clenching his fists. But he kept his voice even. "Just give us a quickie, that's all. Put us on top of the homicide feed for one hour."

"I reserve that spot for videos that might actually ka-ching," Burgess said. He turned to Haylee. "What did they teach you in Brooklyn, anyway? You need the vic's face to be recognizable. I'm surprised you don't know that."

Haylee felt her face growing warm. In the nearby cubes, several detectives and marketing specialists were openly eavesdropping, and she heard somebody laugh.

"I'm planning to vidshop most of the blood away. I can bring the victim up to an eight or nine, easy," she said, trying to sound confident.

As Burgess led them into his office, he said, "Now might not be the best time for you guys to ask for special favors." He sat behind his desk and didn't motion for them to sit, too. Not that they could have—his office only had one extra chair. "You two have been partnered up for a whole month now. Do you have any idea how little ka-ching you've brought in?"

Juke said, "Counting the three bucks I found in the john last week?"

Burgess ignored the attempted joke. He pulled up the squad's stats on his wall. The Juke O'Keefe/Haylee Navarro team was way down at the very bottom. "You two only raised sixteen K. That's thirty-seven below median."

He leaned back in his chair. "Navarro, I did you a rock solid approving your transfer from Brooklyn—"

"I appreciate it—"

"You said after what happened to your fiancé, you needed a change of scenery. I respected that. But maybe you weren't ready to go back on the job. When you can't perform, it doesn't only affect you—it affects your partner and the entire Squad."

Haylee's mouth dropped open. *He's not threatening to fire me, is he?*

Juke stepped in. "None of this is Haylee's fault. The Fernandez case took a week and a half longer than anybody anticipated."

"And yet you still didn't close it."

Juke's eyes flashed. "I would've closed it no prob with half-decent forensic support."

Burgess slammed his hand down on the desk. "Goddammit, O'Keefe, if you want support, quit wasting our resources on gray-dot cases. You're homicide. You're supposed to be a cash cow. Instead all the Department makes off you guys is fifty percent of sixteen grand. That won't keep the lights on around here."

Haylee decided to keep her mouth shut from here on in. Juke would have to fend for himself. She was so not looking forward to telling Burgess she was pregnant. He might fire her, since laws protecting pregnant workers had long since been found unconstitutional. Wouldn't that be tutti: looking for a new job with a belly out to here.

Meanwhile Juke was thinking how much fun it would be to turn Captain Burgess upside down by his ankles and shake him. The only thing this prick cared about was his end-of-year bonus. Juke said, "You know full well I have a better clearance rate than anybody else on the squad—"

"When's the last time you cleared a red-dot? Or a blue, or a yellow—hell, I'd even take pink!"

Juke gritted his teeth. "I'm building up goodwill for the whole squad. The more killers we catch, the better media we get. That helps us with *all* our cases—"

"O'Keefe, here's the deal," Burgess said sharply, hitting some keys on his rollup. "I'm linking the five hundred seed money into your account. You want more than that, you're on your own."

A measly five hundred bucks to solve a homicide with no obvious clues or suspects? It was what Juke had expected, but that didn't make it any easier. "Fine," he said, "but put our video on top of the feed for just thirty minutes. We'll see what kind of response we get—"

"You want the prime spot? Then bring me a deadly home invasion, a serial killer, a vicious pedophile—"

"Actually," Juke said, hating that he was saying it, "based on the efficiency of the killer's blows to Talia's face, we have reason to believe he *is* a serial killer."

Burgess laughed out loud. "Nice try."

Then he leaned forward and pointed a finger at Juke's chest. "No more deadbeat cases. I want to see real dollars on this murder—fast. If you can't ka-ching at least three Reagans by midnight tonight, you're done with this girl. Cold-case her and move on."

Then Burgess got on his *I!* and turned away, dismissing them.

As Juke and Haylee walked out of Burgess's office and back into the squad room, Haylee said, "That went well." She could feel everybody in the room looking at her.

Juke said, "I need you to enhance that video and blast it out to networld as soon as you can."

"What are you gonna do?"

Juke had already been forced to squander a key hour of investigation time. It was infuriating. He buttoned up his jacket.

"I'm going to Talia's speck," he said, as he started out of the squad room. "Gonna bust this case open before lunch."

Chapter Seven

7:32 am

Safiya, Rey, and Diego

Safiya could still remember the exact day when she decided to join the Resistance full-time. It was July 4th, four and a half years ago, a few months after she moved in with Juke.

Safiya had grown up in a poor neighborhood in Elmhurst, with an Italian father and a Black mother who were underemployed all their lives. Multis like Safiya made less money on average than Whites, and were more likely to be owned. Their poverty was self-perpetuating: if you wanted to go to college but had low earnings potential, the syndicates charged you a higher percentage of your future income. The exact formulas were secret, but it was generally believed that if you were Black or Multi, the syndies would hit you with an extra five to ten P, depending on additional factors. After all, Black people were more likely to encounter roadblocks on the job market, and their higher incarceration rates ate into their earnings. So it made sense that the syndies upped the ante.

All in all, it wasn't only a question of racism, it was bizness. With no government regulations stopping them, the syndicates charged higher P's from poor people of all races.

They did give out occasional high school and college scholarships in inner-city neighborhoods; and Safiya, at the top of her class since preschool, had received one. Her two brothers Perry and Cyrus went to prison for ten years for stealing from a syndie electronics store, but Safiya went to college and medical school. She dreamed of doing good in the world and giving back to her community. After med school, she became an internist at Merck Hathaway General Hospital.

But Safiya rapidly discovered that working at a syndie hospital was incredibly stressful. Every day she was forced to inflict heart-wrenching choices on patients who were desperately sick, but broke. These experiences began to change her. She was working hundred-hour weeks and maintaining a relationship with Juke, but she began getting involved in the Rez, going to meetups and flares.

On that hot July 4th afternoon, she stepped into the hospital room that her patient Ginny Martinez shared with another eight-year-old girl. The other girl was asleep, or drugged into unconsciousness, so Safiya and Ginny could have this conversation privately.

She sat down beside Ginny's bed. Even though she was always in a rush, seeing countless patients per day, she always tried to sit when speaking with someone. It reminded her to slow down.

"Hi Ginny," she said.

Ginny turned toward her. Her skin was young and fresh-looking, almost translucent, and her chestnut brown hair was long and lustrous. Her eyes, though, were tired and red-rimmed, the eyes of an old woman.

"How are you doing?" Safiya asked.

"I don't know," Ginny said. "How am I?"

They hadn't prepped Safiya for this in medical school. She supposed she could simply tell Ginny the truth: *If your parents had eighty-five Reagans for personalized cancer treatment, you'd almost certainly survive. But they don't, and they're already sixty percent owned. So bottom line, you're going to die.*

But how do you tell an eight-year-old girl that she could be cured, she could have a long life, the doctors knew how to fix her—but it wasn't going to happen, because basically the world didn't give a shit about her.

This girl didn't need to know that.

As Safiya struggled to come up with the right words, Ginny beat her to it.

"I'm gonna die, aren't I?" she said.

Safiya reached out and touched the girl's beautiful cheek. "I'm afraid so, Ginny. I'm sorry."

Fifteen minutes later, Safiya came out of Ginny's room, went to the bathroom, sat in a stall, and cried. Then she walked out the front door of the hospital and never came back. She joined a free clinic that offered medical care to the homefree, supporting herself by working under the table at restaurants and food co-ops. Above all, she devoted herself to the Resistance.

Juke told her she was doing this out of survivor's guilt; she felt bad making a good living when her brothers and so many of her childhood friends were in prison, owned, or both. But Safiya didn't care if he was right about her or not; she only knew that she *had* to do Rez work, otherwise she felt hollow inside, like she was missing a piece of her heart.

That was the path that led her to where she was today: sitting in the bowels of the 28th Street subway station with Rey, waiting endlessly for a subway to the Bronx, where Talia's speck was. The subways were always slow, because the syndicates had learned from predictive analytics that minimal track maintenance was the most cost-effective way to go. But the long wait was especially exasperating this morning, since Safiya was desperate to beat Juke to the speck.

As she and Rey fidgeted, a street musician set up camp right next to them. He belted out, "I'm gonna make a brand new start of it, in old New York." At eighty years old with a threadbare coat and no socks, he looked way too bedraggled for a new start, anywhere. But he sang full-throated, head thrown back, with the enthusiasm of a twenty-year-old, and the waiting passengers loved it.

Safiya thought about Talia, who had been so eager to make a new start in Canada. Now she was lying dead on the street. Of all the New York Nineteen, Talia had been her favorite. Even after everything she'd been through, escaping war-torn Crimea only to become owned, Talia held tight to her optimism.

Safiya closed her eyes for a moment. She prayed she wasn't responsible somehow for Talia's death.

Sitting next to Safiya, Rey looked around the station to make sure no Dincs were heading their way. He took a deep breath. He desperately needed to talk some sense into Safiya. So he tried to sound reasonable and keep the panic out of his voice as he whispered, "I'm not sure we should go ahead with Chocolate tonight."

This was their code name for tonight's op. It came from their inside joke that the only type of chip that should ever be inserted into people is a chocolate chip. Rey continued, "I think we ought to lay low for a month til Talia's murder gets forgotten. If everything's cool, we go for it then."

"No, we're all set to go right now," Safiya said quietly. "We stole the cars, everybody's trained—"

"But if Talia's murder has something to do with Chocolate—"

"It's probably just some wacko off the street."

Rey shook his head, frustrated. "Come on, you're being stubborn. If your old boyfriend is half as good as you say, he'll find out Talia was planning to de-chip. We should extinguish every trace of this op. Chop up our computers and flush them down the toilet—"

"No!" Safiya snapped, too loudly. A man in a gray metallic suit lifted his head from his I! and watched them. Safiya waited til he looked away, then continued, more quietly, "Even if the cops do find out, it'll take them longer than a day. We'll be safe proceeding tonight as planned."

Rey murmured, "That's so comforting. It's okay if the Dincs jack us, 'cause it won't happen til at least tomorrow?"

"If we wait a month, Chocolate will never happen," Safiya said in a fierce whisper. "We're dealing with nineteen people"—*no, eighteen*—"under incredible pressure. Somebody'll get jacked and neuroed, or snort up at a bar one night and say the wrong thing to the wrong guy. We need to do this *now*, before shit goes south."

"Shit already went south." Despite his efforts to stay calm, Rey could feel his voice rising. "You're so obsessed, you can't see that. Going ahead with this op right now would be insane!"

"Rey, we promised we'd free these people." Safiya put her hand on his arm. "We have a chance to do something incredible tonight. Something that would change the whole world! What if this chance never comes again?"

Rey felt like such a chump. When Safiya got all passionate like this, looking into his eyes, he got swept along by her. He knew he was very likely marching to his doom, and he shouldn't let himself get pulled in—but he knew he would anyway.

The train toward Talia's speck finally creaked into the station, just as the old man sang the grand climax, "It's up to you, New York, New York!" Everybody in the subway station cheered.

Safiya stood up and looked back toward Rey. He stood too, and she squeezed his hand.

"Thanks, Rey. When midnight comes, it's gonna be awesome."

"Assuming the Dincs haven't grabbed us by then," he couldn't help saying, as he followed her onto the train.

Their subway ride to the Bronx was predictably, agonizingly slow. But at last they made it to Talia's stop. They hurried up the stairs, pulling up their parka hoods. Between that and the anti-pollution masks, they'd be protected from the cams.

Safiya couldn't stop thinking about Talia. She asked Rey, "So who do you think did it?"

"Did what?"

She stared at Rey, amazed at how little Talia's murder seemed to have affected him. All he cared about was not getting jacked himself.

But then she thought, *I expect too much from people. He's legit terrified.* "If Talia's murder had something to do with Chocolate… Who did it?"

"Oh," he said. At least he had the decency to look embarrassed. "Well, the most likely guy would be Diego."

She had considered that possibility, but quickly discarded it. It wasn't something she wanted to even think about. "No, Diego loved Talia. You heard him on the phone, he was devastated."

"He could be faking it. I know he acts real sweet and everything, but they've been having problems lately."

"They were about to run off to Canada together!"

"Maybe she changed her mind. I got the vibe he was afraid she might be into some other guy. When's the last time you talked to her?"

Yesterday, and she did seem upset about something—no, this was ridiculous. "It wasn't Diego," Safiya insisted, as they came out of the subway, hooded and masked, and headed for Talia's speck.

* * *

Diego Montoya sat on a bench in the northwest corner of Washington Square, where street hustlers took on all comers at cybersports, and pulled his thin dark jacket tighter around him. He rubbed the thick, jagged scar riding down his cheek, a habit of his whenever he was agitated or scared.

Eight years ago, Diego was celebrating his seventeenth birthday with friends at a neighborhood bar when a bunch of rich preppies from Riverdale walked in, wanting to show everybody how badass they were. They started a fight, pulled a couple guns, and the bartender ended up dead. Diego got this scar along with two bullets in his gut.

He could have gotten the scar fixed if he was willing to surrender three P for ten years. But he was already giving up thirty P to fix his gut and seventeen for a lousy lawyer, because somehow the NYPDinc decided to charge him for the bartender's murder even though it was the fucking preppies who shot him. So Diego had elected not to fix the scar and now he was marked for life.

The irony was that underneath his angry scar and tough demeanor, Diego was mostly a sweet guy, a cat lover like Talia. She had understood that, had found the kindred spirit inside him. At night they'd walk down to the pier and sing old folk songs as they shared a bottle of wine. They dreamed of escaping together to the Canadian Rockies. They'd have a big family: three kids, maybe even four. On weekends they'd all go camping in the mountains.

Here in the U.S., the syndicates hovered over everything, everywhere you looked. They owned the parks. They owned the water you drank and showered in. They owned the sky—or at least, they owned the holos that hung overhead and obscured the sky. Between the holos and the smog, you could go years without seeing a single star and months without glimpsing the moon.

In Canada, Diego and Talia would see the moon and stars every night. They promised each other they would always treasure them.

Their ship did have problems, it was true. A couple of times he got jealous and blew up at Talia in ways that frightened her—and him too. He couldn't always control the anger he'd felt inside him ever since he was seventeen. The fight that caused his scar also gave him a severe concussion, and at times he was scared he still had some kind of weird aftereffects from that.

But still, when Safiya invited Talia to be one of the New York Nineteen, she said she'd only do it if Diego could come too. He jumped at the idea despite the risks. As a forty-seven percenter with no biochip, he might have been able to successfully escape to Canada on his own. But he didn't want to go there without Talia.

Diego thought about her, and the fight they had last night, and his scar began itching like crazy. He willed himself not to scratch, balling his hands into fists and shutting his eyes.

When he opened them, a forty-year-old man in a gold-flecked business suit walking past the bench was staring at him in alarm. Either the fists scared him, or it was Diego's anguished face.

Diego didn't stop to think. Growing up in the Bronx, you didn't let anybody look at you like that. "What the fuck you looking at, asshole?" he said. He felt for the old-school brass knuckles in his pocket—the ones that had belonged to his father before he took off for parts unknown.

The man hurried off. Diego felt a sharp pang of envy for this guy and his fancy suit, along with a sudden urge to chase after him screaming. What he would scream, he wasn't sure.

He was starving, but broke. He needed to talk to somebody before he went insane. He had lost his shit last night—and he better not do anything like that again.

He got on his burner and called the Icelandic immigrant he knew just by his first name, Sölvi. Besides Talia, Sölvi was the only other member of his mini-cell. So that's who he turned to now, even though they weren't all that close.

As soon as Sölvi tapped in, Diego asked, "Did you hear about Talia?"

Chapter Eight

7:58 am

The Red Queen and Karolyn Ford

Down in the basement of the old library, the Red Queen knew instantly that "unknown male, 88%-certainty Mexican parentage"—the same man who was part of the disturbing phone convos earlier—had just called a second unknown male. This second male was determined to have an Icelandic accent so strong he was probably a recent immigrant. Like the other party, he used a GPS-protected burner with a voice-altering app.

The Red Queen listened as they convoed about the death of the female, Talia, who had been mentioned before. Then they began talking about chocolate. That confused the Red Queen for a full sixteen seconds before she realized "chocolate" was code for something.

Then the 88%-certainty Mexican said, "I think we're still de-chipping at midnight," and the Icelandic immie instantly cautioned him: "Careful, ro"—slang for bro, the Red Queen knew—"watch what you say. The electrons have ears, ro."

This was the third suspicious convo, and now there were at least three conspirators involved. Like humans, the Red Queen was a big believer in the number three. Two instances of something could easily be a coincidence, but when you hit three, it was time to quit messing around.

Somebody was planning to de-chip at midnight—and they were serious enough to create a code name for it.

The Red Queen upped the yellow-flag designation on this case to red and immediately double-buzzed the Director and Deputy Director of the New York Division. They hadn't responded to her earlier notification. Carbon units were so unreliable. This time they better get to it right away.

* * *

In her office upstairs from the Red Queen, the new Deputy Director, Karolyn Ford, felt two quick buzzes in her ankle chip. A double-buzz meant a red-flag alert, so she looked up at the flashing red flag on her wall.

Karolyn was forty-two and had transferred in from Tampa three months ago. She was sexy in an icy way, in her perfect makeup, pearls, and fitted navy blue suit with Portuguese pencil skirt. The other New York agents had begun referring to her as the White Queen.

She wasn't born that way. She grew up poorer than dirt, the daughter of one of the last family farmers in Macon County, Alabama. She had to sign away a full forty P for ten years so she could go to the top-flight high school and college she wanted. For many of those years she lived in specks that were too tiny to have tables, so she ate her meals sitting in bed.

But Karolyn never stopped believing she was smarter than all the rich, connected kids she worked with at the Agency. Now she was almost at the very top of her profession, a prime example of how the syndicate investment system provided opportunity to everybody, regardless of race, religion, or class. She knew a lot of people just like her: kids from poor backgrounds who sacrificed and worked hard and were now rising up the ranks in corporate America. If it weren't for the syndies, they'd all be dishwashers or homefree drug addicts or whatever.

Karolyn had zero patience for the Resistance losers who wanted to overthrow the New American Revolution and turn the clock back to the dark days of big government socialism. Didn't these people ever read any history? That ideology had driven the economy into the ground. It created generations of welfare-addicted takers and penalized people who were truly productive and willing to work.

Karolyn's own parents blamed losing their farm on the syndicate system. But she knew that her parents, like so many others, weren't taking ownership of the bad choices they'd made. If they had just purchased GMO heat-resistant seed from the syndicates, their farm might have survived the droughts. Sure, it would've cost them a few P—but it would have been worth it. Their own stubbornness had destroyed them.

But what really glitched her about her parents was that even after all these years, they still hadn't forgiven her for going to work for the syndies. In their minds she'd gone over to the "other side." When she called to tell them about being promoted to Deputy Director in New York—*Deputy Director! New York!*—they never congratulated her. Instead her dad started in about some syndicate outrage back home, and her mom babbled on about Karolyn's sister Tracy. Tracy was a lazy drunk who still lived only a mile from their childhood home and eked out a living doing God knows what, with two little brats who got their used shoes from a syndicate-funded charity. Karolyn had been sending her mom and dad money from her paycheck every month for years, and no doubt a lot of that went straight to Tracy. But despite everything she'd done for them, all the things she'd accomplished in life, her parents still—let's face it—loved her sister more.

It wasn't even a contest.

As Karolyn studied the flashing flag on her wall, she drank her third espressaccino of the morning. During the two decades since she left home, her rising success had been accompanied by a few private vices to relieve the tension, mainly caffeine, sugar, and bot sex. She'd put on a good ten pounds of ice cream weight since moving to New York, and her skirt strained at the hips. There was so much stress in this city, so much Rez activity! A lot more than in Tampa, that was for sure. Her ankle chip double-buzzed at least five times an hour here.

She decided this would be her last espressaccino til at least after lunch. The drug-testing chip the Agency had inserted in her midsection, like they did with all employees, didn't test for caffeine, sugar, or sex—or so they said.

But still, she wanted to cut down. She would do it on her own, because she wasn't about to go to one of those eleven-step programs. The last thing she needed was to sit in some church basement and listen to people blather on about their Hyper Power.

According to this new red flag, two unknown males were talking on their *I!*'s about escaping to Canada. *Big deal,* Karolyn thought. Fifty-one percenters were always dreaming about escaping—it was like breathing for them. Why was the Red Queen even bothering her with this? She'd given the case a quick once-over this morning when she came in. The case was yellow-flagged then. She didn't get why it was now being upgraded to red.

She started going through the convo transcripts again—and then she saw it: the word "de-chip." In not just one but two of the convos now. *Fuck, how did I miss that?*

She quickly read further and saw the convos had a lot of other disturbing aspects too. The parties were extremely specific, talking about "midnight" and "tonight." The woman in the first two convos had stunning leadership metrics: 9.8, at least psycholinguistically, and Karolyn had always found that a reliable measure. Put it all together and you had at least three people, one of them a very strong leader, engaged in a specific and immediate plan to de-chip.

She shot up straight in her chair. What if this wasn't fools ranting but the real deal? *What if the Resistance de-chips somebody tonight—on my watch?!*

All of Karolyn's old fears that she'd never amount to anything, that she'd end up like her parents or her sister, came bubbling up out of the cobwebs of her mind. She should have noticed "de-chip" as soon as she came in this morning. Hell, she should have noticed it *before* she came in, while commuting in her car! But she had so many red and yellow flags to deal with, sometimes things got lost.

She downed the rest of her espressaccino and focused. She still had lots of time before midnight to stop this op. The woman, the 9.8 leader, was the key. It made no sense: how could anyone who was a 9.8 be so stupid she'd join the Resistance?

It hit Karolyn that her Mom would love her more if she was a Rez leader like this bitch. She shook that thought away. She needed to find the 9.8 and neurointerrogate her. That would eliminate the danger.

The wild card in this case, which Karolyn felt the Red Queen hadn't sufficiently focused on, was: who was this "Talia" that the Mexican guy kept going on about, and how did her murder fit into all this?

Maybe Talia had learned about tonight's op and was about to go to the cops for a reward, so one of the conspirators zapped her. Or she was planning to de-chip and escape herself, and that pissed somebody off big-time.

As insanely brilliant as AI was, it hadn't yet reached the point where it couldn't use a little human guidance now and then. So Karolyn told the Red Queen to investigate the recent deaths of any women named Talia and search for any connections they might have to the Resistance.

Karolyn's boss Raja, the Director of the New York Division, was on a conference call with the NYPDinc brass about the recent pro-Rez flares in Brooklyn. As soon as he got off the phone, she'd tell him what was going on. Hopefully by then the Red Queen would have more intel.

Karolyn's ankle chip double-buzzed again: another red flag, somebody hacking vehicle sensors in Red Hook. She decided she better have another cup of espressaccino after all.

She told herself to look at the bright side. Now she had a chance to prove herself to Raja and everybody else in the New York Division. If she jacked this 9.8 woman and terminated a major Resistance conspiracy, she'd be a hero.

Chapter Nine

8:38 am

Haylee

At One Police Plaza, Haylee was hard at work in her cube, editing the fundraising video from the crime scene.

Juke's performance had been so strong she didn't have to cut around it much. Her main task was prettying up the victim. She needed to vidshop Talia's facial blood and bruises so that viewers could feel this beautiful girl's pain without getting so grossed out they'd tap to a different video.

This was the kind of delicate line you had to walk with a lot of crimes. Do it successfully, balancing heartbreaking with sexy, and you could majorly ka-ching.

So Haylee moved the ugliest cuts away from Talia's eyes and mouth to the edges of her face. That matched Juke's verbal description that she'd been beaten in the face, but without losing the loveliness of her deep dark eyes. Hopefully viewers would be as affected by those eyes as Juke had been.

After working up Talia's face, Haylee gave her a little extra cleavage. Then she spent about ten minutes—more than she had time for, really—picking out nice shoes. She finally settled on a sweet pair of Buccis with two-inch purple heels and sparkly silver straps that perfectly complemented Talia's dress.

Haylee doubted the shoes would make any real difference. When it came to getting donations, it was the face and breasts that mattered, not the feet. Anyway, no matter what vidshop tricks she pulled, she was still highly skeptical that she and Juke would ever bring in enough resources to solve this girl's murder.

Haylee felt guilty about that, even if it wasn't her fault. But at least she could give the dead girl a stylish sendoff, she thought as she adjusted the straps on the girl's heels. That had to be worth something.

Once the video was done, Haylee checked the time: 8:52. Not bad. She'd always prided herself on being fast. They needed to ka-ching by midnight, or Captain Burgess would throw them off the case. So that gave the video fifteen hours to do whatever magic it could.

She was about to launch the video into networld when her computer buzzed. It was her ob/gyn's office, informing her there had been a cancelation and the doctor had an opening in an hour and twenty minutes.

All the fears she had been trying so hard all morning to clamp down jumped up and screamed for her attention. She wanted to run someplace far away.

Instead she pinged a yes to her doctor's office. It was all the way uptown in Washington Heights, but she might be able to get there in time if she blasted out the video fast enough.

First she hit the general crowdfunding sites, starting with the granddaddy of them all: Kickass, formerly Kickstarter. Then she sent the video to all the crowdfunding sites that specialized in solving crimes and jacking bad guys, like Crimebusters and LetsFuckEmUp. After that she hit the locally oriented, socially conscious sites dedicated to improving life in New York. With government gridlocked and ceding power to the Big Six, and people giving up on politics, crowdfunding had become a major way for people to get involved.

She also sent the video to general news vlogs and social media sites, though she doubted a garden-variety killing like this one would break through the clutter. Finally she pushed it out to all the Crimean-American linkhubs she could find.

Then she grabbed her purse and threw on her coat. She didn't want to miss this appointment. It might take her weeks to get another one.

She knew she would have to make major decisions about her baby, *soon*. And these decisions would not be hers alone. She'd need to work it out with the syndicate that partially owned her.

She rushed out of the squad room as fast as she could without drawing attention to herself, and ran to the subway.

Chapter Ten

8:52 am

Juke

As Juke rode his Zan toward Talia's speck, he clicked on a forensics database. Then he sent them photographs of the tire tracks on Talia's legs. For fifteen bucks, they should be able to identify the make and model of the vehicle that had run her over.

But a minute later they texted him: "Unidentifiable." *Oh for Chrissake.* Couldn't they at least narrow it down to a few possibilities? He wanted to call somebody at the database, but he knew he'd never reach any actual humans there.

He took another look at the photos himself. He had to admit, the tire tracks did look a little fuzzy. It was almost as if…

Wait—is that possible?

He enlarged the photos. Sure enough, they were double tracks. *Somebody ran over Talia twice.*

As the Zan turned left, Juke closed his eyes and imagined it: *The killer drags Talia's dead body out of his car. He's so furious, he leaves her in the middle of the street to publicly humiliate her. He backs up over her body, then rides forward over it, enjoying the bumps when the car mashes her.*

This was a man with rage so overwhelming he couldn't control it. His homicidal ferocity lasted even after the girl was dead.

Juke stopped breathing and his whole body went rigid. He'd come up against sick monsters like this man before. *My God, this guy is a serial killer after all—or if he isn't yet, he will be.*

Juke checked his ETA at Talia's speck: sixteen minutes. *Too slow.* He put the car on manual so he could drive over the limit. Then he slammed his foot on the gas and roared onto the bridge leading to the Bronx.

Three years ago, in summer, Juke had caught a case where the murdered girl was a poor immie nobody important cared about, like Talia. She even had sad dark eyes like Talia. After four days, Juke and his partner had only raised a hundred bucks, and he had nothing but thin leads to follow. So he abandoned the girl and moved on to a more lucrative case.

He told himself he was just following his captain's orders. But the truth was, he did it willingly.

Less than two months later, the girl's killer went on a rampage at an outdoor concert and murdered fourteen more people, before he finally shot himself. Some of his victims were children as young as five.

Juke almost ended up dead too, shortly afterwards. He was driving home that Sunday night from Queens, distracted and more than a little drunk, and decided to take the wheel himself. What happened next was still fuzzy in his mind. He'd followed his headlights right off the bridge, and he wasn't sure if he'd done it on purpose.

He hadn't wanted to scare Safiya, so he made up a story about a digital malfunction. But he was damn scared himself. In the three years since then, he had sworn to never again abandon a murder victim. He would hew even tighter to his Dad's mantra, and maybe one day he'd start to feel okay again. So now he drove even faster, veering right onto Opportunity Boulevard and racing toward Talia's building, his heart burning. He still believed the killer had known Talia personally, based on the up-close way he had killed her, using his fists. That should make his investigation easier.

But half a mile away from Talia's place, he was forced to come to a screeching halt. The Teng Chao Global Syndicate, which owned Opportunity, was doing road work, installing new underground vehicle sensors that would supposedly be unhackable. According to the holographic traffic sign hovering above them, all cars going in this direction would have a twelve-minute wait.

Juke fumed as more precious minutes of prime investigative time slipped away. He looked past the holo and saw, in the hazy distance, the Koch Syndicate Housing Projects—four tall concrete buildings that used to be public housing. Talia had lived in Building Two.

Somewhere inside Talia's speck, Juke believed, lay the secret to her murder. Out of frustration, he honked his horn. But in a fit of whimsy a while back, Juke had programmed in a cowboy yodel: "Yippie-aye-oh, yippie-aye-ye-ye..." So it wasn't a satisfying sound, and did nothing to quell the restless turmoil building inside him.

Midnight. He better solve this murder by midnight, or it would fry his ass forever.

II

PART TWO

OPPORTUNITY BOULEVARD

Chapter Eleven

8:56 am

Safiya and Rey

As Juke sat in his car, stymied, Safiya and Rey walked up Opportunity Boulevard to Talia's housing project as fast as they could without drawing attention.

An armored tank guarded the entrance. Three heavily armed syndicate cops in bulletproof vests stood outside the tank, stopping vehicles and pedestrians and scanning everybody's hands and irises. That way the Syncs could prevent wanted criminals from entering the projects and wreaking havoc. Also, when they found somebody with an outstanding warrant or lien, they put him in custody and got a cut of the ka-ching that eventually shook loose. They were part security guards, part bounty hunters.

Safiya and Rey needed to somehow enter the projects without getting ID'd. If things went sideways breaking into Talia's speck, they couldn't leave behind any digital crumbs that would bring Juke down on them.

But there was no obvious way to sneak in. The syndicate had placed barriers at the ends of all the side streets to prevent vehicles and pedestrians from entering. If Safiya and Rey tried to jump a pedestrian gate, an alarm would sound.

They hid behind a pile of old tires and scoped the area. Surely, Safiya thought, the many lawbreakers who lived in these projects must have found an alt way to slip in and out. Growing up, she'd had friends in the projects down the street, and their favorite Saturday night entertainment was digging tunnels under the barbed wire fence.

Rey saw it first, through his I*!* cam. "Third street up on the left," he said. "The vehicle sensors are down. Pedestrian digitals'll be down too."

Safiya looked. Sure enough, the sensors were blinking red. Somebody must have hacked in and knocked them out. This was getting more common, as Resistance cells, freelancers, and random teenagers lulzed sensors to make transportation free for all. It was yet another sign the country was ripe for revolution, she thought. All people needed was a spark—and she would give it to them, tonight. "Let's go," she said.

They made their way through the neighborhood, past the barred doors and boarded up windows, past the moms out walking their babies and the old people lying homefree in the bushes. Finally they came to the pedestrian gate at the end of the third street.

They did recon from behind a rusty old pickup. The digitals were indeed down. But Building Two was a good eighty feet away, and the Sync checkpoint was disturbingly close. If they tried to sneak through the gate now, the Syncs would spot them.

"Now what?" Rey said.

"Hang on. We'll wait til they're not looking."

They huddled behind the pickup for fifteen minutes, bouncing from foot to foot to ward off the cold. Finally one of the Syncs stepped away from the tank, heading for a Quarterpotty to relieve himself. Meanwhile the other two Syncs got busy checking a white van full of day laborers.

"Now!" Safiya said. She and Rey raced for the side of the building, where they'd be out of sight of the Syncs.

They leaned against the side wall catching their breath. Then Safiya poked her head out just enough to see around the wall. Nobody was heading their way; the two Syncs were still focused on the van. Maybe they'd found themselves a little payday, some poor sucker who owed a couple hundred bucks in sensor fees.

"I think we're good," Rey said.

Safiya nodded. "How do we want to work this?"

Rey hesitated, then asked cautiously, "What do you think would be best?"

Safiya sighed, annoyed he hadn't answered her directly. She knew exactly how this would play out if they talked it over. They'd end up agreeing Safiya should be the one to break in while he stayed out here and stood lookout. After all, women were less suspicious than men to both humans and algorithms. It one hundred P made sense that when there was a highly dangerous mission where somebody might have to scam their way through, it should be her doing it, not Rey.

But still. This shit got old.

"Fine," she said, trying not to act chunked, "I'll go up there. You wait here for a minute, then hit one of the benches out front. If Juke comes—"

"I'll buzz you right away." Rey held her close and kissed her. "Good luck, babe."

Babe, thought Safiya. *Hardly.*

Out of nowhere, she found herself wondering if Juke and his tall brunette partner were sleeping together. She thrust that thought aside and pulled up her coat collar. Then she came around the wall and headed for the front steps. She wasn't sure how she'd pull it off, but she had to make it inside the building and into Talia's speck without getting caught. Once she got there, she needed to grab Talia's computer and anything else dangerous.

And she needed to do it fast, before Juke arrived.

Chapter Twelve

8:58 am

Karolyn

Karolyn was meeting—finally—with her boss, Raja Chandrasekar, in his large corner office at the Agency. He'd been on the phone for an hour with the NYPDinc Commissioner—and then he made Karolyn wait twenty minutes more, even though she buzzed him this was red flag. It was typical behavior for Raja, a toady to his bosses but an arrogant jerk to his subordinates.

Raja's office was decorated with photos of himself with famous syndicate CEO's. He was fifty, the son of a wealthy syndie family from Seattle, and he'd been running the New York Division for four years. A lot of people thought he was in line to run the entire Agency one day, and if that happened, Karolyn hoped to take his place here in New York. So she bit her lip around him and humored him as best she could.

"There's been no further digital noise?" Raja asked, tapping his fingers impatiently on his desk. Karolyn could tell he was distracted, worrying about the Brooklyn flares, the subject of his call with the Commissioner. Last night's flare had attracted over five thousand Resistance sympathizers, and you could hear the drumming all the way from Manhattan. So Raja just wasn't getting how potentially dangerous this new conspiracy was.

Karolyn said, "Not yet—but it hasn't been that long."

Raja waved his hand dismissively. "We've had a thousand of these de-chipping scares since I've been here. It's always just a bunch of nutcases crying into their booze about how they'll get rid of their chips once and for all by chopping off their legs."

Karolyn saw Raja's eyes drifting toward his rollup, probably thinking about his next meeting. Her voice rose. "Sir, this isn't about nutcases. This woman has 9.8 leadership metrics."

"So? She could still be totally toons. You'd have to be, to try and beat the syndies at the de-chipping game."

"But what if she's for real? What if she's actually figured out a way to do it?"

Raja sighed and reluctantly pushed away his rollup. This was a possibility, however remote, that he couldn't ignore. "Look, the Anthill is already on the case. What more do you want us to do?"

"We should look into the murder of this girl Talia Qirimoglu." The Red Queen had given Karolyn the details, sketchy though they were. "The Anthill hasn't found any connections yet, but my gut tells me it's tied to this conspiracy."

Raja folded his arms. "You think these clowns are still planning an op tonight? Sounded to me like this murder was scaring them off."

Karolyn nodded toward the button on Raja's desk. "We can ask the Red Queen."

Raja pushed the button, bringing the Red Queen into the convo, and said, "Case 20563. What are the chances tonight's op has been called off?"

The Red Queen took a moment to analyze the specificity, intensity, and tension levels shown by the three parties in the intercepted phone calls. She considered the time intervals between communications.

Then, in her refined, aristocratic British accent, copied from old tapes of the twentieth-century politician Margaret Thatcher, she said, "Chances of them postponing or canceling 'Chocolate' are approximately seventeen percent. Their leader is extremely determined."

Karolyn wanted to make sure if this case blew up on them, she was on record as having brought it to Raja's attention. This convo with the Red

Queen was being recorded. So she asked, "Do you think it's possible this Resistance cell may have discovered a way to de-chip without setting off the bio-alarm?"

The Red Queen replied, "Given security concerns, the Anthill has not received precise data on the biochip, so I don't know its vulnerabilities. But if I were to base my answer solely on the confidence, urgency, and seeming intellectual acuity of the cell's leader, and the faith her two known followers exhibit in her, I would put their chances of successfully de-chipping at fifty-four point six percent."

That got Raja's attention, alright. He jolted upright. "Fifty-four? Fuck me."

Karolyn said, "We need to expend every resource to stop these people. It has to be our top priority."

"Absolutely," the Red Queen agreed. "One hundred P."

Raja hit the button, irritated, silencing the Red Queen and returning their convo to privacy. "Fine, you've made your point for the record."

Karolyn said defensively, "I just wanted to know what she thought—"

Raja waved her off. He stood up and began pacing. "If you believe this homicide is connected to the conspiracy, then let's put together a team to investigate it."

Karolyn shook her head. "It would be a tactical mistake for the Agency to get involved directly in a two-bit street murder. Word would get out. Somebody'll tip off the Resistance, and they'll take increased security measures or go on the run."

"Then what the hell do you suggest?"

Karolyn leaned forward in her chair. "We keep our involvement secret by piggybacking onto the NYPDinc's homicide investigation. We find out what they've learned and take it from there."

Raja frowned thoughtfully, then snapped his fingers and grabbed the holographic dart that instantly appeared in the air in front of him. He threw the dart at a target that manifested on the opposite wall. Bull's eye.

Karolyn would have been more impressed, except she knew Raja had rigged the game so he *always* got bull's eyes and his guests never did. What a putz.

Raja asked, "Is the lead detective someone we can trust?"

She knew what was worrying him. There were Resistance moles inside the NYPDinc, and lately they'd been giving the Rez advance warning about Agency ops.

"The detective is questionable," Karolyn admitted. "He's a white knight type, straight out of Marvel. The kind of guy who could easily be a sympathizer—though we have no evidence of it."

Raja growled, exasperated. "Scrucking Dincs. We oughta go in there and neuro every single one of 'em. What about his partner?"

"The Anthill's looking into her, but they don't have a solid read yet." Karolyn put her hands on Raja's desk. "But I do have one guy I'm positive we can trust: the Captain of the Homicide Squad, Gary Burgess. Class A shithead, but there's no way he's a symp."

"How do you know?"

"I've had dealings with him." She gave a quick grimace of distaste. Burgess had tried to pick her up at a law enforcement dinner last month, even though he was about seven percent as attractive as she was. "The Red Queen agrees with me. This is a guy who's just out for himself. He'll jump at the chance to kiss Agency ass."

"Good. Make sure he keeps us posted on everything his detective finds out." Raja fired another dart and got another bull's eye, of course. "And tell him to be on the lookout for the 9.8 agitator. She sounds like the head of the snake."

"You got it," Karolyn said, standing up. "If our 9.8 is connected to Dead Girl in any way, Detective O'Keefe will lead me straight to her. And he won't even know he's doing it."

Chapter Thirteen

9:04 am

Juke, Safiya, and Rey

After a twenty-minute wait, the holographic traffic signal turned green and the cars on Opportunity Boulevard started moving again. *Finally,* Juke fumed. He drove as fast as he could, weaving in and out of lanes. His ETA at Talia's housing project was now four minutes.

***

Meanwhile Safiya was walking up the front steps of Talia's building. She tried to ignore the three guys in their twenties hanging out on the top step drinking their first canned beers of the day. Their cartoonish arm muscles said they hit the roids hard, and their faces were tatted with long blue chains.

Safiya had known plenty of guys like these as a kid. And she had seen similar tatted chains. She liked to think of them as a political statement—*we're living in chains!* But in reality the tats indicated these guys were members or hangers-on of a violent street gang called the CGs. That was short for either Chain Gang or Carrion Gangsters, depending on who you asked.

The biggest of the three CGs, who despite his youth had a beer gut and two missing teeth, gave Safiya's breasts a long appraisal as she came toward him. "Nice!" he said.

She didn't respond. Instead she walked past them, hoping nobody would grab her ass, and put her I! up to the scanner on the front door. Rey had programmed the I! with over fifty thousand skeleton ID's. Hopefully one of them would work.

She stood waiting as the scanner cycled through her IDs. Dammit, nothing was happening—the thing refused to turn green. The CGs watched her, amused. The shortest one, with a thick unruly beard down to his chest, said, "Whatsa matter, honey, fake ID not working?"

The third CG, an acne-ridden, sallow-faced guy in a Cyber Giants cap who was more wasted than the others, began making noises somewhere between laughing and snarling. The CGs stepped up behind Safiya, so close their decaying beer-soaked breath smelled overpowering.

Her eyes still on the door, she tried to gauge quickly how dangerous these guys were. Growing up, she'd heard horror stories about gang rapes in the projects in the middle of the day, with no Dincs or Syncs arriving until hours later. She wondered if she should scream for Rey and try to make a run for it.

Instead, she half turned. "Fucking syndie fuckheads locked me out!" she said, banging on the door. "Two weeks behind on my motherfucking rent, and I got two fucking babies. Gonna kill these fucking motherfuckers. Fuck!"

The CGs glanced at each other, torn between evil and empathy. A moment passed. Finally the big guy with the missing teeth took out his I! and gallantly held it to the scanner. When the green light went on, he held the door open for her.

"Thank you so much," said Safiya.

"No worries," said the guy.

The short, bearded CG added, "And if you want help with your rent, come see me." He tugged at his crotch to make sure she caught his meaning.

The third guy laughed or snarled or both. Safiya hurried inside.

* * *

Rey stayed out of sight by the side of the building for about a minute, then stepped out just in time to see Safiya disappear through the front door. *So far so good,* he thought; apparently she'd made it inside with no hassle.

The Syncs at the checkpoint didn't seem to be paying him any attention. Trying to act like he belonged here, he headed for one of the splintery wooden benches out front of the building and sat down. No way Juke could ride up without Rey spotting him, and he'd be able to alert Safiya in plenty of time. He settled in for a long surveillance.

But the Koch Syndicate had reduced garbage pickups to once every two weeks, and today was Day 13. When the wind shifted direction, the stench of putrefying garbage immediately assaulted him. No matter how hard Rey had tried to transform himself into a tough working-class doob, there was still a part of him that liked things tidy and *clean*, like the suburb where he grew up. Being stuck here surrounded by malodorous despair made him twitchy all over.

He felt in his pocket for the synth coke he picked up at a med store yesterday. He hadn't done any yet, except for one small bump around dinnertime last night that hardly counted. Given all the pressure he'd been under for the past three months setting up tonight's op, it was a wonder he wasn't a complete danghead by now.

It was in the low thirties, the coldest day since last winter. If he had to wait for Safiya in this stinking, freezing cold for who knows how long, he should have a little bump first to help him make it through. He looked around. The three CGs on the front steps looked plain evil, and the short one seemed to be checking him out. If he snorted up out here on the bench where they could see him, he was asking for trouble.

So he went back to the side of the building where he could snort in peace. To be extra safe he went behind a dumpster, despite the stink. He began the complicated process of snorting synth without losing any to the November wind.

Behind the dumpster, with his nose in the synth, Rey never saw Juke riding up.

* * *

At the armored tank, Juke held up his badge. The tall, mustached Sync he showed it to raised a dubious eyebrow. "Not going in that hellhole alone, are you?" he said.

"I'll be fine," Juke replied.

The Sync shook his head, but waved Juke through.

He rode past the CG graffiti, broken booze bottles, and tween girls rehearsing their dance moves. Then he told the Zan to park by the side of the road, in easy view of the Syncs. That way, even if some CGs identified the Zan as a Dinc vehicle, they'd be less likely to smash it up.

He got out of the car and headed for Talia's building.

* * *

Up on the seventh floor, Safiya was having trouble breaking into Talia's speck. She tried Rey's skeleton IDs on Talia's lock—but again none of them worked. *Thanks a lot, Rey.*

Time for Plan B: deactivate the digital alarm with the hack disc she carried, then try to kick the door in. She wasn't sure her networld karate training was up for that, and it would make way too much noise—

"Can I help you?" a man's voice said right behind her, making her jump. Why hadn't she heard him coming?

As soon as she turned, she understood the absence of footsteps. The man was in his mid-thirties, with a look of curiosity on his broad, dark-skinned face—and he was in a wheelchair.

Safiya smiled ingratiatingly. "Oh hi. I'm having trouble with my key."

"I bet you are. This isn't your speck."

"Right, it's my sister's. She must've linked me the wrong key," Safiya said.

"Bugshit." The man pointed at her I*!* "You were running skeletons."

Safiya's blood pounded in her ears. She better make a run for it. But the wheelchair blocked her path to the elevators. She'd have to shove Wheelchair Guy out of the way—not an attractive prospect.

Especially because that bulge in his jacket pocket looked an awful lot like a gun.

* * *

Outside, Juke walked along the cracked sidewalk toward Talia's building. He passed a dying oak tree with big red letters spray-painted on the trunk: "RESIST!" This was hands down the most popular graffiti slogan in New York—unfortunately for Juke, because every time he saw it he thought of Safiya. She had "RESIST!" tatted on the small of her back.

Three years ago, Juke had considered joining Safiya in the Resistance, more seriously than she probably realized. He wanted to believe. He went with her to some flares and read a lot of the material the Rez put out.

But while he agreed with the goals of the Rez, he couldn't help feeling that Safiya and her friends were hopeless dreamers. Even worse: hopeless dreamers who would end up in syndicate prisons. He grew angry and depressed that Safiya was hurtling headlong toward a terrible fate.

Now he came to an oasis in the dreary landscape: a playground with big leafy trees and freshly watered green grass. A shiny new jungle gym with blue swings and red and yellow slides beckoned brightly.

But the playground was fenced in by barbed wire, with a flak-jacketed Sync guarding the gate. A sign above him read: "ENTRANCE FEE $1 PER PERSON Children Under 3 Free."

As Juke came closer, he saw a young mother in a thin patched coat and her two little girls, about two and four years old, gazing longingly at the jungle gym through the barbed wire. "Mom, *please,*" the older girl begged.

"Come on, let's go," her mom said. She tugged at the girl's hand and pulled her away from the playground.

The girl started to cry. *"Stop it,"* her mom said.

The girl's little sister let out a huge wail. Their mom turned frantic. Juke could tell she was about to lose it and scream at them—

"Hey," he said.

The mom turned and eyed Juke warily as he walked toward her. He found two old-school dollar coins in his pocket and handed them to her. "Here," he said with a smile.

She stared at him wide-eyed. Her kids stopped crying to stare too.

"Thank you," she said.

"No worries," he answered, and headed for the front steps to Talia's building.

* * *

Upstairs, Safiya tried to convince the man in the wheelchair she was utterly innocuous. "Maybe I got the speck number wrong," she said. "I'm looking for Swooz Bartle-Henson-Smith?"

"Nobody with that crazy name lives in this building."

"How would *you* know?"

"I'm the building manager."

She tried to think of a comeback, but the man stopped her. "Sweetheart, you don't get it. You want me to let you into this Crimean girl's speck?"

Safiya nodded cautiously. What was this doob's angle? "Yeah."

"No problem. You seem like a nice girl. You won't do anything *too* illegal, right?"

He gave her a crooked smile. It hit her: a tongue job. *Oh God, he's paralyzed and he wants a tongue job.* Her face fell.

He could tell what she was thinking. He put up his hand. "Don't worry, ladybug, I'm not trying to bust your eggs. Give me twenty dollars and I'll let you in."

Safiya sighed, relieved. "I'm broke. Make it ten."

"If it's just ten, maybe I *will* want something extra."

"Fine, twenty," she said. "Let's do this."

She took out her *I!,* so did he, and she ka-chinged him twenty bucks. Then he unlocked the door and Safiya went in.

* * *

The three CGs were still hanging out on the front steps of the building when Juke walked up. They smelled law enforcement right away and stood up, eager to defend their turf.

The big CG with the missing teeth folded his arms and blocked Juke's path. He gave a wide, threatening grin and said to his buddies, "Check out little syndie boy."

Juke held up his hands in a gesture of peace. "I'm not from the syndicate. I'm NYPDinc Homicide."

The short, bearded guy stepped forward. "Yeah, fuck you, Dinc."

Juke held up Talia's photo on his I! "Somebody beat this girl to death. She lived here. Did you know her?"

The big CG said, "Is she another syndie ho like you?"

All three of them laughed. It put them off their guard for a moment, so Juke grabbed the big CG's I! out of his shirt pocket. "Hey!" he said, but Juke was already stepping around him. He pressed the I! to the scanner and unlocked the door.

Then he handed the I! back to the big CG and stared at him, hard and unblinking, ready to fight. The man stared back. The other CGs waited for their leader to make his move.

As the big CG debated within himself what to do, Juke broke off his stare. He turned and opened the door. At last the big CG spoke up.

"Let us know if you need anything. Always happy to help a ho," he said.

The other CGs hooted with laughter. *Whatever,* Juke thought, and went inside.

* * *

Out behind the dumpster, Rey felt a lot better. He'd snorted the whole baggie instead of just half, and the added bump had def been worth it.

Now he walked back to the front of the building and quickly looked up and down Opportunity, but didn't see Juke or his black Zan anywhere.

Confident Safiya was safe for now, he sat down on a bench and bobbed his head to a pop song, "Syndie Cyndy," that kept running through his synthed-up brain. The cold and the smell didn't bother him so much anymore. He kept an eye out for Juke, but figured the guy would never actually show up.

Safiya had probably been exaggerating about him. She'd made her ex-boyfriend out to be a superhero, but no doubt he was just another dollar-grubbing scumbag like the rest of the Dincs. He'd take one look at Talia's bank account and forget all about her murder.

He and Safiya had nothing to worry about from that asshole.

* * *

Juke stepped into the lobby of Talia's building. It was furnished with mismatched plastic folding chairs, a tattered sofa, and a TV monitor so ancient it actually jutted out from the wall instead of being part of the wall itself.

Two white-haired women in their sixties or seventies who looked worn down from years of hard living and antidepressants sat on the sofa eating powdered donuts and watching the news on Foxbook. Three talking heads were earnestly discussing today's youth and why they were so susceptible to Resistance propaganda. Kids today didn't seem to understand the value of hard work and sacrifice. Maybe it was the insidious influence of pop music.

Juke walked up to the two women. "Good afternoon, ladies," he said brightly.

They eyed him up and down.

"My name's Juke O'Keefe. I'm wondering if either of you has ever seen this girl." He showed them the picture of Talia on his I*!*

The woman closest to him turned to her friend. "Dinc," she said.

The other woman nodded, took a bite of her donut, and began chewing slowly. The white powder stuck to her lips. Then they both turned back to the TV.

"O-kaay, thanks for your help," Juke said, as he headed for the elevators.

Behind him the three talking heads were gone, replaced by an anchorwoman in a power suit and a helmet of blonde hair. "We've thrown off our government shackles and everyone is free at last," she was saying. "Free to make your own choices…"

As he waited for the elevator he called Haylee to check in, but she didn't pick up. He hadn't heard from her in a long time, and he wondered what she was up to. He was about to check the tip line for the case when the elevator door opened. A man in a wheelchair rolled out and blocked Juke's way. He eyed Juke suspiciously, no doubt sensing he was some species of cop.

"Can I help you?" the man said.

"Maybe," Juke replied. "Who are you?"

"I manage the building. Who are you?"

Juke badged him. "I need you to let me into 708. Talia Qirimoglu's speck."

The building manager blinked up at him. "Your badge says 'Homicide.'"

Juke waited, watching him.

"Is Talia… Is she *dead?*"

"I'm afraid so. You didn't know?"

The man looked like he was in shock. "No," he managed to say.

Juke wondered why the man seemed so shaken. Had he been friendly with Talia?

"What's your name?"

The guy gulped. "Lonnie Martin."

"Let's go upstairs," Juke said. He got in the elevator and held the door open. Lonnie hesitated, then wheeled inside.

"Seventh floor," Juke told the elevator. The door closed, and they headed up toward Talia's speck.

Chapter Fourteen

9:31 am

Lonnie

As the elevator rose, Lonnie panicked. He'd let that girl into Talia's speck less than ten minutes ago. She was probably still there. *She'll rat me out. And this Dinc will interrogate me.*

His little twenty-dollar hustle would be the least of his worries.

He was furious at himself. He never should have pulled that move, it was way too risky. Now the Dinc would find out *everything!*

The door opened on the seventh floor. "Which way?" Juke asked.

Lonnie gestured weakly toward the left. As they headed toward Talia's speck, Lonnie felt like he was wheeling toward his doom.

And that girl, whoever she was, was in for a nasty surprise too.

Chapter Fifteen

9:32 am

Safiya

As soon as Safiya entered Talia's speck, she was struck by the beautiful drawings of Canadian Rockies landscapes taped to the walls. They reminded Safiya of the sketch Talia was doing on the morning they first met.

When Juke got here, would he guess what these drawings meant—that Talia was planning to escape to Canada? No need to take that risk. Safiya put on her gloves, ripped the drawings down, and stuffed them inside the pockets of her parka.

Then she went to the battered gray refrigerator, which Talia had covered with pastel portraits—*including one of Safiya.* Thank God she'd beaten Juke here. She loved the portrait, which showed her on a mountain cliff at sunrise, but she tore it down and squashed it into a pocket without hesitating.

There were two pictures of Diego with his long scar. One showed him smiling, but the other showed him with angry, slitted eyes. As Safiya ripped the pictures down, she wondered again what Talia and Diego's ship had really been like.

Down lower, on the freezer, were pictures of a middle-aged man and woman Safiya didn't know, probably Talia's parents back in Crimea. Just to be safe, she took them down too.

Okay, now all the potentially dangerous art was gone. But where was Talia's computer?

She began by searching Talia's drawers. The speck was a small studio with only about six drawers in all, so it didn't take long. She found cheap clothes and art supplies, but not much else. She searched the tiny closet—but the Hodu wasn't there either.

Despite the cold, Safiya started sweating. If Talia's computer wasn't in her speck, that meant she probably had it on her when she was killed. Juke and that tall brunette partner could be going through it right now. Maybe he'd already found Talia's graphic novel. Maybe Talia had even uploaded that portrait of Safiya, and Juke was sitting at police headquarters staring at it.

She wondered again, *what would Juke do?*

He might decide, *hey, the bitch broke my heart and I've got a murder to solve.* He could be on his way to Safiya's speck right now to interrogate her.

Even if Juke cut her a break, what about his partner? She would know that if she gave the Agency intel about a de-chipping op, she'd get fifty Reagans easy.

Trying to stifle her fears, Safiya went through the closet and drawers a second time, throwing stuff on the floor so she could see inside better. Still no computer.

She looked up at the ceiling and saw a large, raggedy, open-air vent. It looked like the syndie that owned this place began some sort of repair and never got around to finishing. Could Talia have hidden her Hodu up there to keep it safe? Safiya climbed onto a rickety chair and shone her I! into the space above the vent.

But all she saw was cockroaches running away from the light.

She jumped down off the chair—and heard footsteps and men's voices in the hallway outside. It sounded like they were coming toward Talia's speck from the elevator. For a moment she thought she heard Juke's voice, and she freaked.

But then she realized that was impossible. If Juke had arrived at the building, Rey would have buzzed her. So she started searching the kitchen cabinets, finding nothing but pots with broken handles and second-hand dishes—

Shit, that is Juke's voice! He's right outside the door!

She looked around wildly. She ran to the window—but it was the non-opening kind and she was seven floors up.

Under the bed? No room.

The front door knob turned. *Oh God!*

She ran into the bathroom and shut the door—just before the front door opened.

She turned and looked for a bathroom window—there wasn't one—and saw the Hodu! It was right there behind the toilet seat, all rolled up. She grabbed it and stuffed it inside her parka.

But now what?

She froze, listening.

Chapter Sixteen

9:33 am

Karolyn

At the Agency, Karolyn was studying everything the Red Queen had dug up on Talia. There wasn't much, which indicated the dead girl had encrypted her communications. This made Karolyn even more certain Talia was in the Resistance—and the key to stopping Chocolate.

She looked up from her computer. "What is Juke O'Keefe doing now?" she asked the Red Queen.

"His car's GPS indicates he parked at Talia's housing project. I assume he's searching her place."

Perfect. This O'Keefe might be a symp, but he was doing Karolyn's work for her, investigating the Rez op.

Karolyn drank her espressaccino and smiled to herself. She had Captain Burgess on board already. His cooperation had come at a hefty price—ten Reagans—but it was worth it. Between him and the Red Queen, Karolyn would keep track of Juke's every single move.

He wouldn't be able to wipe his ass without her knowing it.

Chapter Seventeen

9:34 am

Juke and Safiya

When Juke stepped into Talia's speck, he instantly saw it had been trashed. Whoever did this could still be here. He pulled his Heston.

"Get back in the hall," he ordered Lonnie, in the wheelchair behind him. Then he called, "Come out with your hands up!"

Nobody moved.

"Now!"

Still nobody moved.

Weapon out, Juke opened the closet door, then looked under the bed. Nobody there—but something was tugging at him, he wasn't sure what.

Then he opened the bathroom door—and it hit him full force: *Safiya's smell.*

The musky, citrusy, indefinable scent that he used to know so intimately was so strong he felt like he'd been punched in the chest. He stepped backward, reeling.

It threw him so far off his game, he forgot to check behind the shower curtain.

Finally, he got control of himself—more or less. He decided either Talia or the intruder must have used the same soap, shampoo or whatever that

Safiya used. That would explain the smell. He called out to Lonnie, "Okay, clear. Come back in."

As Lonnie wheeled back in from the hall, Juke added, "But don't touch anything. We'll be checking for prints."

"You got it, boss," Lonnie said, with an oddly inappropriate grin. He seemed happy, or maybe relieved, for some reason.

Juke studied him. "You have any idea who broke in here?"

Lonnie shook his head vigorously. "Not a clue."

Maybe this guy was telling the truth…but there was a slight twitch in his left eye. "What kind of video you got in the building?"

The twitch picked up speed. "To be honest, we get hacked a lot. And the CGs are always busting the cams. But I'll give ya whatever we got."

As Juke searched the drawers, he asked, "How well did you know Talia?"

"Not at all. She just moved in a couple months ago."

"Did she have any visitors?"

"No idea. I got hundreds of people living here."

Juke looked up at the wall and saw pieces of tape hanging there. It looked like Talia had put up pictures or something, and this intruder, whoever it was, ripped them down in a hurry. Why? Maybe somebody heard Talia was dead, so they scavenged her place for cash and anything they could eat, drink, snort, or sell. But what could they have found on the wall that would be worth ka-ching?

Maybe the intruder was just some danghead grabbing random stuff. But maybe he was the murderer—and whatever he tore off that wall had held the clue to Talia's death.

Juke pointed at the hanging tape. "What did Talia have on the wall there?"

"You got me," Lonnie shrugged.

As Juke opened the closet door, he asked casually, "By the way, where were you last night?"

Lonnie chuckled. "You figure I jumped outta my chair and whacked her on the head?"

"From what I can see under those jeans, you got the leg muscles for it."

Lonnie stared at him, open-mouthed.

Juke said, "It's okay. I truly don't give a byte."

Lonnie said frantically, "Please. If my syndicate finds out, they'll send me back to the Middle East—"

"Just tell me where you were last night."

"I already did three tours—"

"Where were you?"

"At my buddy's place, in Building 4. Watching the Cyber Jets lose again," he added with a nervous attempt at a grin, obviously trying to ingratiate himself with Juke.

"So what can you tell me about Talia?"

Juke saw Lonnie was wracking his brain trying to come up with something helpful. He prompted him, "You ever see her with any guys?"

"I'm sorry, I honestly can't remember seeing her with anybody. We talked maybe a couple times, but just about the cats."

"Cats?" Juke went back to the bathroom, looking for a litter box. Instantly Safiya's smell tore into him again.

It was stunning how much Talia, or the intruder, smelled exactly like Safiya. Maybe they had the same pheromones.

He hadn't smelled anything like this at the crime scene. Had Talia been dead long enough that her aroma had dissipated? But in Juke's experience, people who had been dead for only a couple hours still gave off some of the same scent they'd had when they were alive. So it seemed likely this smell in Talia's bathroom didn't come from her, but from the intruder. Did this mean the intruder was a woman?

Suddenly he realized he'd been so thrown by the smell a minute ago, he'd actually forgotten to check the bathtub. The cheap brown shower curtain was closed and he hadn't seen past it. He was an idiot. *Somebody could easily be hiding in there.*

Behind him, Lonnie asked, "Everything okay?"

"Sure." But Juke turned and put his finger to his lips, motioning for Lonnie to be quiet. Then he drew his gun.

Quietly, he took one step forward—and thrust open the shower curtain. The bathtub was empty.

* * *

Two feet above Juke's head, Safiya held her breath for so long she felt like she would explode. She was lying all curled up inside an open-air vent in the bathroom ceiling, which was almost as big as the vent in the main room. She had climbed onto the toilet tank and pulled herself up and in.

Down below her, Juke asked the wheelchair guy, "Do you smell that?"

"Smell what?"

Go away! I have to breathe! Safiya screamed silently, cheeks bulging. She knew when she finally let out her breath, it would make a loud noise.

Juke was saying, "Never mind. So she had cats? I'm not seeing a litter box."

"Oh no, they weren't *her* cats," the wheelchair guy said. "See, we have these mean old tomcats in the building that never let anybody touch 'em. But for some reason they took a big liking to Talia." Safiya could tell this guy was babbling on because he was so nervous. "They'd sit in her lap. One of 'em had a messed-up ear, so she bought some antibiotics for him…"

Safiya's lungs burned. *Would this guy never shut up?!*

Finally she heard Juke stepping out of the bathroom—not a moment too soon. She expelled her breath all at once. The noise rang in her ears like thunder.

* * *

In the main room, Juke was thinking about how much Safiya loved cats—*everything* made him think of Safiya today!—when suddenly he heard a noise, like something bumping into something, coming from…the bathroom? But he'd just been in there. Must be the old pipes, he decided.

He searched Talia's speck for another twenty minutes. He didn't find any obvious clues to her murder, or traces of boyfriends or exes. But he did find watercolor brushes and nice ink pens. This led him to believe that what had been torn down from the walls were pictures Talia drew. What had been in those pictures?

He suspected the key to this case lay with the intruder. That person either committed the murder or had a good idea who did. If it was a woman, as he believed from the scent, he doubted she killed Talia herself. The murder had been too physically brutal. Could the woman be the killer's mother or sister, trying to protect him? Or was she part of some sick love triangle?

If Juke and Haylee raised enough money to send in a fingerprint tech, and the intruder wasn't wearing gloves, they might discover her identity. Or the building's security cams could help.

"Let's go check out your video," Juke told Lonnie. He walked out of the speck, and Lonnie wheeled out after him.

Safiya decided she'd wait seven minutes before she left too.

Chapter Eighteen

10:02 am

Haylee

Haylee waited in Dr. Swanson's examination room at the Liberty Medical Center, her anxiety rising. She wouldn't absolutely believe she was pregnant until her gynecologist confirmed it, based on the bloodprick her bot nurse had just taken. The home tests were 99.3 percent accurate; but still, there was that other .7.

Finally Haylee's doctor walked in. In her sixties with undyed gray hair, Marie Swanson was a warm, nurturing presence.

The exam room wasn't so nurturing, though. As soon as Dr. Swanson entered, a timer on the wall with the words "DOCTOR'S VISIT" underneath beeped on automatically. Right now it read 0 MINUTES, but Haylee knew from previous visits it would change to 1 MINUTE and beyond with alarming rapidity. Haylee liked Dr. Swanson, but she always tried to ask her as few questions as possible, because each minute cost dollars. Hell, each quarter-minute.

Dr. Swanson came toward her with a smile. "Hi, Haylee, it's good to see you."

Haylee nodded hello and gulped, unable to speak.

"So...it's a yes," Dr. Swanson said.

Haylee's hand went involuntarily to her belly. "Oh my God."

"You're at forty-three days, and it's a girl."

"Oh my God," she said again.

Dr. Swanson sat down. "I hope this is a good thing?"

"Yeah. It's great." Haylee started to cry.

The doctor handed her a tissue and waited.

Haylee wiped her eyes. "It's from the very last time my fiancé and I made love," she said. She took out her I! and showed the doctor her favorite picture of herself and Harrison. They were on the Brooklyn Heights promenade at night, with the lights and holos of Manhattan in the background. Harrison was a powerfully built guy—all natural, no steroids—with thick dark hair and an easy grin.

"He's a handsome guy," Dr. Swanson said uncertainly. "Are you…still together?"

"Harrison was my partner. A homicide cop."

Dr. Swanson nodded patiently as the timer changed to 1.5 MINUTES.

"We were going after a suspect in Fort Greene. Harrison wanted to wait for backup and body armor and all that, but I didn't think it would be that dangerous. And if we got backup we'd have to cut them in for a percentage, and we were saving up for the wedding, so…"

She took a sharp intake of breath. "The suspect's son answered the door. Little twelve-year-old kid with a mohawk. Harrison asked if his dad was around. The kid was scared shitless, so I told Harrison to put his gun away."

Haylee looked down at the picture of her and Harrison. "Soon as he did, the kid pulled out a gun and shot him dead."

"Oh Haylee," Dr. Swanson said, taking her hand as the timer hit 2 MINUTES. "Haylee, I am so sorry."

"The kid ran. Harrison bled out while I was holding him." She looked up at the doctor. "If we'd just waited for backup like Harrison wanted, or if I hadn't told him to put down his gun, he'd be sitting right here with me."

"You can't blame yourself," Dr. Swanson said. People always said that. But it was bugshit.

"I want to have this baby," Haylee said.

The doctor looked at her.

"I killed Harrison. I'm not gonna kill his child."

Dr. Swanson hesitated, searching for words. "Haylee, I understand you're feeling emotional—"

"I want this baby," Haylee said. She'd known the doctor would recommend an abortion, so she was ready for it. Ten years ago, the syndicates and their politicians had decided that fighting abortion was bad for business. It alienated too many customers and voters, and besides, it detracted from their core message of freedom for all. Even in Haylee's home state of Ohio, abortions were legal for everyone through six months.

Dr. Swanson said, "Haylee, being a single Mom in this day and age—"

Haylee cut her off again. "So I know don't smoke, drink, or do drugs. Are there special pro-oxidants I should take?"

Dr. Swanson looked at Haylee for another few moments and realized there was no way to change her mind. "I'll click you a prescription," she said.

As the doctor unrolled her computer and hit a couple of keys, Haylee asked, "When will we know if the baby needs editing?"

"We'll check for genetic diseases at the ten-week mark," Dr. Swanson said, turning back to Haylee. "In the meantime, there are some major decisions you need to make right away. Before the baby's blood-brain barrier forms."

Haylee said anxiously, "I know. How much does enhancement cost now? I heard the price was going down."

"For the basic package, which elevates the child's IQ by an estimated twenty-five points and also ensures against any weight problems, it's seventy-nine thousand dollars. Payable by the end of your pregnancy."

Haylee gasped. "Seventy-nine thousand?!"

Dr. Swanson said gently, "It's the best I can do. The Big Six control the price."

"But there's no way I can afford that."

"We're partnered up with three of the syndicates. If you want to contract out ten P, I'm sure a deal could be worked out—"

"I'm already at twenty. If I go to thirty and then have some kind of emergency, I could go up over fifty. They'll own me."

"Then maybe we should just forget about it," the doctor said kindly. "Enhancement isn't the right choice for everybody."

Haylee pressed her palms against her temples. *If only Harrison were here. We'd figure this out together.*

She said, "You read so many different things. I mean, how important do *you* think it is to get your baby enhanced?"

Dr. Swanson hesitated, as if measuring her answer. The timer changed to 5.25 MINUTES. "Well, it's an arms race. Most of my patients are doing it now. Which means your daughter would start life at a serious disadvantage without it. She'd almost certainly never get into a top college, for instance. She'd be unlikely to ever be a doctor or an algorithm shepherd. Essentially she'll be a beta in a world of alphas."

Haylee bit her lip, hard. "That's horrible."

"Honestly, if you give up ten P? Your child's additional earnings during the course of her lifetime will more than make up for that." Dr. Swanson paused, then added, "But it's your decision."

"How much time do I have?"

The doctor looked straight at Haylee with her gray, serious eyes. "Less than a week."

"What?!"

"Your daughter's blood-brain barrier will begin to form in six days."

Chapter Nineteen

10:08 am

Lonnie, Juke, and Safiya

In his office on the first floor, Lonnie apologized profusely to Juke for not having any video from this morning. "Somebody must've hacked the building's digitals," he said. "Happens every other day around here."

In fact, the digitals were working fine—but Lonnie had surreptitiously destroyed the video so this Dinc wouldn't see him taking a bribe from that girl.

The Dinc was about to ask follow-up questions, and Lonnie braced himself. His alibi for last night was nowhere near as solid as he'd made it out to be.

But then the Dinc's I! buzzed, distracting him, and a middle- aged, chubby-faced guy appeared on his screen. The Dinc told Lonnie, "I'll be right back," and stepped out of the office to get some privacy.

In the empty hallway, Juke double-tapped his I! and said, "What's up, Captain?"

* * *

It had been seven minutes, so Safiya stepped cautiously out of Talia's speck, looking both ways, and hurried for the stairs. She ran past the urine stench and passed-out dangheads on the third-floor landing, came out onto the first floor, raced up the hallway to the front door—

—and almost ran smack into Juke.

Or rather, Juke's back. He was turned away from her, less than two feet away, saying into his I*!*, "I'm in the Bronx. Why?"

Safiya backed up slowly and quietly, then ran like mad out the back door.

Suddenly Juke smelled that powerful Safiya scent again. *What the hell?* He whipped his head around—

But there was nobody there.

Meanwhile Captain Burgess was saying, "Any progress on that girl with the weird name? Talia Kiramiggle or whatever?"

Juke studied Burgess's face on his screen. Why was his boss asking about Talia when he'd made it clear he didn't give a crap?

But whatever the reason might be, Juke decided to try and get Burgess pumped up. Maybe he'd cut loose some discretionary dollars. "Absolutely, we're making *major* progress. Somebody broke into Talia's speck, and we're pretty sure it was the killer," Juke lied.

"Why?"

"'Cause they tore up the place getting rid of evidence."

"You sure they weren't just looking for synth?"

"They ripped pictures off the walls." Juke knew that was a little thin, so he added quickly, to redirect Burgess, "If we send in a fingerprint tech, we can ID this guy."

"What about video?"

"No luck there. But if you could spring for a few bucks and get us a print tech—"

"How do you know he wasn't wearing gloves?"

Juke felt his anger rise. *Scrucking Burgess.* "It'll only cost us a couple hundred to find out, and it could make the case."

"If you vibe that strongly, take it out of your seed money. What else you got?"

Juke wracked his brain, searching for some creative lie to convince

Burgess he was close to solving the case. But his three seconds of hesitation told the Captain all he needed to know.

"So you got squat, huh?" Burgess said. "Any idea if the killer is a woman?"

Odd question. Especially coming after Juke's suspicion that whoever broke into Talia's speck was female. "Still working on that. Why?"

"Female killers are hot right now. Girls with guns. If you can tie a vixen into this—even if she's not the actual zapper, just an accessory—maybe we could put your video in the prime spot after all."

The prime spot. That could mean hundreds or even thousands of dollars. Juke was on the point of revealing his hunch—but then realized he'd have to explain it was based on nothing but his sense of smell. Burgess would laugh his butt off at him.

"I'll see what I can find out," Juke said.

"Get going, O'Keefe, or I'll move up your drop-dead. Link me if there's any new developments—and remember what I said about girls being involved."

Then Burgess tapped off.

Chapter Twenty

10:41 am

Captain Burgess, Karolyn, and the Red Queen

Captain Burgess shut the door to his office at One Police Plaza and sat down. He activated the voice-altering app on his phone so he'd sound deeper and sexier, then called Karolyn Ford.

The ten Reagans he was getting from this deal was sweet. Even sweeter would be if he could get up inside that tight blue skirt of hers. For a woman in her forties, Karolyn had a sleek interface. She hadn't been too receptive at that dinner last month, but he figured she was worth another shot. She was new in town, and he was pretty sure she was single.

* * *

At the Agency, Karolyn's I! buzzed. She picked up and asked Captain Burgess, "What do you got?"

"You wanna do this over lunch?" he asked.

Yeah, right. Burgess was a pasty, out-of-shape snorp who thought he was the best thing since synthetic salmon. Men like him were the reason she preferred bots. "Some other time," she said. "What's up?"

Burgess passed along Detective O'Keefe's intel. "So what do you geniuses at the Agency think? Want me to send in a fingerprint guy?"

"No, we'll send in one of our own people with a fake badge. That's the best way to keep this under wraps."

"Impersonating a police officer? Isn't that a crime?"

"So jack me."

"I'd love to put you in handcuffs," Burgess said.

Did this gelatinous twit realize how much she outranked him? She could fry his balls anytime she wanted. Her ankle chip buzzed, and Case 20563 flashed on the wall. The Red Queen had new datascoop.

"Contact me the minute your people find out anything more," Karolyn told Burgess, and tapped off.

She hit the AI button on her desk, and instantly Margaret Thatcher's reconstituted voice filled her office. "We have identified Suspect #3, the Icelandic man, to a 99 P certainty."

All the other red flags on the wall disappeared, replaced by a photo of a man in his forties with light hair and weary blue eyes who would have been handsome if he didn't look so beaten down. "His name is Sölvi Hilmarsson. He's forty-two and widowed, employed as a Hodu salesman in Chelsea. Fifty-one percent owned, address unknown. Possibly homefree."

"How did you ID him?"

"He called a woman named Steffany, apparently a friend, from a non-blocked I! Vocal pattern and accent were identical to Suspect #3."

"What did he say to her?"

The Red Queen played the recording. Karolyn agreed that Sölvi Hilmarsson sounded exactly like their suspect from the earlier call, even using 'ro' the same way, to begin one sentence and end the next. He said, "Ro, I'm calling to say good-bye. I'm taking off tonight, ro."

"Why, where are you going?" the woman asked.

"I'm sorry, I can't tell anyone. But listen, cricket, good luck to you," Sölvi said, and then hung up.

Karolyn's blood rose. "So he's still planning to escape tonight. Presumably by de-chipping."

"Yes. I've linked you the GPS data from his non-blocked I! He's walking up Broadway. He just passed 75th."

"I'll pick him up right now." Karolyn took her Ruby Ridge .38 out of her drawer and stood up. This was too important to delegate—and besides, jacking people was her favorite part of the job. She'd grab a field agent for backup and bring in this Sölvi guy herself. With aggressive neurointerrogation, she'd get the names of all his accomplices in thirty minutes, tops.

She smiled grimly. The 9.8 woman was toast, and so was her big top-secret op. "Chocolate"—what a dumb code name.

"Good work," Karolyn said.

"I know," the Red Queen replied.

Karolyn changed out of her heels into sensible flats, holstered her Ruby Ridge, and headed out the door.

Chapter Twenty-One

10:46 am

Safiya and Rey

On the subway back from the Bronx, Safiya buzzed Sölvi. Since he was in Talia's mini-cell, he might have some idea what happened to her. But Sölvi's phone was turned off.

Meanwhile Rey wouldn't stop talking. "I'm really sorry, Safiya," he said, "I have no idea how Juke got by me. I swear, I only left for a second." Then he repeated his story about how some little kid got his kite stuck in a tree by the dumpster, so Rey got it for him super quick, but that must have been the exact moment Juke rode up…

Safiya figured Rey must be telling the truth; he wouldn't invent such an elaborate lie. But still, she couldn't help feeling chunked at him. He'd gotten distracted—and it put her in danger.

Juke would never screw up like that, she thought.

No question: seeing Juke this morning, so close she could smell his aftershave and sweat, had scrambled her brain. Despite his flaws, Juke really was an amazing guy. So dedicated to getting justice for people like Talia. True, he'd never joined the Resistance, choosing to stay part of a corrupt system; but he also never stopped fighting for what was right. She was glad to see that part of him hadn't changed.

She remembered something he'd said in Talia's speck—"From what I can see under those jeans, you got the leg muscles for it"—and smiled. She could picture how his face must have looked: the dry expression, eyebrows slightly raised, a half smile so subtle you had to search for it on his lips...

Then she thought about him kissing her with those lips, rising up toward her in the bed while they made love, his mouth meeting hers...

"This is our stop," Rey said.

She'd been so lost in her fantasy, she hadn't noticed. They got off the train and headed upstairs past a blind man begging for money. He was probably faking the blindness but she ka-chinged him a dollar anyway, for luck.

Rey said, "So what do we do now?"

Hidden inside Safiya's coat pockets was all the stuff she'd grabbed from Talia's speck. "First we get rid of Talia's Hodu and pictures. Then we steal a car."

Rey gave Safiya an incredulous look. She faced him and said, "Nothing that happened at Talia's speck changes anything. We still need one more vehicle for tonight's op. Let's go get it."

Rey couldn't believe this woman. She'd come so close to getting jacked by the Dincs—and she still wanted to keep going? *Does she have no fear?* He wanted so badly to tell her no, he was bailing, if she wanted to go to prison she could damn well go by herself!

But then he thought, *I'll never hang onto Safiya if I act like some burban wimp.*

So he dialed up the bravado and smiled. "Okay, let's go gank that car."

Chapter Twenty-Two

11:37 am

Haylee and Juke

Haylee could barely manage to put one foot in front of the other as she walked from the subway back to One Police Plaza. *Seventy-nine thousand dollars. Either that or ten P.*

Or I'll have a beta baby.

She'll end up a fifty-one percenter, like Talia. She'll be doomed before she's even born.

Haylee made it to her cube and sat there, shaky, too stunned to cry. She put her hand on her stomach. "Oh Hera," she said out loud. That was the name she'd decided to give her baby. "What am I gonna do?"

Haylee wished she could call her mom. But she wouldn't be any help. She was too worn down, stuck back in Dayton in her tornado-damaged house with Haylee's aggro dad.

The one cousin Haylee really liked was back in Ohio too. She was all alone. She missed Harrison so much—

The tears came again, and then she saw Juke walking toward her. She couldn't afford to act erratic in front of him twice in one day. She didn't have a mirror in her cube, but she tried to rearrange her face and tone of voice into something approaching normalcy.

"You solve the crime yet?" she asked.

"Yup. It was the husband," Juke replied.

She lifted an eyebrow. "Talia wasn't married."

"Darn. Well, back to the drawing board then. How's it going here?"

She showed Juke the video, and he was complimentary as usual—one of his best traits, though she was too distressed to appreciate it now. Then he brought her up to speed on the unknown intruder at Talia's speck.

"You think this person left prints?" she asked.

"If it was just some bozo grabbing stuff, then maybe."

"But if it was the killer or an accomplice, then no?"

Juke plopped down in the other chair. "I figure anybody savvy enough to go in and remove evidence was probably wearing gloves. In case we get lucky, I requisitioned a fingerprint tech for two hundred bucks. But it'll take 'em a couple days to get there, they're backed up."

She nodded. Given the case's low priority, that was as fast as they could expect.

Juke continued, "We can pay an extra hundred and they'll get to it tomorrow."

Anger rose up inside her. She was broke, she needed seventy-nine Reagans, and now Juke was about to piss a hundred bucks down the toilet. "We don't have an extra hundred. And we have a midnight drop-dead, so tomorrow won't help us."

Juke stood up. "You're right. We need forensics we can use right now. Let's go talk to the M.E."

"What good will that do? Same problem. No ka-ching."

"Vinnie's on duty. She likes me. Maybe she'll give us a freebie."

Haylee stood and followed him out the door. Juke sensed her anxiety, but misunderstood it.

"Don't worry," he said. "We'll beat our drop-dead, I promise. The sick fuck who killed Talia won't know what hit him."

III

PART THREE

BOTTOMS UP

Chapter Twenty-Three

11:52 am

Cheyenne Littlejohn

After meeting with her fifty-eighth cancer patient since starting her double shift last night, Dr. Cheyenne Littlejohn told the bot receptionist at Merck Hathaway General she was going out for lunch. She changed out of her scrubs, put on a coat and wide-brimmed fedora, and went outside. But instead of hitting a restaurant, she went straight to a drug store.

At thirty-four, with a petite frame, sparkly purple T-shirt, and dangly peace-symbol earrings, Cheyenne didn't look like a doctor. She didn't look like a medical researcher either, or a key member of the Resistance. But she was all three.

Cheyenne had grown up in Berkeley, the daughter of two Resistance-adjacent nurses. At eighteen she made her way to Boston and then New York City, where she trained at Merck alongside Safiya. She felt the same torment at forcing her patients to choose between indentured servitude and death. On their rare days off, they spent long hours walking the city from Harlem to Brooklyn, trying to make sense of their lives. When Safiya quit and joined a free clinic, Cheyenne was tempted to do the same.

But going to med school had left her thirty percent owned, and she couldn't risk becoming a fifty-one percenter herself. Also, she loved when she was actually able to cure people. So she stayed at her job.

She kept in touch with Safiya, though. Their friendship grew even closer two years ago, after Cheyenne's girlfriend moved to Montana to work as a fly-fishing guide for wealthy clients in the private, trout-stocked rivers that were once part of Yellowstone National Park.

Really, Cheyenne felt, Rita had needed to escape the mindburn of New York City life. Increasingly, people had been harassing them when they held hands in public. Rainbow patients got worse deals from the syndicate that owned Cheyenne's hospital. When she walked home from work, holographic news commentators, paid by the syndies, pontificated that "non-trads" were too busy engaging in immoral sex to be financially responsible. In fact, they droned on, that's why so many were fifty-one percenters.

Not that Wyoming would be any more rainbow-friendly than Manhattan. All over the country, the syndies kept driving their wedges between people.

Cheyenne dealt with her girlfriend's defection by joining Safiya's cell and diving into the de-chipping project. Her doctor job gave her access to the bio lab in the hospital basement, and that became her new passion. She worked in the lab every night til dawn, summer and winter and then summer again, with nobody else around except when Safiya came by.

Those long, lonely nights were filled with a thousand failed experiments and agonizing dead ends. But they ultimately led to Cheyenne being here, inside this Walmart Lifestyle Syndicate drug store, trying to save the world.

Cheyenne grabbed a shopping basket and headed for the Vitamin Supplements aisle. Ordinarily she avoided this section—the parade of miracle cures depressed her. They spoke of all the desperate people hoping to heal themselves for twenty dollars so they wouldn't have to get *real* medical treatment and sign their lives away to a syndicate.

But today Cheyenne walked straight up the aisle past a sign advertising "garaflora multis"—whatever that was—and headed for the curcumin display, which filled two whole shelves. She picked out a small bottle with one hundred 550-milligram pills. It was the same brand of curcumin she'd used in her experimental trials. A hundred pills would be more than enough for everybody in the New York Nineteen.

Curcumin was the primary ingredient of turmeric, an Indian spice used in curry. For over a century, researchers had been intrigued by curcumin's unusual properties, especially its ability to bind easily to certain proteins. At one time or another it had been studied as a possible cure for breast cancer, arthritis, and depression. None of these ambitious hopes had ever panned out, but that didn't discourage the alt religion people and the quacks. Every ten years or so, curcumin would become popular again as a cure for something or other. Lately it was on the upswing, touted as combatting drug addiction and other "inflammations in the brain." Cheyenne saw it everywhere. This ubiquitousness made curcumin ideal for her purpose.

Which was to make the syndicate biochips quit acting like fireflies.

Two years ago, Safiya had given Cheyenne a stolen shipment of chips. That's what Cheyenne was working on so feverishly in the hospital basement: trying to decode the biochips' secrets. *How did they set off a bio-alarm inside the bloodstream when people de-chipped?*

At last she figured out their secret.

It was really pretty simple once you understood the basic chemistry. If a fifty-one percenter tore out their biochip, that released a synthetic protein into their blood. It was a modified version of luciferase, the protein fireflies used to light up. But instead of emitting light waves like luciferase did, this new protein emitted radio waves. The waves automatically transmitted to the Anthill. So now the fifty-one percenter's blood became a GPS radio signal. They would be tracked and jacked by syndie police within hours, if not sooner.

As soon as Cheyenne identified the new protein, she began searching for a way to neutralize it. She tested over seven hundred chemicals without success.

But then, one Tuesday night three months ago, just as dawn was breaking and she was about to head home discouraged after another fruitless session, she tried one more compound: demethoxycurcumin, a highly bioavailable form of curcumin. Much to her astonishment, it worked immediately. The new synth protein attached to curcumin like they were long-lost lovers. In fact, the protein quit binding with hemoglobin altogether! That meant no radio waves, no bio-alarm—*and no GPS signal for the syndie cops to track.*

To confirm her findings, Cheyenne did four trials on dogs and two on herself. Every time, ingesting curcumin rendered the bio-alarm completely inoperable.

Now Cheyenne, Safiya, and Rey were basically hoping a megadose of a common spice would free tens of millions of people from indentured servitude—and start a revolution.

Well, it wouldn't be the first time a spice changed the course of history, Cheyenne thought as she walked away from the vitamin supplements aisle, curcumin in hand. Hadn't Columbus sailed to America because he was looking for pepper and cinnamon? Come to think of it, he was probably looking for turmeric too.

She headed for the kitchen supply aisle and picked out a pair of scissors. If Chocolate blew up tonight and she had to go on the run, she would need to cut her hair. She should change her hair color too, so she went to the cosmetics aisle and started looking through all the various coloring bottles. She found one labeled "Marilyn Monroe" and decided that shade of blonde could be kind of fun, actually.

But then she remembered that buying hair coloring products triggered an automatic facial recognition search, since people trying to change their identities often started by changing their hair color. The last thing she needed was extra scrutiny from Agency cops, Dincs, Syncs, Fincs (from the FBI, Inc.), or anybody else.

So she put down the hair dye and went to the checkout machine. Tilting her face so the fedora would hide her from the security cam, she paid for her purchases using her burner. Hopefully that would keep the cops from ever discovering she'd bought curcumin today. Because if they somehow managed to connect her to this op, they would lock her up in a max prison and neurointerrogate every last millimeter of her brain.

A cold shiver went through Cheyenne as she adjusted her fedora. Rumor had it some people never fully recovered from neuro; it fried their brains worse than electroshock therapy.

But still: she had to do this.

She just hoped Safiya would be able to keep her and the New York Nineteen safe.

Chapter Twenty-Four

12:03 am

Vinnie Cho, Juke, and Haylee

Down in the morgue, Vinnie Cho rolled a body out of the drawer and onto the autopsy table. Vinnie—short for Lavinia—was an immie from Korea who'd been doing this work for thirty years. She didn't need any help, even though she was only five foot two and the dead body was six three.

The body had belonged to Dr. Montee Goldman, a plastic surgeon in his forties from the Upper East Side with two gunshot holes in his chest. Vinnie decided that was where she would start. Keep it simple, get in and get out, time was dollars.

As she selected her knife and checked the blade, Juke walked in with the new girl, Haylee. "Hey Vinnie," Juke said, smiling brightly.

"How's it hangin'?" Vinnie greeted him, like she always did. If she hadn't been so totally uninterested in sex with men, it might have constituted harassment. Not that anyone ever got prosecuted for that anymore.

"We got a kickass case for ya. Hot off the street."

"I heard." She picked up a sharpening stone and honed the blade. Yet another annoying economy measure; the M.E.'s office hardly ever bought new knives these days. "But I've been on since midnight. Soon as I do Dr. Goldman here, I'm going home."

"We just need a quick look," Juke said. "Time of death, that's it."

Vinnie gave him a knowing nod. "Plus evidence of sexual assault, stomach contents, and I'm guessing you want me to look under her nails… I don't do this for fun, guys." She brought down her knife and sliced into the dead man's chest.

Haylee backed up several feet. She'd attended plenty of autopsies, even shot a few for her videos, but they still made her queasy.

Juke, seemingly unaffected by the cutting, said, "Vinnie, it'll take five minutes tops, and you'll get paid, I promise. Tell ya what, I'll set her up for ya."

He opened the drawer holding Talia's body and started to pull her out.

But Vinnie pointed her bloody knife at him. "Leave the girl in there," she ordered. "I checked. You've only raised *eighteen dollars.*"

Vinnie nodded toward the far wall, which displayed today's stats. Haylee looked over and saw that, sure enough, the Talia Qirimoglu case was totally dying at $18.25. Meanwhile, Dr. Goldman's case—with DeAndrey Jackson/Davey Campbell as the lead homicide team—had already raised fifty Reagans. *What I could do with my share of that jackpot!* Haylee thought. Jackson and Campbell must have snagged life insurance or a rich widow or both.

Juke said, "Our video's only been out for a couple hours. The dollars'll be coming in, no problem."

"If you don't infect networld in the first fifteen minutes, you never will," Vinnie retorted. "Ask your Marketing Specialist, she'll tell you."

Haylee, on the spot, tried to bluster her way out of it. "That's not necessarily true. If you find some tutti stuff, we'll blast it out to networld and get all kinds of ka-ching."

"We'll give you a sweet cut," Juke told Vinnie. "Five P."

"I don't work on spec," Vinnie said.

"Come on, Vinnie," Juke pleaded. "This girl was a poor immie, just like you—"

"Spare me." Vinnie made another cut into Dr. Goldman and struck gold: bullet number one. She reached in and pulled it out.

Juke said quietly, "Tell ya what. How about we just spot you a quick two hundred cash. You won't have to pay the Department their fifty P."

Vinnie threw him a look. "You want me to risk my consulting contract for a measly two hundred?"

"Make it three," said Juke.

Haylee was pissed. He kept trying to throw money away without consulting her. At this rate, they'd *lose* dollars on this case. Forget about oatmeal; she'd have to stand in line for free breakfasts at a syndie soup kitchen. She had a quick image of herself, eight months pregnant and about to burst, waiting with all the other pregnant women and elderly people for greasy scrambled eggs and stale coffee.

Juke said to Vinnie, "This killer is a sick, angry man who ran over a dead woman twice. He's gonna do it again."

Vinnie looked at Juke. He was a good guy, and she suspected he was still tortured by his old case, the killer who went on to commit mass murder. Vinnie was the only person in the NYPDinc, besides Juke, who had put the whole story together. Out of kindness to him, she kept it quiet.

But still, that didn't make this Crimean girl her problem. She shook her head and was about to tell Juke no one more time when the morgue door swung open and DeAndrey Jackson swaggered in. He was rolling total tough Dinc, in black cowboy boots, big cowboy hat, and his possibly stolen gold necklace. As Detective of the Month for three months running—and the lead on today's hot case—Jackson's arrogance was at an all-time high. He took one look at Juke and laughed.

"Hey Vinnie," he said, "don't tell me this chump is trying to freeload off you again."

"What's up, Jackass?" Juke said, using Jackson's nickname on the squad—though nobody else said it to his face. "You gonna catch the real killer this time? Or just jack the first unlucky sucker that comes along, like you usually do."

Jackson looked sadly at Juke, dripping fake sympathy. "Aw, you're not *jealous,* are ya? 'Cause the doctor's widow just bought in for fifty more Reagans—*up front.* We're talking red-dot now."

Haylee checked the wall again and saw Jackson was telling the truth: the Goldman case was now listed in red, at $100,000 even. She was sick with envy.

But she tried to act like she didn't care. She and Juke were partners, and she had to support him. If she didn't, she'd get a rep for not being loyal, and other detectives would refuse to work with her. That would cripple her NYPDinc career.

So she eyed Jackson disdainfully. "You're taking advantage of a grieving woman. That's disgusting." But as soon as she said it, she thought maybe she was being a little *too* supportive of her partner. She didn't want to get on the Golden Boy of the Month's bad side.

Jackson grinned at her. "I see you've raised eighteen dollars. Impressive." Lowering his voice, he said suggestively, "Too bad you're not partnered with me, vixen. I'd make you rich."

As Haylee tried to think up a good comeback, Juke turned to Vinnie, who was groping inside Dr. Goldman's chest cavity for the second bullet. "One question before we go," he said. "GPS chip in the left ankle. Which syndie does that?"

"Berkshire Vanguard," Vinnie said.

Oh God, thought Haylee. She wanted nothing to do with Berkshire Vanguard today. They were the syndicate that owned twenty percent of her—and now they were reaching into her womb to grab ten percent more.

As they left the morgue and got in the elevator, Juke told her, "We'll go uptown and hit Berkshire Vanguard headquarters."

Haylee's stomach turned queasy. A side effect of pregnancy—or her terror that she and her daughter would get sucked into the same quicksand of poverty and struggle that had defined her mother's life.

She had promised herself she would never let that happen to her.

The elevator door opened and they headed down to the garage to pick up the Zan. Juke took out his I! and said, "Since Talia was high P, her syndie probably collected a lot of information on her. I'll set up a meeting with one of their execs."

Suddenly it hit Haylee that she was looking at this trip to Berkshire

Vanguard all wrong. She stopped in the hallway and stood still, thinking about it. She was about to meet with a big-shot Berkshire Vanguard exec. This could be a huge blessing in disguise!

"You coming?" Juke asked, puzzled.

"Yeah," Haylee said, walking again.

If she made a good impression on this exec, she would call him first thing tomorrow morning and ask for a discount for her baby's enhancement. That kind of deal happened all the time, because people liked having friends in law enforcement. Knowing a cop could come in handy.

Haylee would ask for fifty percent off. Ten P for ten years would be a tough pill to swallow—but five P she could handle. She and her daughter would make it through.

"You are tough and you are ready," Haylee whispered, as she and Juke got into the Zan and set out for Berkshire Vanguard headquarters. All she had to do was charm the pants off this exec, and she and Hera were back in bizness.

Chapter Twenty-Five

12:08 pm

Karolyn and Sölvi Hilmarsson

Karolyn sped toward AppleSoft Syndicate Park, formerly Central Park, with Agent Willard, a guy with short hair from Wisconsin or Iowa or some place like that who didn't talk much. She liked that about him. She didn't want to answer a bunch of questions, she just wanted to grab Sölvi Hilmarsson real quick, drama-free, and bring him into the Agency Debriefing Center. They had all the medical equipment she'd need for her interrogation.

According to her I!, Sölvi's I! was inside the park, south of the lake. She and Willard got out of the car, ka-chinged the gate, and walked in.

They headed toward Sölvi's I!, passing young lovers, bicyclists, and elderly people taking their mid-day constitutionals. A fuzzy sunshine made it through the smog, giving everything a kind of glow. Karolyn heard a lot of chirping; thanks to global warming, there were more birds in the park in November than there used to be. She thought back to the warblers and song sparrows that used to gather on her parents' farm in the fall. When she was six, she rescued a baby sparrow with a wounded leg and nursed him back to health, feeding him with an eye dropper.

But then a neighborhood tomcat snuck in through an open window one night, and that was the end of that story.

At the time it broke Karolyn's naive little heart. But in retrospect, she felt the experience taught her a valuable lesson. The same one Charles Darwin had taught.

Willard said, "Ma'am," and pointed to a man kneeling next to an oak tree by the lake, less than fifty yards away.

"Looks like our doob," Karolyn agreed, and they stepped swiftly toward Sölvi Hilmarsson. She was about to get her big break in this case.

* * *

Sölvi hadn't gone in to work this morning. Hell no! When he woke up at dawn on top of his subway grate in Brooklyn, he decided to pretend he was already a free man. Leaving his sleeping bag with the busted zipper behind forever, he walked across the bridge and up Broadway toward AppleSoft Syndicate Park. He was extravagant, buying a full-on beefburger for breakfast along with lemonade from actual lemons. The sky was gray and the wind was cold but it didn't bother him. Tomorrow he would be in Canada.

When Diego called this morning and said Talia had been murdered, Sölvi was alarmed. Had something gone wrong with Chocolate?

But then he decided if there was a problem, Safiya would have contacted him. Sölvi had an almost religious faith in her, and refused to allow himself to stay scared. No doubt there was some other explanation for Talia's death. As he headed uptown he blinked positive, using the strategy for getting rid of negative thoughts that he had read about on networld.

The blinking worked pretty well until he reached the park. As he ka-chinged a dollar to the gate and went in, his mood darkened. Coming here was always hard. But he knew he couldn't possibly leave the city forever without saying goodbye to Addý.

He headed for the southern end of the lake, where he knelt beneath the oak tree twelve feet to the left of the Alice in Wonderland statue. This was where he had sprinkled his wife's ashes.

He felt the ground with his hands and said out loud, "I love you, *ástin mín,* my darling. Wherever I go, you'll always be with me."

Sölvi and Addý had moved here ten years ago, escaping the flooding and hurricanes back home in Iceland. They had such high hopes. True, like a lot of new immies they had to give up fifteen percent of their income to the syndicates, to pay their entrance fees to the U.S. The government charged immies heavily, to make up for low taxes on its citizens.

But the first three years in America were good for Sölvi and Addý. He had a steady job at a nursing home, and she got work at a synth coke plant. They were even saving money.

Until Sölvi lost his job to a robot. He began bouncing from one low-paying gig to the next. Then Addý had a stroke, like several other workers at her plant. By the time her ordeal was over, Sölvi was owned and chipped—and Addý was dead.

Sölvi's life pretty much ended too at that point. But one night last year, while trudging back to his subway grate to sleep, he heard some loud drumming. He followed it to a flare on the Hodu Brooklyn Bridge. He listened to the impassioned speaker—a young woman in an anti-pollution mask who he later came to know as Safiya—and got hooked, just like Rey.

For a year he passed out flyers for the above-ground arm of the Resistance and shared his life story on networld, trying to give a personal face to the fifty-one percenter problem. His life regained meaning. Then, one warm September evening two months ago, Safiya and Cheyenne Littlejohn came to look for him at his grate. They told him about the New York Nineteen and invited him to join.

This whole idea of de-chipping using a common household spice sounded nuts. But Sölvi trusted Safiya, and Safiya trusted Cheyenne, so he said yes.

Now D-Chip Day had come at last.

Sölvi bent his head down toward the cold soil where poor Addý's ashes had soaked in. He thought about how they used to spoon each other at night for warmth in the long, frigid twinters back home.

Then he noticed a woman in a navy blue suit coming toward him, with a short-haired man in a gray suit at her side. It was odd that people so well dressed would be walking off the path, through the dead leaves.

Ordinarily he might not have paid them much attention. But Talia's murder had made him edgy. He quickly got to his feet.

The man and woman—Dincs? but they were too well-dressed for that—kept coming toward him. Now they were less than twenty-five feet away.

He began walking away from them. Glancing over his shoulder, he saw they were striding faster now, gaining ground. *Shit!* He broke into a run.

They ran too. "Sölvi Hilmarsson!" the woman shouted. "Halt. Police!"

The young lovers, bicyclists, and exercise walkers watched as Sölvi dashed down a hill. Panic drove him to run faster than he had since he was a teenager in Reykjavik, playing soccer with his friends. He put some distance between him and his pursuers. If he could make it through the northeast gate and down to the subway—

He tripped on a tree root and fell headlong. He rolled and jumped back up.

But with his momentum slowed, the man and woman caught up to him. The woman shoved him hard in the back and sent him flying down to the ground. She said, "You're under arrest," and pulled out cuffs.

Sölvi didn't stop to think. During the past two months he had already decided what he'd do if he were caught. One way or another, he would be free.

He reached in his coat pocket and took out a .25 that he'd bought at a hardware store in midtown. He aimed up at the woman and fired.

She ducked. His bullet hit the man in the shoulder.

The man screamed with pain and staggered backward. Sölvi pointed his gun at the woman and fired again.

But his aim was thrown off, because before he fired, she pulled a gun and shot him in the right eye.

Sölvi dropped his gun as his head hit the ground. His other eye opened wide like he was seeing something… or someone.

Addý.

Then he died.

* * *

Karolyn looked down at the dead man, ears ringing. *Why'd this stupid fool have to pull that .25?* She hadn't wanted to zap him. If she hadn't put on all those damn extra pounds, maybe she could've moved faster and stopped him before he pulled it. Starting tonight she was laying off the ice cream for real.

She realized her mind was spinning. She must be in shock from killing this guy, even though she should be used to it by now—this was her eleventh or twelfth time. She took some deep mindlessness breaths and began to settle down.

This was definitely a blow. She had wanted Sölvi alive so he'd flip on his co-conspirators. But all wasn't lost. With luck, his I!—and his burner I! too, if they could find it—would give them clues.

First, she had to deal with the agent—what was his name, Wilson? Williams?—writhing in pain on the ground. More importantly, she needed to keep Sölvi's death secret from his co-conspirators. She didn't want them suspecting the Agency was onto them.

She ordered an Agency ambulance; they had one on call for screwups like this. Then she took off Willard's jacket—yeah, that was it, Willard—and held it tight to his wounded shoulder. If only he would stop his endless moaning. It made it hard to think.

The gunshots, moans, and screams brought curious onlookers. Most of them took off fast when they saw Sölvi lying dead with his eye shot off. But two AppleSoft Syncs stepped toward them from the path with their guns out.

Karolyn stood up to greet them, holding up a fake NYPDinc badge she carried. "It's okay, guys, we're NYPDinc. We were making an arrest and this man resisted. I've called an ambulance."

"Why didn't you tell us you were coming in here?" one of the Syncs asked. He had white hair and looked mid-fifties, but he was still fit.

"Hot pursuit. Sorry about that."

The other Sync, a nervous guy in his twenties, looked down at Sölvi's busted eye socket and started puking. His white-haired partner said, "Ian, if you gotta do that, go in the bushes."

Ian went behind a bush and puked some more. The older Sync turned to Karolyn. "You want to set up a perimeter around the body?"

"No, we'll take him in the ambulance too."

The Sync frowned, puzzled. "What for? I'm pretty sure he's dead."

Karolyn looked the man straight in the eye. "I think it's best," she said.

Then she shut up and watched him. This was the moment. If the Sync wanted to, he could go all Marvel on her and insist the body stay where it was. She'd have to deal with an investigation into her shooting. It would slow her down considerably—and she couldn't afford that.

Or the Sync could decide to just forget the whole thing and let the NYPDinc (as he imagined Karolyn to be) deal with it. That way he wouldn't get caught up in a Sync-Dinc turf battle.

To make the decision easier for him, Karolyn pointed at Sölvi's gun lying on the ground and said, "This asshole shot my partner. He was trying to kill us."

Finally the Sync nodded. "Okay, do what you gotta do."

He walked back toward the path and kept the civilians away. Three minutes later the Agency ambulance came. Two agents in dark gray EMT-looking uniforms jumped out and helped Karolyn load Willard and Sölvi into the back. The ambulance was equipped with a large canvas duffel bag, and they were able to stuff Sölvi's body inside it. They'd get Willard to an ER, then dump the body somewhere.

But first Karolyn went through all the dead man's pockets—and found his burner phone. *Excellent!* Soon they'd have info on every phone contact this guy had. Too bad she'd had to kill him, but it would work out after all.

Chapter Twenty-Six

12:51 pm

Safiya and the Red Queen

Safiya walked swiftly up Broadway toward 74th, alarmed at how late it was. This morning's crises had thrown her so far off her schedule, she hadn't had time to steal a car yet.

She'd already ganked three cars in the past two days and parked them near her speck. But she needed one more, so there'd be room for all her people to ride off to Canada tonight just as soon as they were de-chipped.

There was a Quarterpotty on the corner, so she ka-chinged it and went in. Now that she had some privacy, she took a flesh-colored gel out of her purse and pressed it onto her palm—a perfect fit. You'd have to look very closely to see it wasn't her actual hand.

The gel hand came with its own set of palm and finger prints. Weeks ago, Rey had prepared for today's heist by hacking into the security digitals of an upscale condo building on Broadway. He inserted the gel hand's prints into the digitals, to fool the system into thinking these prints belonged to someone who lived in the building.

So now, Safiya stepped out of the Quarterpotty and headed toward the building. Drawing her shoulders back and trying to appear self-assured, like she belonged here, she walked up to the front door. She placed her gel hand up against the scanner.

This hand needed to work better than those useless skeleton IDs had. She held her breath—and heard a click, as the door unlocked. Success! She opened the door and entered the marble lobby.

A bot security guard greeted her. He was a good-looking guy with thick blond hair and a wide smile, dressed in an impeccable black suit. "Hello there," he said in a faint Italian accent.

Some people talked to bots like they were real—hell, some people had sex with them—but Safiya had always found that creepy. So she didn't say anything. She put her gel hand on the elevator scanner, planning to ride down to the garage.

The guard, however, was apparently programmed for sociability and putting people at ease. No doubt the condo residents paid extra for this perk. "I don't believe we've met. My name's Theo," he said, sticking out his hand.

Safiya looked at the outstretched hand and panicked. *He'll feel the gel! He'll lock down the building so I can't get out and grab me. Chocolate will be dead because some stupid bot wanted to shake hands with me!*

"Nice to meet you," Safiya said, and then sneezed. "I shouldn't shake hands. I have a cold."

Theo raised his eyebrows. "You afraid I'll get sick?"

Her heart raced. "No, but you'll shake other people's hands, and *they'll* get sick."

Theo frowned in thought. Safiya bent her knees, getting set to dash back out the front door before Theo could lock it down.

But then his pleasant smile returned. "Good point," he said.

The elevator door opened, and Theo gave her a little wave as she got in. "Have a nice day."

She was so relieved she forgot her personal rule about not exchanging social pleasantries with bots. "You too," she said, waving back to him with her un-gelled hand as the door closed.

Down on the bottom level of the garage, she headed for a yellow Lex parked in a far corner. Hacking into the building's digitals had enabled her and Rey to identify three vehicles, including this Lex, that hadn't left the garage in over two months. Today the Lex was partially obscured from the security cams by a large SUV, so this was the car they'd chosen. In person, the yellow looked a lot brighter than it had on Rey's computer.

As her footsteps echoed through the garage, it hit her once again how anytime there was a dangerous gig, it seemed to be her doing it instead of Rey. She quickly shook off that thought. She needed to do this fast and smooth, so she wouldn't arouse Theo's suspicions. She strode toward the Lex.

Then her burner buzzed.

She froze. Should she tap in? It could be Rey warning her about something. He was in a nearby Starbucks, watching the building's security video on his rollup.

She pulled out her burner. But it wasn't Rey, it was an unknown number— *shit, I bet it's Diego*. Had Juke found him somehow? She tapped in and said, "Hi, you okay?"

"What's going on?" Diego said, his voice high and frantic. "You didn't send the alert!"

She registered that nothing terrible had happened, he was just scared. With everything else that was going on, Safiya had forgotten to send a noontime alert to the New York Nineteen, like she had promised. "I can't talk right now, it's not a good time." The security digitals were no doubt catching her every word and maybe Diego's as well, and Theo was listening. "But everything's okay."

Diego was too wound up to catch her signals that she didn't feel safe convoing now. "What do you mean?" he said. "Did they find out what happened with Talia?"

"Not yet," Safiya said quickly. She chose her words carefully. "Listen, I'll call you back in five minutes. I'm in the middle of doing something for tonight."

"So Chocolate is still on? Why didn't you send—"

"Sure, it's on. I'll see ya then." She was trying to keep it light so Theo wouldn't get interested. Some security digitals measured people's tone of voice, and if you sounded tense or upset they honed in on you. "Have a great day, I'll call ya."

Diego shouted, "'A great day?' Nobody cares that Talia's dead! Not even you!"

If he did kill her, he was doing a great acting job—but she needed to end this convo quick.

"Diego," she started to say, but caught herself after she'd made the "D" sound. "D—doob, hang in there."

She stuck the I! back in her pocket and walked up to the Lex. Then she dropped her purse, just like she'd practiced. Her lipstick, meditation balls, and other stuff spilled all over the floor.

As she squatted to pick everything up, she took her small gray hack disc out of her pocket and put it on the floor where the cams wouldn't see it. She pointed it at the Lex and turned it on. A red light on the hack disc began blinking.

She started grabbing her things and putting them back in her purse. It took about twenty seconds—and by the time she finished, the blinking red light had turned green. Her disc had successfully deactivated the Lex's security.

Still squatting down, she double-tapped the disc to give the Lex a whole new set of security data that would include her natural handprint. This would enable her to enter the car and drive off. The reactivation process would take about thirty-seven seconds, so while she waited, she began removing the gel from her hand.

Then she heard footsteps. She looked up—and Theo was coming straight toward her!

She was so agitated she had trouble getting the gel off. Finally she did, and stuffed it deep in her purse. She grabbed the hack disc off the floor and held it against her leg. Hopefully Theo and the cams couldn't see it, but it would still be pointed at the Lex and do its work.

As she stood back up, Theo stepped close to her. "Did you drop your purse?" he said, raising his eyebrows just like before. Apparently his facial expressions were a bit limited. Then he smiled.

His smile looked sinister. Had he spotted the hack disc? If she got caught trying to gank a car, she'd do a year in prison. And if they found out about the rest…

She felt like the disc was burning a hole in her leg. Forcing herself to smile back at Theo—oh God, she was *flirting* with him, how disgusting was that?—she said, "Yeah, I'm so clumsy. I spilled all my stuff."

Theo nodded understandingly. "No worries, that happens to me all the time. You get everything?"

"Yup, I'm good, thanks." She prayed he would leave already.

But he didn't. He smiled at her again. Why? She couldn't tell if the bot was interrogating her, making small talk, or coming on to her. For all she knew, part of his gig was to politely offer himself to the single women who lived in the building for afternoon quickies. No doubt he'd noticed she wasn't wearing a wedding ring.

"May I open the door for you?" he asked.

Her pulse raced. Before the car door could be opened, she'd have to place her right hand on the ID scanner, on the car's roof. But her hand was still holding the hack disc. Theo would see it.

Safiya pointed at the Lex's front left tire and asked, "Is that my barrette down there?"

Theo gallantly bent down and looked, as she frantically stashed the disc in her pants pocket.

"I didn't see anything," he said, and stood back up.

"Thanks, I guess it was just a shadow."

Had it been thirty-seven seconds? She placed her hand on the Lex's ID scanner. If the car didn't recognize her hand and announced an ID error, she'd need to come up with some inane line of bugshit and talk her way out of this. Or should she run like hell up the steps and hope to escape before the bot grabbed her and held her down—

The scanner flashed green. As Safiya stifled a sigh of relief, Theo politely opened the door for her.

She got in the car. "Thank you so much."

"You're welcome. I hope I'll see you again soon," the bot said. She could swear he batted his eyelashes.

Safiya backed up, waved goodbye, and started out of the garage. She made it onto Broadway and drove off.

She finally relaxed, knowing Rey would wipe the garage video clean so there'd be no evidence of her theft. She was home free.

* * *

Down in the Agency basement, the Red Queen spent a full four seconds—a long time for her—assimilating the new I! convo the Anthill had just intercepted, between the 88%-certainty Mexican and the woman with 9.8 leadership metrics.

This was the third convo between them that the Red Queen had heard. Once again the woman was insisting they'd go forward with "Chocolate" no matter what.

The red flag was getting even redder.

In all three convos, the man showed a high degree of tension. In fact it had grown, along with his accent; the Red Queen now classified him as 97%-certainty-Mexican. Meanwhile the 9.8 woman continued strong, deflecting the man's panic with cool resolve, almost botlike in her focus.

Except this time, she had made one potentially huge error.

Linguistic pause analysis indicated a slip of the tongue. She started to say a word beginning with a "D" sound, then stopped herself and changed the word to "Doob." It was the single moment in the three convos when a slightly higher tension level seeped into her voice.

What was the word she stopped herself from saying? There was an 81 percent chance it was a name that started with D. That would explain the woman's tension: she realized she was about to make a major security blunder.

The Red Queen instantly advised Karolyn and the Anthill to be on the hunt for a man of Mexican heritage whose first name began with D.

Given the 9.8 woman's tension level and likely security slip-up, the Red Queen almost downgraded her leadership metrics to 9.7. She was still in the top .05% of humans, in terms of leadership skills; but the good news was, she had been rattled.

The Red Queen would bring this woman down.

Chapter Twenty-Seven

1:08 pm

Jeannie Bardach and the New York (Nineteen) Seventeen

With Talia and Sölvi both dead, only seventeen members of the original New York Nineteen were left.

They were all supposed to get an alert from Safiya an hour ago, at noon, confirming Chocolate was still a go. So when twelve o'clock came and went with no message from her on their I!'s and Hodus, they began worrying. By one o'clock they were downright frantic.

Several of them shared an identical physical tic, compulsion even, which showed itself now. They kept rubbing and squeezing their skin above their biochip, feeling its tiny edges with their fingers. It was so infuriating that such a tiny chip, less than one tenth of a millimeter in diameter, could hold them captive.

Jeannie Bardach, the sixty-two-year-old mother of the imprisoned teenage hacker, felt her chip and got so scared she would never, ever get rid of it that she began having trouble breathing. Desperately gulping oxygen through her constricted airways, she was positive it was a heart attack.

But of course there was no way she could go to a hospital. So she downed a glass of cheap, semi-rancid Australian wine, lay down on her kitchen floor, and tried to relax. She shut her eyes and imagined peaceful ocean waves, but that reminded her of taking Nicholas to the beach when he was little, which reminded her of her fear that she'd never see him again. She got even more panicky.

Further uptown, Diane Patterson and Mychal Collins, a married couple in their thirties hoping to escape together, walked up Ayn Rand Street arm in arm, sticking close to the buildings for protection from the wind. They tried to distract each other from their fears by talking about the babies they'd have in Canada, once they didn't have to worry about paying a five percent penalty for each child.

At the corner of 68th, they found themselves outside an old church. The holo out front said it was owned by the Walmart Lifestyle Syndicate, the syndie that owned Diane and Mychal. Walmart Lifestyle, based in Arkansas, drove the hardest income-share bargains of any of the syndies. They were also more likely to throw people in prison for minor economic offenses, and more relentless in their messaging that most fifty-one percenters were responsible for their own problems.

But the church's weathered spires and stained glass windows were still intact and spoke of an earlier, kinder era. Diane and Mychal looked up at the windows longingly. Then they went inside, sat down in a back pew, and prayed.

Throughout the city, the New York Seventeen waited desperately to hear from Safiya that they were safe, and that tonight they would escape to freedom. Where the hell was she?

Chapter Twenty-Eight

1:24 pm

Juke and Haylee

Juke and Haylee rode through heavy midtown traffic toward the New York headquarters of Berkshire Vanguard. The glacial pace was driving Juke nuts, especially since they had so little time til drop-dead. Less than eleven hours.

He looked over at Haylee, checking the crowdfunding stats on her I*!* and hoping for some miracle. "How are we doing? Over a hundred bucks yet?"

"Don't ask."

Clearly she wanted to be left alone. He looked out the windshield at a giant holo of an American flag waving in the wind. Underneath it, red, white, and blue letters flashed: "LAND OF THE FREE." The constant flashing was irritating, so he turned his gaze to the side window.

A clown was performing on the sidewalk, balancing six rollup computers on his head while juggling six holographic soccer balls with what looked like six hands. It was impossible to tell his real arms from his digital ones. The tourists watching his act were delighted. Juke saw three stern-looking Chinese women start to giggle.

Despite everything—the traffic, the pollution, the ubiquitous homefree people—Juke loved New York. He breathed in the aroma of Middle Eastern spices. You could find anything here: Kurdish creameries offering goat yogurt, Mexican-Japanese fusion joints serving cicada tacos, MacDonald's restaurants selling spicy mockburgers, trendy Uighur bistros specializing in organically raised yak gyros at fifty bucks a pop. On the corner was a med store advertising everything from jenkem to old-school hashish. Next to that was a Broadway theatre playing the new hit musical, *MacBugs!*

No question, New York was an amazing place. Except for one thing: the fact Safiya was here and he never saw her.

He shook his head, irritated at himself. *God, how long will it take me to get over her?* If three years wasn't enough, would it take five? Fifteen? Fifty? He'd always thought of himself as a pretty tough guy. This was getting ridiculous.

The Zan interrupted his thoughts, saying in the deep growly voice he'd programmed , "You have arrived at your destination."

Unfortunately, now that the NYPDinc was a corporation like any other, free parking for cops was a thing of the past. Just like handicapped parking. So Juke told the car, "Zan, park if you find a spot within a quarter mile, otherwise circle the block until we come back."

"You got it, boss," the Zan said.

As Juke and Haylee got out of the car, Haylee looked up uneasily at the Berkshire Vanguard Syndicate skyscraper looming above them. She was trying to stay positive about her upcoming meeting with a high-level executive who might help her, but this place freaked her out.

She'd been here twice before, once when she signed her initial income-share deal and a second time, during her senior year of college, when she applied for a year-long internship and was hoping Berkshire Vanguard would award her a fellowship. Several unsmiling executives interviewed and neurotested her, coldly evaluating her intelligence, career choices, and likely future income. She had never felt so small in her life. Ultimately they turned her down.

Now she followed Juke past the Corinthian columns into the grand, elegant lobby. She gazed up at the fifty-foot-tall, bronze, holographic letters spelling out "BERKSHIRE VANGUARD: WE GIVE YOU THE FREEDOM TO CHOOSE," and didn't notice the bot-sweeper coming her way. She ran right into it.

"Shit!" she said, as she tripped and fell.

The bot-sweeper moved off without a word as Juke helped her up. "You okay?"

She moved away from him, embarrassed. "Yeah, I'm fine."

But he eyed her closely. "You've barely said a word since we left the M.E.'s office. Is something bugging you?"

"I'm just tired."

"This is your syndicate, isn't it?"

She blinked. "How'd you know?"

"Just a guess. A lot of people get squirrely about their syndicates. You're scared of them, aren't you?"

She gave a quick laugh like, *don't be silly*. But Juke just looked at her, and finally she relented. "I guess I am a little nervous," she said. As they headed for the elevator, she added, "Don't antagonize them any more than you have to, okay?"

"Why, what can the syndicate do to you?"

"I don't plan on finding out. When you talk to them, just remember: you catch more flies with honey."

"Whatever you say, partner."

Haylee followed Juke into an empty elevator. He said, "Twenty-eighth floor," and they headed up. Then he turned to her. "So what's your P, if you don't mind me asking?"

Haylee was taken aback. P's were private. She hadn't told Harrison her P til they'd been working together for six months. Hell, she hadn't told him til they were already sleeping together.

But Juke had always seemed like someone she could trust, and he'd proven that by not busting her for her little bout of insanity this morning.

Besides, why should she be ashamed? Everybody was at least partially owned. So she told Juke, "They get twenty P of my gross for another seven years."

He nodded sympathetically. "You have any restrictions?"

She shrugged, playing it down, her reticence returning. She didn't want

Juke's sympathy. "Not that many. Drug testing, and there's a penalty if I have kids…"

Oops—she hadn't meant to talk about that. She didn't want to give anybody at work any hints she was pregnant. So she veered to a different topic. "Not that I'm complaining. Berkshire Vanguard paid for college—*and* high school. Without that I'd be gigging at Starbucks."

The elevator door opened and they came out into the hallway, walking past patriotic murals from the American Revolution and *Atlas Shrugged.*

Juke said, "Must've been nice in the old days, huh? Back when high school was free, and you didn't have to make a syndicate deal to go to college."

"Yeah, right," Haylee said sarcastically. "Except taxes and student loans were insanely high and the government controlled everything."

"You believe that?"

What a weird question, Haylee thought. "Of course. Don't you?"

Juke looked at Haylee and thought how different she was from Safiya. Like most of America, she probably got her news from Foxbook. It was one reason he thought the Resistance didn't stand a chance. He got a sudden urge for a drink.

Of course, maybe Haylee had a point and he was romanticizing the old days. He'd read that when the syndicate investment system was first introduced as a way to help poor and middle-class kids go to college, everybody, liberals and conservatives alike, thought it was a great idea. It seemed way better than student loans, where you could be on the hook for insane dollars even if you didn't have a job.

But when the Depression hit, and people began selling off pieces of themselves for all kinds of reasons besides education…

Haylee broke into his thoughts, asking, "What P are you?"

"Zero," he answered.

She stared at him. "No way."

"I went to a cheapo networld high school and skipped college. Didn't want anybody owning even one percent of me."

"But how'd you get into the NYPDinc without going to college?"

"I bribed somebody," Juke said, his standard response. Haylee laughed, like they all did. Actually he did bribe somebody—his Dad's old boss—but no one ever believed him.

They entered a large, open reception area. Behind the front desk was a female receptionist—well, female bot receptionist—dressed in a red business suit. If she were human, you'd have said she was in her mid-twenties. When Juke lived with Safiya, she and her friends used to have constant discussions about whether bots should be considered brothers and sisters in the Rez, or just bots. To Juke it was simple. They were bots. "May I help you?" she asked pleasantly.

"Yes, thank you," Juke said. Despite his views about bots, he always talked to them as if they were people; it felt less complicated. He pulled out his badge. "I'm Detective O'Keefe. We're here to see Michael Billingsley."

Haylee's eyes opened wide, startled. *Michael Billingsley?* She remembered that name well. He was one of the execs who turned her down for the fellowship. But he was the one she liked—the only one who looked her in the eyes and smiled. When her application got rejected, she was told one of the execs had voted for her. She'd always felt sure it was Billingsley.

What incredible luck he was the exec they were meeting with! All her optimism returned.

"Mr. Billingsley is expecting you," the receptionist said. "This way, please."

She led them back through the cube area toward Billingsley's office. They passed a video of a blissful couple holding hands on the beach, with gentle waves and a sparkling blue chyron: "BERKSHIRE VANGUARD: WE MAKE YOUR DREAMS COME TRUE."

Haylee looked up at the slogan and thought, *Please make my baby's dreams come true.*

Juke thought, *Boy, these people sure have a lot of slogans.*

But hopefully Berkshire Vanguard would give him the break he needed. Syndies gathered mountains of intel on their high-percenters, to make sure they weren't hiding income. Juke had used this data to solve murders before.

If Talia's murder wasn't random—and Juke was pretty sure it wasn't—then the key to this case might lie somewhere in Michael Billingsley's files.

Chapter Twenty-Nine

1:32 pm

Karolyn

Karolyn rode in the ambulance from AppleSoft Syndicate Park to the nearest ER, siren blaring. Sölvi Hilmarsson's body was stashed in the duffel bag in the back, next to the still moaning Agent Willard. Karolyn was in a hurry—*only ten hours to stop Chocolate!* So she and the two agents with EMT-looking uniforms dropped off Willard and kept the siren on while they headed for a building supply store to buy a cinderblock and rope. She'd decided to go old-school: put the cinderblock inside the duffel with the body and dump it in the East River. That would be quickest.

As the other agents entered the store, Karolyn stayed behind in the ambulance. She needed to get started analyzing Sölvi's burner phone. It took longer than usual to power up, and while she waited she checked out the bloodstains on her suit and decided it was ruined. Fortunately she had another suit in her office closet. That got her thinking about the new bot lover she'd bought off the interdrone that was sitting in her closet too, just waiting to be turned on. She closed her eyes briefly as she thought about it.

It used to bother Karolyn that whenever she zapped somebody, she got a huge craving for sexual release. But then she decided it wasn't that killing turned her on; she needed a distraction so she could wipe out of her mind all the terrible things she'd just witnessed. That blood spurting from Sölvi's eye socket… His other eye opening wide as he died, like he was staring at her—

Suddenly Sölvi's phone exploded in her hand.

She screamed and dropped it—but not before burning plastic ripped into her hand and forearm. Red-hot sparks jumped all over her wool coat. She yanked it off, tearing the buttons. More sparks ate into her neck and chin. She clawed them off her.

But she unintentionally kicked burning remnants of the I! onto the duffel bag, and that started sparking up too. Shit, what if Sölvi's body caught fire and the cops came? The NYPDinc cooperated with the Agency—but there were limits.

Suddenly somebody pounded on the ambulance door—two burly sub-contractor types. They must have heard her scream through the windows.

"Are you okay? Open up!" one of them shouted, rattling the door handle.

"Go away!" she yelled, as she kicked the I! remnants off the duffel bag and tried to stamp out the sparks. The duffel was smoking.

"Open the door!" the other guy shouted. They jiggled the handles and the burglar alarm screeched.

She pulled her Ruby Ridge and held it up to the window, pointing it at the two men. "Get away from here—now!"

They stared at her wide-eyed and backed up. But now everybody in the parking lot was watching her. She finally found the alarm switch and turned it off, but they kept looking. The ambulance was filling up with smoke.

She used her ruined suit jacket to smother the burning I! remnants. Then she found two jugs of saline solution in the back of the ambulance and dumped them on the duffel. She hoped that wasn't a burning body she was smelling.

Gradually everything got back to normal, more or less. Except she felt like an idiot.

But how was she supposed to know the goddamn phone was rigged to blow up if an unknown party turned it on? In all her years with the Agency, she'd never seen that before.

Somebody with major skills had rigged this phone. Karolyn was more certain than ever her adversaries were extremely dangerous. She better find these anarchist psychos.

Fast.

Chapter Thirty

1:45 pm

Safiya and Rey

As soon as Safiya got back to her speck, she sent the New York Eighteen—she didn't know it was seventeen now—a new song on their I!'s and Hodus. It was a recent hit by the Love Slaves, "Gimme Gimme Gimme." The first verse was about holographic sex, but the second verse began: "Gimme chocolate gimme sweet I suck it off your feet."

This was the secret signal confirming Chocolate was proceeding tonight as planned. She could only imagine how terrified all her people had been when they didn't receive the song at noon—especially poor Jeannie, who always got so anxious when things didn't go exactly according to plan. Safiya had a soft spot for Jeannie, because she had loved ones doing heavy prison time too. Safiya's brothers Perry and Cyrus had four more years to go. She hoped there would be a better world waiting for them when they got out.

And then there was the world's sweetest couple, Diane and Mychal, so hoping to start a family. She pictured them holding each other close, trying to reassure each other. She felt guilty for not sending them the confirmation when she was supposed to, but she had so much to deal with today!

As her kittens reminded her now, meowing for food. She spooned ground-up bugs out of the can for them and thought to herself: *taking these little guys in was a mistake.* Here she was, a leader of the Resistance, planning an op that could alter the future of the entire human race—and she had to stop everything to feed Tubby and Tubman.

But they sure were cute, she had to admit, as she watched them eat their bugs and lap down their milk. She'd gotten them from an elderly neighbor who was spending a month in jail for not reporting six hundred dollars of income to his syndicate. If she hadn't stepped in, Tubby and Tubman would have gone to the pound.

Safiya was always saving kittens and stray cats. Maybe not as satisfying as saving people, but a lot easier.

She drank some milk herself and considered her next move. She felt uneasy. She'd thrown Talia's Hodu down a Quarterpotty toilet. But what if it had contained an important clue to Talia's murder? Maybe she was keeping Juke from catching the killer.

She decided to buzz Sölvi again, to see if he had any ideas about who killed Talia. But his burner was still turned off.

If she had a half-decent theory on the murder, she would tell Juke, anonymously. But she couldn't come up with one. After her recent convo with Diego, she was even more convinced it wasn't him; he could never have done such a great job of faking his innocence.

Though if he wanted her help escaping the cops and getting to Canada, then of course he's play innocent with her, even if—

No. It couldn't be Diego, it just couldn't.

The murder must be connected to tonight's op. But how?

She couldn't stop herself from asking, once again, what Juke would do if his homicide investigation led him to Chocolate—and to her. Especially if he discovered that she had destroyed key evidence, intentionally obstructing him. Would he feel she'd betrayed him yet again? Maybe he would be so angry, he'd jack her himself.

More likely, he'd go off somewhere and get drunk while somebody else jacked her—his partner, probably.

She desperately needed to stay one step ahead of Juke and keep him and his partner from finding out about tonight. Or if they did find out something, she needed to know about it. She tried to think what Juke's next move would be. He'd probably hit the morgue and hustle his M.E. friend, Vinnie…

All of a sudden, despite everything, Safiya smiled. She remembered the darkly funny texts Juke used to send her from the morgue, like: "The vic has an ax in his head. Guess he 'axed' for it." Or: "A couple CGs went bowling last night. Guess what they used for a bowling ball?"

At first these missives had disturbed her. But then she realized Juke was just letting off steam because he cared so deeply.

From what she'd seen this morning, he seemed like his old self. She wondered how he was doing now—

Behind her, Rey walked into the kitchen. Hearing his footsteps, she felt vaguely annoyed—and guilty.

She loved Rey. For a year now he had stood beside her in the Rez and supported her when she was down. He was a good comrade and terrific hacker, and they'd pulled off a lot of cool ops together. Taking over TikTagram for a day had been a PR masterstroke. If she sometimes felt there was a little something missing, that he could be a bit needy at times and maybe overdid the med coke now and then, still, as she'd learned all too well from being with Juke, no ship is perfect, no matter how much you love the person—

"The kittens peed on the rug," Rey said.

She clenched her teeth. *Seriously?* Cats had always been an issue between them. She sometimes wondered if he was jealous of the attention she gave them. "I'll clean it up later," she said.

She closed her eyes, willing him to leave. But he plunked himself down at the counter. "So what do you think is gonna happen?"

How many times had he asked her that today? She didn't answer, just leaned down and poured a little more milk into the kittens' bowl. Rey acted tough in Rez meetings, advocating radical action, but now that they were dealing with a legit holy-crap crisis, he was turning out to be…well, a typical man. In her experience, when the chips were down women were stronger and more composed.

Of course, there were exceptions to this rule, like…

Rey's Hodu dinged from the bedroom. "Wonder what that's about," he said, and headed back there to check.

* * *

As Rey walked away from Safiya, he thought about how cold she'd been to him today—ever since she saw Juke. She was treating Rey like a scared kid or something. He sensed she was comparing him to her old boyfriend.

It's not fair, he thought, *I'm just being sensible.* This whole scheme to go ahead with Chocolate tonight despite Talia's murder… He was going along with it, but let's be honest, it was insane! They should be lying low instead.

And sure, Safiya was the one who actually stole the cars—but he did the hacking. If she got caught, they'd *both* get jacked. So how did that make him a scared kid or whatever?

Okay, yeah, Juke had slipped past him at Talia's speck. But that could have happened to anybody.

I deserve more credit, Rey thought. Sure, Safiya was a mega, but what he contributed was pretty darn important too.

Rey had always felt a nagging vibe, even during the first thrilling weeks of their ship, that Safiya wasn't totally giving herself to him. She was holding back somehow. He'd shrugged it off, figuring he was just being insecure. But now he wondered if he'd picked up on something real—and that something was named Juke. She still had feels for Juke, Rey decided unhappily, as he unrolled his computer to see who or what had dinged him.

* * *

Safiya decided to watch Juke's video about Talia again. Maybe she'd find clues to which direction his investigation was heading. As Tubby and Tubman nibbled at her shoes, she hit the icon and Juke came onto her phone screen, saying, "Hi, I'm Juke O'Keefe, NYPDinc Homicide."

When he gazed into the cam with his passionate brown eyes and said, "Please. Help us catch the monster who killed this girl…" Safiya couldn't take her own eyes off him.

If it was any other cop, she'd figure he was faking compassion to make a sale. But with Juke she knew it was real. She was so glad he hadn't turned cynical after their breakup.

All at once she got an overwhelming desire to throw caution to the wind and go see him. She would call him , assuming he still had the same number. They could meet somewhere private, away from his partner, away from everyone, and she'd tell him everything. She'd beg him to stop investigating this murder, for her sake. Just this once, let it go.

But that would make him an accomplice in their de-chipping op. If they got caught and neurointerrogated, Juke would get thrown in prison too and suffer the same tortures they did. It wouldn't be fair to him.

She had ended their ship and broken his heart. She still remembered the despair in his eyes when she walked away from their speck, wheeling her suitcase, on that freezing December morning. How could she possibly ask him to risk his life for her now? He'd almost certainly say no—but if he said yes, that would be even worse.

Suddenly Rey came back in from the bedroom excited, carrying his rollup. "I just got a hit on your ex-boyfriend's car. He's at 43rd and Scalia, heading uptown."

Safiya was taken aback. "How'd you find that out?"

"One of the interdrones I hacked into located him. Any idea where he might be going?"

"No. At least he's not heading toward us."

"We need to bug his car right now," Rey said, grabbing his coat. "That way if he and his partner find out about Chocolate, we'll know. We can get in the Lex and run."

Safiya frowned. "How would we bug his car?

"I'll download an eavesdropping app on this burner." He took a burner phone from the back of the silverware drawer. "Soon as he parks somewhere, we'll hack into his car and hide this under the front seat."

"I feel funny spying on Juke," Safiya said.

Rey stared at her, incredulous. "Are you insane? Your Dinc ex-boyfriend and his buddies could put the whole revolution in danger. They could lock us up for the next twenty years."

Safiya knew he was right. She stood up and got her coat, and they walked out the door.

Chapter Thirty-One

1:59 pm

Haylee and Juke

Michael Billingsley, President of New York operations for Berkshire Vanguard, had a corner office on the 30th floor. Outside his windows, drones and holos punctuated the gray Manhattan sky.

Every wall of Billingsley's office shimmered and changed colors, creating an air of constant movement and excitement, except for the wall facing him. This was painted the exact shade of dark green that made him the most relaxed, according to his neuroscan. His desk, chair, and coffee cup were all made of glass, encrusted with jewels that were digitally secured. If anyone tried to remove them from the room, an alarm would sound.

He was seated behind his desk when Juke and Haylee entered, escorted by the bot receptionist. A confident man in his mid-forties, his body was carefully shaped by thirty-six minutes a day with his personal trainer. In contrast to his aggressively hypermodern, multicolored office, he wore a gray pinstriped suit and dark red tie that could have come straight out of some presidential debate from the previous century.

He stood and greeted Juke and Haylee with firm handshakes. "Detective O'Keefe. And Ms. Navarro. I'm so glad to meet you."

Haylee recognized Billingsley immediately, especially his warm smile.

She was too nervous to do anything but smile back. Juke said, "Thank you for your time."

"Of course. Please, have a seat."

Juke and Haylee settled into their glass chairs—which were a foot lower than Billingsley's, Juke noted. No doubt a ploy to make his visitors feel inferior.

Billingsley sipped coffee from his jeweled cup and shook his head sadly. "Such a terrible tragedy. Talia was a beautiful girl. I'm so glad you've taken an interest."

"How well did you know her?" Juke asked.

"As head of Manhattan operations, I try to meet all our clients at least once." He eyed Haylee curiously, squinting a little. "You know, you look familiar."

Haylee said, "I was wondering if you'd remember me. I'm a client. We met a few years ago."

Billingsley beamed at her. "I thought so. I never forget a pretty face."

Juke thought, *talk about corny*. But it didn't seem to bother Haylee any; she smiled awkwardly at Billingsley and blushed. Juke was amused and a little irritated. *I guess if you're rich it doesn't matter how corny you are,* he thought.

"So how are things going for you?" Billingsley asked Haylee.

"Great. My deal with Berkshire Vanguard has totally worked out for me."

Juke belatedly understood Haylee wasn't just flirting. She was kissing this guy's ass. As someone who had never been owned, even partially, Juke was constantly surprised by the psychological hold syndies had on their clients.

Billingsley said to Haylee, "I'm so thrilled to hear that."

Juke broke into their lovefest. "Mr. Billingsley, could you give us some background on Talia?"

"Of course," Billingsley said pleasantly. He consulted Talia's file on his Hodu Supreme. "We began investing in Talia five years ago, when she came to the U.S. We helped her get residency status."

"What P did you take?"

"Twenty for seven."

That meant twenty percent for seven years, Juke knew. "And how did you become a majority owner?"

"Talia came back to us a year later when she injured her back and required surgery. Then she became addicted to painkillers, so she had to go to rehab…" He lifted his shoulders in a sad shrug. "Things added up."

Juke nodded. "Any violent episodes in her past? Was her back injury caused by somebody getting physical with her?"

"No, she got caught in the Oklahoma City Earthquake."

She was lucky she survived, Juke thought; ten thousand people didn't. "What information do you have on Talia's boyfriends?" Remembering the female scent of the intruder, he added, "Or girlfriends?"

Billingsley looked at his computer and frowned. "I'm afraid we don't have anything."

Juke was taken aback. "Are you sure? Any info about roommates?"

"I'm sorry. She lived by herself."

"When was Berkshire Vanguard's last contact with her?"

Billingsley checked his computer again. "Three months ago. She was teaching neuroyoga part-time and trying to make it as a visual artist." He gave a little laugh. "As if we'd ever recoup our investment that way. So we sent her to one of our corporate partners, a club in Soho called Bottoms Up."

Juke glared at him, not bothering to hide his disapproval. "You forced her to work as a stripper?"

Sitting next to Juke, Haylee gave a start. *Don't glitch this guy off,* she thought. *I need him!*

But Billingsley just smiled indulgently. "No, she was a hostess. And it was a mutual decision. Don't believe everything you link. Your partner here will tell you we're not evil tyrants, like the so-called Resistance movement makes us out to be."

Haylee smiled her agreement. "Absolutely," she said.

Billingsley stood up. "Now is there anything else I can do for you? I'm afraid I'm late for a client meeting."

"Thank you so much for your time, Mr. Billingsley," Haylee said, standing too.

But Juke stayed seated. "Actually, there is something important I'd like to ask you."

Billingsley and Haylee both waited.

"As I'm sure you can imagine," Juke continued, "murder investigations require a great deal of resources—"

Billingsley held up his left hand to stop him. "I'm afraid I can't help you with that."

But Juke kept pushing. "Sir, a donation of three thousand dollars would jumpstart our investigation, and be an excellent way to show the world your syndicate really cares about its people—"

"The world is already quite aware how much we care. We donate more money to religious institutions than any other syndicate."

Juke needed to puncture this asshole's smugness. "Sir, your syndicate owned this girl. You owe it to her memory to find out who killed her."

Haylee's throat tightened. *Oh God, let's get out of here before Billingsley blows up.*

But if he was getting riled, he didn't show it. He said evenly, "Berkshire Vanguard has a strict policy against giving charity to our clients—even after they're dead. It undercuts our core principle that people need to take personal responsibility for their actions."

Juke finally stood—but he didn't turn to leave. He was four inches taller than Billingsley, so he looked down at him. "Talia Qirimoglu was not 'responsible' for getting savagely assaulted and murdered."

Billingsley eyed Juke coolly. "Detective, ten years ago, when I lost my finger…"

He held up his right hand; sure enough it was missing a finger, the pinkie. Juke hadn't noticed.

"…The pain was excruciating," Billingsley continued. "But I never got hooked on cheap narcos. Talia was a woman who made bad choices. I imagine one of those bad choices led to her death."

Juke's fury rose inside him so fast, sweat popped on the back of his neck.

What a sanctimonious prick. Easy to make good choices when you've got so much money you drink out of jeweled coffee cups. Men like Billingsley bought and sold human beings. They drove good people to their deaths.

Juke told Billingsley, "You're full of shit. You have no idea what led to Talia's death—so don't dishonor her memory with stupid assumptions."

Then he walked out of the room before he started assaulting this idiot.

Haylee gave Billingsley a sickly half-smile and left too.

No way she'd ever get a discount after this. She was totally, permanently sunk.

And so was Hera.

God, she wanted to kill Juke.

Seventy-nine thousand dollars. What the hell would she do now?

Chapter Thirty-Two

2:17 pm

Karolyn, the Red Queen, and Dr. Marie Swanson

After dumping Sölvi's body, Karolyn raced back to Agency headquarters. She cleaned her wounds from the I! explosion and changed into her spare suit, identical to the ruined one except it was black. Now she almost felt like herself again as she hurried up the long basement hallway to the tech department. Some agents claimed they could still smell the aroma of the old books that used to line these walls. But she didn't smell anything herself and figured they were just rich-kid elitists with liberal arts degrees imagining things.

"Karolyn," she heard someone say. She turned, and Raja was walking toward her. Great, this was the last thing she needed: her insufferable boss slowing her down.

Raja said, "So the Icelandic guy, he's…"

"He's no problem." She didn't elaborate; he wouldn't want to know the details of where the body went.

"Too bad you weren't able to bring him in alive."

Karolyn heard the reproach in his voice. If they didn't stop tonight's Resistance action, Raja would probably set her up as the fall guy.

"We still have Sölvi's non-burner phone," she said, taking it out of her pocket. "We should be able to get datascoop from this—"

"Don't turn it on!" Raja threw up his hands in front of his face to protect himself.

"Of course not." She wasn't sure if he was seriously scared or just messing with her. "I'm giving it to the tech guys and telling them they better hack it before midnight."

"What else are you doing?"

"We have fingerprints coming from Talia's speck. The Red Queen is on Code One, and I'm about to check in with Captain Burgess."

They came out into the big open area dominated by the gleaming scarlet body of the Red Queen, in all her metallic, angular glory. Raja said, "The Director is extremely concerned about this matter."

That brought Karolyn up short. Raja had already informed the Director of the entire Agency about her investigation, without telling her?

He continued, "If this chatter is real—if the Rez really finds a way to de-chip people—"

She interrupted him. "Sir, believe me, I get how important this is."

"I'm not sure you do." He turned toward her. "The Board met last week."

Twice a year, the top national executives from the Big Six met at a hunting lodge in northern New Mexico. These meetings were so hush-hush, for security reasons, that Karolyn hadn't even known this one had already taken place.

Raja said, "They decided gen pop is psychologically prepared to accept an expanded chipping program."

Duh. "That's not exactly a secret. The Invest In People Act will allow syndies to chip just about everybody—not just fifty-one percenters."

"Right, but the program is expanding in other ways too. Exciting ways." Raja gave her a cagey look. "The new generation of biochips doesn't only have GPS data. They do drug and alcohol testing and dopamine and depression detection. They even test for a cocktail of aggression hormones, starting with testosterone. That could help us prevent violent antisocial behavior before it occurs."

Karolyn's hand went reflexively to her belly, as she wondered if the chip in her midsection tested for more things than she'd realized. Did the Red

Queen and Raja know about her little bot love breaks? "That's a pretty impressive list of chip attributes."

"And it's only the beginning." Raja put his hand on the Red Queen, feeling her hard, curveless surface. "We expect these chips will be used within five years, ten at the outside, to regulate mood. The goal is a happy, more productive population, untroubled by unnecessary stress and unaffected by Resistance propaganda."

He eyed Karolyn meaningfully. "But for that to be possible, we need absolute chip integrity and security."

She tried not to show how pissed off she was getting. Enough already, she got the point. "Sir, is there anything else you'd like me to do?"

"Convo with Captain Burgess immediately. I'll contact the Human Hill to see if anyone's heard any de-chipping rumors." The Human Hill consisted of all the CEO's of New York operations for the Big Six.

Raja continued, "The Rez is planning this op for midnight, so we need to kick ass—now." He threw Karolyn a look. "We don't have time to take any breaks."

Karolyn's face reddened. *He does know about the bot love.*

* * *

Back in her office, Karolyn called Burgess to light a fire under him. When he picked up, she said immediately, "What do you got?"

Burgess cleared his throat. "Funny, I was just about to call you."

Karolyn sat up in her chair. "Did O'Keefe find something?"

"Not yet, but I'm sure he will. The reason I was calling was, one of our Deputy Commissioners called me in. And he said, for the amount of interagency cooperation you're asking for…" His voice trailed off, then he hit her with the punch line. "Ten Reagans isn't really enough."

Karolyn's anger level went to ten in a second. "Are you fucking kidding me? All I asked you to do is call your detective and find out what he's up to!"

"Sorry, Karolyn, this is one of the Deps talking."

"Which one?"

"That's kind of internal information. Anyway, he said twenty-five Reagans would be more appropriate."

Karolyn was willing to bet Burgess hadn't talked to anyone. But he'd divined how important this case was to her, and he was chunked at her for rejecting his advances, so now he was shaking her down for more.

She said, "Go to hell. Ten is all you get."

"Well, I don't know. I'll have to check with the Dep—"

"You better hold up your end or I'll have your ass," she said, and tapped off.

At first she just felt furious. But then she began to second-guess herself. What if Burgess took revenge by firewalling her out of the loop, or slow-playing her? She couldn't have that. The moment O'Keefe found out anything, she needed to know it.

Maybe she was misreading the balance of power here. At all her other postings, the local cops were intimidated by the Agency. But in New York, people were more arrogant.

Her mood darkened even further when she heard back from the IT techs. They hadn't discovered anything noteworthy yet on Sölvi's unexploded phone. Then the fingerprint techs buzzed her that Talia's speck didn't have prints from anybody connected to the Resistance.

Karolyn threw a shoe at the wall. It was a gym shoe, not one of her Streizas, she wasn't *crazy;* but still, she threw it.

Should she call Burgess back and say yes to the twenty-five Reagans? But if she gave in to him after initially saying no, he was the type of guy who'd brag about it. Word would spread, and it would be a disaster. She was new in town, and she'd look like some small-town Southern rube. Raja would find out.

Her computer buzzed, distracting her. It was her bot assistant, who she'd named Benedict because his elegant, mildly sardonic voice reminded her of the late, great—and sexy as fuck, she loved Englishmen—Benedict Cumberbatch.

"You have a call from Michael Billingsley, CEO of New York operations for Berkshire Vanguard," Benedict informed her.

Karolyn took the call immediately, and Billingsley appeared on her screen. *Whoa, talk about sexy,* she thought. This guy could make her forget about bots once and for all. Strong chin, a confident air—and sitting behind a glass, jewel-encrusted desk. *Nice.*

"Mr. Billingsley, what can I do for you?"

"It's a pleasure to meet you, Ms. Ford," he said with a smile. "You're new here, aren't you? I've heard great things about you."

"Thank you." Karolyn hoped the burn marks on her neck and jawline weren't showing up on Billingsley's screen.

His face turned serious. "Listen, I got a snap from Raja about this Resistance de-chipping op. Obviously extremely disturbing, and I want to help any way I can."

"I appreciate that."

"Raja said it may be related to the murder of a young woman named Talia Qirimoglu. So I wanted to let you know the NYPDinc just interviewed me about her."

"Really." She lowered her head a little so the marks on her neck would be less visible. "Why did they come to you?"

"Because we owned Talia."

Of course. She should have remembered that. She needed another espressaccino. "Did you get a sense of the direction of their investigation?"

"My impression was they had zilch. Grasping for straws."

Karolyn nodded. "I thought as much."

Billingsley leaned forward, and his face grew on her screen. Ordinarily that made people look less attractive, but the opposite was true for him. "The real reason I'm calling you…I didn't get a good feel about the lead detective, Juke O'Keefe. Some of the things he said seemed a little…"

"You're concerned he may be a sympathizer?"

Billingsley's smile returned. "I guess you're already on top of that, huh?"

I'd like to be on top of you, Karolyn thought, then got annoyed at herself. She should use that bot for release before she did something stupid.

"O'Keefe is a problem," she admitted. "We need somebody in place on the homicide squad that we can trust." She def did not trust Burgess. She rubbed her chin pensively, then worried it might draw attention to the burn marks so she pulled her hand away. "Did you meet O'Keefe's partner, Haylee Navarro?"

"Great minds think alike," Billingsley said. "I think she could be very useful for intel purposes. She got upset when O'Keefe tried to give me a hard time. She's twenty P, and she seemed like someone who's eager to please authority figures."

This was a much-used cliché in high-level syndicate circles. Execs were always discussing how to make gen pop "eager to please authority figures."

Karolyn said, "Thank you for the tip. We'll definitely consider her."

"Good." Billingsley gave her that smile again. "Please ping me if there's anything else I can do. In fact, I'd love to keep up to date on the case, so give me a ping regardless."

Karolyn blinked. She was positive: he was coming on to her. "Will do," she said, and tapped off.

She was about to connect with the Red Queen, then realized the Red Queen had been connected all along. "So what do you think?" she asked.

In her Maggie Thatcher voice, the Red Queen responded, "Based on his vocal upticks but relative lack of tension level, there's an 89 percent chance he's available for a fling but only a 16 percent chance he's interested in something long-term."

"That's not what I was asking about."

"I know," said the Red Queen. "I was messing with you."

Karolyn rolled her eyes. Sometimes she found the Red Queen's dry British humor grating. "Tell me about O'Keefe's partner. How do I get to her? What's the best and fastest way to turn her into an asset?"

"I'm working on that."

"Well, work fast."

"If I may make a suggestion, Karolyn—"

"By all means."

"I'm detecting a 9.85 level of stress. Despite what Raja said, now might be a good time for one of your little fifteen-minute breaks."

So the Red Queen knows too. Karolyn looked toward her closet where her new bot lover waited patiently, ever ready. She could one hundred P use him right now. She could already feel her blood rushing downward, anticipating a release.

But what if her belly chip somehow told Raja what she was up to? While there was obviously nothing illegal about bot love, and nothing against it in Agency policy, she preferred to keep her sex life as private as she could. Despite all the social advances of the past century, women still faced a double standard about bot love, just like they did for every other kind of sex. Maybe the vibe wasn't as heavy as it used to be, but it was still there.

Karolyn sighed. "Not now, but thanks for the advice."

She looked out her window at the gray New York sky. Sometimes she missed the simplicity of life in Macon County. She could always go back there and marry some local guy, get a low- level admin gig, find some cheap hobby like birdwatching…

She shook her head. *Who am I kidding?*

She had spent her whole life rising out of the Alabama mud. Nothing and nobody would ever push her back down into it.

She was going to be a fucking Agency star. Her years of living on fried bugburgers were over.

"Give me everything you have on O'Keefe's partner," Karolyn told the Red Queen.

* * *

At that very moment, at the Liberty Medical Center, Dr. Marie Swanson finally got her first break of the day. She desperately needed it; she'd been working six hours straight and she'd seen forty-four ob/gyn patients. Eating a hummus sandwich at her desk, she dictated notes about all forty-four of them into her rollup.

Her notes immediately went into the national medical records system.

* * *

Twenty-eight milliseconds later, the Red Queen announced, "Excellent timing. If I believed in God, I'd say He just sent us a sign."

"Meaning what?" Karolyn said.

"I've just received new data. Haylee Navarro is pregnant—with her late fiancé's child."

Karolyn sat up straight. "Really. Does she intend to keep it?"

"Yes. *And* she's hoping to enhance it."

Karolyn broke into a grin. "No shit," she said.

"No shit," the Red Queen agreed.

If the Red Queen could have grinned too, she would have.

Chapter Thirty-Three

2:20 pm

Juke, Haylee, Safiya, and Rey

Juke stalked out of the Berkshire Vanguard building, still seething at Billingsley. Haylee had to step fast to keep up with him. She was mad too, though for different reasons.

They strode down the crumbling sidewalk toward the Zan, which had been circling the block this whole time. Haylee's I*!* said it was now stuck in traffic around the corner.

Juke ranted, "Billingsley has a lot of balls talking about 'core principles.' Talia wants to be an artist, so what does he do? Makes her work in a strip club."

Haylee was in no mood to be supportive. She had specifically asked Juke not to raise hell with Billingsley. Maybe Juke hadn't meant to screw her—but he did. She said petulantly, "I bet Talia's whole artist thing was bogus. She was just trying to renege on her contract."

"Oh, for cake's sake."

"That's what people do. She was probably working some black market gig so she wouldn't have to pay the syndicate their percentage."

"Who can blame her?"

"When people cheat the syndies, it's not fair to the rest of us. Drives up our rates."

"Good thing I'm not owned," Juke said, "I'd kill somebody."

He almost fell into a pothole, which glitched him off even more. The damn syndies never bothered to fix their sidewalks. He turned the corner and saw his gridlocked Zan up ahead.

Then he noticed a tall, slender guy in a buzzcut and anti-pollution mask walking across the street. He seemed to be heading straight for the Zan—but at the last moment, just when he reached the driver's side door, he veered off.

Juke felt like he'd seen this guy somewhere, recently. "Does that doob look familiar?"

"What doob?" Haylee said.

"In the black T-shirt." The guy was walking rapidly away. "It looked like he was gonna try to get in our car."

"He was just dodging traffic."

Juke decided Haylee was probably right and he had imagined it. They got in the Zan and started downtown to Bottoms Up, the strip club where Talia had worked. They rode past a hot chocolate shop…

* * *

…Where Rey was hiding in the back corner.

Safiya had buzzed him the instant she spotted Juke walking toward the Zan. Thank God she did, because Rey was about to hack in and leave his bug. Now he was petrified the Dincs would run into the shop after him. He was up on his toes, all set to dash out the back door.

Finally Safiya texted Rey the all-clear. He slipped out the front door and looked both ways before ducking into the stolen Lex idling nearby with Safiya in the front seat.

"Jesus, that was close," he gasped as they rode off.

As the terror left him, he began feeling exhilarated. For once it had been him taking point on a dangerous op instead of Safiya, because if Juke had seen her he'd have recognized her. *Rey* was the brave one this time!

Then he looked up ahead and saw Juke's black Zan, only five cars in front of them. His fears roared back. "Turn right. Let's get the hell out of here."

"No, we'll follow them. We still have to bug their vehicle," Safiya said.

He started to protest, then stopped. She was right, of course. Nothing had changed. They needed to follow Juke and his partner until they parked somewhere and got out. Then Rey could sneak into their car and get it bugged at last.

They didn't have time to program the Lex's carbrain to follow the Zan, so Safiya shifted out of automatic, grabbed the steering wheel, and drove.

She followed Juke downtown, trying to stay five cars behind and wishing the bright yellow Lex they'd stolen wasn't so conspicuous.

* * *

Up ahead, Juke and Haylee got stuck in traffic again, and Juke wanted to punch somebody.

Haylee checked the LED display. "We should go over to Tenth. They have a special today: two and a half dollars per mile."

Juke shook his head emphatically. "Forget it, that would take an extra eight minutes. We need to get to Bottoms Up, *now*."

Haylee didn't answer. Her I*!* had just buzzed with an extremely strange message from Captain Burgess: *"Come back to the office. Don't tell Juke where you're going."*

Don't tell Juke?! She texted back, *"What's this about?"*

Burgess responded, *"Come right now."*

Haylee's heart pounded. Had Burgess found out somehow about her meltdown this morning? Was he going to suspend her?

But why would he keep that secret from Juke?

As she tried to puzzle this out, Juke said, "Let's see what networld says about Bottoms Up—"

"Oh no!" Haylee said suddenly, banging her forehead with her hand. "Dammit!"

"What's wrong?"

"It's almost three. I have to go." Juke frowned at her. She continued nervously, "I completely forgot. I'm having coffee with Harrison's mom."

"We have a drop-dead. You'll have to reschedule."

"I can't, I'm really sorry. I promised her, we're meeting in Little Taiwan."

Juke shook his head, disgusted. Would he ever find a partner as dedicated to solving murders as he was?

But then he realized he was being a jerk. Haylee's fiancé had just been killed, and she wanted to spend time with his mom. *How can I give her grief for that?*

"No prob," he said. "You can have the car, I'll take the subway."

Haylee said, "You don't have to do that, I'll oob it." Ubers usually took less than a minute to arrive in midtown.

Juke waved her off. "No, the car's all yours. Subway'll be quicker to Soho anyway." The Zan stopped dead again—more gridlock—so he got out. "Buzz me when you're done."

"Thanks," Haylee said.

She watched Juke walk off toward the subway stop. She felt bad lying to him. But she had to follow the Captain's orders, right?

Unaware of Haylee's turmoil, Juke headed down the gridlocked street—

* * *

—Straight toward the yellow Lex, five cars back. "What's he doing?" Rey said, terrified.

Safiya gripped the wheel tight. "I don't know."

Now Juke was only three cars away. Rey said, "He must've seen you!"

Safiya thought Rey might be right. She was boxed in on both sides, so she couldn't drive off and escape. She tried to read Juke's body language through the windshield.

"Stay low. Look down," she whispered. She took out her I! and held it in front of her face, hiding from Juke.

"Come on, drive!" Rey said, seeming not to notice that their car had zero room to move.

"Just stay low!"

Rey had no choice. He sank lower and held his breath as Juke came closer.

* * *

Walking down the row of gridlocked cars, Juke pulled out his I*!* and asked, "Which subway station is Bottoms Up?"

The I*!* told him. As he tried to decide whether it would be quicker to take the local or go four blocks further and take the express, he came to a yellow Lex.

He walked past it and kept on going.

* * *

Safiya and Rey let out huge sighs of relief.

"That was lucky," Rey breathed.

Safiya nodded, then looked up ahead. "His partner's turning right."

Rey got a sudden urge to go buy some synth, but of course now wasn't the time. They still needed to bug that car. The traffic eased up and they made it to the intersection. They caught up to the Zan and followed it downtown, staying a careful distance behind.

Rey decided Juke and his partner must have split up so they could follow two leads at once. He wondered how their investigation was going, and how soon it would lead them to Chocolate. He pictured Juke sitting in a brightly lit cubicle at the police station, typing away on a computer. The name "Rey Matoshi" would appear on Juke's screen. He would smile victoriously and jump up... He and his partner would bang on the door of Rey's speck, guns drawn...

Safiya broke into his dark fantasy. "Too bad Juke got the case. Every other detective in the city would've given up by now."

Rey snapped, "I'm sick of hearing how wonderful your ex-boyfriend is. If he was so tutti, why'd you break up with him?"

Please God, thought Safiya, *just let me make it through tonight.*

Through midnight.

They barely spoke another word to each other as they followed Juke's partner for twenty blocks. Then the Zan pulled into One Police Plaza and disappeared down into the police garage.

Safiya banged her hand on the steering wheel. No way they could slip down there undetected by Dinc security and leave their bug. They'd have to wait here on the street until Juke's partner rode the car back out again.

"I wonder what she's doing in the police station," Rey said.

Safiya wondered too, and a chill went down her spine. She had a bad vibe Juke's investigation was getting way too close to Chocolate.

Meanwhile, during the past few minutes of silence, Rey had decided he'd acted like a jealous ass just now. Sure, he was under pressure, but still. He had learned during the past year that Safiya was quick to forgive when he apologized, so he put his arm around her and kissed her. "I'm sorry if I was a little on edge before," he said.

"No worries." She kissed him back and let her shoulders relax.

Maybe all her fears were for nothing. At this very moment Juke could be arresting some random sexual predator for killing Talia, and his partner was returning to headquarters because the case was closed.

Juke and the NYPDinc would move on to a different murder. Chocolate would be safe.

Chapter Thirty-Four

3:02 pm

Haylee and Karolyn

Her stomach churning, Haylee knocked on Captain Burgess's door.

"Come in," his voice called.

She forced a confident smile onto her face and entered Burgess's office. He wasn't alone. An attractive woman in her early forties, wearing perfect makeup, pearls, and an expensive black suit, sat across the desk from him.

The woman rose to shake Haylee's hand. "Hi Haylee, my name's Karolyn Ford. I'm glad to meet you."

"Likewise," Haylee said, nonplussed.

Burgess stood up too. "I'll leave you ladies to discuss whatever you need to discuss. I see zilch, hear zilch, know zilch." With a wink Haylee couldn't decode—except it seemed fake, masking some sort of tension between him and this Karolyn person—Burgess walked out and closed the door behind him.

"Please, have a seat," Karolyn said.

"Thank you." Haylee sat in the guest chair. Karolyn rolled Burgess's chair out from behind the desk, so they could talk without having a barrier between them.

As Karolyn sat down, Haylee glanced up at the earnings wall and saw she and Juke still hadn't hit the two-hundred-dollar mark. Shit, was Karolyn from the Finance Unit, here to read her the riot act?

Karolyn said, "I'm sorry to pull you away from your case. How's that going?"

"Financially or investigatively?"

Karolyn smiled. "Both, I suppose."

Haylee tried to sound relaxed. "Same answer for both. We're in process. The first twenty-four hours is key."

Karolyn nodded appreciatively, as if Haylee had said something very wise. "Indeed it is." Then she held out a bowl of Alphas and Omegas—or "M & M's", as old people called them—that Burgess kept on his side of the desk and never offered to visitors. "Would you care for some… chocolate?"

Haylee got a weird vibe that when Karolyn said the word "chocolate," she gave it extra emphasis and eyed Haylee extra keenly. But that made no sense. Haylee must have imagined it. "No thanks," she said. She shifted uncomfortably, then realized fidgeting was a sign of weakness so she made herself sit still.

"I see you're not one for small talk," Karolyn said approvingly. "So I'll lay my chips on the table. I'm from the Syndicate Agency for Public Safety."

The Agency? What do they want with me?! Haylee quickly tried to think of anything questionable she might have done or been involved in.

Karolyn put up her hand. "Don't worry, you're not in trouble. In fact, we have a proposal for you that I think you'll find quite thrilling." She leaned forward. "We understand you'd like to enhance your daughter."

Haylee's jaw dropped. "How did you know I'm…? I haven't told anyone."

"Except your doctor. Don't worry, your secret is safe with me."

Safe with you and who else? Haylee thought. *Does Burgess know?*

Karolyn said, "I'm a strong believer in enhancement. It's the most important gift a mother can give to her child. We'd like to help you with that."

Finally Haylee was pretty sure she understood what was going on. This woman might technically work for some branch of the Agency, but really she was a syndie salesperson. She was here to talk Haylee into making a deal.

"Ms. Ford—"

"Call me Karolyn."

"I'd love to enhance my daughter, but I don't know if I can give up another ten percent."

"What if you don't have to give up anything?"

What the fuck?! "What's the catch?"

Karolyn said, "We've done a little research on you, Haylee. You've led an exemplary life. Graduated college in just three years and then went into law enforcement. You're a solid upstanding citizen."

Haylee was more puzzled than ever. "Thanks, I guess."

"Based on your social media and networld history, you're a supporter of the New American Freedom. You appreciate all the tremendous advantages that true liberty has brought into our lives." Karolyn paused. "Would you agree that's accurate?"

Why was this woman talking politics all of a sudden? "Sure," Haylee said.

"Then there's no catch." Karolyn smiled, pleased. "All we want you to do is help us defeat the forces of radical anti-American extremism. We need somebody inside the NYPDinc we can trust." She stood up. "I'm going to tell you something I expect you to keep secret from your partner."

Before Haylee could protest, Karolyn continued. "We have reason to believe the murder of Talia Qirimoglu is connected to a major Resistance conspiracy that's scheduled to reach fruition tonight—at midnight."

Haylee stared up at her. Was this for real? "What kind of Resistance conspiracy?"

"They're attempting to de-chip some fifty-one percenters and help them escape to Canada."

"But de-chipping is impossible. It triggers their bio-alarms."

"These people believe they've found a way around that."

Haylee was speechless. On Foxbook they said the bio-alarms were invulnerable. But this Agency woman seemed to be taking the threat seriously.

Karolyn asked, "Have you learned anything in your investigation that would support a link between the murder and this conspiracy?"

"No, not at all."

"Have you come across a Mexican-American man who was close to Talia? His name may begin with the letter D."

Haylee shook her head. "No."

"How about an Icelandic immie named Sölvi Hilmarrson?"

Haylee started to feel dumb, wondering what else she and Juke had missed. "I'm sorry, no."

"We believe the leader of this operation is a strong woman in her twenties or early thirties."

Haylee suddenly flashed to Juke's theory that the person who broke into Talia's speck was a woman. But that was pretty thin; she had no idea if Juke was right, or if the woman was "strong," or how old she was.

Besides, she didn't feel right giving intel to this Agency woman behind Juke's back. So she said, "We haven't come across anyone like that, that I can think of."

Karolyn eyed Haylee closely. Maybe she had noticed Haylee's hesitation. "Are you sure?"

"Yeah."

Karolyn nodded slowly. "Okay. No worries. But now I'd like you to keep on the lookout for any information regarding these three individuals. They're the key."

Haylee frowned. "And you want me to hide all this from my partner, even though it might help him solve the murder."

Karolyn said, "Would you agree with me that Juke has strong pro-Resistance sympathies?"

Haylee considered that. Juke had sounded an awful lot like a sympathizer when he went off on Billingsley. Also, his obsession with solving the murders of poor people said he was the kind of bleeding-heart who—

Karolyn interrupted her thoughts. "Your silence is an answer."

"But he's a good guy. And my partner. And sort of my boss. If he ever found out I was hiding things from him about his own investigation…"

Karolyn smiled at her again and sat back down. "You're being overly dramatic, Haylee. We won't damage your investigation. Keep working it just like you would. We may even help you and Juke solve it." She tapped the arm of her chair. "All you'll need to do is keep us updated throughout the day—especially on anything that may indicate seditious activity." She paused. "And we might ask you to run an errand or two."

Haylee said, "I need to think about it."

"How much time do you have until your baby daughter's blood-brain barrier forms?"

Haylee had a feeling this woman already knew the answer. "Six days."

"Exactly," Karolyn said. "We're offering you a simple deal. If you help us stop tonight's Resistance op, we'll pay for your baby's enhancement. The entire sum." She put a hand on Haylee's shoulder. "Your girl will have a bright future."

Haylee's heart jumped. Hera could be born with all the advantages rich kids had. She could go to a good college one day, the whole world available to her.

And Haylee wouldn't sink into hopeless debt. She'd been hoping for a discount—but now she might get the enhancement for free!

Karolyn stood up and tapped her I!, linking her contact info into Haylee's I! "It's been a pleasure meeting you, Haylee. I know you'll make the right decision. But you need to make it fast. Very fast."

Haylee got up. Her thoughts swirled, but she said mechanically, "Nice to meet you too."

Then the marketing consultant part of her brain snapped to attention. "You know, if you contribute, say, five thousand dollars to our investigation, we could get you results more quickly."

Karolyn said, "If we see you're working hard for us, we'll consider it. But for now, we'll help you behind the scenes."

She shook Haylee's hand again—but this time didn't let go. "Remember. Don't tell Juke or anybody else about our little talk. If there's a leak in the Department, and the Resistance finds out we're onto them…"

She looked straight into Haylee's eyes, and her own eyes went cold. "Believe me, Haylee, you don't want to be blamed."

Haylee was pretty sure that was a threat. A rock of fear rose toward her throat.

Karolyn patted her on the arm and left.

Chapter Thirty-Five

3:27 pm

Juke

Even with the easy availability of AI sex, bot sex, and VR sex, people still liked to see a naked body gyrating in person every now and then. When Juke walked through the main room of Bottoms Up with Teddy Rhodes, the club manager, the place was packed even though lunch hour had passed and happy hour hadn't yet begun. Several strippers worked the poles in semi-transparent digital outfits that shimmered and sometimes disappeared. Erotic holos lit up the dark corners. A steady stream of customers headed for the private booths where human, mechanical, and electronic stimulation were available. This wasn't Juke's scene, but he was impressed.

Teddy Rhodes was a big guy in his late thirties, a six-two former athlete who'd put on weight. A lot of weight. He had bright red hair and a red shirt with extra buttons left open to reveal a broad hairy neck. He carried himself with swagger, and Juke got the impression he saw himself as much handsomer than he actually was.

Teddy shook his head sadly and said, "Talia had a real pretty face. I tried to help her out."

"In what way?" Juke asked, as they sat down at the one empty table.

Teddy paused while a stripper stepped up and shook her booty in his face.

No doubt currying favor with the manager was a big part of these girls' gigs. Her hairless body revealed itself when her digital black G-string turned red, then pink, and then transparent. Juke had heard the girls controlled this using implants in their hands. The sexertainment industry touted this as yet another example of the freedom strippers had to control their own bodies.

Teddy turned his attention back to Juke. "For a two P stake I was gonna get Talia a nice boob job, lift her ass a little, she coulda made major dollars on the poles. I do that for a lot of the girls."

What a nice guy, Juke thought. "But she didn't go for it."

Teddy shrugged. "She wanted to stay a hostess. I guess she was pretty heavily owned already." He tapped the table, bringing up the drink menu. "What can I get ya?"

"Nothing, thanks. Was Talia having problems with anybody?" Teddy looked blank, so Juke prompted, "Guys chopping on her…"

"She never mentioned any problems. If she did, we woulda dealt with it, believe me." Teddy pointed to one of the bouncers, a heavyset Filipino guy carrying a gun on his hip, like so many New Yorkers did. "We treat our girls right."

Juke doubted that, but didn't contradict him. A new song came on, a cover of the classic hit "Rehab." The strippers danced sinuously, matching the song, and the holographic lovers thrusted and moaned.

Juke asked, "Any boyfriends or exes?"

"If so, she kept it low."

"Who was Talia close to here? Any of the dancers?"

Teddy thought about that. "Talia was a sweet kid, you know? Big smile for the customers. But she kinda kept to herself. The retro-artiste type." His lips curled with a trace of derision. "Always drawing pictures on napkins."

Then he added with grudging respect, "Actually, some of 'em were pretty good. I told her, 'Don't throw 'em in the trash, give 'em to me and I'll sell 'em for ya. We'll split the cash.'"

Juke asked, "When did she leave here last night?"

"Her shift ended at one, so I guess a little after that."

"And when did you leave?"

Teddy threw him a look. "Maybe two-thirty. Hey, I didn't have nothing to do with Talia. She wasn't my style."

Juke knew if Teddy left at two-thirty, that still gave him plenty of time to kill Talia and dump her before the body was found. "I'll need to look at your video."

"We don't have any."

Juke eyed him in disbelief.

"Club policy," Teddy said. "This is the one spot in the whole city where you can go a little wild and you won't get caught in the net the next day."

"What about customer videos?"

"If anybody uses a cam the sensors catch it, and we delete the video." To demonstrate, Teddy brought out his I! and tapped the cam icon. Within milliseconds, three different ceiling sensors shone bright red beams straight down at his phone. The Filipino bouncer hurried their way, attracted by the beams, but Teddy waved him off.

"Now what else can I help you with?" he asked Juke. "I'm supposed to be auditioning some new girls. You want a private room, on the house?"

Great, no video, Juke thought, frustrated. *Now what?*

But then he got an idea. "What do you do with your trash?"

"My trash?" Teddy asked, puzzled.

"Yeah." Juke stood up, energized. "Your trash."

* * *

In the alley behind Bottoms Up, Juke and Teddy examined the contents of the club's four large garbage cans. They were searching for the napkins Talia drew pictures on last night.

Juke believed somebody had torn down pictures from the walls of Talia's speck because they held clues to her murder. Hopefully these napkin pictures would have clues too.

Unfortunately, the syndie that picked up garbage didn't do recycling—it wasn't cost-effective. So rotting food, plastic cups, busted vibrators and wadded up tissues were all mixed together. Juke and Teddy uncovered a bunch of used napkins, but none of them had been drawn on. They had a variety of interesting body fluids stuck to them, but that was it.

Teddy said, "Doob, I gotta get back to work. I can't leave you out here going through our garbage—"

"*Wait.*" Juke saw a fugitive flash of black and white, deep down inside an empty bag of freedom fries. He reached in and pulled out several crumpled up white napkins.

They had black ink drawings on them!

He eagerly smoothed them out, protecting them from the wind. The first napkin had a drawing of a stripper working a pole.

"Talia was talented, huh?" said Teddy. "Except she drew the tits too small."

"You recognize this girl?"

"No, but nobody with tits that small would ever work here."

The next napkin had a picture of a cat rubbing its back against a dumpster. Somehow the cat managed to look both blissful and lonely at the same time. Teddy was right, Talia had serious skills.

Next came a landscape. With just a few pen strokes, Talia had created a mountain range and lake so real you could almost hear the birds calling. At first Juke thought it was the Pacific Northwest or western Canada. Then he decided it was probably Crimea, the land of her birth.

There was one more crumpled napkin at the bottom of the bag. Juke brought it out.

When he opened it up, he saw a picture of a young man with dark, medium-length hair—and a long, thick, jagged scar going down his right cheek.

Juke's pulse quickened as he stared at the picture. Between the scar and his fierce scowl, this man looked dangerous. Juke believed the woman who drew him was scared of him. He was depicted in an anime style, but Juke sensed he wasn't fictional. He was all too real.

Looking over Juke's shoulder, Teddy said, "I recognize this doob. I mean, not his face so much, but that scar. He was here last night."

"When?" Juke asked, trying to contain his excitement.

"About twelve-thirty, one." Teddy paused, thinking back. "And he was talking to Talia. She seemed upset."

Juke looked at the scarred man again. He saw jealousy—and anger.

The kind of anger that could turn into uncontrollable, murderous rage.

IV

PART FOUR

BUGTOWN

Chapter Thirty-Six

3:38 pm

Cheyenne

When Cheyenne Littlejohn got off work at Merck Hathaway General Hospital, she headed home. She'd been on duty for eighteen hours straight, but she was way too keyed up to lie down. She wanted to get things ready for tonight.

She brought out the nineteen new, sharp knives she had acquired during the past month. They were all the exact same brand, with black easy-to-hold handles and five-inch blades. She'd purchased them one or two at a time at twelve different stores, paying with cash.

She boiled a pot of water on the stove and put the knives in. She waited ten minutes until they were sterilized, then put them in plastic bags.

In truth, they could have used any old knives sharp enough to cut through human skin. But she and Safiya had decided having new knives would make tonight's op feel safer and more professional to the New York Nineteen. Anything that increased their comfort level was important.

Also, they planned to video tonight's de-chipping and blast it out to networld. Shiny new knives would look good on video.

After bagging all of them, Cheyenne turned her attention to the nineteen old-school I*!* chargers she'd bought. She put them on the kitchen table and counted them. She knew she was being obsessive; chances were, everybody would remember to bring their chargers like they'd been told. No way all nineteen of them would forget. But she was bringing these with her anyway.

Using I*!* chargers had been another one of Cheyenne's brainstorms. They would be instrumental in removing people's biochips.

Cutting through the skin at the point where the biochip had been inserted was relatively easy; all people needed to do was find the scar and start cutting. But then they'd start bleeding and things would get messy. Some people might freak out—like Jeannie, who got scared at the sight of blood. That would make it hard for them to find their chip and remove it. While the chips were implanted close to the skin, they were tiny. Cheyenne didn't have trouble spotting them—but she was a trained doctor.

I*!* chargers solved this problem elegantly. They had thin magnetic rods at the end, an eighth of an inch long, intended for insertion into the I*!*'s porthole. But Cheyenne had found a new purpose for them. After you cut through your skin, you could insert an I*!* charger into the cut and wiggle it around until the chip, made of carbonized silicon, attached to the magnetic rod. Then you simply withdrew the charger and you were done.

The other great thing about the chargers was almost everybody had one, at least as a backup. Just like everybody had a knife and easy access to curcumin. If Chocolate was successful tonight, fifty-one percenters everywhere would be able to duplicate it. The de-chipping process would be simple enough that a high school kid could do it after watching a three-minute video.

Cheyenne put the *I!* chargers, curcumin, and bandages in one shopping bag, and the knives in a second bag. Now she was all set.

Eight hours to go.

Chapter Thirty-Seven

4:02 pm

Haylee, Karolyn, the Red Queen, and Juke

As Haylee left One Police Plaza, she got a text from Juke asking her to get to Bottoms Up as quickly as possible. He even used exclamation marks, something he'd never done before. He must have had a breakthrough.

She got in the Zan and headed for the club, mind racing. She could spy on Juke and inform the Agency about his every move. It wouldn't be that hard.

But what if he found out? He'd never forgive her.

And no other detective would ever want to work with her. Betraying your partner for financial gain was *the* number-one, cardinal sin. Haylee could kiss her NYPDinc career goodbye.

And then what? Maybe Karolyn Ford would help her find a gig at the Agency; but she didn't know the woman well enough to count on her.

And what if Juke truly was a sympathizer and she got him in trouble—real trouble, prison- type trouble. She'd never forgive herself. Aggro though he might be, Juke had been kind to her.

But.

What about the tiny baby girl growing inside her, who depended on her, whose whole destiny would be decided in the next six days? Didn't she owe it to little Hera to give her a powerful boost toward happiness?

She wished she could take a Lazy Susan, or even half of one, to relax. She wished there was somebody she could call for advice. The Zan was stuck in traffic. Out of frustration, she beeped the horn, but that annoying cowboy yodel—"Yippie-aye-oh, yippie-aye-ye-ye"—didn't cut it; she needed something way more fierce.

A holographic video loomed in the sky in front of her, advertising a new CBS drama, *Criminal Bots*. The video showed two cops side by side, a man and a woman, and made her think of Harrison.

Then the holo dissolved into a promo for *Ten Minutes*—formerly *Sixty Minutes*. The promo showed a cartoon of a grossly fat little girl sitting in a corner of the classroom, all alone. She wore a stupid-looking purple beanie and had a blank expression on her dull-looking face. Underneath her was a big caption in flashing red letters: "WITHOUT ENHANCEMENT, IS YOUR CHILD DOOMED?"

Haylee gasped. It was like this holo was meant just for her.

In fact, it was. Karolyn and the Red Queen were tracking the GPS on Haylee's I*!*, and they had arranged for this holo to be looking down on her.

Haylee's eyes teared up. *Screw it!* she thought, *just screw it!* She took out her I*!* and called Karolyn.

A moment later Karolyn appeared on her screen. She smiled. "Hello, Haylee."

"Hi," Haylee said. "I'm in."

* * *

When the Red Queen learned of Haylee's decision, the supercomputer wasn't surprised.

"Any two-bit algorithm would tell you that for human beings, motherly love is the most robust motivator there is," said the Red Queen.

Karolyn had never had the slightest desire for squirmies herself, but she suspected the Red Queen was right, in general.

* * *

Haylee parked outside Bottoms Up, and a petite Chinese hostess escorted her to Teddy's office at the rear of the club. It was small, with a ratty old sofa and no windows, but it boasted one aggressively high-tech feature: life-size holos of all the strippers who were currently performing danced through the room. There were four of them, so the office felt pretty crowded.

Haylee walked through a blonde stripper to the desk, where Juke was inserting napkins into plastic baggies as Teddy watched. Haylee registered Teddy as a beefy guy with red hair who looked at her breasts instead of her face. "What's going on?" she asked.

"I'm protecting the evidence," Juke said, holding up one of the baggies. The napkin inside it had an ink drawing of a guy with a big scar on his cheek. "This may be our killer."

Haylee thought, *hey, this scarred guy looks kind of Latino! What if he's the Mexican-American doob with the D name that Karolyn's looking for?*

"What's his name?" Haylee asked.

"Don't know yet," Juke replied.

She followed him out of the office through the noisy club, and he told her Teddy's story about Talia arguing with this scarred guy last night. Haylee got more and more excited. If they jacked this guy and it helped stop the Resistance plot, Haylee would get her baby enhanced, just like that!

As they walked outside, Juke said, "We need to blast out a video featuring the scarred man. We'll see if anybody recognizes him."

Haylee looked around. Above them, a huge holo of a naked girl shook her red neon butt at passersby. "I'll shoot you standing in front of this girl, that'll triple our clicks."

She'd shoot the video real quick, then sneak off somewhere and secretly report to Karolyn on what Juke had found—

"What the hell?!" Juke said suddenly.

Haylee got a scary vibe he was reading her thoughts. But then she realized he was looking down the block, where she'd parked the car. A tall, slender young man in a buzzcut and anti-pollution mask had just ducked down behind it.

She recognized him. This was the same guy they'd seen outside Berkshire Vanguard.

Meanwhile Juke remembered all at once where he'd seen this doob even before that: hurrying away from the crime scene this morning, with the curly-haired girl who looked like Safiya.

Was his mask hiding a scar? Juke ran toward him, pulling his Heston. Haylee ran behind Juke and reached for her gun too, then remembered it wasn't there.

The guy in the mask was looking away from them. But he must have sensed them somehow, or a lookout shouted a warning into his phone—because all of a sudden he popped out from behind the Zan and took off running.

Juke called out, "Freeze! NYPDinc!"

The guy kept running, jumping over a huge pothole and veering left onto Spring Street. Juke and Haylee followed, yelling at him to halt. He swerved right on Adam Smith, shouting to several teenage Starpunks smoking weed on the corner, "Dincs! Help, the Dincs are after me!"

The Starpunks looked confused at first, then figured it out when Juke and Haylee came racing toward them. One of the Starpunks, a big girl carrying an extra eighty pounds, got in Juke's way and opened her arms wide.

"Hey, ro—" she said, just before Juke barreled into her. She started to go down, and her head would have crashed into the sidewalk hard except Juke was somehow able to grab her and do a staggering dance that kept them both from falling.

"You're cute," the girl said, holding onto him.

Juke finally extricated himself, and he and Haylee ran on. Behind them the Starpunks yelled, "Dincs! Dincs! Dincs!"

Juke could still see the man in the mask, but now he was a full block away. He turned right, and when Juke and Haylee got to the corner they couldn't see him anymore.

"You link into the street vids, I'll chase him," Juke told Haylee and took off.

At the next intersection he looked left and caught sight of the guy again. He chased him, getting closer. Then a bugburger truck got in Juke's way, blocking his view for a few seconds, and the guy vanished.

Juke was pretty sure the guy had entered one of two stores near the corner: "Freedom Guns" or "Rosa's Readings: Modern Neuropsychic Science." He tried Rosa's, dashing inside past astrological charts, tarot cards, and neuroscan technology. The woman in her forties behind the counter had the classic fake Roma thing going, complete with babushka and too much jewelry, but she also had the black-rimmed glasses of a science geek. Presumably this was Rosa, combining the best of old and new.

"Did a guy run in here?" Juke asked.

Rosa didn't answer right away, and he sensed scheming in her eyes as she tried to figure out a way to ka-ching off this situation. But she made a mistake: her eyes darted briefly toward the back door. He didn't need tarot cards or neuroscans to divine what that look meant—the masked man had run out the back.

Juke ran out the back too, and looked up and down the street. Which way did he go? There were stores in both directions. Juke guessed left. As he ran he asked people if a guy in a mask had just run by. "He killed a girl!" he shouted, trying to get people on his side.

But everybody claimed ignorance. He ran back to Rosa's and dashed off in the other direction, but still no luck.

How had the masked man disappeared so completely? Maybe he had an accomplice who picked him up in a car—the same person who'd warned him to run in the first place. Juke checked the vehicle sensors and saw they were blinking red on this street, and his suspicions felt confirmed. The accomplice had picked up the masked man here, knowing that without sensors it would be harder for the NYPDinc to get video of him getting into the car.

When Haylee rejoined him, she had already spent ninety dollars on footage from nearby streets. She'd gotten video of the masked man running away from Bottoms Up and into Rosa's. But there the trail died, thanks to the useless sensors.

None of the cams had caught the guy up close or straight on. But Juke and Haylee would blast the video out to networld anyway. Maybe somebody would recognize his haircut or clothes.

Who was this doob—a random terrorist trying to stick a bomb inside the first Dinc vehicle he could find? Juke didn't think so. The guy was actively targeting Juke's car, trying to sneak into it not once but twice.

This morning somebody broke into Talia's speck to destroy evidence. Now this afternoon somebody tried to break into Juke's car. Juke had a sudden vibe these two actions might be linked. *What if the masked guy wanted to _bug_ my car, not bomb it?* Maybe he wants to find out what's going on in Talia's murder investigation.

But why—is he Talia's killer?

And who is his accomplice? Maybe it's the woman who smelled like Safiya, who broke into Talia's speck. And maybe that was the same woman who'd been at the crime scene—the one who, from a distance, looked like Safiya. For a second Juke got the crazy idea this mystery woman really *was* Safiya. But then he laughed at himself and put that thought aside. Like Safiya would ever get caught up in a murder.

Especially a murder as brutal as this one.

Juke wondered again, *are the man with the mask and the man with the scar the same person?* It seemed likely.

In any case, between the napkin pictures and the masked-man video, he had two excellent leads now. That midnight drop-dead was looking a lot more doable.

But he needed to move fast.

Chapter Thirty-Eight

4:49 pm

Rey and Safiya

Speeding away from Rosa's in the Lex, Rey looked back to make sure Juke wasn't on their tail. "That's it! We're not doing *that* again!" he said.

He's right, Safiya thought. With Juke on the alert now, they could forget about bugging his car.

She put a hand on Rey's arm. "You did a great job getting away."

His breathing quieted a little, and she sensed his panic receding. "Thanks for saving my neck," he said.

She smiled at him. "You got it."

"Where are we going?"

Safiya was driving manually, because she wanted to stay on streets with disabled sensors, and she didn't know how to tell the Lex's carbrain to do that. "I figure we stick to the dead zones, then double back home and stay low."

"That's the plan?" Rey said, incredulous. "Go home and stay low?"

She checked the dashboard clock. "Look, we only have seven hours to go."

"Right. Sure, just seven hours, no prob." He started laughing, high and loud, and didn't stop.

"Rey." His laughter got worse, and she realized he was having some sort of hysterical reaction to fear. *"Rey!"*

She took her right hand off the wheel and punched him on the shoulder, harder than she meant to. But he stopped laughing, thank God.

"You okay?" she said.

Rey rubbed his shoulder. "Never been better. Viva the revolution."

"Hang in there, babe. You and me are gonna make history tonight."

Rey wasn't so sure he cared about history anymore. He wanted to fucking *survive.*

And he never wanted to see Saifya's pain-in-the-ass ex-boyfriend again. That guy was a nightmare.

Chapter Thirty-Nine

5:08 pm

Karolyn, the Red Queen, Haylee, and Juke

Haylee sat in a toilet stall in the women's room of Bottoms Up, with graffiti of a princess kissing a robotic frog on the wall behind her. "Juke is waiting for me, so I only have a minute," she said into the phone. "But I'm sending you video of the masked man right now."

Karolyn, sitting in her office watching Haylee on her phone screen, thought: *so far this new asset is absolutely working out.* Haylee had signed on barely an hour ago, and already she was delivering strong data flow.

Haylee continued, "I couldn't tell if the masked man was Mexican or Icelandic or what."

Karolyn didn't bother informing her the Icelander was dead. The Red Queen cut in, "What about the man with the scar? Could you determine his ethnicity?"

Haylee looked puzzled, like she was wondering who had just spoken. Karolyn said, "Sorry, I should have introduced you. My fellow agent, Margaret, is also on this convo."

"Hi, Margaret," Haylee said. "The guy with the scar def looked Mexican, but I couldn't tell for sure from the drawing."

"You need to send us a photo of that drawing," the Red Queen said. "You should have done that already."

Haylee's mouth fell open, flustered. "The drawing is in Juke's pocket. I'll link you a photo as soon as I can."

"That's fine, Haylee," Karolyn said soothingly. "You're doing an excellent job. Just keep it up and I guarantee you, we'll keep our end of the deal."

After the convo was over and they'd tapped off, Karolyn said reproachfully to the Red Queen, "This girl is helping us. Why were you so hard on her?"

"That wasn't my intention," said the Red Queen. "I believe I sometimes act a bit insensitive."

"I've noticed."

* * *

Haylee joined Juke outside Bottoms Up. They headed for the holo of the naked girl, preparing to shoot the new crowdfunding video they'd been distracted from.

Haylee was still neurospiked about her convo with Karolyn and that cold, nasty woman with the British accent, Margaret. She replayed it in her mind. Karolyn kind of scared the crap out of her—and Margaret was worse.

Juke smoothed his hair. "Ready, Vancouver?"

Focus, Haylee told herself. Centering her cam on Juke, she saw that the naked neon butt behind him wasn't completely in the shot. "Move a little to the left."

"Here?"

"Perfect. Okay, Humphrey: *go.*"

Juke gazed earnestly at the cam and began. "Flash update on the Talia Qirimoglu case: we've identified a person of interest." He brought out the baggie containing Talia's drawing of the scarred man. He held it flat against his jacket so it wouldn't blow away, and made sure the man was easy to see through the plastic.

As Haylee zoomed in for a close-up, he continued, "Last night Talia drew a picture of this man on a napkin. You'll note the pronounced scar on his cheek. He was seen arguing with Talia at the Bottoms Up club in Soho shortly before she was murdered. We need to know who he is. Be careful:

he may be dangerous."

Way to draw people in, thought Haylee.

Juke said, "The man with the scar may be the same person as *this* man with the mask." In Juke's other hand he held up his I*!*, showing the clearest screenshot they had of the masked man. Haylee zoomed in again. "At 4:55 p.m. today, this man was observed acting suspiciously right here, outside Bottoms Up. We believe he was attempting to obstruct the murder investigation. My partner and I chased him east on Spring Street…"

Juke pointed down the street, and Haylee shot in that direction. "He turned right on Adam Smith, then left on Mulberry before he got away."

She swung the cam to Juke as he continued, "If you have any information on the man with the scar *or* the man with the mask"—she pulled back to get both the napkin and the I*!* in the shot—"please click the blue button on the upper left corner of your screen."

"Pitch the red button too," Haylee called out. Sometimes Juke got so caught up in an investigation, he forgot to do the most important thing: ask for money.

"And to help us fund this investigation," Juke said, "please click the *red* button on the upper right."

He stepped closer to the cam. "Let's do this, my friends. There's a killer on the loose—a murdering, raping sonufabitch who will probably do it again if we don't catch him. And if he does kill somebody else, their blood will be on our hands."

He gave it a moment, then said, "Thank you, everyone."

Haylee pumped her fist. "Give this man an Oscar. Fucking tutti!" Actually it *had* been tutti, but she wondered if she was being extra effusive because she felt bad sneaking around behind Juke's back.

"Thanks, Vancouver." Juke dropped his pose. "How long will it take you to send that out?"

"I'll blast it right now, raw and uncut." She hit a few keys, did some quick editing, and within thirty seconds sent the video to everywhere in networld that had received the first video.

She also, without telling Juke of course, sent it to Karolyn.

As they headed for the Zan, she said, "I'll juice up the video and blast the new, improved version in twenty minutes."

"Thanks, Haylee, you're the best," Juke said.

Once again she felt that twinge of guilt.

He added, "While you're at it, send the picture of the scar-faced guy to the NYPDinc database. Maybe we'll get a match."

We'll get more than one, Haylee thought, *try a few thousand.* Talia's expressionistic, anime style meant her drawing would resemble a lot of guys with medium-length dark hair and scars on their cheeks. That scar could even be a tat.

They needed to narrow down their search. Karolyn seemed sure a Mexican-American guy was involved, so Haylee decided to give Juke a hint. "Do you think the guy in Talia's drawing looks Latino?"

"Hard to say."

"He looked Mexican to me. Maybe we should put that out there."

Juke threw her a sidelong glance. "You are seriously leaping to conclusions."

Haylee's face reddened, and she let it go. They got in the Zan, and Juke carefully placed the plastic baggies in the tray between the front seats.

Haylee considered the evidence they had so far. None of it, to her, indicated any connection to the Resistance. She wished there were some subtle way to ask Juke about that. But Karolyn had been emphatic in ordering her not to talk to him, and she didn't want to do anything that might jeopardize the deal she'd made.

"So what do you think?" Juke asked, startling her out of her thoughts.

"About what?"

Juke gave her a *duh* look. "Our new video. Will it infect people?"

She needed to forget about Karolyn for now and get back to being a crime marketing consultant. "Well, the napkin is a cool clue, it might get some bounce. But we still have the same problem we've always had. We need to give gen pop a reason to care about Talia, otherwise they'll never click our video in the first place."

Juke banged his hand on the dashboard in frustration. "Maybe we'll get lucky. Except for Dr. Goldman, there weren't any big murders today."

Haylee lifted her shoulders in a shrug. "Like Burgess said, we need the boo hoo."

"That guy is a total zero."

"But he's right. We need a grieving Mom or kid sister. Or Talia devoted her life to taking care of little baby orphans. We need some kind of hook—"

While Haylee was talking, she thought: *this is hopeless, just another worthless case.* But then her eyes fixed on the baggies Juke had put on the tray. The top one contained Talia's drawing of the cat rubbing his back against the dumpster. Haylee stared at it.

"Cats," she said. *"Cats!"*

"Yeah, what about 'em?"

"Talia fed starving cats!" Haylee could feel her excitement growing. She grabbed Juke's arm. "That's our hook!"

Juke gave her a puzzled look. "What are you suggesting exactly?"

"It's obvious. A cute cat video!"

He stared at her. "Cute cat videos don't generally have dead people in 'em."

"Well, they should. This is brilliant!" She waved her hands, mapping out the shot. "We start with a shot of tiny, adorable kittens. We hear you, in voiceover: 'Talia Qirimoglu loved cats. She fed all the poor homeless kittens in the neighborhood.' Then we vidshop Talia playing with the kittens, giving them milk. And then…"

She put her hand to her heart, hamming it up. "We show sweet Talia, brutally murdered, lying on the street… *with the kittens she loved so much licking her poor dead face.*"

Haylee punched the air. "Then we show you with the napkin, the guy running. Then back to the kittens. Not only did this monster kill a beautiful, saintly girl… He's made these kittens really sad! Boom! If we play this right, we'll get thousands of cat lovers hitting the red button! And maybe somebody will even hit the blue button and lead us to the killer. Win, win!"

Haylee's face shone as she thought about the real win: the huge prize that awaited her baby daughter if they caught the killer and stopped the

Resistance plot in the process.

Juke eyed Haylee, taken aback by her enthusiasm. He'd never seen her this stoked. Was it just the prospect of doing a really unusual video that got her going?

"Come on, it's a cupcake idea," Haylee said. "You know it!"

Juke shook his head. "You should be directing movies. You missed your calling."

But the way he said it, they both knew he had just given in. Haylee said, "Where can we find cute kittens? We could hit the pound, but I'd rather not shoot in an institutional setting."

The idea came to Juke so quickly and naturally, it surprised him.

Safiya always has kittens.

When they were together, they constantly had abandoned kittens running around their speck. It was one of the things he found so amazing about Safiya, that this tough Resistance leader melted around kittens. She basically ran her own little pound. He was willing to bet she still did.

And even if she didn't…

It would be the perfect excuse to see her.

And he realized now, with absolute clarity, that he *needed* to see her. He needed it like he needed air, or dreams.

He could still feel her smell hitting him this morning and taking his breath away. For three years he'd stayed away from her, trying to forget her. It hadn't worked. He needed to see Safiya and…

Well, he wasn't sure what he'd say or do, or what would happen. But he needed to see her and get closure, or get together again—the thought made his heart jump—or *something.* He needed to figure out some way to get on with his life.

Maybe if he got some kind of resolution with Safiya, he could finally stop obsessing about the murder case that, in his mind, had caused the end of their relationship. He wasn't sure if that made logical sense, but it was how he felt.

He looked up at the gray November sky. He needed to make his move now. *Right now.* Before he found some stupid cowardly reason not to, and spent another year or however long mooning over her.

Midnight was coming fast, though. How could he justify taking time away from the investigation, if it turned out she didn't have cats after all?

Scruck it, she *would* have cats. Or know somebody who did. Anyway, going to see her wouldn't even be a detour. Two months ago he ran into an old mutual acquaintance who said Safiya lived in the Lower East Side now. That meant she was less than a ten-minute drive away. The thought of how close she was—and what he was about to do—sent a charge through him, all the way down to his toes.

"I know where we can get kittens," he told Haylee.

Then he told the Zan: "Residence of Safiya Bassani-Jones, Lower East Side."

Chapter Forty

5:18 pm

The Red Queen and Karolyn

The Red Queen analyzed the video footage of the masked man and classified it as useless. The images were below recognition threshold.

She wasn't thrilled with Talia's drawing of the scarred man either. "Anime," she said dismissively, in her snobby British tone. "So imprecise."

But Karolyn was much more excited. "Scarface looks Mexican to me. Haylee thought so too. I bet he's Suspect #1."

The Red Queen said dubiously, "Are you sure you and Haylee aren't both indulging in wishful thinking?"

"Just go with it, okay? Art appreciation isn't one of your strong points. Get me datascoop on every man in New York under sixty with a scar or tat on his right cheek—"

"Both cheeks. Sometimes people get that wrong."

"Fine, both cheeks. And highlight everyone of Mexican heritage whose name begins with D."

The Red Queen had access to the same NYPDinc database Juke was using, and several Agency and syndicate databases besides. She quickly compiled a list.

Of the seven million men between seventeen and sixty who lived or worked in the metropolitan area and weren't currently incarcerated, over six thousand five hundred had a scar or tat on one cheek. Three thousand one hundred sixty-eight of these men had hair approximating the hair in Talia's drawing. One thousand two hundred twenty-seven had documented Mexican heritage.

And eighty-nine of those had first names beginning with D.

Karolyn and the Red Queen went to work.

Chapter Forty-One

5:32 pm

Haylee and Juke

Riding toward Safiya Bassani-Jones' speck, Haylee thought about how she would incorporate cute cat footage into her homicide video. It was such an obviously tutti idea, she was amazed nobody had ever done it before. Hell, if her deal with the Agency didn't pan out, maybe she could still ka-ching off this murder after all! Hopefully Safiya would have super-cute kittens.

"So who is this Safiya person?" she asked Juke.

"A friend."

"Yeah? What kind of friend?"

"Ex-girlfriend."

"Oh." Noting the tightness in his voice, she didn't push it. She did tease him, though. "You look like you could use a drink."

"I probably could," he said, with a wry half-smile.

He's pretty sexy when he smiles, Haylee thought, then stopped herself. The last thing she had time to think about now was a man.

Especially a man she was working with, who she was keeping secrets from.

Meanwhile, Juke checked the GPS. They were only five blocks away from Safiya's speck. Now that he was about to learn his destiny with her, his heart started racing.

He closed his eyes and took a deep breath to calm himself, but it didn't work. All kinds of images of Safiya flooded his mind, starting from when he first met her twenty-three years ago, just after his father died. She was a scrappy kid from the poor part of Elmhurst who was amazing at handball, uncannily dropping her shots in the corner where Juke couldn't reach them. She was smart too; even though she was two years younger than Juke, she was in his math class. Safiya was the curly-haired kid in elementary school who just seemed to know everything, when he felt so confused.

For twelve years they lost track of each other. But then one warm summer evening, Juke ran into her again at a retro movie theatre. He could picture, and practically taste, their first kiss two weeks later. It was on the Hodu Brooklyn Bridge, on a rare night that was so clear you could see the moon.

Then Juke pictured, without wanting to, Safiya's unhappy face during their terrible last months together. Ending on that freezing post-Christmas morning.

He ran his hand through his hair.

"Do you think a lot about your fiancé?" he asked.

The words were out almost before he thought them.

"I'm sorry," he said. "That's way too personal."

"It's okay," Haylee said.

He turned toward her and gazed straight into her eyes. He wasn't sure why he was saying this now, but it had been on his mind all month. "Haylee, I just want to say, I heard about what happened. It's not your fault, you know. Nobody in the Department blames you."

Haylee's throat got so tight she could barely breathe. She felt her eyes getting wet and fought it. "Okay, so now you *are* getting a little personal."

Juke nodded. He understood only too well the guilt she felt. "Did you ever hear about the Libby McDowell murder?" he asked.

She looked at him, puzzled. He continued, "Probably not. She was a poor immie like Talia, except younger. Fifteen. One night three years ago she was hanging out at a flare in Washington Square, drumming, smoking weed…and she got hit by a sniper from long range. It was my case."

Haylee wasn't sure where this was going, but it was better than talking about Harrison. "Did you catch the guy?"

"I spent four days on it and got a couple possible leads, but nothing obvious, and we weren't raising any money. So I took another case that was worth twenty Reagans." He paused, then said bitterly, "The one time in my life I ever did something like that."

Juke looked out the window at a Lebanese street vendor. Haylee wondered if he would keep going.

Finally he said, "Five weeks later somebody shot up a street concert in Battery Park. He took out fourteen people."

Haylee remembered reading about that. It was some nut job who hated loud music or something.

Juke was still looking out the window. "Turned out it was the same guy. If I'd worked one of those leads a little longer, just a day or two, I'm pretty sure it would've led me straight to him. I could've saved all those people."

"I'm sorry," Haylee said. She wanted to say more, but wasn't sure what would help.

Juke rubbed his eye, then looked back at Haylee. "The thing is, all you can do after something like that? Is from then on, just… try and do the right thing."

I am, Haylee thought fiercely. *I'm having Harrison's baby.*

Juke's I! buzzed, and both of them welcomed the distraction. He checked the phone and said, "The NYPDinc database has four thousand two hundred ninety-one guys with scars or tats on their cheeks."

"Damn, that's a lot of guys."

"I'll link them to Teddy Rhodes at Bottoms Up, see if he recognizes anybody."

Haylee watched as Juke linked, thinking that guy Teddy would never care enough about some dead girl to look through that many photos. She wished she could tell Juke about the Mexican and D clues.

She unzipped her coat, feeling hot and overcrowded in the car. She understood Juke had told her that story partly for himself, but also to make her feel better by sharing his pain.

But that just made her feel worse about lying to him and keeping secrets.

Meanwhile the Zan parked in front of a bodega. "Your destination is six houses down," the car said. "This is the nearest available parking spot."

Juke turned to her. "Why don't you stay here while I make sure she has cats?"

She saw how nervous he was, so she lightened the mood by teasing him. "You want time alone with her, huh?"

"She might not even be in." He looked in the mirror and smoothed his hair.

"Hey doob," she said. "You're devastatingly handsome. Good luck."

She watched as Juke's face turned red.

Then she said quietly, "Juke, what you just told me… is that why you do all these dog cases?"

"That's part of it."

"Well, in my opinion… you've done enough penance."

Juke took a deep breath and got out of the car.

He stepped around a patch of herbs growing out of a three-foot-square hole in the sidewalk. A small handwritten sign on a wooden post said: "Community Garden." He recognized the writing as Safiya's and felt a catch in his throat.

He came to Safiya's tenement building and found the names "Bassani-Jones/Matoshi" next to Apartment 3D. Was Matoshi a boyfriend? Juke felt a powerful urge to take off right now without even buzzing Safiya and get back in the car.

God, quit acting like a sixteen-year-old, he told himself. He put his finger on Safiya's old-school buzzer, a relic from the early part of the century, and pressed.

Chapter Forty-Two

5:38 pm

Safiya and Rey

Safiya and Rey had made it back home three minutes before Juke arrived. Safiya fed the ever voracious kittens fishmeal, and she and Rey began fixing sandwiches and coffee, because with all that adrenaline they were starved too—

Suddenly the front-door buzzer sounded. Rey spilled his coffee and Safiya almost dropped her half-made sandwich.

Rey said, "It's the Dincs! They sensored us!"

Safiya tried to stay calm. "No, the sensors were down where I picked you up."

"Well, they found us somehow!"

The buzzer sounded again. Rey jumped up and looked out the sooty back window, past the fire escape, to the street three floors below. "There's no Dinc cars back here. We should make a run for it."

Safiya said, "It's probably that girl from next door, wanting to see the kittens again." She reached for the buzzer.

"Don't touch it! Don't let them know we're here!"

"If it's the cops, they'll come up whether we talk to them or not."

She pressed the buzzer as the kittens meowed at her feet. "Hello?"

Nobody answered; maybe they'd gone away. "Hello?" she said again.

Behind her, Rey was so scared she could hear him gasp for breath.

Then a voice came up over the intercom. "Hi Safiya. It's Juke."

Oh shit.

Was he here to interrogate her? Jack her? Take her off to a syndicate prison?!

"Safiya?" Juke's voice said.

"I'll be right down," she said.

As soon as she released the button, Rey said, "What's he gonna do?"

"No idea. If you don't hear from me in five minutes, go out the fire escape and make a run for it."

Rey took her arm. "You can't go down there. Come out the back with me. We'll start for Canada right now—"

"And leave the New York Eighteen behind? Let me just see what he wants."

Safiya gently removed Rey's hand from her arm and stepped out the door.

Chapter Forty-Three

5:39 pm

Juke and Safiya

Standing outside and looking into the foyer, Juke parsed Safiya's words. *"I'll be right down."* Did she not buzz him upstairs to her speck because she had a boyfriend there?

No, not necessarily, maybe she just felt awkward seeing him again—

Oh my God.

There she was in the foyer, coming toward him. He forgot how to breathe. *She's so beautiful. Those eyes...that curly hair...*

But she wasn't smiling.

He gave her a smile and she tried to smile back, but it looked totally forced. She seemed beyond nervous—

She opened the door and stepped outside. Now she was standing so close to him, close enough to touch. Should he do that—touch her? Hug her? His entire self inhaled that scent he loved and missed so much.

He ended up leaving his hands at his sides. "Hi Safiya."

"Hi Juke."

Her face looked so uncertain. A little scared, maybe? He felt there was something about her emotions he was missing. *I haven't seen her in so long, I can't read her anymore.*

"It's great to see you," he tried. "You look good."

"You too."

He could sense she was waiting for him to get to it, so he did. Maybe that would make them both less uncomfortable. "You're probably wondering why I'm here."

"You saw us, didn't you?" she said, with a bitterness he didn't understand.

"Saw who? When?" he asked, puzzled.

"You followed us," she snapped, anger rising, but Juke thought he detected hurt as well. "Why are you playing games with me?"

"What are you talking about?"

"Oh, shove it up your ass." Juke stared at her. "You're forgetting, I know all your stupid little investigator tricks."

He took a stab in the dark. "Safiya, are you in some kind of trouble?"

She said through tightened lips, "What do you want from me?"

"Your kittens."

That stopped her. "My what?"

"I need some cute kittens," he explained. "And I know you always have kittens around, and I'm in a hurry, so I thought I'd come by."

"What do you need kittens for?"

Juke felt on solid ground again, at least temporarily. Even after their ship hit the rocks, Safiya never lost interest in his cases. So he pulled up a picture of Talia on his I*!*

"I'm investigating this girl's murder. Her name was Talia, and she loved cats. She fed all the stray cats in her neighborhood. So we're gonna make a video and try to get cat lovers to ka-ching us."

Finally the storm on Safiya's face broke. She exploded with laughter. "That's really what this is about?"

Juke eyed her. "Yeah. Seriously, you're okay?"

"Yeah, I'm fine." She gazed at him. "And you haven't changed, have you?"

"Neither have you," he said, and then smiled. "Except I think your hair's even curlier."

"The humidity," she said. "But don't you ever get sick of it?"

"Of your hair?" He reached out and almost touched an errant curl on her shoulder.

Maybe his flirting made her anxious, because her lips tightened again. "Of making cat videos to solve murders. Being a part of this insane system that just about destroyed you three years ago."

Juke shook his head. "Didn't take us long to get into the same old argument, did it?"

"I'm sorry," Safiya said. She touched his arm. "I shouldn't have gone there."

Her touch raced through him, but he did his best to keep his cool. "It's okay, no worries." He gave her another smile. "So, you got any kittens? I thought I heard some meowing on the intercom."

After a moment, Safiya replied, "I'm sorry, no."

"I'm stunned. Safiya Bassani-Jones, with no kittens?"

"I did have two, but I gave them away last week."

"Who'd you give 'em to? Maybe I can go see them."

"I gave them to a girl who was moving to Connecticut."

"Well, that's a little far," Juke sighed. "Guess I'll have to hit the pound after all."

Safiya nodded, and as they stood together awkwardly on the steps, Juke was afraid their convo was at an end. It had definitely been weird. *She thought I was following her. Why?* Well, whatever—it was a misunderstanding. Maybe he should see if she wanted to get together for hot chocolate. Did she have a boyfriend? God, she smelled good. What was *she* thinking?

"So how's your investigation going?" Safiya asked. "You have a suspect?"

She wants to keep talking. That had to be a good sign. He spoke rapidly, eagerly. "We do. Talia was seen arguing with a guy last night. She drew a picture of him." Reaching in his jacket, he pulled out the plastic-wrapped picture of the man with the scar. "Scary looking doob, huh?"

Suddenly he realized Safiya was staring at him oddly. Suspiciously. *Fearfully.* "What's wrong?"

"Nothing," she said, but her voice squeaked a little. She backed away from him, toward the door. "I gotta go. I was just getting ready to go out."

Juke was hurt and confused. What was she hiding from him? Why had she switched so quickly from "let's talk a little more" to "gotta run"?

He said, "Can I drive you somewhere?"

"No thanks."

He started to put the napkin away, but then it hit him: had something about the picture upset her? It seemed unlikely, but –

He held up the napkin again. "Do you know this guy?"

"No, of course not," Safiya said.

Her shoulders lifted, and the right side of her mouth went higher. Juke studied her. Maybe he couldn't totally read her anymore, but this look he remembered, all right. She gave it to him on Christmas Eve three years ago when he asked if she was thinking of leaving him and she said no.

She was lying then and she's lying now.

"Who is he?" Juke said.

"I told you, I don't know him." She looked at Juke—sadly? desperately? "It's good to see you, Juke. Maybe we can talk sometime."

He nodded. Then she stepped back inside and shut the door behind her.

Juke watched Safiya until she was out of sight, going up to her apartment. Then he turned and ran toward the Zan.

Chapter Forty-Four

5:46 pm

Haylee and Juke

Haylee watched Juke from inside the Zan, puzzled by why he was running. As soon as he threw open the car door, she asked, "How'd it go?"

He didn't answer. Instead he told the car, "GPS phone tracking," and entered Safiya's address into the LED.

"Does she have kittens?" Haylee asked.

Juke checked the LED screen. "Sorry, we won't be making that cute cat video."

"Why not?"

"Just a sec. I think she's about to call somebody." The local-access recon technology he was using was new and didn't work properly the last time he tried it. Theoretically it could identify the locays of GPS-protected phones— as long as one party in the convo was local, within a couple hundred feet. Safiya's speck should be close enough.

He waited as Haylee gave him a bewildered look. Then, on the screen, the word "TRACKING" came up. *So far, so good.*

He said, "Someone inside Safiya's building is making a call. They're using a burner, which means it's probably her." He felt weird as hell spying on Safiya, but she should have been straight with him.

There was a time when the two of them had shared their deepest secrets, but that time was long gone.

A street map with a flashing red X appeared on the screen. "It's working!" Juke said. "That's the locay of the person she's calling. He's using GPS masking, but this overrides it."

Juke magnified the map. The flashing X vanished, and he was scared the new technology was screwing up again. But then the X reappeared. Safiya was talking to somebody located in a warehouse building on Liberty Drive, next to the East River in the Bugpacking District.

He told the Zan: "5821 Liberty Drive. Forget the speed limit and run the siren."

The Zan said, "Are you sure? That could be dangerous."

"I'm sure. Keep the siren going til we get within a quarter-mile."

As the siren blared and they sped off, Haylee shouted above the noise, "What' s going on? Who was Safiya calling?"

Juke shouted back, "I think she called the man with the scar. I think she knows him."

The Zan darted and swerved through the Friday rush hour traffic, racing toward the warehouse.

Haylee grabbed her stomach. "I'm gonna lose my lunch."

"Puke out the window," Juke said. "We'll lose this guy's locay as soon as he gets off the phone. We gotta catch him before he runs."

Chapter Forty-Five

5:52 pm

Karolyn, Cheyenne, and the New York Seventeen

Karolyn had been hunting for Scarface too, ever since Haylee called from the Bottoms Up bathroom.

Haylee said that Teddy Rhodes, the strip club manager, claimed he saw Scarface last night. Karolyn checked Teddy's networld links and quickly deduced he was mainly into girls and dollars.

She buzzed the guy, identifying herself as Juke O'Keefe's boss at the NYPDinc, and offered him a Reagan to help her catch Talia's killer.

"You want me to go through all those four thousand photos O'Keefe sent me?" Teddy said. "It'll cost you a lot more than one Reagan. I got a club to run."

"No, not four thousand. Eighty-nine." Then she linked him the photos of the eighty-nine Mexicans whose names started with D.

Ten minutes later, he buzzed her back. "The club was crazy last night and I wasn't really paying attention to this doob. But I checked your pics and found six guys it coulda been." He gave her the names: a Domingo, two Donatos, a Diego, a David, and a Dimas.

Karolyn said, "Okay, if one of these guys pans out, we'll link you your Reagan. And one more thing: if you don't tell O'Keefe I called you, I'll link you a second Reagan."

There was a pause while he considered that.

"Office politics," she explained.

"Whatever," Teddy said. "I didn't like that O'Keefe guy anyway."

Karolyn tapped off, encouraged. The Agency could easily track down these six suspects without the NYPDinc finding out. If she needed their help for some reason, she'd go through Haylee.

The Red Queen believed the most promising of the six was Domingo, an ex-con who lived only ten blocks from where Talia's body was dumped. He had an aggravated assault conviction and he'd been videotaped drumming at a Resistance flare, so he checked off two boxes: violent and possibly Rez-connected.

Karolyn dispatched teams to grab the other five suspects. She rode off to Domingo's speck herself, taking an agent named Adams—another gray-suited Midwesterner, like Willard—for backup.

Unfortunately, Adams was way more talkative than Willard had been. He spent the entire trip recounting some pointless anecdote about somebody or other he'd jacked back in Kansas, as if Kansas even mattered. Luckily they were riding in a brand new Dutch Boer, so they got to Domingo's speck fast, before this snorp drove her nuts.

Domingo lived on the second floor of a bodega. Karolyn was plotting how to take him by stealth when the Red Queen suddenly spoke from the car's LED screen with a clipped British urgency.

"Karolyn. Haylee Navarro's I*!* is on the move. I assume that means she is too. Her vehicle is running red lights and going sixty in traffic, heading for Bugtown."

The Red Queen put up Haylee's route on the Boer's dashboard. Haylee was racing east like a mad bot on 54th. *Why didn't she contact me?* Karolyn wondered. "Any idea what's going on?"

"It may have something to do with a call we just intercepted between the 9.8 woman and Suspect #1, the probable Mexican-American. We haven't succeeded in interpreting their convo yet. I believe he was telling her his locay, but it was in code."

"Okay, we're on our way right now," Karolyn said.

Adams broke in. "But what about Domingo? Shouldn't we check him out first?"

Karolyn didn't bother answering. She'd send another agent to pick up Domingo. She ordered the Boer, "Bugpacking District. Follow the car highlighted on the LED. Go fast and ignore all traffic rules."

The Boer had driven Karolyn before, so it knew better than to argue. It took off and raced uptown honking and swerving, siren screaming.

Karolyn didn't want to call Haylee, since Juke was probably in the car with her. So she texted, *"Where's the fire?"*

A little later the response came: *"Hot pursuit of scar suspect."*

She wondered if "hot pursuit" was an intentional pun on "fire." How smart was Haylee—and how much could Karolyn rely on her? She texted, *"Where are you going?"*

After a moment the answer came back: *"5821 Liberty."*

Karolyn smiled. Haylee was indeed proving an excellent asset. "5821 Liberty Drive," Karolyn told her car.

The Boer ignored the next red light and squealed into a left turn without even slowing down.

* * *

Down in Chelsea, Cheyenne Littlejohn opened the trunk of her ancient Qilin, one of the first Chinese cars to make it big in the U.S. after the tariffs were lifted. She put in the two shopping bags containing curcumin, knives, and I*!* chargers. Chocolate was hours away, but Cheyenne wanted to be one hundred P ready. After devoting two years of her life to this op, she didn't want it getting derailed by some silly last-minute oversight.

Further south on Houston Street, Jeannie Bardach treated herself to a final New York meal of borscht and kasha knishes at Yonah Schimmel's. She'd been coming here for over fifty years, and she would miss this place.

She'd miss a lot of things. New York was still one of the greatest cities in the world. But it didn't belong to people like her anymore. It was time to go.

In midtown, Bobby Morelli, at twenty-six the youngest of the New York Seventeen now that Talia was dead, debated which dumpster to hit. Four years ago he'd gotten in over his head with an algorithm-forge startup. He was hoping when he started over debt-free in Canada he could relaunch— this time avoiding his previous mistakes. He promised himself tonight would be his last dumpster dinner ever. So it might as well be a good one!

He decided to walk up to 54th and Lex, where the dumpster outside Phnom Sí sometimes had decent Cambodian-Mexican food. He was opening the lid when Juke and Haylee rode past, siren screaming.

Chapter Forty-Six

6:13 pm

Haylee, Juke, and Karolyn

As Haylee and Juke raced to Bugtown, they smelled a not unpleasant earthy aroma. The odor of dead bugs was way milder than the odor of dead cows and pigs that hung over meatpacking plants throughout the world—yet another way that increased bug consumption had turned out to be a great thing. Maybe bugs didn't taste as good as other forms of meat, but they were cheap, and most people thought they were every bit as good as mockburgers.

But even though the bug smell didn't bother her, Haylee felt queasy as the Zan roared down Liberty, then skidded around a corner toward a warehouse at the far end of Bug Row. All the turmoil in her gut from the fast driving better not cause a miscarriage. Logically she knew it wouldn't, but her stomach was way too far gone for logic.

Juke ordered the Zan: "Park behind the building." It turned sharply two more times, then screeched to a halt. He jumped out of the car and turned to her. "You gonna be okay?"

Why was he eyeing her like that? *Is my nausea so obvious?* She willed herself not to throw up and said, "Yeah, let's jack this doob."

After a moment, Juke took Haylee's Heston from his jacket pocket and held it out to her. "You might need this."

So that's what he'd been asking: if she would go berserk and start shooting people. She was grateful to get her Heston back, but it was embarrassing that he doubted her. "Thanks," she said, and holstered the gun.

Above them, the sky was darkening. They hurried through the cold past a bunch of other parked cars, most of them old and dinged up, and reached the side door of the bug warehouse. It was unlocked, so they walked in.

This particular bughouse used to be owned by the Nestlé's Food and Wellness Syndicate. But it wasn't in operation now, so it was empty of bugs—at least the packed, dead kind. Haylee figured it was the same old story: foreign buggers getting paid pennies an hour, taking jobs away from Americans. Factories in Guyana were winning the global bug wars.

Juke and Haylee headed down a wide industrial hallway with exposed pipes. The hallway was empty, but hard technospunk boomed through the walls. They turned right up ahead and the music grew louder.

Juke got a sharp hit of nostalgia. He hadn't been to a shmub since he was with Safiya. They used to go together about once a month.

New York shmubs typically lasted a week or two before they got shut down. Somebody would find a big empty space, bribe the relevant Dincs and Syncs, bring in truckfuls of booze and entertaining drugs, hire a band, and put out the word.

Shmubs were often Resistance-connected, with a share of the profits going to the movement, so it had been risky for a cop like Juke to be seen there. He always wore a mask. But he enjoyed the offbeat people he met, and he and Safiya had good times. He didn't relish hitting the scene now in a different role, as a despised Dinc. It would be weird as shit jacking a guy Safiya knew and apparently liked.

But there was a good chance this guy killed Talia.

Juke and Haylee turned right again and encountered a thick metal door. Juke tried to open it, but it was locked.

He knocked. A small electronic slot, no doubt created for this event, opened up in the door. An I! appeared in the slot, its cam peering out at him.

He tried the same magic words he'd used back in the day. "Friends of

Safiya Bassani-Jones."

There was a pause, then the I! was withdrawn and the door opened. As they went in, Juke whispered, "Safiya's gonna love me for this."

Haylee asked, "She's not Resistance, is she?"

Juke gave her a sidelong glance. "I don't know and you don't want to know."

Haylee immediately understood she'd stepped over the line. She had no right to ask Juke that kind of question about his girlfriend—even his ex-girlfriend. "Sorry, didn't mean to pry—"

Suddenly she got an exciting but terrifying thought: could Safiya be the strong Rez leader in her twenties or early thirties that Karolyn had asked her to find?

The room they were coming into was warm with sweat, dancing, and hundreds of bodies, but Haylee got a chill in her spine. *What the fuck do I do if it's her?*

No way she wanted to rat out Juke's ex and get her thrown in prison for years for seditious conspiracy. Juke obviously still had major feels for her. If he ever found out Haylee was responsible for—

"Let's go," Juke said, leading the way into the chaos of the shmub.

Haylee tried to breathe her fears away. She needed to find a man with a scar on his cheek.

* * *

Karolyn and Adams careened wildly toward 5821 Liberty Drive in the Boer. Adams grabbed the dashboard tight, petrified, but Karolyn was unaffected, talking to Raja on the phone. "If the NYPDinc jacks Scarface," she said, "we need to immediately take custody of him."

"Bad idea," Raja said over the phone. "If we grab Scarface from the NYPDInc, somebody would leak it. The Rez would find out."

The Boer hung a sharp left at fifty, sending Adams reeling into the side door. Karolyn said, "The Red Queen calculates it's worth the risk. We'll neuro the truth out of Scarface a lot faster than the NYPDinc would."

Finally Raja said, "Okay, if you really think so, go ahead."

Then he tapped off. Karolyn knew if there was a leak, Raja would blame her for it. He'd blame her for everything. A slow-moving roach truck was blocking their way, so Karolyn banged the horn, causing the Boer to scream: "Pull over before I fucking shoot you! Pull over before I fucking shoot you!"

The roach truck got the message and pulled over. The Boer raced around it toward Bugtown.

* * *

Juke and Haylee made their way through the huge bughouse room, packed with people in their twenties and thirties. On a makeshift wooden stage, three women with chains tatted on their bald heads banged on drums and synthesizers, blasting out the technospunk. The crowd danced wildly, throwing themselves at each other, banging asses and other body parts together, then bouncing off to new partners. Off to one side, long wooden planks sitting on cement blocks comprised the bar. Shmubbers lined up fifteen deep to purchase their drinks and drugs.

Haylee thought Juke looked pretty at ease. But for her this scene was new and strange. She didn't see herself as a stick in the mud, but these people took clubbing to a new level.

As they searched the room for the scarred man, Haylee bumped into one of the dancers, a doob with a large fishhook stuck into his bare chest. He mistook her bump for an amorous advance and responded by banging his hip hard into hers, knocking her to the floor.

While she checked her gun, making sure it was still properly holstered, the guy jumped on top of her. Apparently he had mistaken her falling for yet another demonstration of amorous interest. She tried to push him off her, while Juke hurried over and gave his arm a quick pull.

The guy, confused by the mixed signals he was getting regarding Haylee's romantic intentions, asked them, "Fish balls?"

"Not tonight, thanks," Juke said.

The guy saluted them with his left fist. "Break the chains!"

Then he turned away, looking for other people to bang with. Haylee watched him go, wondering what the hell fish balls were—some new drug, probably—

All of a sudden, several feet past the guy, she saw him: *the man with the scar.*

He was ordering something at the bar, and she could only see his profile; but that profile showed a long, thick scar going down his right cheek. He had the same dark hair and pointed nose they'd seen on the napkin.

Juke saw the man too. He told Haylee, "You go behind him."

Blood pumping, Juke gripped his Heston as they moved silently on the guy. They had to do this carefully—jacking somebody in a Rez shmub where everybody hated Dincs was no joke.

Juke thought, *here goes nothing,* and put his hand on the man's shoulder. The man spun around—

And Juke saw he was missing the other half of his face. It had been shot off or bombed or something.

This was a hundred P *not* the same guy who was on Talia's napkin. Fighting down his physical revulsion, Juke said, "Sorry, I thought you were somebody else."

The man looked at Juke incredulously out of his one eye. "You kiddin' me? There's somebody else who looks like this?"

Juke and Haylee walked away from the half-faced man. "Well, now I definitely feel like puking," Haylee said.

The band kicked it up a few clicks, with all three women screeching loudly like crazed parrots. The crowd loved it and screeched too.

Haylee covered her ears with her hands and wondered if being pregnant made you unusually sensitive to noise. It seemed like she was the only person in this whole shmub who found the caterwauling unbearable. Even Juke seemed to get a kick out of it.

As Juke looked around the room, Haylee watched him. In so many ways he had been the perfect partner to her this past month. He'd been patient at a time when she desperately needed it, when she was far from her best. This morning he could easily have snitched her out. Any other detective—

DeAndrey Jackson, say—would have done that without a second thought to cover his butt. Haylee would have been suspended, maybe permanently.

But Juke stood by her.

And now what am I doing to him?

Surrounded by everybody dancing and partying, Haylee felt so alone. How could she possibly take care of a baby all by herself? It seemed hopeless.

The only thing she knew for sure was: *my baby needs this deal to work out.*

"Let's keep moving," Juke said. She was glad to be distracted.

They walked through the room, stepping between and around the dancers. There were a lot of guys who looked like the napkin man from a distance—same medium-length dark hair. But up close, none of them had the scar.

As they reached the back wall, Haylee shouted into Juke's ear over the music, "Maybe he already left."

"We'll do one more sweep through the room," Juke said—

And then they saw him.

This time there was no doubt. It was their suspect. He had that same jagged scar going down his right cheek.

He was drinking by himself, sitting in a chair against the wall, maybe so he could see anybody who approached. He wore a dark leather jacket over broad shoulders. His narrow face looked tough, but drawn and worried.

He hadn't noticed them yet. But he would; with their lack of partying spirit, they stood out. So they didn't waste time figuring out a strategy— they just stepped to him fast. Juke drew his Heston, holding it close to his jacket so nobody but the scarred guy would see it. The guy's dark brown eyes widened with terror, his toughness no match for the gun barrel.

"Come with us real slow or I shoot you," Juke said.

"Who are you?" the guy said.

Juke jammed his gun into the guy's gut. Haylee stood next to Juke, ready to pull her gun too. "Get up," Juke said.

The guy froze.

"Move."

The guy stood up. All around them people danced, unaware of the drama so close by.

The guy's right hand reached for his pocket.

Juke grabbed his wrist and twisted. The guy gasped in pain, and Juke jammed his gun harder into him. Haylee drew her weapon and stuck it in his side. Two teenage girls in skull masks looked over curiously, but bodies and jackets hid the guns from their view. They turned away, evidently deciding Juke, Haylee, and the guy were doing some kind of dance. Juke reached into the guy's pocket, found a .25 Waco, and pocketed it.

"Let's go," Juke said.

With two guns poking him and his own gun gone, the scarred guy obeyed. They walked toward the back door, with him in the middle and Juke and Haylee flanking him real close.

About twenty-five feet from the door, two burly security guards in red neon "Fuck the Syndies" armbands stood watch. Juke, Haylee, and the scarred guy had to pass right by them.

"Don't say a goddamn word," Juke growled into the guy's ear as they drew close to the guards.

The guy kept quiet—but threw the guards a desperate, beseeching look.

The guards were confused, trying to make sense of this strangely uptight threesome walking so close together. Then the guard nearer to them figured it out.

"Dincs!" he shouted. "The Dincs are here!"

Instantly everybody who heard this above the technospunk stopped dancing and looked over.

A tall, muscular blonde wearing Viking armor ripped off her helmet. "It's the Dincs!"

Any chance of sneaking out quietly was gone. Juke and Haylee brought up their guns. Juke whipped his gun around in a semicircle, trying to threaten everybody in the crowd at once. Haylee trained her gun on the guards, who were reaching their hands toward their pockets, clearly itching to draw their own weapons.

With his free hand Juke grabbed hold of the scarred guy. He backed up toward the door, pulling the guy along as a shield. "Back off!" he yelled. "Back!"

But the crowd surged toward them, furious, barely held off by Juke and Haylee's guns. They came from every side, looking for an opening to attack.

"Fight the fascists!" the Viking woman screamed, and some guy shouted, "Kill 'em! Kill the Dincs!"

The crowd roared. If they got between Juke and Haylee and the door, that would be the end. Juke and Haylee would get trampled and shot.

Juke swung his gun behind him, trying to keep a pathway open for escape. "I'll shoot!" he yelled.

Now everybody was shouting. "Kill the Dincs!" "Break the chains!"

As Juke and Haylee moved backwards, the scarred guy stumbled and Juke yanked him back up. The guy seemed almost as scared of the mob as they were. They were less than five feet from the door.

But then a large man wearing nothing but thick metal chains wrapped around his powerful frame braved Juke and Haylee's weapons and stood at the door, blocking them. He reared back his head and howled at the ceiling, louder than any wolf. His eyes rolled upward. He had to be totally snorted up.

Juke pointed his gun at the man. "Open the door!"

But the man thrust his huge fists above his head and howled even louder. The crowd went wild. They closed in, smelling blood.

Haylee's throat got so tight she couldn't breathe. *My baby will never even be born,* she thought. She stuck her gun in the man's neck and screamed, *"Move!"*

For some reason her scream brought the man down to some semblance of semi-sobriety. Maybe he responded to the wildness in it. He took off and ran.

She covered Juke with her Heston as he opened the door and pulled the scarred guy through it. Then she dashed outside too.

The Zan was where they'd left it, forty feet away. Juke raced toward it, as quickly as he could while towing the scarred guy, and Haylee ran behind them.

The mob poured out the door after them. The two guards were in the lead, guns out, looking for a way to shoot at Haylee and Juke without hitting the scarred guy.

Haylee fired shots in the air to hold them back. It worked for a few moments, but then a new wave of people led by the Viking woman ran outside and pushed the mob forward. There were over a hundred of them, coming fast.

The scarred guy was absolutely terrified now. He raced with Juke and Haylee toward the Zan.

Juke scanned himself in and opened the car's back door. He was about to throw the scarred guy in there—but then he heard tires screeching close by. He looked up—

A car stopped right in front of the Zan, completely blocking it. *Juke and Haylee would be trapped!* The car was a yellow Lex. Juke couldn't see the driver, but the passenger window rolled down—

—and a masked man with a buzzcut—*the* masked man, Juke was sure of it—yelled out to the scarred guy, "Hey, ro!"

Juke and Haylee both pointed their guns at the masked man. The scarred guy took advantage of the diversion, wrenching himself free from Juke's grasp and running away from them toward the Lex.

The crowd cheered him on: "Go, ro, go!" Then the two guards started shooting at Haylee and Juke. The sound of their gunshots rose high above the crowd's yells. Haylee shot above the nearest guard's head and wasn't sure if she'd been aiming at him or above him. She could feel herself losing it, her heart pounding.

As the guards shot at them, the scarred guy jumped into the Lex's back seat and the car raced off. He was getting away.

But at least now the Zan wasn't trapped anymore. Juke scrambled into the car and yelled at Haylee, "Get in!" She dove for the door.

But the Viking woman raced forward, grabbed Haylee's coat, and wouldn't let go. The mob was closing in. Haylee pointed her gun. "Get off me!" she shouted.

The Viking woman ignored Haylee's shaking gun and shouted back, "Break the chains!"

Haylee heard more gunshots. Suddenly she saw the twelve-year-old boy with the mohawk shooting at Harrison. The horrifying bang reverberated in her ears as blood spurted out of Harrison's chest. She aimed her Heston at the Viking woman and started to squeeze the trigger—

"Haylee!" Juke shouted from inside the car.

Haylee went blank for a moment, then snapped back into reality. She took her finger off the trigger and did a quick half-turn, sliding out of her coat and leaving the woman standing there holding it. She jumped into the Zan—

—just as somebody fired a shot through her window, breaking the glass.

"Code red!" Juke yelled to the Zan, and its siren started shrieking.

A thick, hairy arm reached in through Haylee's open window and yanked her hair. She screamed and smashed the man's elbow with her gun, and he backed off.

The crowd converged and banged on the Zan so hard it rocked. But the car swiveled right, swiveled left, and at last broke free and sped away. The guards and other people in the mob shot at them, but the Zan veered right to get off Bug Row and out of range of the bullets.

Haylee's terror began to recede. But immediately it was replaced by a new panic.

That guy with the scar def looked Mexican. He was the man Karolyn wanted— and we let him get away.

They better find him again—fast—or Haylee and her baby were fucked.

Chapter Forty-Seven

6:42 pm

Karolyn

Karolyn and Adams were racing around the corner toward 5821 Liberty when they heard gunshots. Karolyn buzzed Haylee but got no answer. They turned into the parking lot and saw a large, agitated crowd milling around.

Adams said, "These people look like Rez. We should get backup."

"There's no time." Karolyn told the Boer to park on the edge of the lot. She didn't want this mob to see her expensive car and vent their frustration on it.

She got out of the car and used her *I!* to track Haylee's *I!* The signal monitor said Haylee's phone was somewhere in the middle of the crowd. But as Karolyn waded into the mass of bodies, she didn't see any sign of her asset. She heard snippets of convo: "…Dincs grabbed the guy!" "They shot at us." Somebody yelled: "Fuck the Six!", and people yelled the standard callback: "Break the chains!"

What a bunch of losers, Karolyn thought. She was maybe the oldest person here, and conspicuous in her black business suit with the gray-suited Adams at her side, but she kept going. In front of her, a South Asian security guard was bragging to the crowd about how he shot out the Dincs' car window. "And the doob with the scar escaped," he said. "Big-ass bright yellow Lex drove up and took him away."

The doob with the scar? So Haylee and O'Keefe found him. Karolyn hoped the guard would be too rocking about his glorious success to pay attention to her attire. "What happened to the fucking Dincs?" she asked him. "I hope they got blasted."

The guard said proudly, "They'll never come back *here,* that's for sure. They were bugshitting their pants."

That sounded like Haylee had made it out alive. Maybe her I*!* would have intel about where she was heading next, or about Scarface. Stepping around some rowdy shmubbers, Karolyn tracked Haylee's I*!* to a tall blonde woman dressed in some weird suit of armor. She was holding up the I*!* in one hand and Haylee's coat in the other and boasting to everybody who'd listen about how she ganked the I*!* from one of the Dincs. "Got it off the bitch's coat. If she comes back for it, she can suck my pits."

Karolyn stepped up to the armored woman and pointed at the I*!* "I'll give you twenty dollars for that. I'll wipe it and use it as a burner."

The woman said, "Can't use an NYPDinc phone for a burner. Nobody's decrypted their digitals."

Shit, she wasn't as dumb as she looked. Karolyn was tempted to grab the phone out of her hands, but didn't want to start a riot. "I know how to do it. I'll give you thirty."

The armored woman eyed Karolyn and Adams and said slowly, "You know how, huh?" Her voice rose. "Where you from in those flunky suits? The Fincs? The Agency?"

The South Asian security guard and a bunch of other shmubbers looked their way. They moved closer, menacing, ready to tear the crap out of Karolyn and Adams.

Karolyn laughed. "Don't be 'noid, doob. I'm D.C. Rez. We got every PDinc in the country decrypted."

She was confident she could talk her way out of this. But next to her, Adams whispered, "Let's get outta here"—and he was too loud, the moron. The mob heard him.

The armored woman yelled, "Agency! We got two agents here!"

Karolyn held up her hands to calm everybody down—but the guard grabbed her wrist.

Her instincts kicking in, Karolyn pivoted toward him and drove the thumb and forefinger of her free hand into his eyes. He screamed in agony and fell backward.

"Come on!" she yelled to Adams, and they raced toward the Boer. But the mob blocked their way, yelling and shouting, and somebody shoved Adams to the ground. She was tempted for a moment to leave him there—first Willard, now Adams, why couldn't these guys take care of themselves? But she pulled her Ruby Ridge and let loose with three shots in the air, trying to give him time to get up.

It didn't work. After beating the Dincs just now, this mob wouldn't be stopped by a few air shots. They surged forward, breaking into a run. Karolyn aimed low at the armored woman, racing at the front of the pack, and shot her in the knee. Her spurting blood and howls of pain slowed the mob enough for Karolyn and Adams to make it into the Boer. They roared off.

But the mob was shooting at them now. Multiple gunshots blasted in their ears. They made it less than fifty feet before one of their rear tires got hit and exploded. The Boer screeched forward on the other three tires, then smashed into a parked truck.

Karolyn and Adams crawled out of the car, dazed. But as the mob ran toward them firing and yelling "Fuck the Agency!", they jumped up and ran.

Karolyn couldn't feel those extra pounds anymore—she put her head down and kept going. Their fear was a more powerful motivator than their pursuers' hatred, and four minutes later, when they reached 53rd Street and looked behind them, the mob was nowhere in sight.

Adams bent over double, trying to catch his breath. "Boy, that was lucky," he gasped.

Lucky, Karolyn thought with disgust. If it wasn't for Adams' stupidity, they never would have had any problems in the first place. Now Scarface was in the wind, and so was her NYPDinc asset. She checked the time—*7:06. I have less than five hours!*

Somewhere out there in the dark haze of the night, the Resistance was planning their operation. Somehow, Karolyn needed to stop it.

I <u>*will*</u> *stop it. I won't fail.*

"God, it's freezing," Adams said.

"Shut up."

With Adams scurrying to keep up, Karolyn headed down 53rd and buzzed the one colleague she could always count on—the Red Queen. "I need you to find a bright yellow Lex, last seen at 5821 Liberty."

"I'm on it," the Red Queen said. "I take it the suspect successfully evaded you?"

"He was gone before we got there," Karolyn shot back.

"I didn't mean to imply it was your fault."

She gritted her teeth. "What do you have on the six Mexican D's?"

"Between the Anthill and your human colleagues, we've narrowed it down to three possibles: David, Diego, and one of the two Donatos. We're attempting to locate them."

"Keep working that," Karolyn said.

"Absolu," said the Red Queen. "And meanwhile, let's find that bright yellow Lex."

Chapter Forty-Eight

7:07 pm

Juke, Haylee, Safiya, and Rey

As soon as Juke and Haylee escaped the bughouse mob, they began searching for the yellow Lex. With no money in their case account, they couldn't put out an APB. They'd have to do this on their own. Juke was about to tell the Zan to go south on Liberty when he heard a squeal of tires to the north. Of course that might be coming from some other car, but it was the only clue they had. So he told the Zan to turn around and go fast in that direction.

As they stared through the windshield, watching for a flash of bright yellow, Juke asked, "Did you see who was driving the Lex?"

"No. All I saw was that guy with the mask."

He nodded. "At least now we know the guy with the scar and the guy in the mask are two different people." He thought about the brutality of the murder. "Maybe they killed Talia together. Some weird sex thing, or…"

Haylee looked away from Juke, upset. Now that the scarred guy was on the run, she'd have to tell Karolyn everything she knew about him. Karolyn would demand it. And that would mean telling her about Juke's ex.

Damn it. She felt awful for Juke. When he learned his investigation had brought down Safiya, he'd be crushed.

But what else could Haylee do?

And if Safiya really was the woman Karolyn was looking for, and she'd been stupid enough to launch a big conspiracy against the syndicates, that was on her. Radical Rez people weren't peaceful protestors; they were violent extremists breaking the law. She'd just seen for herself how dangerous they were.

Haylee felt in her pockets for her I! so she could text Karolyn, then realized she'd left it behind. Shit, she'd have to buy a new one. She was about to ask Juke to borrow his—though it would feel weird using Juke's I! to rat out his ex-girlfriend—when a raucous choir of car horns began yelling and quacking up ahead. What was that about?

"Go faster," Juke told the Zan.

The Zan said, "But I'm already going—"

"Go faster."

This time it was Haylee who said, "But—"

"*Faster,*" Juke repeated yet again, and the Zan finally followed orders, going as speedily as its piece-of-junk engine could go, throwing them backward against the seat.

Juke said, "All those horns—I bet the Lex is up there, running."

* * *

Only law enforcement vehicles could go over the speed limit on automatic. So when Safiya, Rey, and Diego had raced away from the bughouse in the Lex, Safiya took the controls, because they needed to go fast. Now she was ignoring the car horns as she veered in and out of lanes doing fifty—impressive for a Friday night.

As Rey checked behind them to make sure the Zan wasn't on their trail, Diego spoke up from the back seat, still breathing heavily with fear. "I thought I was dead! Where are we going?"

Safiya felt guilty toward Diego; Juke must have located him by tracking her phone call. She said, "We'll keep you in a safe house till midnight. In Syrian Harlem, up on 130th."

"God, I can't wait to get out of this fucking city," Diego said.

Safiya had a disturbing thought—*am I helping Talia's murderer escape?!*—but shut it down. "Hang in there, Diego. It'll be okay—"

"They're coming!" Rey yelled, pointing behind them. "The Dinc Zan. It's right there!"

Safiya checked her mirror—shit, the Zan was pulling around a bus and coming up hard! *What do I do?*

Rey sprang into action, hitting the unlock button, rolling down his window—and pulling out his gun. Safiya shouted, "Rey, what are you doing?! *Stop it!*"

"They're coming at us!" Rey shouted back.

Behind them the Zan called out: "Pull over!"

"Go faster!" Diego yelled.

"Put down the gun!" Safiya yelled at Rey.

"He's gonna jack us!"

"Pull over! Pull over!"

"Oh God oh God," Diego breathed, as Rey raised the gun.

Safiya reached out her right arm and tried to yank Rey back from the window. She screamed, "You can't shoot Juke!"

"He's your enemy now!" Rey screamed back. He stuck his gun out the window and fired at the Zan.

* * *

As soon as the masked man inside the Lex drew his weapon, Haylee spotted it. "He's got a gun!" she shouted, grabbing her Heston.

"Wait—don't shoot!" Juke yelled, horror taking over his face. "Safiya's in the Lex!"

The Zan screamed, "Pull over! Pull over!"

Haylee shouted, "He's gonna shoot us!"

"No he won't! Safiya will stop him!"

"Pull over!"

"You don't know Safiya anymore!" Haylee yelled.

"Stand down! They won't shoot!" Juke screamed—

—and the masked man shot at them.

His shot went wild, but the sound of it exploded in Haylee's brain. Within a millisecond she was gone. Juke was saying something to her, but she didn't hear it.

She fired at the masked man, again and again, and he fired back.

* * *

Inside the Lex, Safiya shouted at Rey, frantic, "Stop shooting! You idiot!"

But he didn't stop, didn't even answer. So she yanked the wheel and veered into the right lane, throwing him off balance so he couldn't shoot any more. Then she swerved into a right exit that was coming up fast.

But she lost control. The car fishtailed once, then twice, and smashed into a tree.

* * *

As soon as Safiya cut toward the exit, Juke shouted "Manual!" He grabbed the wheel and swung hard into the exit behind them.

The Zan fishtailed just like the Lex had. It was fishtailing a second time when its rear bumper smashed smack into the Lex's side. The Zan's digitals instantly died—and Juke and Haylee were thrown into the dashboard.

* * *

Most cars didn't have airbags anymore since they weren't required, but the Lex was high-end. Its airbags deployed as soon as it hit the tree. So Safiya, Rey, and Diego made it through the initial crash relatively unscathed.

But when the Zan crashed into the Lex's side, the airbags were useless. Rey's head banged into the dashboard. Safiya hit the windshield hard enough to possibly cause a concussion, though for now the adrenaline was pumping.

Rey said, "I can't find my gun."

"It's on the floor," said Diego, whose body had been thrown half into the front seat.

"Leave it!" Safiya said.

Rey went for it anyway. Safiya tried to grab it first—

Then they both heard Juke saying, "Hands up!" He stood outside Rey's open window with a fresh, bleeding gash on his forehead and a gun pointed at Rey's face.

Juke's partner, the tall brunette, stood at the other window with a gun trained on Safiya.

Safiya looked around desperately for help, but they were parked outside office buildings that were dead at this hour of night. And what would she do if she saw somebody—ask them to call the cops?

Juke reached through Rey's open window with his free hand and unlocked the door, then opened it. "Get out—all of you. Leave that gun on the floor."

Safiya's brain stopped working.

"*Move,*" Juke ordered.

Finally Safiya managed to say, "We're coming."

She got out of the car, for a moment locking eyes with Juke's partner, who backed up but kept her gun aimed at her. Rey and Diego got out on the other side.

Rey said to Safiya, "He doesn't give a scruck about you. We're dead."

Juke said, "Put your hands on the car. Safiya, get on this side."

It was jarring to hear Juke say her name so coldly. Stumbling, head throbbing, she made her way to the other side of the car. She stood beside Rey and put her hands on the car roof next to his.

Rey said, "We shoulda run when we had a chance."

God, shut up, Rey, she thought.

Diego shouted at the cops, "What do you want from us? We didn't do anything!"

Standing behind Safiya, Juke said, "Besides shoot at us."

Rey said, "Your partner was pointing her gun at us!"

"And now it's pointed at all three of you," Juke said. "She's got a quick trigger finger and a bad case of PTSD, so I suggest you don't make any sudden moves."

As Juke described, Haylee was aiming her gun at them. She kept her face dead serious—but inside, victory surged through her.

No question: the scarred guy had a Mexican accent. And Safiya was a strong leader in her twenties or early thirties. Haylee could tell that just from one moment of looking her in the eye.

As soon as Haylee got the chance, she'd call Karolyn and tell her everything. And she could quit feeling guilty. These people had shot at her! They tried to kill her!

Despite the tension of aiming the gun, Haylee felt her stomach start to calm down. Maybe little Hera knew she was being taken care of. Her mom had figured it out.

Meanwhile Safiya studied Juke as he searched Rey for additional weapons. Juke patted him down from head to toe and found nothing, then removed Rey's mask and examined his face. Safiya wondered, *has he figured out Rey's my boyfriend?*

Juke moved on to Diego—and found something in the very first pocket he checked: old-school brass knuckles. The weapon looked quaint in an era when people were so quick to reach for their guns.

"What's this for?" Juke asked.

"Protection," Diego spit out.

Juke thought about saying something like "Protection from Talia?", just to see how the guy handled it. But he decided to hold his fire. After verifying Haylee had him covered, he turned on his I! flashlight to examine the brass knuckles for traces of blood. He believed the damage to Talia's face had been caused by naked fists, but it wouldn't hurt to make sure.

He didn't see any blood. But as he put the knuckles in his pocket, he caught Safiya looking at Diego strangely. "What's up?" he asked her.

"What the hell is that supposed to mean?" Safiya said, defiant.

"You gave your pal here a funny look."

"Fine. So jack me for it."

Juke couldn't believe he and Safiya had come to this, but so be it. He finished searching Diego, confiscating his burner, and now it was her turn.

He paused, said, "Sorry about this, Safiya," and put his hands on her.

"If you were sorry, you'd have your partner do it," she said bitterly.

"I'll switch with her if you want."

If he can handle this, so can I. "Whatever. You know I never carry a gun."

"I know you didn't use to."

His hands reached inside her coat. She tried to make her mind go numb as they went through the pockets in her shirt, her pants… Then they went back up to her shoulders and felt their way down her sides. They slid around her hips, back to front…

She smelled that mixture of aftershave and sweat. Having his hands on her was a strange form of agony, so familiar and yet so sick and off-kilter. He went down her legs, feeling for an ankle holster. Then he stood back up.

"Now what?" Safiya said. "Gonna take me in for neuro? Fry my brain?"

"You got a better idea?"

She heard his I! buzzing. "Better answer that. Could be your syndicate bosses."

"Safiya, I'm investigating the brutal murder of a young woman. Your friend is our prime suspect."

"I know him. He didn't kill her."

"I saw the look you gave him. You have doubts."

The brass knuckles did throw her, it was true—but just for a moment. "No, I don't. He loved Talia."

"That makes it more likely he's the killer."

His hands still flat against the car, Diego said, "I would never hurt Talia. I wanted to live my life with her—"

Rey turned to Diego. "Don't talk to this Dinc."

Juke's partner said quickly, "Hands back on the car."

"Do it," Juke said.

Rey complied, as Safiya told Diego, "Rey is right. Don't say a word till we get you a lawyer."

Juke told Diego, "Play it that way and we'll have to assume you're guilty and take you in."

Safiya snapped, "Cut the crap. You're forgetting I know all your moves."

Juke looked at her. "Let me ask you something. Did you know Talia?"

Safiya's silence made it obvious she did.

"Then why don't you help me find out who killed her?" Juke asked.

She took her hands off the car roof and turned to face him. Immediately Juke's partner ordered, "Hands on the car."

"Go to hell," Safiya said. She looked straight into Juke's eyes. "Juke, if I knew anything that could help you, I would've told you by now. Honestly, none of us have any idea who killed Talia."

"Where do you know her from?"

"I'm not getting into that."

"How do you know this guy?" Juke said, pointing to Diego.

"It doesn't matter."

"Gonna stonewall me, huh? That was you this morning at Talia's speck, wasn't it?"

Safiya gave a start. *How did Juke figure that out?*

Rey said, "None of your bizness."

Juke ignored him. "What were you doing, Safiya—removing the evidence?"

"Not evidence of murder."

"Evidence of what then?"

Safiya didn't answer.

"What about *this* doob?" Juke said, pointing at Rey. "Somebody helped him escape from us this afternoon. Was that you?"

Safiya said, "Juke, you have to trust me."

"I'll take that as a yes. What were you two trying to do—bug my car?"

She clamped her jaw tight.

Juke's I*!* buzzed again, but he kept looking at Safiya. "Are you going out with this guy?"

Rey broke in. "Got a problem with that?"

Juke's partner spoke up from behind them. "Listen, fuckwads, this man you're aiding and abetting had a fight with Talia right before she was murdered. You better come up with something pretty damn tutti, or we're taking all three of you in."

Juke nodded. "What she said. And because of my association with Safiya, I'll have to turn you guys over to another detective." He paused, looking at her. "You sure you want that?"

Was he being sympathetic or just playing her? She couldn't tell. But she turned to Rey and Diego. "Maybe we *should* talk to him." Rey opened his mouth to protest, so she said quickly, "He's a good cop, at least he used to be. He'll be more fair to us than anybody else." *And less likely to jack us for sedition!*

Rey said, "Or else he's still chunked at you for dumping him, and he can't wait to hurt you—*and me.*"

"All I care about is catching this girl's killer," Juke said.

Rey laughed harshly. "You're a Dinc. All you care about is ka-ching."

Diego asked Safiya, "Are you really sure you trust him?"

She stared at Juke for a long moment. His eyes looked so cold and hard. A cop's eyes. In truth, she didn't know what she thought.

But she said, "Yes. I trust him."

Was it her imagination, or did his eyes soften?

Diego scratched his scarred cheek. "Is he a sympathizer?"

"Yes, no question," Safiya answered.

Rey retorted, "What about his partner? Is she a sympathizer too?"

Juke said, "All we're trying to do here is get justice for Talia."

"So in other words she's *not,*" Rey said.

Juke didn't contradict him, and the partner stayed silent too. Great. Safiya said, "Juke, here's what we'll do, assuming my guys are good with it. We'll talk to you—but not your partner."

"No," Juke said. "I don't keep secrets from her."

Safiya eyed the woman. She looked uncomfortable for some reason. Safiya couldn't read her.

But what choice did Safiya have? If Juke took them to the station, they would be neuroed, starting with Diego. The NYPDinc would learn *everything* about Diego and Talia and tonight's op. Safiya, Rey, and the New York Eighteen would be doomed. Maybe Juke wouldn't want that to happen—but it would.

Not only that, Chocolate would be dead.

Safiya turned back to Juke. "Listen to our story. Then use your discretion about what you tell your partner." She pointed to the wall of the office building across the street. "For now she goes over there."

"No, not that far. I need her to hold a gun on you guys," Juke said. "We'll talk here by the tree, and she can hang by the driveway." He turned to Haylee. "If you're cool with that."

"No prob," Haylee said. "I can kill 'em from there."

Safiya lifted her eyebrows and said to Juke, "She's a real charmer. You guys an item?"

Juke's I! buzzed again, but he continued to ignore it. He turned to Safiya, Diego, and Rey.

"A girl's been murdered," he said. "I'm gonna find her killer. It doesn't matter worth a damn how much I loved Safiya or still love her. If any one of you lies to me or refuses to answer a question, I will jack *all* of you. I'll charge you with destroying evidence, resisting arrest, and shooting at an officer of the law. Everybody got that?"

Safiya nodded, and Rey and Diego grudgingly did too.

But what Safiya kept hearing inside her head was: "how much I loved Safiya or still love her."

After everything that had gone on between them, was it possible Juke still loved her?

And how did she feel about him?

She shook her head and tried to shut out these thoughts. She wasn't a lovesick teenager. She had a revolution to protect.

* * *

As Juke began his interrogation, Haylee backed up toward the driveway, her gun out and ready.

She would do what she had to do.

Chapter Forty-Nine

7:17 pm

Karolyn and the Red Queen

So *infuriating!* Karolyn and her idiot partner Adams couldn't find *anything:* not the yellow Lex, not Haylee, not even the Zan. The Zan must have had an accident or malfunction that killed its digitals, including the GPS. Meanwhile another night of heavy smog was making drones worthless for surveillance.

Haylee didn't have her I! anymore, so Karolyn called Juke. She planned to say she was Haylee's doctor and needed to talk to her immediately. But Juke never answered his phone, and even worse, it was locay-protected. This was probably wise; there had been several instances lately of people hacking-and-tracking Dincs they had a beef with and shooting them. But it meant Karolyn couldn't use Juke's position to find Haylee too.

Karolyn called Raja, who gave her grief for way too long before finally sending out agents to hunt for the Lex.

She was desperate to chase after the Lex herself. It couldn't have gone far. She didn't want to wait for a car from Agency headquarters in midtown, that might take fifteen minutes, so she tapped for an oob. But three whole minutes sludged by before one arrived—and then it was a rickety, lime green, fifteen-year-old Munch, descended from the VW Bugs of the previous century. The oob came with its owner in the front seat; he must have been on his way somewhere else and decided to make a few quick bucks. He was a middle-aged Icelandic immie—annoying, since she wasn't in the mood to think about Icelanders right now, after that mess with Sölvi Hilmarsson. Even more aggro, the oober refused to take control of the driving and go above the speed limit to hunt for the Lex, even when Karolyn offered him a hundred bucks.

Since Adams wasn't exactly the swiftest chip in the circuit, Karolyn was pretty much on her own. She was stuck in a slow Munch with an irritating Icelander and a useless Midwesterner, heading south on Liberty with no idea if that was the same way the Lex went. She slammed the dashboard and yelled, "Fuck!"

"Please keep your voice down," the Icelander said.

Karolyn couldn't take it anymore. Besides, she needed to make a call and couldn't have any civilians listening in. "Get out of the car," she told the Icelander.

He looked puzzled. "What?"

Karolyn drew her Ruby Ridge and stuck it in his neck. "Doob, don't make me zap two Icelanders in one day."

The oober stared at her wide-eyed and decided she just might be serious. He ordered the Munch to pull over, jumped out, and ran. He would probably call the Dincs, but so what? She'd had to commandeer the Munch on a matter of vital syndicate security.

Adams frowned at her reproachfully, but she ignored him—that was getting easier and easier—and ordered the car back on the road. Keeping her eyes open for the yellow Lex, she tapped into the Red Queen and asked, "Why hasn't Haylee Navarro buzzed in?"

"Confidential snitches often have second thoughts," the Red Queen pointed out.

"What about motherly love conquering all, like you said?"

"It's possible she's dead."

Karolyn wanted to scream. "If Haylee is dead or tripping, we need somebody else at the NYPDinc we can count on—and forget about that weasel Burgess."

"May I suggest a Plan B," the Red Queen said. "A homicide detective named DeAndrey Jackson who's helped the Agency in the past, before you arrived. He's absolutely not weasel-ish—but you'll need to pay him a sizable amount."

Karolyn scowled. "Fine. We'll have him put out an APB on the Lex—and also hunt down David, Diego, and Donato. I want every uni in the city working this."

"Agreed. But we should still keep our involvement secret if possible."

"We can't worry about that anymore—it's almost midnight!"

"Even so. I'm going to buzz you in to Michael Billingsley."

The seeming non sequitur confused Karolyn. "The Berkshire Vanguard guy? Why?"

"Because you're into him." Karolyn's face grew warm with embarrassment and annoyance, since Adams was listening. "Also, he had a promising strategy to propose."

Ten seconds later Billingsley, as hot as Karolyn remembered, was on her I! screen. "Good to see you again," he said.

"Likewise," said Karolyn. "I understand you have a good idea for me."

He smiled, revealing two rows of perfect teeth. "If the Red Queen says so, it must be good."

"What is it?"

Billingsley turned serious. "I'll keep it quick, 'cause I know you're in a hurry. This man with the scar—it sounds like he's the guy that killed Talia. And you also think he's part of this de-chipping conspiracy?"

"That's right."

"Then how about if Berkshire Vanguard offers the NYPDinc fifty Reagans to hunt for Talia's killer. And fifty more if they succeed. We'll say we're doing it as a gesture for our client Talia. Nobody needs to know our real goal is to bust open the conspiracy."

Karolyn didn't have to think twice. "Thank you very much for being so generous."

"Hey, always happy to help the Agency." He leaned forward. "Karolyn, please call me anytime you want something."

Def flirting again. "I'll see you around."

"I certainly hope so. Oh, and one more thing before you go. Who at the NYPDinc will get this money?"

"It won't be Juke O'Keefe," said Karolyn. "He doesn't know it yet, but we're getting a different detective to take over. O'Keefe is off the case."

"Excellent," Billingsley said, beaming.

Chapter Fifty

7:22 pm

Juke, Haylee, Safiya, Rey, and Diego

Juke made Safiya sit on the ground under the tree, next to her boyfriend and the scarred guy. Even with Haylee backing him up, he stood in front of them and kept his gun out. He didn't trust the two guys—and he wasn't a hundred P sure about Safiya either.

How would he play this if he didn't know her? That's what he needed to do: take his emotions out of it.

By the driveway, Haylee had her gun out too. As Juke's interrogation began, she bent forward and strained her ears. Maybe she'd hear things she could pass along to Karolyn, as soon as she got hold of a phone.

But really, Haylee told herself, she already had more than enough information for Karolyn. She had Safiya's name and address. Even if for some reason Juke let Safiya go, Karolyn would have no trouble tracking and jacking her.

Haylee's gun felt heavy in her hand, and she shifted it. She hoped Juke would never find out she was the snitch.

Meanwhile Juke turned to the scarred guy. He didn't have a gut feeling yet about whether this guy was guilty. Sure, Safiya vouched for him, but Juke had seen plenty of people get fooled by killers. "What's your name?" he asked.

The guy hesitated. Juke put his age at twenty-eight, but maybe the scar made him look older than he was. "What's your name?" he repeated.

"Diego Montoya," the guy said grudgingly.

Juke would check that later. For now he wouldn't ask for proof; he needed to get a conversational rhythm going. He thought of interrogations as pieces of music, with rises and falls and even choruses. Safiya had found that weird and used to tease him about it.

"What was your relationship with Talia?"

Diego answered belligerently, "I told you. I loved her."

"So you were lovers."

"Yes," Diego said, exasperated.

Juke tried to bring the tension down a notch, slow the tempo a bit. "How long have you known her?"

"We met at rehab a year ago. We've been together ever since."

"Really. There's no record of your ship with Talia on networld."

"We wanted to keep it on the deep low."

This was not an uncommon desire among Gen Deltas; a lot of them rebelled against networld in one way or another. But Juke wanted to hear Diego explain his own reasons for it. "Why'd you stay low?"

Safiya said, "'Cause the less interaction people have with the system, the better off they are."

"Please don't speak for the suspect," Juke said. Ignoring Safiya's pissed-off look, he turned back to Diego. "Where were you last night?"

"When?"

"Starting at ten."

Diego hesitated. Juke wondered, would he lie about being at Bottoms Up last night?

Safiya's boyfriend told Diego petulantly, "I still think you shouldn't talk."

Diego ran his hands through his hair, then said, "I was out walking."

"Just walking?" Juke said.

"I don't have the ka-ching to do anything else."

"You didn't stop in anywhere?"

Finally Diego cracked. "Okay, I went into the strip joint where Talia worked. We talked for a while. That was it."

"Where'd you go after that?"

"I walked home. Went to bed."

"Anybody see you?"

"I don't know. Not really."

"Do you have any roommates?"

"Yeah, but he's doing ninety days." Diego added bitterly, "The doob owed two hundred bucks for parking tickets and the syndies jacked him."

Juke felt he had Diego in a good rhythm now. He was talking pretty fast and even volunteering info. Juke was irritated when a van exited Liberty and came toward them. He hoped it wouldn't stop to check out the car wreck and interrupt them.

Fortunately the van drove past. He turned to Diego again. "What did you and Talia talk about?"

"Last night? I don't remember."

"Get real, Diego. She's dead. Those were the last words you ever said to each other. Whether you killed her or not, I know you've replayed the entire convo a hundred times in your head." For three years, Juke had replayed his last scene with Safiya.

Diego didn't deny it, but said, "We didn't talk about anything special. Just movies and stuff."

"You argued with her. People saw it. That's why we tracked you down."

"No, you tracked me 'cause my scar makes me look like a bad-ass."

"You gonna answer me or not?"

"It was just a normal convo," Diego said, a pleading tone entering his voice. "Ship stuff."

Juke could tell he was lying. "Quit playing games or the deal's off. I'm taking you in."

Safiya's boyfriend said to her sullenly, "I told you, he's just another Dinc."

Safiya said, "Juke, if you ever believed me on anything, you gotta believe me on this. Diego didn't do it."

"How do you know him?"

Safiya said, "Through the Resistance."

Juke blinked. Diego's eyes widened in alarm. The boyfriend was terrified too. He said, "Safiya—"

She broke in, "I lived with Juke, okay? He knows I'm Rez. And I'm sure he guessed Diego is too."

Juke said, "If you're so certain he's innocent, why'd you try to help him run away?"

The boyfriend said, "'Cause you Dincs will frame him for murder so you can make bank and move on to the next case."

"You're right—some Dincs would do that. But Safiya knows I'd never frame anybody."

Safiya said, "Juke, if you place Diego under police scrutiny, it would have unintended dangerous repercussions. Not just for him." She looked up at Juke. "For me too."

A chill went through Juke. *Finally, there it is.* He'd suspected it might be something like this.

Now he needed to keep pushing, pretending he'd never met Safiya before. She was just another witness, maybe an unwitting accomplice to the murder. "So the three of you are involved in some Resistance operation, and you're afraid I'll find out."

Diego looked desperate. The boyfriend glared at Juke with hate-filled eyes.

Safiya said, "If you pursue this with Diego, I could end up in prison for twenty years for seditious conspiracy. Is that what you want?"

Juke said angrily, "You have no right to lay this kind of trip on me. This man fought with his girlfriend, he has no alibi, and now he's lying to me."

"He's not lying—"

"Bugshit. He's hiding something, and so are you, and I need to know what it is so I can find out who killed a young girl with no family who drew beautiful pictures and loved homeless cats and deserved a whole lot better than getting beaten to death and dumped in the street and run over like she was a rotten piece of meat. And you better believe whoever did this to her will do it again to another woman unless I stop him. I'm sorry for whatever happens to you but I'm taking him in." He turned to Diego.

"Diego Montoya, you're under arrest."

Diego said, "If I tell you the truth, you'll just think I'm an even bigger suspect. I'm a jealous boyfriend or whatever."

"Either tell me right now or put out your hands to be cuffed."

Safiya's boyfriend told Diego, "It's a trick. He'll cuff you no matter what—"

Diego turned to Juke and said, "We were arguing about her after-shift work."

"Her what?"

Diego looked down, feeling a private pain, then looked up again. "Every night after her shift, she was supposed to do one or two guys. That was part of her job for the club, what she got paid for. Obviously I wasn't too happy about that."

Juke stared at Diego. "Okay, so doob, you do realize you're a moron."

Diego's head snapped back. "What do you mean?"

"Why didn't you tell me this in the first place? You just gave me a great murder suspect. Whoever she was with last night."

"She wasn't with anyone. She was gonna refuse to do it."

Juke frowned, puzzled. "You must've been happy about that. So why were you fighting?"

Diego looked ashamed. "I thought she *should* do it. She shouldn't make waves on her very last night."

"What do you mean, 'her very last night'?"

Juke caught Safiya and her boyfriend looking suddenly agitated. About what? Meanwhile Diego didn't respond. He seemed stricken, like he knew he'd talked too much.

Juke asked, "Was Talia quitting her gig?"

Diego lifted his head and looked Juke straight in the eye. "That's all I'm gonna say. If you want to jack me, go ahead. I don't give a fuck." He turned to Safiya and her boyfriend. "Don't worry, I won't ever snitch on you guys."

Diego was looking in Safiya's eyes to reassure her. Juke watched him and thought: *I kinda like this guy. I hope he's not the killer.*

But he probably was. It was always the boyfriend. Who else could have killed Talia?

But then it hit him: *what about the guy Talia said no to last night?*

"Who was Talia supposed to be with last night?" he asked, trying to hide his growing excitement.

"She didn't know. She hadn't gotten her assignment yet."

Damn. But there was something here, he could feel it. "Were any of these after-shift guys giving her problems?"

"She never mentioned anything. The way she described it, it was always pretty much a one-time thing."

Juke thought for a moment. "How did she get her assignments? On her I!?"

"No, her boss would tell her what to do."

"You mean Teddy, the red-haired guy?"

"Yeah. One hundred P prick," Diego said. "Whenever Talia tried to get out of doing that stuff, he'd give her a hard time, start screaming at her."

"Last night, did Talia tell him she wouldn't do it?"

"She said she was gonna tell him as soon as her shift ended. She was nervous about it."

Juke felt a tingle going up his spine. Evidently Safiya felt something similar, because she said, "Oh my God."

Diego and the boyfriend looked confused. Diego said, "What is it?"

Juke said, "What if Teddy got pissed off at Talia when she refused to turn tricks for him? She knew it was her last night, so she told him to take this gig and shove it. And he did what pimps do: he knocked her senseless. Then he went even further."

Diego stared at Juke. "I'm gonna kill him."

Juke needed to go to Bottoms Up and question Teddy—*now.*

But what should he do with Safiya, Diego, and… "What's your name?" he asked Safiya's boyfriend.

Diego cut in, "I'm gonna kill that motherfucker—"

"Quiet." Juke held up his hand and asked the boyfriend again, "What's your name?"

"What, am *I* a suspect now?" he said, belligerent.

"You will be if you don't tell me your name."

Safiya said, "It's Rey Matoshi."

The boyfriend sputtered furiously, "What are you doing—"

Safiya spelled it out for Juke. "R-E-Y M-A-T-O-S-H-I."

Rey's jaw tightened in disbelief, while Juke said, "Okay, Safiya and Rey. I'll let you go for now. But I want you to stay here in the city and be available for questioning."

"What about Diego?" Safiya said.

"He's a murder suspect who ran. I can't release him."

Diego's face twisted, panicking. Safiya protested, "But I told you, he's innocent—"

"Obviously I can't take your word for it."

"But you just said, Teddy killed Safiya—"

Juke said, "Diego, here's what I'll do for you. I won't take you in to the station." He squatted down to Diego's level, so he wouldn't tower over him. "My partner and I will hold you in the back seat of our car while I investigate the lead you gave me, about Teddy. It's a good lead. If it works out I'll let you go too. No one will ever know you were a suspect."

"You need to let me go before midnight," Diego said.

"Why?"

Diego didn't answer. His eyes glistened, near tears. What was going on here? "Is this related to what you said about it being Talia's last night?"

Diego still didn't answer.

Safiya said, "Juke, it's irrelevant, I promise."

Treat her like you don't know her. "Not good enough. Tell me what it is."

"It won't help you—"

Juke stood up. "Enough of this. You're all material witnesses in a homicide. I withdraw my offer to release you and Rey."

Safiya clenched her fists. "Why won't you believe me?"

"'Cause I believed you three years ago when you said you wouldn't leave me."

Shit—he hadn't meant to say anything like that. Safiya's lips parted, startled. He backtracked, trying to get less emotional. "I need to know what's going on here. I can't investigate the way I need to if you leave me in the dark."

Safiya eyed him, exasperated. He looked right back at her. He wasn't sure if he was bluffing or not, but he took a set of handcuffs out of his jacket. Then he called back toward the driveway, "Haylee, get me two more handcuffs from the car."

Haylee started toward the car, keeping her gun ready.

Then Safiya said quietly, "Diego wants to leave at midnight 'cause he's escaping to Canada."

Rey snapped, "Shit, Safiya—"

"Rey, trust me, okay?"

"You're putting *my* life in danger! You have no right to tell some fucking Dinc—"

"Juke is an honest man—"

"Are you in love with him?!"

Juke gave a start. He watched Safiya closely.

Her eyes widened. She hesitated, then said, "No I'm not, but I'll tell you one thing. He would never make his girlfriend gank a car 'cause he was too scared to do it himself!"

Rey threw Safiya an outraged look. *There's def a story there,* thought Juke.

What was her tone of voice when she said, "No I'm not"? *Did she mean that? Was she sure? She paused before she said it...*

Haylee came toward them carrying the two sets of handcuffs. Juke waved her off. "Never mind, Haylee. Go back to the driveway for now."

Haylee stopped, looking like she wanted to say something. But then she backed away, her gun still trained on Safiya and the two men.

Juke turned to Safiya. "Was Talia escaping too? That's why it was her last night?"

"Right."

"But how could she escape? She was a fifty-one percenter. What about her bio-alarm?"

Out of the corners of his eyes, Juke saw Diego and Rey listening, stunned, as Safiya revealed the whole truth—a truth that could destroy them. "We found a way to remove biochips without activating the alarm. Tonight we're gonna de-chip eighteen people—it would've been nineteen with Talia—and get them across the border. Then we'll show every fifty-one percenter in the whole country how to do it. We're hoping to free tens of millions of people and start a revolution."

Juke stared at her in shock and amazement. She'd always had big dreams, but—"Holy crap, Safiya."

"Now you know why we can't let the NYPDinc or anyone else get hold of Diego. If they neuro him, he'll give us up—no matter how hard he tries to resist."

"So he's one of the fifty-one percenters escaping tonight?"

Diego spoke up. "No, I'm at forty-seven. But Talia didn't want to leave without me, and Safiya said I could come along."

Safiya said, "Diego needs to get out of the country quick, 'cause what if the NYPDinc tries to frame him for Talia's murder? Not you, but a different cop."

Juke said, "That won't happen. Nobody else cares about Talia's murder."

"But if they find out he was involved in tonight's op, they'll throw everything at him."

Juke rubbed his head. Safiya was right: Diego was in big danger. But on the other hand, he was still a prime murder suspect.

Safiya said, "I'm sorry, I shouldn't have told you all this. Now *you're* involved. You could get in trouble too—"

"Not your fault. I'm the one who pushed it."

Then Juke turned to Diego. "You gotta understand, in my experience it's always the boyfriend. Your girlfriend was with other guys. For all I know you killed her 'cause she decided she didn't want to run away with you."

"That's not what happened!"

Rey said to Safiya, "This Dinc is un-fucking-believable."

Juke pointed his gun in Diego's direction, not straight at his face but close enough to show he meant bizness. "Stand up. And nobody get any ideas."

Diego sat frozen with fear, eyeing Juke's gun.

Safiya looked into Juke's eyes. "Juke. Diego just lost the woman he loved. Take him if you have to, but please. Take care of him."

Juke saw Safiya as a little kid again, the scourge of playground bullies, making sure the younger and smaller kids got their turn at handball. Had he been in love with her even way back then? He tried to wipe the thought from his mind. "I'll do everything I can to catch Talia's killer by midnight. I have my own reasons for wanting that. If I find out for sure the killer is Teddy, or somebody else, I'll let Diego go. But no promises."

He tossed the handcuffs to Diego. "Put these around your wrists. I'll snap them."

He turned back to Safiya and Rey. "You two better get moving. And if I were you, I'd stay away from the yellow Lex. After that scene at the shmub, somebody may be looking for it."

* * *

Over by the driveway, Haylee wasn't able to catch much of this convo. But she did hear the words "bio-alarm" and "de-chip." *Excellent!* Her intel would be perfect for Karolyn.

She was relieved when Juke let Safiya and her boyfriend walk away. It would be less traumatic this way. Juke wouldn't be there to witness it when Karolyn grabbed Safiya and hauled her off to the psych ward, or wherever the Agency took people.

Haylee gave her head a shake, not wanting to imagine the painful scene. Everything was falling into place for baby Hera. Haylee needed to focus on that, and not worry about what happened to Juke, Safiya, or anybody else.

V

PART FIVE

LOW DOWN

Chapter Fifty-One

7:53 pm

DeAndrey Jackson, Karolyn, Safiya, and Rey

DeAndrey Jackson was rocking. *One hundred Reagans* from Berkshire Vanguard to catch the Crimean girl's killer! Scrucking amazing. Two red-dot cases in one day—at this rate, he'd be the highest-grossing detective in NYPDinc history!

A woman from the Agency named Karolyn Ford had buzzed him with the good news, along with marching orders. He was supposed to locate three scar-faced Mexicans who were prime suspects. He'd nicknamed them Davy, Dimwit, and Doofus. Even more important for some reason, he was supposed to track down a bright yellow Lex, last seen in Bugtown. The woman gave him a midnight drop-dead and stressed that Agency involvement needed to be kept on the deep low.

The Agency clearly had some agenda that had nothing to do with the murder, but he didn't pry. As long as he got paid! Using the Berkshire Vanguard money, he rerouted fifty NYPDinc patrol cars to hunt for the yellow Lex and another nine to go after the scar-faced Mexicans. With the Agency's superintelligence assisting the search, Jackson figured he had enough resources to wrap this up by midnight, no problem.

But it wouldn't hurt to be extra careful. He wanted a good ship with this new Deputy Director; she could be the source of much ka-ching in the future. So he decided to spring for twenty more patrol cars.

Jackson smiled to himself. That yellow Lex was his.

* * *

Karolyn had been riding south on Liberty for twelve minutes with no yellow Lex sightings. So after she got off the phone with Detective Jackson, she and Adams got in the front seat of the Munch and she took the wheel. She immediately did a squealing U-turn and headed north.

Sure, Jackson had promised to dispatch dozens of Dinc patrol cars, but she believed in the old saying, attributed to the great American wit Rush Limbaugh, "If you want something done right, you better do it yourself." Chances were the Lex was long gone from this part of town by now, but she would keep looking.

She got a grim pleasure from how her driving terrified Adams, sitting in the passenger seat with his knuckles whitening on the dashboard. Served him right for almost getting her killed before.

"Keep your eye out for the Lex," she told him.

"Yes, ma'am," Adams said, fighting his horror as the Munch swerved between a Chinese tour bus and a love bot rental van, almost getting clipped by both.

Karolyn straightened the wheel and continued north.

* * *

The yellow Lex sat on 198th just off Liberty, next to the tree it had crashed into. Juke, Haylee, and Diego were gone, heading for Bottoms Up. But Safiya and Rey still stood by the Lex's damaged hood, arguing.

Safiya knew this was toons. They should have left here already. But their mutual anger and confusion kept them stuck to this spot, unable to move. Rey was saying, "Chocolate is dead, okay? It's over."

"Bullshit—"

"The Dincs are onto us. The Agency'll be next. We need to get outta New

York—"

"We can't just abandon everybody—"

"It's your fault. How could you tell your ex-boyfriend our entire op without talking to me first?"

Safiya was furious. "You're *jealous?*"

"It's not about that—"

"You want to give up on everything we ever fought for because you're chunked at me?!"

"I could go to prison because of you! We should be a team. Instead you—"

"Cut the ship drama. We need to oob it out of here." Safiya took out her I*!* to make the call.

Rey narrowed his eyes. "You don't respect me."

"Oh, for cake's sake."

"It's true. You think I'm a weak bougie boy from the burbs. A coward. That's pretty much what you said."

No question, Rey didn't have the same Rez passion she did. His family hadn't been ripped apart. He didn't have two brothers in prison. Tightening her lips, she tried to figure out their next move. Maybe hit that safe house in West Hanoi, hide out till it was almost midnight. "Rey, not now, okay?"

He grabbed her arm so hard it shocked her, and forced her to look him in the eye.

"Safiya, I've loved you since the day we met. But I was just a rebound ship for you. I get it now."

"That's not true," Safiya said.

"You never loved me. You're still in love with him."

She wanted to say, *Rey, you're wrong. I do love you.*

But…he was right. She was seeing it clearly now.

She didn't love Rey. She never should have let him move in with her. It was a mistake, unfair to both of them.

"Rey, you deserved better."

He didn't reply. He let go of her arm, then opened the door to the Lex and got in. The airbags hung limp and the car smelled of something like polyester smoke. But when he started the engine, it still worked.

"What are you doing?" Safiya said.

"Going to Canada."

"Rey, you can't take the Lex. You heard what Juke said. People might be looking for it."

But Rey just slammed the door.

"Rey!"

He took off, getting back on Liberty heading north.

She watched as he drove away. She felt all alone in the cold November wind.

But then she remembered she wasn't alone. The New York Eighteen needed her. She quit feeling sorry for herself and walked westward on 198th, making plans.

She stopped, alarmed, when she heard an outbreak of car horns behind her. That could be Dincs chasing after her and Rey. But when she looked, all she saw was a lime green Munch racing northward, swerving in and out like a highly caffeinated mosquito, annoying all the vehicles around it. No way any Dincs or agents would be riding in a lime green Munch.

Safiya pulled her coat around her and walked on.

* * *

Roaring north, Karolyn was about to slow down and switch to automatic so she could call Jackson again. But then Adams gasped.

"Hey!" he said, still scared but excited now too. He pointed up ahead. "About ten cars up, on the right!"

Karolyn caught sight of it: *a bright yellow Lex.*

She hit the gas and raced toward it even faster.

Chapter Fifty-Two

8:24 pm

Juke and Haylee

Juke drove downtown manually, since the Zan's digitals were still knocked out. Haylee sat beside him, twisting her body around to keep her gun pointed in Diego's direction. He was in the back seat, handcuffed, and looked wiped out. But she didn't intend to get fooled. He had moved awfully fast when he pulled his .25 back at the shmub.

Keeping the prisoner secure was an unusual job responsibility for a Crime Marketing Consultant. But the electronic barrier between the front and back seat wasn't working.

Haylee thought about what Juke had told her before they got in the car. He said Teddy Rhodes tried to pimp Talia out last night, and she said no; so now Teddy was their prime murder suspect.

Juke claimed this was the only thing of interest Diego had said earlier. But Haylee had heard enough of the interrogation to know Juke was lying to her. She was glad: it made her feel better about lying to him.

"Can I borrow your I*!* for a minute?" she said. She needed to hurry up and buzz Karolyn already.

But Juke shook his head. "I need you to stay focused on security."

She knew she was pushing it, but she said, "I want to check your phone to see if we got any tips from gen pop."

"Not now."

Panic rose in Haylee's chest. It must be after eight already, and she hadn't spoken to Karolyn since before the bughouse. What if Karolyn found another way to stop the Resistance conspiracy—without Haylee's help? *Would Karolyn decide not to ka-ching Haylee?*

It was infuriating that in this digital age, she couldn't find a quick way to contact Karolyn. How could she convince Juke to give up his stupid phone? That seventy-nine thousand dollars—her daughter's future—was just sitting there, waiting for her. But she needed to grab it!

Haylee took a mindlessness breath and tried to relax. For right now there was nothing she could do. She had to hope Karolyn wasn't getting anywhere without her.

Chapter Fifty-Three

8:25 pm

Karolyn and Rey

Karolyn zipped around one car, veered around another—

—and pulled up alongside the yellow Lex.

The Lex's left side was severely dented, and from Karolyn's vantage point it looked like the front hood was damaged even worse. Her adrenaline surged. This was the right car—it must have gotten in a crash during that Bugtown mess.

"Only guy I see is the driver," Karolyn said.

Adams said, "Yeah. Asian doob."

So he wasn't Mexican Scarface. But maybe he was the guy who'd rescued Scarface.

She rolled down Adams' window. "Tell him to pull over."

Adams leaned his head out and waved to get the Asian guy's attention. When he looked back, frightened, Adams gestured for him to pull over.

Instead the guy sped up. So did Karolyn. "Show him your gun."

"Shouldn't we wait for backup—"

"Show him your fucking gun."

Adams drew his Ruby Ridge and aimed it. The guy's eyes widened and he instantly raced ahead, roaring around a minivan and getting in front of the Munch. Karolyn banged into his rear bumper but it wasn't a fair fight—the

Lex was more than twice as big.

"Shoot his tires," she said.

"But—"

"Shoot his fucking tires!"

Adams aimed at the nearest tire and fired. He missed. The Lex swerved right to get around another car.

Adams aimed again—just as Karolyn broke sharply to avoid a syndicate metrobus. His arm jerked back, and instead of hitting the tire he hit the Lex's back window. The bullet smashed through it—and through the Asian doob's left arm.

* * *

Inside the Lex, Rey screamed. Blood and bone shards sprayed from his forearm. He tried to keep driving but almost immediately bashed into a concrete guardrail.

He wrestled the Lex back onto the road. But it banged into a Hodu delivery truck on his left, careened back right, and busted through a rusty metal guardrail. Then it stopped, half on the shoulder and half in a muddy ditch.

Pain washed up and down Rey's arm and back. Who could be riding in that green Munch—Dincs? Agency? It didn't make sense!

But the Munch parked behind him on the shoulder. They were coming for him! He was finished!

Or maybe not. Maybe there was a God after all. Because suddenly he noticed something black and shiny on the floor of the Lex, right in front of him. It had been disgorged by the glove compartment when it sprang open during this new crash, and it was an answer to his prayers: a .38 Hoover.

He grabbed the gun, rolled out of the Lex, and ran along the ditch.

But then his foot got stuck in the mud and he fell.

The two people from the Munch, the gray-suited man who had shot him and a woman dressed in black, ran toward him, guns out and pointed at his head.

"Drop your weapon!" the woman yelled.

In that moment, Rey knew he had a choice. He could put the gun down and live.

But they would take him in to the Agency or the NYPDinc and neurointerrogate him. He'd be forced to give up Safiya and Chocolate. He would destroy her, along with everything they'd ever dreamed of together.

He couldn't do that. He refused to. In the final moments of his life he would not be a coward.

He lifted his gun and pointed it at the two onrushing figures. But sprawling awkwardly in the ditch, he couldn't aim properly. He shot in between them.

The woman fired and hit him in his right arm—his shooting arm. His elbow shattered. He screamed and dropped the gun. They were coming closer. In a second they'd be able to reach down and grab his gun away. They would have him.

"No!" Rey roared. He grabbed the gun with his damaged left arm and aimed again—

The man in the gray suit shot him in the chest.

Rey felt a sledgehammer punch and gasped. Then he felt himself falling away.

He had only a couple milliseconds of life left, but time slowed way down. *Safiya will know. She'll know I fought to the end.*

I gave my life for the Resistance.

I gave my life for her.

* * *

"Brilliant move," Karolyn said, walking up to the body with Adams. She knew right away the guy was dead. "You didn't have to zap him."

"He was shooting at us," Adams said defensively.

"So shoot him in the arm, like I did."

"But you're supposed to aim for center mass—"

"Oh shut up."

Being careful to avoid the blood—she didn't want to ruin two outfits in one day—Karolyn felt in the dead guy's pockets. She found a burner. Handling it gently to avoid blurring any fingerprints, she tried to turn it on, but it was protected.

"Well, at least it didn't explode," Adams said.

Christ, she couldn't stand this guy. She pressed the dead man's fingers against her I! to make sure his prints would come out clearly and took pictures. Then she held open his eyes and got iris pics. She sent them all to the Agency tech department. They should have this body ID'd in less than a minute.

On her way back to the Munch, she told Adams, "I'll take the burner to the tech guys. You stay here with the body and call it in. Make sure none of this gets out into networld."

Adams said, "I'm sorry I killed him."

She nodded. "You should be. Now we can't interrogate him."

"No, I mean, I've never killed anybody before."

The pain on Adams's face glitched her off. It made her feel like a coldhearted bitch, that she didn't feel terrible anymore when people died right in front of her. *Well what do you expect, it's been a long day.* "For fuck's sake, get over it."

Karolyn got in the Munch, leaving Adams behind, and checked the dashboard clock: 8:40. Three hours and twenty minutes to go. She did a U-turn in traffic and raced back toward Agency headquarters.

Chapter Fifty-Four

Haylee and Juke

Haylee fidgeted as the Zan turned onto Ayn Rand—only five minutes from Bottoms Up, thank God. She figured as soon as they hit the club, Juke would go inside to interrogate Teddy, leaving her to guard Diego. Then somehow she'd get hold of a phone and call Karolyn at last. If Juke didn't leave his I! with her, she could always borrow one from a passing pedestrian.

Juke began questioning Diego again. "How many times did Talia say no to Teddy about after-shift work?" Haylee listened, alert for any data she could pass along.

"I don't know, maybe four or five times," Diego answered.

"Did Teddy ever get violent with her before?"

Diego frowned, thinking. "She never said anything about that."

Haylee was taken aback by this response. If Diego wanted to take suspicion off himself and put it on Teddy, he should have answered the exact opposite: *yeah, Teddy smacked Talia around, she was terrified of him.*

Juke said, "Can you think of anything else she said last night that might help us?"

Diego thought for a moment, then burst out crying.

"What is it?" Juke asked.

Diego brought his cuffed hands up to his face and wiped away tears, trying to control himself. "I can't believe some fucking piece of shit killed her and now I'll never see her again."

The sobs poured out of him.

For a moment Haylee thought: *I wish I could video this, it's the boo hoo we've been looking for!* But that thought quickly passed. It suddenly hit her that Diego's words were stunningly familiar.

Except for a pronoun or two, she had probably said those exact same words herself, about Harrison.

Juke turned to her. "I think there's Kleenex in the glove compartment."

She couldn't understand what Juke was saying. She was in some other world, sorting out her feelings. Then she opened the glove compartment almost robotically, took out a couple tissues, and put them in Diego's hand. As she did that, she looked in his eyes.

"Thank you," he said. He wiped away some more tears, then loudly blew his nose.

"I'm sorry for your loss," Juke said.

Diego said, "We were gonna get married. Be together forever." The tears came again. "I just feel so alone."

And in that moment, Haylee knew Diego was innocent.

She just knew. One hundred P.

His face, his tears, his tone, his words, even his snot-filled nose when he cried… *My God.* They mirrored every single thing she felt about Harrison, and her own life.

This man wouldn't be acting this way if he had killed Talia. *He couldn't.*

They stopped at a red light, and Juke's I*!* buzzed. With the Zan's digitals busted, the call didn't show on the dashboard. He took his phone out of his pocket and looked at the screen. "It's Jackass."

The light turned green. As Juke drove on, he handed Haylee the I*!* She saw the bald head, big smug face, and probably-stolen-from-a-murder-victim gold necklace of DeAndrey Jackson.

Juke said, "Put Jackass on public, but hold the I*!* so he can't see Diego, just me."

"Got it," Haylee said. Diego sank down lower in the back seat to stay out of sight, and she turned the I! so its cam pointed at Juke's face. Then she double-tapped, and a moment later Jackson's booming voice filled the car.

"O'Keefe," he said, "how's my favorite Marvel superhero? I see you and your poor grieving partner raised almost three hundred bucks today." He laughed. "Impressive."

Haylee decided she wasn't jealous of this shithead—she purely and simply loathed him.

Juke said, "What do you want, Jackass?"

"I buzzed you before but you didn't pick up. Captain Burgess asked me to let you know you're off the Talia Qirimoglu case."

Staring at Jackson on his I! screen, Juke didn't notice the car in front of him was slowing down. "Watch it!" Haylee yelled.

Juke hit the brakes just in time, and the Zan screeched to a stop.

Jackson taunted, "What's the matter, O'Keefe, you forget how to drive?"

"What do you mean, I'm off the case?"

"Berkshire Vanguard just gave the NYPDinc a hundred Reagans to solve Talia Qirimoglu's murder."

Haylee's jaw dropped. Juke looked equally dumbfounded.

Jackson continued with malicious pleasure, "I get fifty up front, another fifty when I close. Not bad, huh?"

"This is still my case," Juke said.

"Eat roaches, dickwad."

Haylee turned the cam toward herself, to show Jackson her face. "Juke and I are the ones who contacted Berkshire Vanguard. That money belongs to us!"

A mean glint shone in Jackson's eyes. "Sorry, vixen, the BV exec you met with wasn't impressed by your partner. He heard about my fabuloso rep, so he told the Captain he wants me."

Haylee said, "It's not fair. We've been working this case all day. We're making serious progress!"

"What kind of progress?"

"Forget it. I'm not telling you shit."

"Don't be like that, babe. Help me out and I might throw ya a couple Reagans."

She could feel her face burning with rage. Juke shook his head slightly, indicating she should keep quiet, and motioned for her to turn the cam back around toward him. She did, making sure to keep it pointed away from Diego.

Juke said, "Billingsley was emphatic they wouldn't donate a single dollar for this homicide. Why'd they change their minds?"

"Who cares? Never look a gift pit bull in the mouth. So how's your search for Scarface going?"

In the back seat, Diego sank even lower as Jackson continued, "We got Dincs hunting for him all over town. It's narrowed down to three guys: Donato Guzman, David Herrera, and Diego Montoya. Any of those names ring a bell?"

Diego's face registered terror. He was practically down on the floor by now. Haylee was stunned, and she knew Juke was too, but he kept a poker face. The cam was on him and Jackson was watching.

Juke scratched his neck and said, "Never heard of those guys."

"You got any leads for us?"

"We're working on it."

"You two wouldn't be hiding anything from me now, would you?"

Haylee couldn't see Jackson's face, but she heard the suspicion in his voice. Her pulse jumped.

What if Jackson finds out we caught Diego—and we're keeping him secret? Jackson would rat them out and Burgess would be livid. This was a red-dot case now, and the brass didn't cut you slack with that much ka-ching at stake. Burgess would so fire her. He might be glitched enough to charge her and Juke with a crime—obstruction, harboring a fugitive, even sedition. *And I'm pregnant—*

Juke said, "We're not so sure anymore the guy with the scar is the killer. We're following up on another suspect we like better."

"Who's that?"

"We'll let you know."

Jackson snorted derisively. "In other words, you've got squat for evidence. What do you have against Mexican Scarface being the zapper?"

Haylee knew Juke couldn't explain his reasons, not without revealing more than he wanted to. "Like I say, we're following a different lead."

Jackson laughed. "You're wasting your time, doob. Scarface is the perfect suspect—evil-looking and Mexican. We bring him in, get a confession one way or the other, take the ka-ching, and call it a day. That's how it works IRL, Marvel man."

Juke said, "So you're okay with jacking the wrong guy? Knowing the real killer is still out there and might do it again?"

"More bizness for the NYPDinc!" Jackson boomed. "Tell ya what. Find me Mexican Scarface and I'll shoot ya three whole Reagans. You too, vixen," he called out to Haylee.

Juke found a parking spot a block away from Bottoms Up. Hands free now, he took his I*!* back from Haylee. He put it inches from his own face, so Jackson would see him in close-up.

"Jackson," he said, "you truly are a jackass."

Then he tapped off and turned to Haylee. "You stay here with Diego while I talk to Teddy, okay?"

She nodded, staggered by everything she'd just heard. Juke handed her his I*!* "While I'm in there, check my buzzes. Anything from Jackass or Burgess, ignore it."

In the back seat, Diego was a puddle of fear. "If they catch me, they'll torture me into confessing—even though I didn't do it!"

"They won't catch you," Juke said. "My partner and I will jack the real killer before those lame-dicks can even find you."

Haylee watched as Juke reached in the back seat. He pulled up the hood of Diego's jacket, so it hid his scarred cheek. "Stay low."

Diego's eyes darted back and forth from Juke to Haylee. Her chest felt tight. "You really think you can prove Teddy did it?"

Juke put a hand on his shoulder. "Yes. I promise. And you'll go free before midnight."

Diego gulped and nodded hopefully. Juke turned to Haylee. "You good?"

"Sure," she said.

Juke got out of the Zan and headed off to Bottoms Up. From the back seat, Diego said to Haylee, "God bless you both."

Haylee looked down at her right hand. Juke's I! was sitting right there—at last. Now was her chance.

Hera's chance.

Her hand clenched the phone.

She wanted so badly to make this call. Her finger was an inch above the I!, poised, ready to buzz Karolyn.

Behind her Diego blew his nose, still filled with snot from when he was crying. Haylee's finger couldn't seem to move. It wouldn't go down that final inch to touch the phone. *Fuck!*

If she called Karolyn now, she'd be helping to frame this poor guy for murder.

This guy who was just like her, who had lost the one he loved.

Haylee's baby would owe everything to a devil's deal that put an innocent man in prison, probably for life.

What kind of karma would that be for her baby?! And for her?!

Her stomach heaved again, worse than before. She put down the phone.

"I'm sorry, Hera," she said out loud.

"What?" said Diego.

"Nothing." Haylee put her hand on her stomach and mourned the child that would never be. "I hope Juke nails this motherfucker."

Chapter Fifty-Five

9:04 pm

Juke

Bottoms Up was going strong. Through the closed door of Teddy's office, Juke heard the new hit "I Want 20 P of Your Love" booming through the club. A holo of two pink-haired strippers playing with each other's breasts sprawled across the ratty old sofa against the wall. Juke turned his chair away so they wouldn't distract him while he conducted his interrogation.

He studied Teddy, who sat behind his desk acting utterly unconcerned, scratching the red belly hairs that poked through an opening in his shirt. Juke needed to somehow nail this sonufabitch for the murder right now, before the NYPDinc got hold of Diego. If that happened, Diego and Safiya weren't the only ones who were screwed. He had just become part of Safiya's conspiracy. The NYPDinc and the Agency would make an example of him, since he was law enforcement. He'd get neuroed too, and thrown in prison for God knows how long.

Why was he risking all this for a woman who broke up with him, a woman who no longer loved him?

Or did she?

Scruck that, forget your hopes and fears right now. No victim too small. That's all you need to think about.

He said to Teddy, "So basically this club runs prostitutes."

Teddy said, "It's not hardcore ho-ing or anything, it's just topping off your income a little bit. One guy a night at the end of your shift. Maybe two at most."

Juke guessed that meant three or four. "Do all your hostesses do this?"

Teddy chuckled. "Two hundred bucks for fifteen, twenty minutes of overtime? Who wouldn't do it?"

One of the pink-haired strippers got up from the sofa and danced through Juke's body, then shook her booty practically in his mouth. Teddy smirked at his discomfort. Juke waited for the booty to wiggle away, then said, "Except you don't let the girls keep all those dollars, do you? What's your cut?"

Teddy shrugged. "Not much. Most of it goes straight to the syndie that owns this place."

"When did you meet with Talia last night?"

"I don't know. One o'clock?"

"Why didn't you tell me before about your meeting?"

"Why should I? It had jackbyte to do with the murder."

"I'm a cop. You lied to me." He threw Teddy an intimidating glare.

But Teddy shrugged again. "Sorry, ro."

Handcuffing this smug neurotrash would be a joy. "What did you and Talia talk about?"

"She said she couldn't do her after-shift work last night, 'cause she was having her period."

"Were you cool with that?"

"Me personally? Sure." Then came that shrug. Juke began to think it was a tell that meant he was lying. "But lately she was slacking off a lot. Always sick or tired or her grandmother was visiting from out of town or some other bugshit. I got bosses too, you know. The syndies are always coming in here checking up on me, ro."

A heavy, faux-marble paperweight of a sculpted nude sat on Teddy's desk. Juke picked it up and checked the bottom for blood. "Sounds like Talia was making things difficult for you."

Teddy gave him a grin. "You get all kinds of vixen drama managing a strip club, let me tell ya."

"So you must've been pretty chunked at her last night."

Teddy stared at Juke with what Juke assumed was fake astonishment. "Wait a minute. You don't suspect *me*, do you?"

"You met with the victim right before she died and then you lied about it."

Teddy looked offended. "Hey, I'm doing you a favor talking for free. I bet I could charge you good money."

Juke ignored a holo of a big-breasted Latina woman bouncing into his line of vision. "You met with Talia where—here?"

"Yeah, I always meet my girls here."

"And if they refuse to do after-shift work, what do you do?"

The shrug again. "Nothin'. Maybe I give 'em worse shifts the next week."

"You don't yell at 'em?"

"If they give me attitude, sure."

"Maybe push 'em around a little to keep 'em in line?"

"No. Nothing like that."

"Why not? Who's gonna stop you?"

"You got it all wrong. I'm like a big brother to these girls."

"See, I don't think so." Juke stood up so suddenly his chair toppled to the floor, and leaned over Teddy's desk. "I think you throw them down on your cum-stained sofa, next to your holos. And then"—Juke grabbed his crotch—"you make them show you some company spirit."

He got in Teddy's face, menacing. "But Talia wouldn't give it up—the fucking vixen. You grabbed her arm so hard you left bruises, and you punched her. Again. And again. And—"

Teddy rolled his chair back, away from Juke. "You need to leave right now."

"I'm sure you didn't mean to zap her—"

Teddy stood up. He was bigger than Juke and probably had a gun in that desk. "I said get out."

"We'll get forensics, Teddy. We'll find her blood in your car, from when you transported her to Freedom Street—"

"You got a warrant to search my car?"

"We'll get one."

"Oh yeah? I bet you don't have the ka-ching for a warrant."

The jerk was right—judges charged two hundred, maybe three on a weekend night. Juke said, "Trust me, ro, you'll be a lot better off if you play it real."

Teddy reached into an opening under his desktop and pulled out the gun Juke had suspected. It was a big one, a cannon, which didn't surprise Juke either.

Teddy said, "This is the last time I tell you. Get the fuck out."

Juke said, "Theodore Rhodes, you're under arrest. Put that weapon away right now or I'll charge you with resisting."

Teddy sneered. "You don't have the evidence to jack me."

"We'll let the judge decide."

"I'll push this button and my bouncers'll come in and throw your ass out. Try to pull any stunts, and my syndie will sue the NYPDinc for false arrest. You'll really be in the shitter then."

Juke stood there fuming. It was true, he didn't have sufficient evidence against Teddy—certainly not enough to withstand a full-on legal assault by the syndies.

"Oh, and by the way, have fun searching my car. I took the subway last night."

Juke said, "So you borrowed somebody's car. Thanks for the tip."

He turned and walked out the door. He was going to nail this fuckhead.

He didn't need a lousy warrant. He knew exactly where to find proof that Teddy killed Talia, and he was going there right now.

Chapter Fifty-Six

9:11 pm

Karolyn, the Red Queen, Safiya, and Cheyenne

Karolyn was briefing her boss—except it felt more like an interrogation, with Raja sitting behind his desk wearing a reproachful frown. The clock was ticking and she was desperate to get out of there.

Raja asked, "So what's the story on this guy you zapped? Not the Icelander, the new guy."

Karolyn's jaw tightened. "I didn't zap him. Agent Adams did."

Raja waved her correction aside. "Whatever. Who is he?"

"We don't know yet. His prints and irises came back negative."

Raja raised his eyebrows. "Negative? He's never gone to school or applied for a job, or—"

"It's possible he hacked law enforcement databases and erased his tracks."

"But that would require—"

"—serious technical sophistication. But tonight's op has already shown a fair amount of that. Also, he may have received help from sympathizers inside law enforcement."

Raja said, "Too bad he's dead, otherwise we could ask him ourselves."

Karolyn gritted her teeth at the implied—or not so implied—criticism. "We're hopeful his I*!* will give us something, as soon as we crack it.

Meanwhile we have over seventy NYPDinc and Agency vehicles searching for Scarface. We've narrowed it down to two suspects—David Herrera and Diego Montoya." The third, Donato Guzman, had been caught fifteen minutes ago, but he had an airtight alibi for last night: he was out of town selling T-shirts and hallucinogens at a religious confluence.

Raja snapped his fingers and grabbed a holographic dart out of the air. He fired it at the dartboard and got his usual bull's eye. Karolyn thought he must have some psychological flaw, to be so obsessed with playing a game he would never lose.

Raja said, "Scarface is the key to this whole thing. Him and the 9.8 woman."

"I'm fully aware of that—"

He pointed a dart at her. "You need to redouble your efforts to find them—especially since you've killed everybody else who might've helped us."

"Yes, sir," Karolyn said, as she imagined snapping Raja's neck.

Before she went back to her office, she sidetracked into the kitchen. She grabbed a pint of loquat fudge that she'd stashed way in the back of the freezer, behind a bag of frozen fava beans nobody ever touched.

She felt like eating the entire pint straight out of the carton. She needed it, to deal not only with Operation Chocolate but Raja. What a manipulative cockroach.

She sat at her desk and got out a spoon. When she got home tonight, no matter how this case turned out, she would have a nice long session with her new bot. Maybe she'd even rent another bot for the night and be with two of them at once. According to an article she'd read in the *Post-Times*, this was a new trend among upscale professionals—

"If I may interrupt," said the Red Queen. Karolyn jumped, startled. It felt like the Red Queen had been reading her mind. What was in that belly chip, anyway?

"You got something for me?" Karolyn asked brusquely.

"Indeed I do. We've partially cracked the I! of the man you killed."

"That *Adams* killed!"

"Pardon me. I was using 'you' in the plural sense, as in 'you and Adams.'"

"Just tell me already."

"The dead man's I*!* had quantum-layered security protocols, except that the ID authentication subsystem he installed contained a micro-vulnerability in its neural verification matrix that we were able to exploit."

Karolyn slammed her spoon on the desk, impatient for the Red Queen to get to it already. Sometimes the Red Queen got unnecessarily technical about her achievements. Self-aggrandizing, Karolyn thought. She had never fully understood the Red Queen's personality, assuming she had one. "So who is he?"

"His name was Reiji Matoshi. Rey for short. His romantic partner—or at least, the woman he's on record as living with—is named Safiya Bassani-Jones."

Karolyn leapt out of her chair. "Give me her address."

"Done. Check the wall."

On Karolyn's wall was Safiya Bassani-Jones' address in the Lower East Side, about fifteen minutes away—or five minutes, the way Karolyn was planning to have her car drive. She wouldn't bring backup this time—she didn't want some idiot like Willard or Adams messing things up for her.

"Show me this woman's picture."

The Red Queen put up fifty or so networld photos of the woman on the wall. She was beautiful, about thirty, with light brown skin and thick curly black hair cascading past her shoulders.

"Is she a fifty-one percenter?" Karolyn asked.

"No. Zero."

Safiya had intense, earnest eyes. Karolyn sensed she was smart, and someone who wouldn't get pushed around easily—

Wait a second. Karolyn stepped closer to the photos and stared at them. Had she just hit the jackpot?! "I bet this woman is the 9.8!"

"I don't have sufficient data—"

"Just look at her face!"

"Correlating faces with personality types is a feature the Anthill and I are still working on."

Karolyn studied the photos of Safiya. A few had other people in them, with their names typed out underneath. Two photos from a few years ago showed her with a tall man about her age with gray eyes and a searching gaze. Their body language said they were very close, most likely lovers. Karolyn leaned forward to read the man's name—

Holy shit! She practically shouted, "Safiya was with *Juke O'Keefe?!*"

"Thought you'd enjoy that," said the Red Queen, in her driest British tone. "What does this mean?"

"There's a high-percentage chance that Juke O'Keefe isn't just a sympathizer. He could be part of Chocolate himself—their inside man."

Karolyn walked out the door without another word. She would grab a ZMW, the fastest vehicle in the Agency pool, and race to Safiya's speck.

Meanwhile she'd buzz Jackson, the homicide Dinc, and order him to arrest Juke on the deep low and interrogate him.

Karolyn skipped the elevator and ran all the way downstairs to the garage. She could feel it: everything was about to crack wide open. She would be an Agency hero.

And she'd make sure she got the credit. Fuck Raja.

Meanwhile the Red Queen realized the loquat fudge was slowly melting on Karolyn's desk. For half a millisecond she considered calling Karolyn back to her office, then decided no. The woman was on a roll.

And the sooner she got to Safiya Bassani-Jones' speck, the better.

* * *

Safiya and Cheyenne Littlejohn sat in the front seat of Cheyenne's Qilin, riding to Safiya's speck. The women had met up in Chelsea after Rey drove off.

"I'm sorry about Rey," Cheyenne said.

Safiya nodded. "You were never his biggest fan."

Cheyenne wasn't sure what to say. She had always thought Safiya could do better. Safiya never talked about Rey the way she once talked about Juke. Her face didn't get that same glow.

"Where do you think Rey will go?" Cheyenne asked.

"Hopefully he'll make it to Canada. And meet someone who gives him the love he deserves."

Cheyenne was silent for a moment. She looked up at the pollution meters on top of the light poles; yellow this afternoon, they had turned red again. Then she said, "You know, I think we might have to go to Canada too."

Safiya turned toward her friend. She had hoped to keep tonight's op secure enough that she, Rey, and Cheyenne could stay in New York afterwards, continuing their work in the Resistance. But now it looked like that would be impossible.

"I feel bad, Cheyenne. This isn't what you bargained for."

Cheyenne sighed. "Well, the hell with it. I wouldn't want to raise a family here anyway."

"But we're gonna make America great again."

Cheyenne rolled her eyes. Even all these years later, that old line still lived on as an ironic joke.

Safiya put her hand on Cheyenne's arm. "I mean it, Chey. When the whole world sees how easy it is to be free—all you need is a knife, an I! charger, and some curry!—people everywhere will liberate themselves. They'll take to the streets and head for the border and inspire this country to rise up, 'cause everybody will realize the syndies aren't this huge monolith. They can never stop millions of people fighting together as one!"

Cheyenne said, "Whenever you give a speech like that, I know you're about to ask me for something."

"Well, actually…"

"Go for it."

"Now that Rey took off with the Lex, we don't have enough cars to transport everybody to Canada."

"So you want my Qilin?"

"Kind of."

"No prob," said Cheyenne. "I'll need it up in Canada anyway."

Safiya grabbed her hand. "Thank you."

Outside the car window, three homefree teenage Starpunks sat on the sidewalk, huddling together against the cold. Safiya and Cheyenne rode past a gray high-rise with barbed wire covering the windows, a jail for new inmates who hadn't been processed yet. Safiya thought about her brothers locked away upstate, toiling at syndie prison factories for ten cents an hour.

Cheyenne said, "I just wanted to be a doctor. Heal the sick."

"That's what we're doing," Safiya said. "Healing this whole damn country."

The Qilin turned left. As they entered the Lower East Side, Friday night was in full swing. Safiya and Cheyenne watched as young women in short skirts and stylish multicolored masks navigated the crumbling sidewalks in their high heels. Young men in dark masks and tight blue jeans headed for the bars. Older couples walked briskly, facing down the wind as they headed to the movies.

For years, gen pop had gradually, if grudgingly, accepted greater and greater syndicate power. Those endless miles of holos hiding the moon and stars? The syndicates paid the city a fee to put them up, and that helped keep taxes low.

But there had always been a countercurrent, and in the past few years it had grown stronger. Flares that used to attract a hundred people now got ten thousand. There were Rez sympathizers everywhere, even within the syndicates themselves.

Safiya believed the syndies had finally overreached their powers. *Owning* people, and trying to put biochips inside *everyone*—to Safiya, this was the tipping point. America, the world's beacon of freedom, birthplace of the Declaration of Independence and the Bill of Rights, would come back to its senses and rediscover its ideals. The people out here on these streets tonight would be in the vanguard of the new revolution.

And that revolution would begin—she checked her I!—in two hours and thirty-eight minutes.

The Qilin turned left again and found a parking spot three blocks from Safiya's speck. Safiya and Cheyenne put on their anti-pollution masks and got out of the car.

Cheyenne opened the trunk, obsessively inspecting the two shopping bags one more time to make sure they had everything they'd need for

Chocolate. Then they each took a bag and headed toward Safiya's building.

***

Karolyn had no problem getting inside Safiya's building, since it was syndicate-owned and the Red Queen had access to the digitals. She walked upstairs and headed down the third-floor hallway to Safiya's speck.

Holding her Ruby Ridge under her jacket, she knocked on Safiya's door. When no one answered, she took out her hack disc and double-tapped. After a few seconds the green light came on. She opened the door and entered the dark speck.

Suddenly she heard a small scraping noise. She pointed her gun at it. Then came another sound from the floor behind her. She whirled.

There was a tiny meow. Her eyes adjusted to the darkness and she saw two small kittens. She kicked them out of the way. She liked cats fine—but not now.

Gun out, she moved through the speck and cleared it. Then she turned on her I! flashlight and began searching the place for intel about Chocolate.

She left the room light off, so it wouldn't shine under the door into the hallway. When Safiya returned home, she'd never suspect somebody was inside her speck, waiting for her.

Karolyn was going to ambush this bitch.

Chapter Fifty-Seven

9:24 pm

Haylee and Juke

Haylee sat in the front seat as Juke drove to One Police Plaza, with Diego still in back. She couldn't believe she was in this situation. Juke had told her his plan: sneak into the morgue and get hold of Talia's body. Then they'd search under Talia's fingernails and elsewhere for incriminating red hairs from Teddy. If they found his hairs, they'd go straight to Captain Burgess.

We better find them or we're dead, Haylee thought. *Slinking into NYPDinc headquarters with a wanted fugitive hiding in the back seat? This is insane!* She was an idiot for letting herself get involved. It was Juke's fault; his absurd Marvelness had rubbed off on her. She should rethink her decision and call Karolyn after all.

Juke's I! buzzed again. He shut it off, so he wouldn't have to deal with Jackson or Burgess ordering him again to get off the case, or asking where he was. He looked up at the massive concrete headquarters building and wondered, *how the hell do we make it inside there with nobody seeing Diego?* Since the Zan's digitals were busted, he'd have to drive into the garage through the guard entrance.

He stopped the car outside the building and turned back to Diego. "Lie down and get as small as you can."

"Okay." Diego's voice was anxious and thin. He lay down in the back seat and drew his knees up into a fetal position.

Juke shrugged off his jacket and handed it to Haylee. "Cover him up."

Haylee looked like she would protest. But instead she laid Juke's jacket and Diego's own jacket over him.

Juke said, "Tuck them in so they don't fly off somehow."

Haylee followed his instructions, tucking the jackets in close around Diego.

"We good?" Juke asked.

"I hope so," Haylee said.

Juke checked to make sure Diego was fully hidden, then turned to Haylee. "I'm really sorry I put you in this position. If we get caught, I'll say this was completely my idea. I'll tell Burgess you fought me all the way."

Haylee nodded, lips tight. Juke was grateful she was sticking with him, at least so far. He'd clearly underestimated her. He took a deep breath and drove down into the garage.

But when they got to the gate, he recognized the guard. "Oh, great."

"What's wrong?" Haylee asked, alarmed.

Juke nodded toward the guard, Charysse, a woman with too much makeup in her late thirties. "I know her. She loves to talk." When Charysse got going, it could be almost impossible to shut her up. They'd made out one night a couple months ago in a Cuban bar when they were both blitzed. He had regretted it ever since.

As Juke rolled down the window, Charysse smiled flirtily at him. "Hey Juke, I was just thinking about you." She noticed their damaged fender and frowned. "You get in an accident?"

"Nothing major," Juke said, eager to get away.

But Charysse was in no hurry. She peered into the car to check out Haylee, and Juke was scared she'd see Diego too. "Is this your new partner? Hi, I'm Charysse."

Haylee gave her a sickly looking smile. "I'm Haylee."

Charysse leaned against the car, getting ready for a nice long chat. "You guys gonna get the reward?"

Juke said, "What reward?"

She blinked at him. "I'm surprised you haven't heard, it's from Homicide. There's some Mexican guy with a big scar on his face who's on the run. Ten Reagans to whoever brings him in."

"Sounds good," Juke said.

He started to drive off, but Charysse stopped him. "So what are you doing after work? It's been a while."

Juke avoided her eyes. "Sorry, working late. I'll give you a call sometime, okay?"

Charysse gave him a hurt look and stepped back into the guard booth. "Sure, Juke. No stress."

She tapped a computer key that lifted the gate. *Thank God.* Juke saw Charysse in his mirror, watching him drive off. He was afraid the jackets would slide off Diego's legs, but they made it down the ramp into the garage without incident.

Juke parked, then turned to Diego. "We're leaving you here while we go inside. If I were you, I wouldn't do anything stupid like running. You're handcuffed and there's cams all over this place. And even if you made it out, you got a city full of cops hunting you down."

From beneath the jackets, Diego said, "You're going to the morgue now?"

"That's right."

"You gonna see Talia?"

Juke nodded. "Yes."

"Please give her something for me."

Juke waited.

"It's in my shirt pocket. You missed it when you patted me down. I was gonna give it to her the next time I saw her."

"I'll get it," Haylee said.

She reached in the back seat, lifted up the jackets, and unbuttoned Diego's shirt pocket. She found a small jewelry box. Without even opening it, she knew what was inside: an engagement ring.

Diego said, "Put it on her finger, okay?"

"Okay," said Haylee.

"Please tell Talia…I'll miss and cherish her forever."

Oh Lord, Haylee thought. She'd made the right choice, no question. If she ever snitched on this man, God would send her to hell forever. Even if there was no hell, God would create it just for her.

"I'll tell her," Haylee said.

Juke said, "Let's go. Charysse may be watching us on one of those cams."

Haylee got out of the car and followed Juke into the building. "We'll take the stairs," he said quietly.

That made sense; less chance of running into people. They went up one floor to the building's basement, where the morgue was located, then started up the long hallway—

—and heard Captain Burgess's angry voice saying, "Juke! Answer your damn I*!"*

Footsteps—from Burgess?—were coming toward them. But Haylee couldn't see him. He must be around the corner. *Does he see us on a cam?*

Juke grabbed Haylee and pulled her into an alcove where a phone booth once stood in the previous century. They stood huddled together in the narrow space as Burgess approached. Judging by his footsteps and voice, he was in this hallway now. He was saying, "Where the hell are you, Juke? I've been calling you for an hour."

Haylee finally got it: Burgess must be talking into his phone.

Juke and Haylee squeezed themselves against the alcove wall as tightly as they could, and Burgess came into view. He walked by them so close, they could have reached out and punched him without moving their feet. He said, "Juke, you need to get yourself back to headquarters—now. There's something we need to talk about."

Burgess went quiet for a moment. Haylee couldn't see him anymore, since he was further down the hall, but she guessed he was tapping off the phone. Then he said, apparently to himself, "Fucking O'Keefe. Pain in the fucking ass."

For some reason that seemed hilarious to Haylee, terrified though she was. She had to stop herself from laughing out loud. After Burgess was gone around the corner and they had a few seconds of quiet, they came out of the alcove and hurried toward the morgue.

"What was that about?" whispered Haylee.

"He must've found out I interrogated Teddy. He's gonna ream me out about still working the case."

"He's right, you know."

Juke looked at her questioningly.

"You *are* a pain in the fucking ass," she said.

Juke gave a half-smile in reply. They came to the door of the morgue. Haylee took a deep breath, hoping whatever M.E. was working this shift would be an ally—or at least not an enemy. Juke opened the door and they walked in.

They got lucky: the morgue was empty. The shift M.E. must be out on break. "Let's do this fast, before they get back," Juke said.

Haylee said, "If we get caught we can say we weren't really working the case, just doing a satanic ritual with the body."

Juke found the drawer holding Talia and pulled it out. Then he lifted off the sheet that covered her.

Looking down at Talia's body, Haylee couldn't suppress a grimace. Talia looked just like she did this morning, except stiffer. The blood was frozen on her face and her dark eyes gazed upward at nothing. But her cheekbones were still beautiful.

Juke said, "You gonna be okay?"

"Just tell me we're not gonna chop her up."

"Only if we have to."

"Not funny."

"You check the left hand. I'll check the right," Juke said.

Haylee winced as she lifted Talia's cold, dead hand. She bent down and looked under Talia's fingernails for red hair. If Talia fought back and grabbed or scratched Teddy's head, or for that matter his pubes, this was where his hair would most likely be lodged.

Juke did the same thing with Talia's other hand, examining each finger closely. All it would take was one red hair, just one, and they could bring Teddy down.

But after they spent a minute searching, Juke finally said, "I'm not seeing anything. What about you?"

"Me neither," Haylee said regretfully. If they'd found definitive evidence against Teddy, it would have made things so much easier. "Talia's nails were so short, nothing got caught underneath."

She put Talia's hand back down. But then Juke asked, "You got the ring?"

Haylee took out the jewelry box. "Will we get in trouble for this? Somebody might remember she wasn't wearing it before."

Juke looked at her and she felt ashamed. Shit, they had to do this, whether it was risky or not. It was the closest thing to a decent funeral Talia would ever get.

She opened the small box and took out the ring. It was pretty cheap looking, but she excised that thought from her mind. No doubt it was as much as Diego could afford. She picked up Talia's left hand, this time without wincing, and placed the ring around her stiff finger. It fit perfectly.

She held Talia's hand. "Diego wants you to know: he will miss and cherish you for as long as he lives."

Juke said, "Amen." He leaned down and kissed Talia on each eye. Then he watched as Haylee put Talia's hand down at her side.

He could see that Haylee was super stressed, despite her attempts at humor before. He hoped he could really count on her.

Well, he had no choice. He was stuck with her now and needed to trust her, like she was trusting him. "Okay, let's keep rolling. Did Teddy seem like a guy who would go for oral sex or straight sex?"

Haylee was taken aback, then realized what he was getting at. "Definitely oral."

"What I thought." Juke proceeded to open Talia's mouth as carefully as he could. Between her body being frozen and the rigor mortis setting in, he had to put real muscle into it. He was afraid he'd break her jaw.

"You see anything?" Haylee asked.

He shone his I! light into Talia's mouth and peered in, examining her tongue and between her teeth. "No pubic hairs. Red or otherwise."

He straightened back up. Haylee said, "So now what—a pelvic exam?

Funny, they never taught us that in crime marketing school."

But Juke wasn't listening to her. He was staring at the four small purple bruises on Talia's left arm.

"What's up?" Haylee said.

Juke's heart started pounding with excitement. He stepped around Talia's body so he could stand right in front of Haylee. "Grab my arm above the elbow," he said.

Haylee gave him a confused look. "Grab it," he repeated.

"Okay…" She grabbed his arm.

"Harder. Squeeze it."

"Why?"

"Cause pain."

"Whatever you say, partner." She squeezed.

"Harder."

She squeezed harder. Juke gritted his teeth against the pain.

"Harder!"

She squeezed even harder, putting her whole body into it.

Finally he said, "Okay."

She let go, and he checked his arm. Sure enough, there were five welts on it. "Yes!" he said, thrusting his fist in the air.

"What the hell is going on?" Haylee asked.

Juke told her, "You left five welts on my arm, including your thumb."

Then he pointed at Talia's left arm. "There's only *four* bruises on Talia."

Haylee looked at the dead woman's arm, above the elbow. It was true: there were three finger bruises in close proximity, then a thumb bruise further away.

Juke watched as Haylee put it all together. It took a moment—but then her eyes opened wide with shocked understanding.

She said, "Are you thinking that…"

Juke nodded. "That's right. The killer was missing a finger."

"But—it doesn't make sense!"

"Sure it does." Juke started talking rapidly. "Why did Billingsley pay all that money? To get me off the case, so he could control the investigation.

He's making sure the NYPDinc goes after somebody else—a convenient fall guy."

"But why would a multimillionaire syndicate CEO who could have half the girls in the city… Why would he murder a poor Crimean immie?"

"Same reason guys usually kill girls: she wouldn't have sex with him."

"But he barely knew Talia. She was just a client."

"Teddy said the syndicate was always coming into the club and checking up on them. I bet that was Billingsley. So last night he comes in and decides to have a little fun with the cute hostess. Why not? He owns this girl, he can do whatever he wants with her. But then the stupid immie bitch has the fucking balls to tell him no! Are you kiddin' me? Who does this sub-prime think she is? She's a fifty-one percenter and he's a fucking star! He starts punching her and he's so mad and drunk he can't stop. Then he dumps her in the street and runs her over, just to show what he thinks of her. She's nothing but a piece of garbage."

Haylee looked down at the four bruises. Juke knew she didn't want to believe it. The idea of going up against a powerful executive from Berkshire Vanguard must scare the crap out of her. It scared him too. But there was the evidence, staring straight up at them.

This evidence wouldn't be enough to get Burgess and Jackson on their side. They'd never confront a syndie exec unless he was literally holding the smoking gun, and maybe not even then. But those four bruises were enough to convince Juke—and also, he could tell from her stunned face, Haylee.

Juke said, "We better put Talia away and get outta here before the M.E. comes back. Open the drawer for me."

Haylee opened Talia's drawer without a word. Juke wheeled the body back in. "Rest in peace, Talia," he said.

Then he shut the drawer and told Haylee, "Let's go."

"But now what? We can't fight the syndicate by ourselves."

"We're gonna have to," he said as he led the way toward the door—

Suddenly it opened, and Vinnie Cho walked in. The M.E. stopped short, staring at them. "Juke, what are you doing here?"

He gave her his most charming smile. "Getting a little peace and quiet with the dead folks. It's a crazy world out there."

"I was just up in Homicide," Vinnie said. "Burgess and Jackson are looking for you."

"Yeah, they're pissed off I won't give up the case." He put a hand on her shoulder and noticed she tensed up. "Vinnie, I got something huge for you. Me and Haylee just got proof they're on the wrong track—"

Vinnie stepped away from Juke and interrupted sharply, "You don't know?"

"Don't know what?"

"When they find you, they're gonna jack you."

Haylee gasped. Vinnie watched her reaction while Juke said, "Jack us for what?"

"Burgess said something about you being a sympathizer."

Juke puzzled for a second, then got it. *A sympathizer. They must've found out about Safiya's plot—and her connection to me!*

Safiya was fucked, and so was he—and Haylee. They needed to get out of here. He turned to Haylee, who looked like she didn't know what had hit her. "Haylee, we gotta run."

Then he turned back to Vinnie. "Thanks for the warning. Please, don't tell anybody you saw us."

"You might have other people to worry about besides me," Vinnie said.

"What do you mean?"

Vinnie hesitated, her eyes flicking between Juke and Haylee.

"Come on, what?" Juke pressed.

Finally Vinnie said, "Burgess was acting cagey about your partner here." She gestured at Haylee. "He hinted that she might be an Agency spy."

Haylee's eyes widened. Juke looked at her—

—*and she looked away.*

He knew in an instant there was truth in what Vinnie had said.

"I owe you, Vinnie," he said grimly. Then he tightened his jaw and faced Haylee. "Let's go."

Haylee said, "It's not true—"

"Let's go."

Juke and Haylee walked into the hallway. He shut the door to the morgue—

And threw Haylee up against the wall. She was too surprised to scream. He tore her Heston out of its holster.

"So you've been spying on me," he said.

"No—"

He grabbed her coat collar. "Don't lie, I saw it in your eyes. That's why you wanted my phone—so you could report in to your masters—"

"That's not true—"

"The Agency is using you to stop a Resistance plot—"

"Please, just listen to me—"

"No, the only question is how I shut you up—"

"Yes, I met with the Agency!" Haylee yelled, wrenching free from his grasp. Then she lowered her voice. "They offered me seventy-nine thousand dollars and I said yes because I need to get my baby enhanced—I'm pregnant!"

"That's no excuse for—"

"But then I saw Diego was innocent and I couldn't do it. So I haven't told them anything! Not a single fucking word!"

"You expect me to believe that?!"

"Believe what you want! Now the Agency is gonna jack me too! Go ahead and shut me up, knock me out, whatever, 'cause then I'll have an excuse for why I didn't rat you out!"

Haylee stopped to breathe. Juke stared at her for a few moments, then said, "You want me to knock you out?"

"No. Come on, let's get outta here."

"I can't take you with me."

"Why not?"

"Because I don't trust you."

"If I wanted to screw you, all I gotta do is start screaming right now! Let's go already, before Burgess comes back."

Juke watched her, trying to figure out if she was playing him somehow.

She sounded like she was telling the truth—but then again, she'd obviously been fooling him all night. When had she met with the Agency? Probably when she claimed to be with her dead fiancé's mother.

He decided that for now he would act like he believed her. "Congratulations," he said. "On being pregnant, I mean."

Haylee returned his gaze. "Yeah, it's my lucky day."

Then she snapped into action, hurrying down the hall, and he followed. They didn't say anything more until they made it back to the Zan. Diego still lay beneath the jackets in the back seat. "Did you find out anything?" he asked, voice muffled.

"We'll tell you after we get outta here," Juke said. He asked Haylee, "You okay driving? I gotta use my phone."

"So now I'm a fugitive," Haylee said.

Juke watched her. Her hand went to her chest like she was having trouble breathing, and he was afraid she'd freeze up. But she started the car and raced up the ramp.

"Easy!" he said. "Don't draw attention."

But maybe she *wanted* to draw attention. Could she be trying to get them caught without him knowing she'd planned it that way?

She slowed down and they made it to the exit. The gate was up and it looked like they'd be able to ride through. But then Charysse came out of the guard booth and waved them down. They had to stop, because she was blocking the Zan.

As she stepped toward them, Juke shoved a smile onto his face and opened the window. "Hey girl, what's up?"

She frowned, looking confused. "I don't know, doob, you tell me." She pointed to the holo behind her, at the edge of the guard booth.

The holo was an NYPDinc news feed, with words streaming past in blue: reports of armed robberies in progress, bar fights, a cybersports riot at the Garden. At first Juke didn't get why Charysse wanted him to look at the feed.

But then he saw it: just below eye level, his own name traveled by, followed by Haylee's. There was a warrant out for their arrest. Any

NYPDinc personnel who had contact with either of them needed to report it immediately to their superiors. Extra reward money if they were apprehended before midnight tonight.

Juke started laughing. Charysse eyed him, bewildered, and so did Haylee. "Jackson is hilarious," Juke said. "I can't believe he actually did that!" He slapped his knee like this was the funniest thing in the world. "It's a joke, Charysse. He's messing with me 'cause I put a Cyber Patriots holo in his cube. He's a big Giants fan."

Haylee started laughing too. She said, "You know what I'm gonna do tomorrow? Superglue his Hodu."

Finally Charysse began laughing along with them. "You homicide guys are all insane," she said, putting her arm on the car, ready to kid around some more.

Juke was trying to figure out the best way to get rid of her when suddenly her perplexed frown returned. "What's that in the back seat?" she asked.

Uh oh. Juke half turned and saw Diego's booted left foot and ankle poking out from under the jackets. "It's just our clothes," he said. "Catch ya later, Charysse. Maybe we can go out tonight if you're still around at midnight."

But Charysse said, "Stay here for a sec. I'm gonna check upstairs, if you don't mind."

She headed back to the booth. Juke saw her hand reaching for the computer. He was pretty sure she was about to tap a key that would bring down the heavy metal gate. Then he and Haylee and Diego would be trapped.

He tried to think of some way to stop her, but came up empty. Her index finger was almost at the computer key—

"Hey Charysse!" Haylee called.

Charysse looked startled, because Haylee had never addressed her before—at least never this loudly. Her hand pulled back a little from the computer.

Haylee said quickly, "Me and Juke and Jackson were thinking of going to this new Cuban club on Broadway tonight. You ever hear of it?" Haylee grabbed Juke's *I!* and held it out to show Charysse a picture of the club.

Actually, as Juke knew, the I/ screen was blank, but Charysse couldn't tell from where she was.

Charysse hesitated. Then she stepped closer to look at the screen.

Haylee slammed her foot on the pedal and the Zan roared off in the direction of the exit gate. Charysse stared after them a moment in stunned surprise, then ran back to the booth and tapped her computer. The gate started coming down just as the Zan raced toward it.

The gate bashed into the Zan's rear bumper. The bumper fell halfway off as the car bucked, then tore out of the garage.

Juke told Haylee, "Get on Columbus. The sensors were down before."

Haylee took a sharp left, a right, and made it onto Columbus. Luckily the sensors were still down.

Juke looked at Haylee. "Well done," he said.

"Yeah. I'm a total idiot."

Haylee started to shiver and almost hit a parked car. Juke said, "Careful, Haylee. If we get in an accident—"

"They'll catch us, Juke! They're gonna jack us and throw us in prison. What do we do?!"

"For now," Juke said, "just keep driving."

Chapter Fifty-Eight

9:37 pm

Jeannie

In her sixth-floor walkup in midtown, Jeannie Bardach, the oldest member of the New York Seventeen, repacked her backpack for the fourth time today. She moved her son's frog puppet into a side pocket and took out a pair of socks, trying to make a little extra room. She'd decided there was one more thing she wanted to put in her pack.

She hoped she would never have to use it, but… *just in case.*

She managed to stuff it inside.

Chapter Fifty-Nine

9:39 pm

Safiya, Cheyenne, Karolyn, and the Red Queen

As Safiya and Cheyenne walked the final block to Safiya's building, they scanned the street and sidewalks for any signs of law enforcement. There were none, so they went inside.

* * *

Upstairs, in Safiya's speck, Karolyn used her I! light to search the main room. On the kitchen counter she found an old-school notepad, where Safiya or someone else had written: "38 sandwiches, juice." As Karolyn considered what this might mean, her I! buzzed and turned red.

She didn't want to make any noise, so she texted, *"What's up?"*

The Red Queen texted back, *"A man was seen hiding in Juke O'Keefe's back seat."*

Holy shit! "Scarface?"

"There's a 91 percent chance it's Scarface. Jackson has mobilized the NYPDinc to search for them."

"Excellent," Karolyn texted.

The vibe she had before, of everything coming together, hit her even more strongly now. Soon they'd have three of the main conspirators—Scarface,

Safiya, and Juke—in custody.

She wondered briefly about Haylee—was she dead? Or did she change her mind and decide not to work with Karolyn after all? If so, she was an idiot. She'd end up a fifty-one percenter one day—and so would her unenhanced daughter.

Well, so be it. People got what they deserved—

A door slammed shut down below. She heard footsteps coming up the stairs toward the third floor.

Karolyn took out her gun.

* * *

Heading up the stairs, Safiya told Cheyenne, "I meant to buy peanut butter and jelly for everybody."

"We'll survive," Cheyenne said.

"Canada's a long drive. I don't want us to stop somewhere and risk getting scanned."

"Do you have anything in your kitchen we can take with us?"

"Just yogurt and stuff. Maybe some crackers."

Safiya opened the door to the third floor.

* * *

Inside Safiya's speck, Karolyn tried to figure out: was that one person or two coming up the steps?

She heard a woman's voice and strained her ears—was this the woman she'd heard in the convos, the 9.8? The damn kittens were meowing, making it hard to hear. She wanted to strangle them.

Somebody opened the door from the stairwell, down the hall. Whoever this woman was, she was heading toward Safiya's speck. Ruby Ridge in hand, Karolyn stood behind the door and waited.

* * *

As Safiya came onto the third floor, her I! buzzed—not her burner, but the one she used for innocuous non-Rez stuff. She was tempted to ignore it. But it was too late at night to be a marketer, and curiosity got the better of her. With Cheyenne beside her, she pulled the phone out of her pocket and saw Juke's face on her screen.

It felt so strange seeing him on her I! Why was he calling—had he arrested Talia's killer, the guy from the strip club? She tapped in. "What's up?"

* * *

Inside Safiya's speck, Karolyn heard the woman's footsteps approaching even closer. Then the woman said, "What's up?"

The kittens meowed louder. Karolyn gripped her gun tight.

* * *

Out in the hall, as Safiya walked toward her speck with Cheyenne, Juke's face on her screen looked alarmed. He asked, "Where are you?"

Safiya said, "I'm going home. Why?"

She was at her front door, about to put her hand on the scanner to unlock it, when Juke yelled into her I!, "The Agency knows about you! RUN!"

Safiya stopped, her hand an inch from the scanner. Then she heard her kittens. They were meowing like crazy and scratching at the door. Something about the noises they were making didn't sound right.

Safiya put a finger to her lips, telling Cheyenne to stay silent. Then she kept on walking past the door to her speck. Cheyenne followed her.

They headed down the hall, not too fast, not too slow. Safiya wished she had a gun.

* * *

Inside the speck, Karolyn heard whoever had stopped at Safiya's door—two people, she was pretty sure, including the woman—walking past the speck and heading down the hall.

Why had they stopped and then kept going? Was the woman Safiya?

Karolyn opened the door quietly and carefully, gun ready. She poked her head out—nobody in sight—and stepped out into the hallway.

She started down the hall—and tripped on a kitten, which had slipped out of the speck between her legs. Karolyn didn't fall down, but it rattled her enough that she lost a couple seconds. Then she kept going down the hall, with the kitten yelping loudly behind her.

* * *

As Safiya hit the back stairwell with Cheyenne, she heard the kitten yelp. The only way she could've heard it so distinctly was if the kitten was in the hall—and that had to mean one thing: somebody had opened the door to Safiya's speck and let the kitten out.

Safiya whispered to Cheyenne, "Run!"

They tore down the stairs at full speed.

* * *

Karolyn heard people running down the back stairs. Now she was sure the woman was Safiya and she'd been spooked somehow. She raced into the stairwell after them. Shoes clattered below her as she ran down to the first floor.

A blast of cold wind hit her—somebody must've opened the door to the outside. The door was still in the process of closing when she got to it. She banged it all the way open, waving her gun, and ran out there.

She was in a courtyard at the rear of the building, with a fence at the end. The fence had an open gate, and two women with shopping bags, one tall and one short, were running toward it.

Karolyn yelled, "Halt! Police!" and raced toward them, firing three shots in the air.

But the women kept running through the gate. The tall one with long curly hair—Safiya!—slammed it shut behind them.

Karolyn ran toward the gate. The stupid thing had an old, rusty latch that required two hands to open up. She had to set down her Ruby Ridge for a moment.

Behind her, a man's voice said, "Fucking Dinc!"

She grabbed her gun and whirled. A toothless old man lay in the bushes with a bottle in his hand. Slurring his words and leering at her, he said, "I remember the moon and the stars."

Asshole. Karolyn undid the latch and ran out into the street. It was dark out here, with all the street lights off—another Resistance hack job, no doubt. She checked in one direction: a long straightaway. She didn't see anyone running or hear the clatter of shoes. She checked the other direction: a main street less than fifty feet away. That had to be where Safiya and the second woman went.

Karolyn ran that way. There was a big, deep hole in the sidewalk, so deep she couldn't see the bottom, so she jumped over it and kept running.

She came to the main street. It was well lit. She looked for women with shopping bags, especially a woman with long, curly, black hair. She didn't see any bags—but two women, one with her hood up covering black hair, were hurrying down the sidewalk away from her.

Karolyn ran at them, gun out, yelling, "You're under arrest!"

The women turned around, startled.

Neither of them was Safiya.

* * *

As soon as Karolyn turned onto the main street, two heads appeared out of the deep hole in the sidewalk she had just jumped over.

Then Safiya and Cheyenne tossed their shopping bags out of the hole and pulled themselves up onto the sidewalk. They dashed down the long straightaway, away from the main street, and ducked into an alley.

They raced three blocks back to Cheyenne's car and took off.

* * *

Ten minutes later Karolyn was still searching fruitlessly, getting more and more infuriated. *What a nightmare.* Based on how well Safiya had pulled off her escape, Karolyn was now positive she was the 9.8. Karolyn would have to tell Raja that she'd had the leader of the conspiracy, Syndicate Enemy Number One, in her clutches—but she let her get away.

Karolyn might as well tat the word "Scapegoat" on her face.

A happy couple moseyed up the sidewalk in front of her, arm in arm, and Karolyn got a sudden urge to shoot them just to let off steam. *Get hold of yourself, you're a mess.*

Then the Red Queen called. This better not be more bad news. She tapped her I*!*

"We've intercepted a convo between O'Keefe and Safiya," the Red Queen said. "He alerted her she's a target and told her to run."

At first Karolyn was exasperated. But then she realized this was a huge gift. She wouldn't have to admit to Raja that she'd let Safiya escape! She could claim Safiya never showed up at her speck, because she'd been warned.

Karolyn said, "If Safiya knows she's a target, she probably won't go back to her speck. We can leave an agent there just in case—Adams if he's available." That would be a suitably useless job for a dimwit like him.

"I'll alert Agent Adams," said the Red Queen. "What have you been up to? Your GPS indicated you were running."

Oh scruck, thought Karolyn, and quickly changed the subject. "Is the NYPDinc making progress finding O'Keefe?"

"They're on it. Detective Jackson has every officer in the city searching for a black Zan with a damaged fender and rear bumper."

Karolyn checked the time: *10:17.* Panic surged through her. Finding Juke would definitely help—but he wasn't the 9.8, Safiya was. Karolyn felt strongly that to destroy Chocolate, she needed to find and destroy Safiya.

Especially because Safiya had made a fool out of her. The skinny gutter rat would pay for that. When she finally caught Safiya, she'd neurointerrogate her within an inch of her life. She pictured Safiya escaping out the courtyard, her hair flying behind her—

Suddenly Karolyn got an idea. "I assume you're running facial recognition on Safiya?"

"Yes, but no hits. Undoubtedly she's wearing a pollution mask."

"I want you to run hair recognition too. Maybe we can find her current locay."

"I'm afraid that software is not well developed," the Red Queen said.

"She's an ideal candidate for it. Her hair is very striking."

"We don't know if the subject has cut her hair since the last photographs we have, or if she's wearing it tied back—"

"I bet she still wears it the same way. If anything, I bet it's even longer."

"Really," said the Red Queen.

"I suspect she's somewhere in or around the Lower East Side right now."

"And what makes you suspect that?"

Karolyn fumbled for an answer. "Well, that's where she lives."

The Red Queen paused for a couple milliseconds longer than usual before she spoke again. "By the way, you never mentioned. Why were you running?"

Karolyn could feel her face turning red and hoped the Red Queen wouldn't notice—but of course she would. Karolyn said gruffly, "It was a false alarm. Call me as soon as you get results."

Karolyn ended the call and pulled up Safiya's file on her I!, trying to figure out where the bitch would be scurrying to now.

* * *

Safiya and Cheyenne rode away from Safiya's speck, going as fast as they could without being conspicuous.

As Safiya checked behind them to make sure nobody was following, Cheyenne thought about the past two years, all her lonely nights working in the hospital lab until dawn, desperate to come up with some possible way to defeat the seemingly invulnerable bio-alarms. She had felt such stunned joy when, against all odds, she succeeded at last.

But it would all be for nothing if they got caught before midnight.

Meanwhile, Safiya wanted so badly to call Juke and find out what was going on, and how much the Agency knew. But now that the Agency was involved, she needed to be even more careful with any I*!* communications. *I can't contact him unless it's absolutely necessary.*

Hopefully, if Juke found out anything she needed to know, he'd figure out a way to reach her again. Despite all her fears, a warmth spread through her as she thought about how Juke had saved her.

Though maybe it wasn't mainly about her; maybe he was just protecting himself and his investigation from Agency interference—

Dammit, she had to quit thinking about Juke. She turned to Cheyenne and said, "We need a new center of operations for Chocolate."

"How about that place in Syrian Harlem?" Cheyenne suggested.

"Too far uptown. Soon as we de-chip everybody, we need to get them out of the city fast. The cars we stole are all parked about two blocks from my building."

"We can use my place. It's pretty close."

Safiya shook her head. "No, if they know about me, they'll know about you real soon."

As Cheyenne processed that disturbing thought, Safiya suddenly said, "I got it." She pumped her fist. "I have the security digitals for the food co-op, from when I used to work there—under the table, so the Agency won't have a record. It's only nine blocks from the cars. We'll turn off all the lights in the co-op and do the de-chipping there."

Cheyenne nodded. "We can even make those PB and J's."

* * *

Karolyn stopped at a Starbucks for her eleventh espressaccino of the day— why did she torture herself by counting? While she waited for them to make it, she hit the bathroom. Then her I*!* buzzed.

She tapped in, and the Red Queen said, "I have your hair photos, extracted from today's security videos in Manhattan. We went for long, black and curly."

"How many women are there?"

"Thirteen thousand four hundred seventy-nine."

Karolyn groaned.

"Digestive issues?" said the Red Queen.

Karolyn had forgotten the Red Queen was watching her sitting on the toilet. She took her jacket off the hook and covered her lap with it, even though the I*!* cam wasn't pointed there. She said, "Start with the photos from within a mile of Safiya's speck."

"Done. That brings the number down to two thousand six hundred fifty-seven."

Was it Karolyn's imagination or was the Red Queen laughing at her? Her *I!* screen was too small for her to see more than a couple photos at once, so she transferred them onto the walls of her toilet stall, where she could see thirty at a time. Hopefully there would be enough clarity that she could distinguish if any of these women was Safiya.

She studied the pictures carefully, going through hundreds of them, trying not to get too chunked about time passing—time she didn't have.

Somebody knocked on the bathroom door. "Anybody in there?" a girl called.

"Just a minute," Karolyn said—

—and then, on about the thousandth picture, she got a hit.

She was looking at the rear of a woman's head, with long, curly, black hair rolling down her back. It looked exactly like Safiya's hair had looked when she was running toward the courtyard gate.

The photo was from sixteen minutes ago. Karolyn enlarged it so it covered the whole front wall of her stall. The curly-haired woman was running down Lafayette Street with a petite woman, heading away from Safiya's speck. No question: the curly-haired woman was Safiya.

"How interesting," said the Red Queen. "They're running away from Safiya's apartment. I wonder what that was about."

Karolyn ignored the Red Queen's dig and focused on the petite woman. She had straight brown hair tied in a ponytail. Karolyn zoomed in and saw she was wearing dangly peace-symbol earrings.

"Could you run hair recognition on this woman, correlated with the earrings."

"Give me twenty seconds."

While Karolyn waited, the girl knocked on the door again. "Are you almost done?"

"No," Karolyn said.

Then another photograph appeared on Karolyn's phone and the bathroom wall. It was a front facial view of the woman with the peace-symbol earrings. She had high cheekbones and looked vaguely Native American.

The Red Queen said, "This woman's name is Cheyenne Littlejohn. Ninety-six percent certainty she's the same woman who's in the other photo. And sensor reports indicate that forty-two minutes ago, Littlejohn's Qilin parked three blocks away from Safiya's speck. It left there nineteen minutes ago and now it's on the move, going up Lincoln."

Karolyn told the Red Queen, "I'm going after her. Program my car."

She hurried out of the bathroom, passing the teenage girl who'd been waiting. The girl threw Karolyn a surly look. She wore chains and a "Fuck the Six" T-shirt. If this dumbass was Karolyn's daughter, Karolyn would have slapped some sense into her.

Meanwhile the Red Queen was going to remind Karolyn to wash her hands after using the toilet, but decided this wasn't the right time.

Karolyn grabbed her espressaccino off the counter. It was lukewarm by now, so she downed it and ran.

Chapter Sixty

10:35 pm

Haylee, Juke, and Diego

Driving up Columbus with Juke beside her and Diego lying down in back covered by jackets, Haylee thought: *oh God, am I really on the run from the NYPDinc? And the Agency?!* She'd spent her whole life following the rules. Her elementary school teachers always commented on how well behaved she was. But now—

Juke interrupted her thoughts. "Our best shot at finding evidence against Billingsley is his car."

Haylee tried to focus. "You're thinking Talia's bloodstains, from when he dumped her."

"And he may have attacked her inside the vehicle."

Diego sat up. "I'm gonna kill that fucking—"

"Get back down," Juke snapped. As Diego subsided, he continued, "The question is, where's his car now?"

From his prone position, Diego said, "I can find it."

Juke turned and looked at him. "How?"

"Rey taught me and Sölvi how to hack into vehicle sensors. If you get his license plate from the Dinc database, I'll use my burner and find the last sensor his car tripped."

"Works for me," Juke said.

Haylee gave a nervous laugh. "How many laws are we gonna break tonight?"

"Park in that spot up there, by the subway," Juke said.

"Why?"

"We're ditching the car. I'm sure Jackson has a million people searching for it. Even with the digitals dead, he'll find it eventually."

Haylee pulled over. Outside the subway entrance, a fifty-year-old man with a long beard was yelling about Jesus. She couldn't tell if the man was for him or against him.

Juke took out his handcuff key and turned to her. "Okay, listen. I'm gonna take the cuffs off Diego and put them on you."

"What?!"

"And if you want I'll shoot you in the arm or punch you hard in the head, somewhere that'll leave a mark."

She stared at him.

He kept his gaze steady, but his voice lost its edge. "This isn't your fight. You have a baby to look after. You can pretend you were knocked out, like you said back at the morgue. We'll leave you here in the car, handcuffed. It'll be proof I forced you to do all this crazy stuff at gunpoint. You won't go to prison for it."

Could this idea possibly work? "But won't the Agency neuro me and get the truth out of me?"

Juke hesitated. "I guess it's possible."

"And then you'll one hundred P go to prison."

"I'm hoping if I prove Billingsley is the killer, the rest of this crap will all go away."

Haylee was getting nauseous again, she'd been awake since four this morning, and she wasn't sure she was thinking straight. But she sensed that proving Billingsley was the killer would be the one thing that would save all of them—not just Juke, but herself too.

And she also knew she couldn't walk away from Juke and Diego now. She told Juke, "Fuck the cuffs. Let's do this." She stepped out of the car, and after a moment Juke and Diego, minus handcuffs now, stepped out too.

Juke handed her an anti-pollution mask and put another one on himself. Diego pulled a mask from his jacket pocket.

Juke said, "We'll ride the subway and do our hacking while we're on the move."

They walked past the bearded yeller—Haylee still couldn't tell where he stood on Jesus—and headed downstairs.

Chapter Sixty-One

10:38 pm

Safiya, Cheyenne, Karolyn, and the New York Seventeen

Safiya and Cheyenne zigzagged through heavy traffic to the Lower East Side and told the Qilin to park on Randy Weaver, six blocks from the co-op. The car said they could park closer; but Safiya wanted to be extra careful, in case they were being followed.

* * *

Two minutes later Karolyn roared up Randy Weaver in the ZMW, honking people out of the way. She saw Cheyenne's Qilin and parked behind it. Then she jumped out of her car and started searching the cold November night for Safiya and Cheyenne.

This block had a lot of bars, and on a Friday night it was full of partiers and homefree people, which made Karolyn's task more difficult. As she waded through the crowd, smelling the sweat, cheap beer, and cheaper perfume, she thought: *hopeless masses wasting their lives, just like everybody I grew up with.* It was like the great Ayn Rand had said: some are born to be masters, others are born to serve. The world had always been that way. Outside agitators like Safiya who riled these people up with unfulfillable dreams were the ones responsible for their unhappiness.

But where the hell *was* Safiya? The Red Queen was checking all the vehicle sensors and street cams in the area, but Safiya and Cheyenne seemed to have disappeared.

* * *

Safiya clicked on her underground *I!* app, created by the Resistance, that gave real-time updates on hacked sensors and disabled street cams. Following the app's instructions, Safiya and Cheyenne crossed 4th Street at the one spot the cams didn't cover; ran on a narrow walkway between two buildings; climbed a fire escape to a roof; jumped three feet to another roof; dashed down a second fire escape to a block on Fountainhead where all the sensors were down; climbed a four-foot fence to avoid a loudly barking dog; and finally made it to the rear door of the Low Down Food Co-op, which was closed for the night. Somehow they managed not to lose anything from their shopping bags.

Safiya scanned them into the store. Keeping the lights off so as not to attract attention, they went up to the employees' break room on the second floor.

Cheyenne looked around. The two sofas were a little moth-eaten, and empty coffee cups and candy wrappers cluttered the tables. But there were kids' drawings on the wall and the place had a homey vibe. "Not the most sterile place in the world, but it'll work," she said. "We'll need more chairs."

"You go find 'em, okay?" Safiya said, as she checked the time: *10:55.* "I need to contact everybody right now and tell them where to come."

She prayed she wasn't leading her people to their doom. Maybe Rey had been right and she should have postponed the op. But there was no turning back now, not with the Agency hot on their trail. If they didn't escape to Canada tonight, they all faced certain catastrophe during the coming days.

Safiya got on her backup burner and began contacting her people— carefully, so as not to draw the Agency's attention.

* * *

Several blocks away, Karolyn hurried down Randy Weaver hunting for Safiya. The Red Queen said into her I!, "There's a sixty-four percent chance they've gone inside a building within a three-block radius of their vehicle. Ninety-six P chance it's within five blocks."

"Do you think they still plan to go ahead with Chocolate at midnight?"

"Based on everything we know about Safiya Bassani-Jones, absolutely. It's likely she'll undertake the de-chipping at the home of somebody involved in the Resistance. I advise authorizing a Sed Red and dispatching enough agents to go door to door on all known sympathizers."

The Red Queen was right; it was way past time for a seditious activity red alert. "Make the order. I want fifty agents working this area within ten minutes. Link me the addresses of all known symps right now and I'll start."

* * *

The seventeen surviving members of the New York Nineteen were at coffee shops, bars, and street corners within a few blocks of Safiya's speck. They were ready to converge on it when the time came.

Then all at once their burners buzzed with song recommendations.

For security reasons, each of them received a different song. But they all had essentially the same comment in the social media section, with enough linguistic variations to throw off any law enforcement bots searching for a common pattern.

A typical comment was received by Jeannie Bardach, as she sat nursing her coffee at an all-night Starbucks. The comment, from "Midnite Rider," said: "For real punkydunk tunes, hit the back of Low Down!"

Jeannie figured out immediately what this meant: Safiya was telling her to go to the back of the Low Down Food Co-op instead of Safiya's speck.

Jeannie was alarmed. *Why the change in locay? Did something go wrong with Chocolate?*

But she knew what she had to do. She hoisted her heavy backpack and walked out of the coffee shop. Low Down was only seven blocks away, on

Waverly. She still had plenty of time.

Jeannie and the other fifty-one percenters tried to stifle their fears as they headed for the new locay carrying all their remaining worldly possessions on their backs.

Only fifty-nine minutes to freedom.

Chapter Sixty-Two

11:02 pm

Juke, Haylee, Diego, and the Red Queen

Juke, Haylee, and Diego waited for a subway in the center section between the two tracks. They would take the first train that stopped, no matter which direction it was going, so they could get far away from the black Zan they'd left on the street up above.

As they waited, Juke tapped into the NYPDinc database to retrieve Billingsley's license plates. Billingsley owned a Bond convertible and a Genghis SUV, the latest trendy vehicles of the super-rich. It was unlikely he transported Talia in the convertible; her body wouldn't have fit. So Juke gave Diego the plate number for the Genghis, then handed Diego's confiscated burner back to him. Since it was GPS-protected, they didn't have to worry about the cops finding them if he used it.

Diego started hacking immediately. An uptown train stormed up, and they got in and sat across from a couple arguing in some Eastern European language. Juke watched Diego's fingers furiously tapping the burner screen. Before the train even made it to 28th Street, Diego said, "Got it."

He looked up from the phone. "The Genghis rode up Patrick Henry Street thirty minutes ago. It hit the sensors at 208 and 246 Henry, but not 294. It hasn't tripped any other sensors since then."

Juke said, "Any cross streets it could've turned onto between 246 and

294?"

"No."

Haylee said, "So Billingsley probably parked the car on that block."

Juke studied his I! "There's a strip club called Brain Dead at 262 Henry. I bet that's where he is."

Haylee said quietly, so the foreign couple wouldn't hear them, "You think he kills a girl and the very next night he's out trying to get laid?"

"Sure. He never got to screw Talia, so he's still horny." Then Juke remembered Talia's fiancé was sitting right beside him. "Excuse my language."

Diego nodded grimly. "No worries."

Diego was beyond getting offended. He'd lost everything in the past twenty-four hours: first Talia and now his chance at freedom, because after everything that had happened, he was pretty sure Chocolate was doomed. He expected to be either jacked or killed by the end of the night.

But before that happened, he wanted revenge. He looked up at the holographic subway map.

"We're going in the right direction," he said. "Patrick Henry is in two stops."

* * *

Ordinarily the Red Queen didn't share intel with the NYPDinc, but this was a Sed Red. So she buzzed Detective Jackson and told him, "The sensor system has been hacked."

Her video feed showed that Jackson had taken over the entire homicide squad room to coordinate the citywide search for Juke, Haylee, and Scarface. He had several cops with him whose body language said they were his crew.

Jackson waved his hand dismissively at the Red Queen's news. He was clearly not one to be intimidated by superhuman intelligence. "So what? The sensors are always getting hacked."

"The hacker used the same burner that was used by Suspect #1—Scarface."

Now she had Jackson's full attention. "What did Scarface hack into?"

"The current locay of Michael Billingsley's vehicle. This was less than two minutes after Detective O'Keefe searched for Billingsley's license plate."

Jackson squinted at his I! screen, puzzled. "You think they're after Billingsley? Why?"

The Red Queen wasn't sure why, though it must have something to do with Talia's murder. There was a 58 percent chance Juke and Scarface wanted Billingsley's help tracking down a lead; but beyond that the data was insufficient and the Ps got muddy. There was even a three percent chance they suspected Billingsley himself of the murder.

But she decided none of this speculation would be useful for Jackson to know about. His psych profile indicated he was most effective when you kept things very simple for him. So she said, "The point is, that's where Juke, Scarface, and Haylee are heading. You need to send your people there."

"I'm not sending anyone," said Jackson. "I'll nail that dickhead Juke myself. Can't wait to see his face when I shove my boot up his sorry ass."

Jackson's sidekicks laughed. He nodded to the two lucky cops standing closest to him—Sammy and Reese, guys in their twenties who hit the synth steroids hard and looked up to him like he was their father. "Let's go."

The Red Queen gave Jackson the locay of Billingsley's car, and the three cops grabbed their Hestons and headed out the door.

* * *

Juke, Haylee, and Diego came out of the subway station and walked swiftly past a row of bars and restaurants to the 200 block of Patrick Henry. When they got to Brain Dead, they searched for Billingsley's silver Genghis SUV. It didn't take long. They found the car right behind the club, in a small, roped off, VIP parking lot.

Juke checked the area. There were no security people out here—but there were cams. Probably a guard inside the club kept an eye on the video feed, so they'd need to work carefully and fast.

Juke asked Diego, "I don't suppose Rey taught you how to hack into a car?"

315

Diego said, "Actually, he did. That was part of our training."

They were standing in the shadows twenty-five feet from the Genghis, where the cams wouldn't see them. "Can you do it from here, where it's dark?"

"I'm pretty sure, yeah."

"Then do it."

Diego took out his I*!* and got to work, as Juke and Haylee kept watch.

Chapter Sixty-Three

11:16 pm

Michael Billingsley, DeAndrey Jackson, Juke, Haylee, and Diego

Inside Brain Dead, a Vietnamese stripper who called herself the Tibetan Tornado shook her enormous breasts in Michael Billingsley's face. He appreciated it, of course; but even so, he looked around her breasts toward a waitress at the far end of the club.

He was more into waitresses and hostesses than strippers. He always felt they were fresher, more innocent. That made it even more fun when he rode them hard.

The drug cocktail Billingsley took allowed him to stay erect for pretty much forever. He liked girls with long hair, so he could yank it back while he pumped them. He made the girls tell him over and over again how much they loved it.

The best part was, these vixens were fifty-one percenters, so they'd do whatever he wanted. They'd lick his toe jam if he told them to.

In fact, maybe he'd do that tonight. Why not? He deserved it, after everything he'd been through in the past twenty-four hours.

There was so much pressure on syndie execs like him now. At the meeting last week in New Mexico, the Board kept talking about a "tipping point." The syndies were getting more and more power each day, yet the Resistance was growing stronger too.

No wonder he needed a little extra fun.

His I*!* buzzed. It was Detective Jackson, his bought and paid for investigator. Jackson would make sure Mexican Scarface confessed, in return for a few extra Reagans under the table. He was probably calling to say he'd already captured the guy. *Excellent.*

Billingsley pushed the Tibetan Tornado's 44s aside and stood up. He went out the front door and headed outside to where it was quieter, so he could have an actual convo.

* * *

While Jackson waited for Billingsley to pick up, he rode fast, siren blaring, in a silver Shark with gold rims. No ancient black Zan for him, thank you very much. Sammy and Reese sat in back.

When they got within a quarter-mile of Billingsley's Genghis, Jackson turned off the siren. He wanted to sneak up on Juke and stuff his .38 Heston right in that self-righteous douchebag's face. Everybody in Homicide treated Jackson with deference except for Juke, who acted like Jackson was lower than chewing gum stuck under his shoe. He was always accusing Jackson of busting innocent men or whatever.

Now Juke would regret it. Jackson felt the gun in his pocket and smiled.

* * *

In the VIP parking area, Juke and Haylee hid in the shadows with Diego as he hacked away, fingers flying on his burner. Finally it beeped, and the Genghis did too.

Diego told Juke and Haylee, "The car's unlocked. I rigged it so the light won't come on when the door opens."

"Nice," Juke said, and turned to Haylee. "Okay, go to the edge of the darkness, then run *fast* through the lighted area. We'll hope none of the guards are watching the security video for those three seconds. We'll head for the right side of the car—it looks like it's hidden from the cams."

"Got it," Haylee said. She didn't even bother with a mindlessness breath; she was way too freaked out for it to make a difference.

Juke said, "If Billingsley transported her or tried to have sex with her, it was probably in the back seat. We'll look there first." He turned to Diego. "You stay here. If anybody comes, start shouting or create a diversion."

As Diego watched the surrounding darkness, Juke and Haylee dashed to the SUV and crouched low, by the back door. Hopefully no guards would come rushing out of the club.

Juke opened the door with no problem. It was a slider, so they were both able to see inside the SUV as soon as Juke turned on his I! light.

There was red everywhere—but it wasn't blood. The back seat had been removed and replaced with a soft red carpet. "His fuckmobile," Haylee said, disgusted.

Juke looked around. "Won't be easy finding red blood on a red carpet."

He shone his light all around the inside of the car. Haylee's heart sank; there were no obvious signs of a struggle, much less a murder.

Then Juke's light passed over the rear of the driver's seat, near the top. All of a sudden she saw it: *a big reddish-brown smear.* Trying to contain her excitement, she grabbed Juke's I! and pointed it at the smear. "Look!"

They stuck their heads into the back of the car and checked more closely. They found another reddish-brown smear by the inside door handle, and even more at the bottom of the door.

" This must be where he dragged her body out," Juke said.

He did it, Haylee thought, stunned. *The fucking pig. He really killed her!* He was so arrogant, so positive he was above the law, he didn't even bother to clean out his car after he killed Talia in it.

Juke turned to Diego, still standing in the darkness by the fence. He gave Diego a quick "keep quiet" gesture, followed by a thumbs up.

Then he tapped Haylee's arm. "Vancouver, you ready to make the biggest video of your life?"

* * *

The song "Do Me Do You Do Me" boomed through the open front door of the club, so Billingsley had to walk almost half a block till it was quiet enough to talk on the phone. Then he asked Jackson, "Hello, Detective, what's the word?"

"Are you on Patrick Henry Street?"

Odd question. "Yeah, why?"

"Where on Patrick Henry?"

"I'm outside a club called Brain Dead."

"Get back inside and stay there. We think O'Keefe and Scarface are looking for you. We're not sure why."

Billingsley felt a sudden surge of fear. "They're looking for me?"

"Yeah, they hacked the sensors and found your car. Just go back in and stay safe. We'll be there in less than five minutes and deal with those assholes."

Jackson tapped off. Billingsley stood there on the sidewalk in shock. Why was Juke after him?

Was it possible the Dinc *suspected* him?

He better make sure the Genghis was safe. He couldn't let Juke look inside.

He hurried toward the back parking lot of Brain Dead.

* * *

Juke knelt inside the Genghis next to the bloody smears. Haylee stood just outside the car's open door, aiming Juke's I*!* cam at him. "Okay, Humphrey, go!"

Juke's heart raced. In ten years with the NYPDinc, he'd never brought down anybody nearly as big as Billingsley. A thought came from nowhere: *Safiya will be proud.* He cleared his throat and began, quietly and urgently. "I'm Juke O'Keefe, Homicide—"

"Louder. Getting a lot of noise from the club."

Juke raised his voice. "I'm Juke O'Keefe, Homicide. I'm here in the back seat of a Genghis SUV owned by Michael Billingsley, the CEO of New York operations for the Berkshire Vanguard Syndicate. This large reddish-

320

brown stain, and this one here"—he pointed, and Haylee aimed the cam at them—"are blood. The blood of Talia Qirimoglu, the innocent young woman who was beaten and killed last night—*by Billingsley*. Don't let the NYPDinc and the syndicates cover up this crime. It's time for the people of New York to stand up!" *Shit, I sound just like Safiya,* he thought, but kept going. "Talia may have been poor, but she had the right to live. We can't let the syndicates murder people and get away with it! Michael Billingsley must pay for his brutal—"

"Hands up!" a voice shouted.

Michael Billingsley stood at the open door right next to Haylee, with a gun in his hand. He swung it back and forth between Haylee and Juke.

"Both of you—hands up!" he screamed.

Chapter Sixty-Four

11:21 pm

Diego, Haylee, and Juke

In the darkness, twenty-five feet from the Genghis, Diego panicked. *Fuck!* He'd been so intent on watching Juke, straining to hear him above the music, he hadn't spotted the well-dressed man running into the parking area until it was too late. Now the man was aiming a gun at Juke and Haylee.

The man hadn't seen Diego in the darkness yet, but his body was angled so Diego was in his line of sight. If Diego tried to make a run at him, the man would see him as soon as he moved. Diego would have to cross the lighted area, giving the man plenty of time to swing his gun and shoot him.

Who *was* the man? In that suit, he couldn't be a Dinc.

Suddenly Diego realized: that's Billingsley—*the man who killed Talia!*

* * *

Billingsley's black Smith & Wesson—a classic, like his suit—jumped back and forth rapidly between Haylee and Juke. But in Haylee's eyes, the gun was moving in slow motion.

She expected to flash back to Harrison getting shot. Instead she just went numb. When Billingsley yelled at her a second time to put her hands up, she did.

But then she remembered that the I*!* cam in her right hand, above her head, was still turned on. Her trance fell away—she had a job to do. She didn't know if it would do any good, but she angled the I*!* downwards toward Billingsley so he'd be on cam, and kept shooting.

Inside the SUV, Juke had his hands up too. He said, "It's too late, Billingsley."

Billingsley said, "Step out of the car."

Juke moved slowly toward the car door, feeling the Heston's weight in his right jacket pocket, looking for the chance to pull it.

"Faster!"

Juke said, "You know they have security cams out here—"

Billingsley spit angrily, "Like I care! Out of the car now!"

Juke got out of the car.

* * *

In the shadows, Diego froze. The situation was even worse now. With Juke standing beside Haylee, Billingsley faced them both at the same time; and Diego, beyond them, was even more directly in Billingsley's line of sight. If he tried to lunge across the lighted area, Billingsley would see him coming the entire way—and wouldn't even have to swing his gun sideways to shoot him.

* * *

Juke kept his hands up. If he got close enough, he'd try to bring his hands down hard on Billingsley's gun arm.

But Billingsley was staying about eight feet away—too far to charge safely. Juke needed to throw him off balance. He said, "Doob, security's gonna come out here any second."

"You don't get it, you dumb Dinc," Billingsley said. "My syndicate owns this club. We own these guards. We own these cams. I can zap you right now and nobody'll say a goddamn word."

Haylee knew what she needed to do: blast this I! video she was making to networld. Right now. Livestream it. Maybe somebody nearby would see it and come running. Or she would tell Billingsley, and he'd realize he couldn't shoot them with the whole world watching.

But she couldn't order the I! to begin livestreaming, because Billingsley would hear her. I!'s made people wait fifteen seconds to confirm their streaming requests, in case they were planning to stream sex or suicide and got second thoughts. During those fifteen seconds, Billingsley could shoot her.

So she decided to livestream manually. That required three taps of the I!, and it was tricky tapping in the right places when she was holding the I! up above her head where she couldn't see it. But she did her best. She gave the first tap—

Billingsley caught her. He pointed his gun at her face and yelled, "Drop your I!"

Haylee hesitated.

"Drop it!"

She lowered her hand to her legs and dropped the I! onto her foot. From there it bounced lightly to the pavement. She figured that way the I! wouldn't break, and it would keep recording.

Not that it would help Haylee much if she was already dead.

* * *

Billingsley was infuriated. He hadn't wanted to zap these Dincs, but now he had no choice.

If this came out publicly, the Board at Berkshire Vanguard would be seriously pissed. They hated when their execs got involved in any scandals. If only he and the Agency woman could tie this whole problem to the Resistance op somehow—

Wait, that might work really well!

They could say Billingsley was a hero, singlehandedly taking on terrorist, pro-Resistance Dincs. Who would argue with that?

He began to feel a lot better. "You idiots," he sneered, "why didn't you just jack the Mexican guy and collect your Reagans?"

Juke said, "'Cause the world isn't just about Reagans."

Billingsley laughed. "Seriously? What are you, a high school girl?"

"Why did you kill Talia?"

Billingsley shook his head, amused. "Trying to keep me talking, huh? Sorry, won't work. Say good-bye, chump."

He leveled his gun at Juke's face, about to shoot.

But Haylee broke in. "You're the real chump, Billingsley. Why didn't you clean your car?"

Billingsley smiled. "I thought it would be fun to fuck a girl on top of the dead girl's blood."

* * *

Diego, hiding in the shadows, heard that. He couldn't take it anymore.

He gave a bloodcurdling scream and ran headlong toward Billingsley.

* * *

Billingsley heard Diego's scream before he saw him. He swung his gun around.

But before he could shoot, Juke lunged, trying to close the eight-foot gap in a single jump. Billingsley stepped back fast. Diego was coming too. No time to aim. Billingsley turned and cracked Diego in the head with his gun, knocking him off-balance. Then he spun back toward Juke, raised his weapon, and fired—

—just as Haylee pulled her gun and shot him in the shoulder. The bitch! His arm jerked wide, and he missed Juke.

Billingsley staggered, shoulder burning, but didn't go down. He fired back at Haylee. The bullet skimmed just over her head as she ducked and fired again.

This time she hit him square in the chest.

Billingsley clutched his chest with his left hand, but still managed to point his gun at Haylee again. He started to squeeze the trigger.

But Juke slammed into him. He crashed to the ground and dropped the gun.

Billingsley tried to get up—but couldn't. A choking sound rose from his throat.

He looked up. Diego stood over him now, eyes full of hatred.

Diego said, "Die, you piece of shit."

Billingsley blinked, blinked again, and then died.

Haylee stared down at this man she had just killed. Her gun fell from her hand to the pavement. "Oh my God."

Juke put his hand on her shoulder. "Looks like we just joined the Resistance. Let's get out of here."

Haylee still looked blank. Juke gently slapped her cheek. "Snap out of it. We don't have time."

She leaned down and grabbed her gun, along with the *I!*, which was still videotaping. The three of them ran toward the street.

But then they saw DeAndrey Jackson, flanked by Sammy and Reese, crossing the street in their direction.

Jackson yelled, "O'Keefe! Halt!" He and the two other cops drew their guns and ran straight at them.

Juke, Haylee, and Diego turned and dashed back to the VIP parking lot. But the rear fence was fifteen feet high with barbed wire. They were trapped—unless they went through the club. Juke yelled, "Come on!" and they rushed for the back door. But it was locked.

Juke shot the lock off and opened the door. They dashed inside.

The club was full of people, including at least three bouncers and security guards that Juke could see. They'd heard the gunshots above the music, and they pulled their weapons and moved on Juke, Haylee, and Diego.

Juke yelled as loud as he could, "Behind us! They're shooting!"

That confused the bouncers and guards enough so they hesitated and looked toward the back door. Sure enough, a second later Jackson burst in with his sidekicks. All three of them held their guns high.

The bouncers and guards moved to confront them. Twenty or so strippers, waitresses, and customers hit the floor so they wouldn't get caught in the gunfight. Others ran out the front door.

Juke, Haylee, and Diego hurdled two waitresses and ran out the door too. Jackson, Sammy, and Reese raced for the door right behind them, waving their badges and shouting the bouncers and guards into submission.

But just before the door, Jackson tripped over a prone stripper, who screamed. A new wave of escaping clubgoers kept Jackson and the other cops pinned inside the club for another ten seconds or so.

Finally Jackson was able to toss people out of the way and run out into the street. He and his sidekicks split up and gave chase in both directions.

Juke, Haylee, and Diego were gone.

Chapter Sixty-Five

11:24 pm

Everyone

The Lower East Side had been a hotbed of political passions ever since the original American Revolution in the 1700s, when local rabble rousers ran the rich, powerful Delancey family out of town for supporting the British. This countercultural spirit still held strong in the new millennium. On any given night you'd find drumming circles morphing into pro-Resistance flares; crowded specks hosting old-school teach-ins; and underground cells hacking vehicle sensors and other tools of syndicate power. Along with parts of Brooklyn, the Lower East Side was the rowdiest, most rebellious area that the New York Division of the Agency had to deal with.

Karolyn and all the other eighty or ninety agents who had been rushed in for this Sed Red emergency were trying to knock on every sympathizer's door within a five-block radius of where Cheyenne's Qilin had been found. But that was a lot of doors—well over a hundred. All the agents had accomplished so far was to frighten a lot of residents and break up some parties that were clearly a lot more about snorting and sexing than about supporting the Resistance. They hadn't found any trace of Safiya or Cheyenne.

But Karolyn kept racing from speck to speck and banging on doors. She could feel it: she was so close to destroying Chocolate. She was going to win.

She *had* to.

She checked her list and ran to the next locay.

* * *

Jeannie Bardach was the first of the New York Seventeen to arrive at the co-op, at 11:24. During the next twelve minutes the others followed: Bobby Morelli, the youngest of the group; the married couple Diane Patterson and Mychal Collins; and everybody else. The members of the six different mini-cells met each other for the first time.

The only one who didn't show up was Sölvi Hilmarsson. Since he was in the same mini-cell with Talia and Diego, and their identities had been compromised, Safiya guessed that Sölvi had gotten jacked or worse. That would explain why his burner had been off. She hoped she was wrong—but she knew they couldn't wait for him or they would all go down.

As each of them arrived, Safiya immediately sent them upstairs to the break room. Cheyenne gave them their doses of the crushed-up curcumin pills, which they washed down with bottled water from the co-op shelves. The last fifty-one percenter got her dose at 11:39.

This meant they were still on track to de-chip at midnight. Within twenty minutes the curcumin would enter everybody's bloodstreams in sufficient quantities that it would be safe to begin de-chipping. When the chips were removed, they'd still release synthetic protein into the blood—but it would bind with the curcumin instead of hemoglobin, so it wouldn't send radio signals to the Anthill. There would be no bio-alarms.

Cheyenne set her timer for twenty minutes and got her sterilized knives and I! chargers ready.

Meanwhile Safiya walked through the dark main room on the second floor, stepping around bins full of grains and beans. This floor had mainly bulk items, and shoppers with carts had to use the elevator. She looked out the front window onto the street. This close to midnight, the street had thinned out. A young man and a young woman walked up the sidewalk carrying guitars. Otherwise all was quiet. No sign of trouble.

Hopefully it would still be this way twenty minutes from now.

* * *

Karolyn was racing up a hallway, hand on her gun, hunting down another sympathizer, when her I*!* buzzed with a call from Jackson, "Yeah," she said, still running.

Jackson said, "They zapped Billingsley."

Karolyn stopped dead. "Who did?"

"Juke, Haylee, and Scarface."

"Why?"

"No idea. They ran. We're looking for them."

Oh God, I'm totally fucked!

A syndicate CEO, killed on her watch—by a guy *she* was tracking. A guy she should have caught by now!

She yelled at Jackson, "Well, what are you talking to *me* for? Find them. Catch them! Alive or dead, I don't care!"

She tapped off and slammed her fist against the speck door of the next symp on her list. *Unbelievable.* Her career, her life, that she'd worked so hard for, shot to hell in a single night by these *fools.* It was so unfair!

She hammered the door again and again, harder and harder, and smashed through the cheap wood. The destruction sent a surge through her veins.

Even better, letting loose with her rage like that freed her mind—and she got a sudden hit of inspiration.

She knew how she could locate Safiya and Cheyenne!

She stuck her gun in her pocket and tapped the Red Queen. "Here's what I want you to do—"

But then the busted door swung open and a beefy guy in his thirties, named Erik according to her symp list, came stomping out into the hall. He had a gun aimed at her face, his eyes were red, and he looked snorted. "What is your problem?" he said.

"Never mind," said Karolyn, heading back toward the stairs. She needed to talk to the Red Queen.

But the symp came after her, waving his gun. "Don't move another step or I'll shoot you. You just broke my door."

Karolyn so did not have time for this right now. With her back still to him, she drew her Ruby Ridge. She turned around and shot him, then turned around again and ran down the stairs.

* * *

Juke, Haylee, and Diego were heading downtown on a creaky Koch Syndicate metrobus. They had escaped from Jackson and the other cops by jumping on the bus outside Brain Dead, then ducking down when the cops ran past. They ka-chinged the bus old-school to avoid leaving a digital trace.

As Juke looked out the window to make sure the cops didn't come back, Haylee watched the video of Billingsley on Juke's phone. Billingsley's confession rang out loud and clear: *I thought it would be fun to fuck a girl on top of the dead girl's blood.*

Haylee said, "We should bang this out to networld right away—"

Diego interrupted, holding up his burner. "I just got a song recommendation from Safiya."

"A song recommendation?" Juke asked.

"We use that for messaging. They're at the Low Down Co-op on Waverly."

Juke stood up. He told Haylee, "I need to go there. I gotta make sure she's safe."

Haylee felt dizzy, like she was on a deranged, runaway carnival ride and couldn't get off. Nothing made sense anymore. Cops and syndies were killing people, framing them, and what the hell would happen to her? She had to put her faith in Juke. "Alright, let's go."

They jumped off the bus at the next stop, and Diego used his GPS-protected burner to call an oob. To avoid surveillance, he checked the "Security encrypted, private driver" option.

But Diego's efforts to maintain security weren't enough…

* * *

…Because the Anthill could read the oob driver's I*!* screen.

Three seconds later the Red Queen buzzed Jackson, who was back in his Shark with Sammy and Reese hunting the streets for Juke.

The Red Queen said, "Diego just called an oob. He's being picked up at 23rd and Galt."

Jackson immediately ordered his car: "23rd and Galt, code red."

The Shark raced south, siren blaring.

* * *

After zapping the symp, Karolyn ran out of the building onto the corner of Waverly and Fountainhead. She got on the phone with the Red Queen, speaking rapidly, positive she'd figured out the best way to beat Safiya and Chocolate.

"How many people do you think Safiya is trying to de-chip tonight?"

"I have no way of knowing," the Red Queen said.

"But this is a major op, so it's probably at least ten, right?" Actually, Karolyn thought at least twenty; she was guessing the "38 sandwiches" on Safiya's notepad meant Safiya was feeding everybody who was getting de-chipped.

The Red Queen considered Karolyn's question for a few milliseconds. "There's a seventy-three P chance it's ten or more. Why?"

Karolyn said triumphantly, "We should look for concentrations of fifty-one percenters in this immediate area. If we find ten or twenty of them in the same locay, then we'll know that's where they're de-chipping!"

It took the Red Queen a long time to reply—half a second, at least—and Karolyn was sure she would shoot the idea down. Karolyn was prepared to do the almost unthinkable: overrule the Red Queen.

But then the Red Queen said, "Excellent idea. The Anthill will access all the syndicate databases and get us this intel as quickly as possible."

Karolyn could have sworn the Red Queen sounded impressed.

"How long will that take?" Karolyn asked.

"This is data we haven't accessed previously. I'd estimate five point two minutes."

"Well, hurry!"

* * *

In the break room, Cheyenne prepped her tools while the New York Seventeen waited nervously. Some of them were quiet, others tried to make jokes, and a couple of them counted down the seconds. *"Five four three two one... Fourteen minutes to freedom!"*

Safiya came back into the main room and looked out the windows. Everything was still quiet, except for a drumming circle in the distance. She could hear people in the other room counting down to twelve minutes.

But then she saw someone hurrying out of a building on the corner: a woman in a dark business suit. She passed under a street light, and—*oh shit.* Safiya recognized that black pencil skirt with the side vents. This was the agent who jumped over her when she was hiding in the pothole—who broke into her speck and shot at her!

Should I abort the op? Tell everybody to run out of here and try to escape?

Down on the sidewalk, the agent was talking into her phone, gesticulating. Her gaze swept over the co-op building, and Safiya jerked back from the window. But then the agent kept looking up and down the street. Safiya sensed she didn't know exactly where Chocolate was happening—but she knew it was close by. No doubt a lot of agents and Dincs were about to pour into this area. They'd pull out all the stops to shut tonight's op down.

Safiya's mind raced. If she went ahead and de-chipped the New York Seventeen, they'd all have to walk through this neighborhood for nine blocks to reach the getaway cars. But how could seventeen people— nineteen, including her and Cheyenne—possibly make it all the way to the cars safely if the area was crawling with law enforcement? The streets were already pretty empty, and they'd be even emptier after midnight—except for an army of agents and Dincs. It would be child's play for them to grab the New York Seventeen off the streets.

Safiya couldn't bear the thought of all her most fervent dreams, her life's mission, going down the drain. But how could she give these desperate people their freedom for five minutes, only to have them jacked and carried off to prison as soon as they went outside—

Wait a minute. The drumming circle in the distance got louder, and suddenly Safiya knew what to do. It would be a desperado move, but—

She checked the time: 11:51. *Nine minutes left.* If she was gonna do it, it had to be right now.

She grabbed her burner, got into her Break the Chains account, set her message to Five-Alarm, activated the voice changer, and said urgently into the mic: "There's an Agency action happening now! Flash flare needed immediately on Waverly Street between Fountainhead and Atlas! *Flare now!* Bring your drums!"

Then she blasted her alert out to networld.

* * *

The oob carrying Juke, Haylee and Diego raced down Galt Street. Juke had given thirty-six dollars in trad cash—all he had left—to the oob driver, an old guy with dreads who smelled of pot and said he liked riding around the city late at night. Juke asked him to drive manually and floor it, since the sensors were down on Galt. The guy obliged. At this rate they'd get to Low Down in two minutes.

Juke turned and watched as Haylee, sitting behind him, gave one more tap to Juke's I! With that tap, she blasted out the video of Billingsley's confession to networld.

"We did it!" shouted Haylee. "Now everybody will know the truth about the fucking scum who killed Talia."

Juke nodded tightly. Haylee was right; whatever else happened, at least he'd solved the case. *No victim too small.* Juke had accomplished his mission.

Except now Safiya was in danger.

Just then he became conscious of a police siren, coming closer. He turned around.

Jackson's Shark was coming straight at them.

Chapter Sixty-Six

Midnight

Everyone

Safiya was looking out the window, desperately hoping her flash flare would work, when Cheyenne called out from the break room, "Safiya, we're starting!"

She decided to try and act like everything was normal. Scaring Cheyenne and the others now wouldn't do any good. So she called, "Coming!", and headed into the break room.

Cheyenne had given everyone their equipment: sterilized knives, I! chargers, and bandages. Whatever part of their bodies held the chip—shoulder, ankle, thigh—was bare. They'd each practiced this minor surgery at least five times during their cell meetings. But they'd practiced on dolls and discarded bots. Now they would be actually *doing* the surgery, on themselves.

"Everybody ready?" said Cheyenne.

The New York Seventeen called out: "Yes!" "D-Chip Day, baby." "Free at last!" Mychal Collins and Bobby Morelli had been assigned to videotape the de-chipping, so they took their I!'s out and started shooting Cheyenne.

The plan was for Cheyenne to do Jeannie while everybody else did themselves. So Cheyenne picked up a knife and bent down over Jeannie's right forearm.

"Okay, people," she said. "First I want you to close your eyes, take a deep breath, and imagine a quiet mountain lake in western Canada. The water is rippling gently."

After everyone closed their eyes, she waited a few moments. Then she continued, "Now open your eyes. I want you to find your incision scar and put your finger on it. Feel it."

Cheyenne did that with Jeannie, and everybody else followed suit on themselves.

"Now cut through the skin. As soon as you've made it through the skin, let up. There will be blood, and a little bit of pain, but it's okay. Ignore it. Feel that lake."

Cheyenne cut through Jeannie's skin. Jeannie gave a barely audible gasp. "Easy," Cheyenne whispered, and Jeannie took a deep breath and hung in there.

Cheyenne looked around the room. Everybody was cutting. She saw winces of pain, and blood flowing. But no one was screaming or passing out. So far so good.

This would make for a great video. Fifty-one percenters everywhere would watch it and think: *hey, I could do this too!*

"When you're done," Cheyenne said, "please grab your I*!* chargers and hold them high."

Cheyenne waited for everybody to hold their chargers high so they could go on to the next step.

* * *

As Jackson's Shark closed in on them, Juke tried to come up with some plan that didn't involve a gunfight on the busy street. But it was hard to think straight with the Shark shouting, "Pull over, dickwad, NYPDinc. Pull over, dickwad, NYPDinc."

The old oober pulled over to the curb and told Juke, "You're gonna have to pay my speeding ticket, ro."

In the back seat, Diego watched the Shark come to a halt right behind them. "They're gonna kill me!"

The oober didn't get what Diego was so stressed about. "Pacify yourself."

Haylee said to Juke, "What do we do?"

Juke told her, "Don't pull your gun—yet."

Meanwhile Jackson walked toward them with Sammy and Reese. All three of them had their Hestons out, pointed at the Dharma.

Now the oober was thoroughly frightened too, his pot high gone. "Hey, this isn't just about a speeding ticket, is it?"

Juke said quickly, "You look like a sympathizer, ro. Do me a favor: keep your doors locked for just one minute." Then Juke buzzed Jackson's I*!*

But Jackson ignored the buzz. With Sammy and Reese backing him up, he stepped to Juke's window and aimed his gun at Juke's face. "Out of the car, O'Keefe," he said loudly, so Juke could hear it through the closed window. "You too, Vixen and Scarface."

Juke put his hands up and called back through the window, "We'll be happy to come out. No resistance. But first watch the video I just snapped you."

Jackson rattled the door handle. Juke was relieved to see the old man had kept it locked. Jackson snarled, "Step out of the car before I bash this guy's windows in."

Juke said, "Billingsley killed Talia. He confessed. That's what's on the video."

Jackson looked stunned. Juke could see he was trying to figure out if it was true—and if it was, what he should do.

"You're full of shit, O'Keefe," Jackson said.

"That video is in networld now. You really want to jack us and look like the world's biggest moron?"

Jackson hesitated. He so wanted to nail O'Keefe and collect all those Reagans for bringing in Scarface.

Maybe he should just zap all three of them. That might be simplest. Karolyn had said she wanted them dead or alive. He could say Juke and Haylee were resisting arrest. It would be an easy sell, because they were acting like desperados: on the run with a murder suspect and involved in killing a big-shot syndicate exec.

But what if Juke was telling the truth, and Billingsley really did confess to murder? Would zapping these three make Jackson look bad?

* * *

All over the Lower East Side, Resistance members and sympathizers received Safiya's five-alarm flash flare alert on their Hodus and I!'s. Over a hundred of these people had just had Karolyn or another agent banging on the doors of their specks, so they were wide awake and pissed. When they got Safiya's signal, they were ready to flare.

They threw on their coats, snapped the five-alarm to everybody they knew, banged on their neighbors' doors to wake them up, and hurried for Waverly Street between Fountainhead and Atlas.

As Karolyn stalked the streets searching for signs of Chocolate and waiting to hear back from the Red Queen—it had been five minutes already, dammit—she noticed the street around her starting to fill up. Most of the people were in their late teens and twenties, but there were some bearded old guys in the mix too, and middle-aged women in jeans and boots. Was there a party somewhere?

Then a man in an anti-pollution mask shouted, "Break the chains!" and people shouted back, "Fuck the Six!" As the call and response continued, somebody started playing the protest song "Scruck Scruck Scruck!" on a synthesizer, and people took over the street, dancing and drumming on whatever percussive objects they had brought with them.

Karolyn was furious. She understood exactly what was happening. Safiya had organized this flash flare to distract law enforcement from Chocolate.

Karolyn's I! buzzed red. The Red Queen started to say something, but Karolyn interrupted, "Text me. I can't hear you over this flare."

The Red Queen texted, *"17 51-percenters on second floor of Low Down Food Co-op 1.5 blocks south on Waverly."*

Karolyn texted, *"Get me backup,"* and started running.

* * *

Sammy and Reese kept their guns trained on Juke, Haylee, and Diego. On the sidewalk nearby, Jackson watched the video Juke had snapped him.

Sure enough, just like Juke had said, it contained a confession from Billingsley—and a disgusting one at that. Even Jackson was grossed out. Kind of.

He decided he better tap Karolyn and ask what she wanted him to do. She picked up right away, but he couldn't hear her. There was singing, drumming, and shouting on her end. He yelled into his I!, above the noise: "Billingsley killed Talia! He confessed! You want me to jack Scarface, zap him, or let him go?"

Through the closed windows of the Dharma, Diego could hear every word Jackson was yelling. He went pale. Haylee sat there in shock that Jackson was so ready to kill an innocent man. Juke watched Sammy and Reese carefully, ready to draw his gun the second they made a mistake.

Meanwhile, on Waverly Street, Karolyn ducked into a doorway so she could hear better. She saw on her I! that Jackson was calling from only a minute and a half away. She needed backup immediately. That was way more important than Scarface now. She yelled into her I!, "Forget Scarface, we'll jack him later! I need you at the Low Down Co-op on Waverly immediately. Major seditious activity in progress!"

"What about O'Keefe and Navarro? I got them in custody too!" Jackson yelled.

"Just get over here—now!" Then Karolyn tapped off.

Jackson was seriously glitched. What would happen to all the ka-ching Karolyn and Billingsley had promised him for catching Scarface? She better pay up anyway. And when would he get to bust Juke?

Scruck it, he'd get his chance later. For now, Jackson pointed his gun downward at Juke's window and pulled the trigger. The bullet smashed open the window, then went through the floor of the car.

The oober stared at Jackson wide-eyed. Juke, Haylee, and Diego waited, not breathing, to see what Jackson would do next. He was just enough of a dick to shoot them all for the hell of it. Sammy and Reese kept their Hestons pointed at Juke, so he couldn't make a move for his gun.

Jackson leaned down and smiled at Juke. "I just did that so I wouldn't have to shout through the window."

Juke tightened his jaw and didn't speak. Jackson leaned in even closer. Juke could see the open pores on his nose. "I'll be back. Gonna jack you both for resisting arrest and aiding and abetting a fugitive." He winked at Haylee. "Sorry, vixen. Treat me real nice and maybe I'll go easy on ya."

Jackson straightened up and said to Sammy and Reese, "Let's roll."

The three cops swaggered back to the Shark and roared off.

Inside the Dharma, they all took a moment to breathe. Then Juke said to the oober, "Did I guess right about you being a sympathizer?"

The old man was too shaken to say more than one word. "Why?"

"'Cause there's a Rez action right now on Waverly—and if you drive us there real fast, we can help them."

The old man put his foot on the gas and they raced down Galt, following in the Shark's wake.

Haylee told Juke, "It sure is interesting being your partner."

"You'd rather have Jackson?"

Diego said, "Those Dincs are going to the co-op too. Are you okay shooting 'em? 'Cause I will if you won't."

Haylee felt in her pocket for her gun. "I'm fine with shooting 'em," she said.

* * *

Karolyn was standing in a doorway half a block from the co-op but hidden from the store windows when a car roared up. Three men were inside, and at first she thought they were Jackson and his guys; but they all wore suits and she recognized them as agents. Shit, one of them was that waste of neurons, Adams. On the other hand, she'd seen him kill somebody today, and she had a feel more killing would be necessary; so maybe he was the right man for this gig.

Before the agents even stepped out of the car, she told them, "We're going in the back. I'll give you orders on the way."

They started for the store—and the Shark roared up, with Jackson and his guys. Including herself, she now had seven agents and Dincs for this action. More than enough. Karolyn gave them all their orders, and they hurried toward the co-op.

* * *

Inside the break room on the second floor, everybody held up their I*!* chargers, ready to go. Bobby and Mychal were still getting it all on video.

Cheyenne said, "Okay, guys. Now you want to insert the magnetized end of your charger into your wound—not too deep. Wiggle it back and forth, gently. Just like you did on the bots." She demonstrated, inserting her I*!* charger into the bloody wound in Jeannie's arm. "Very soon you'll feel that little pull as your charger attracts the chip, and the chip attaches to it. Then bring the charger out gently, so the chip doesn't fall off."

Cheyenne felt the little pull inside Jeannie's arm, as the chip attached. A thrill went through her. She brought out the charger with the chip stuck to it, and held it aloft.

"Jeannie Bardach," she announced, "is now a free woman!"

Jeannie said, "*Oh my God!*"

"Okay, everybody get going," Cheyenne said.

All around the room, the fifty-one percenters got to work. One by one, they began succeeding. Cheyenne went from one person to the next, confirming they had de-chipped. There were shouts of elation everywhere.

But Safiya couldn't enjoy any of it. She kept listening for the sound of agents assaulting the co-op. She peeked out the back window of the break room—

Oh shit! The Agency woman was heading their way! With three other agents, all men, coming across the parking lot, guns out.

The last fifty-one percenter, a hot chocolate barista in his thirties, pulled his chip out and held it in the air. Everybody in the room started cheering.

But Safiya yelled, "Everyone shut up and listen!"

In the sudden silence that followed, she said, "The Agency is coming. Go out the front door. Make your way to the corner of Patriot and Houston. Cheyenne will put you in the cars and get you to Canada."

Cheyenne said, "But—"

Safiya looked out the back window. The agents were almost here. "Go!"

Then Safiya saw the woman agent aim her gun at the back door. She shot at the lock three times.

As soon as Safiya's people heard the gunshots, they didn't need any more convincing. They ran.

But she couldn't run with them. She needed to give them time to escape.

Except she didn't have a gun. She'd never carried one—*stupid*, she thought; she should have known she'd need one someday.

So she did the next best thing. She grabbed the bloody knives and stuffed them in her shopping bag. By the time the back door opened downstairs, she had sixteen. Standing behind the railing at the top of the stairs, she peered down at the door, one knife gripped tightly in her hand. Her heart hammered in her chest. She'd have to throw it as hard as she could and hope for the best.

The woman agent came through the door first. Safiya didn't hesitate. She hurled the knife with all her might—and her very first wild throw hit her target in the arm!

As the agent's blood gushed, she screamed and pulled back.

Safiya fired another knife through the open doorway, and another one, to keep the agents scared enough to hold back.

Meanwhile Cheyenne and the New York Seventeen ran to the front stairwell. They charged down the steps to the front door. But when they got there, they saw three Dincs through the glass door pane: Jackson, Sammy, and Reese.

"Open the door!" Jackson yelled, waving his gun.

Cheyenne drew away from the door, back toward the stairs.

Jackson shot the lock off and opened the door. People screamed. A few of the New York Seventeen ran into the main room downstairs, but most of them, including Cheyenne, raced back up toward the second floor.

Jackson started to give chase. Suddenly a voice behind him shouted, "Jackson, stop right there!"

Jackson turned. So did Sammy and Reese.

Juke came toward them, gun drawn. "Drop your weapon, Jackass! You guys too!"

Jackson laughed at him. "You gonna hit all three of us? Drop *your* weapon, asshole."

Juke said, "Look to both sides, Jackass."

Jackson looked. To his right was Haylee, gun out. To his left was Diego, gun out. They both aimed straight at him, looking like they were itching to shoot.

Standing next to Jackson, Sammy and Reese lost their nerve and dropped their Hestons.

Jackson snarled, "O'Keefe, you're going down for this."

"Drop it now. I'm in a hurry and I don't mind zapping you."

Jackson stared at Juke, hatred burning in his eyes, but he finally tossed his gun to the pavement.

Juke, Haylee, and Diego stepped up to the three Dincs. Juke said, "Now hit the ground."

As the Dincs lay down in the entryway, Juke told Haylee and Diego, "Cuff their ankles so they can't run and take their keys. Kill 'em if you have to."

Then Juke ran upstairs.

* * *

Safiya kept firing her sixteen knives at the back door, one after another. She threw them at intervals, every six or seven seconds; and she threw them any time the Agency woman showed her face or shoved her bleeding arm through the open door and shot at her.

Between throws, Safiya was able to grab more ammunition—the last three knives. But way too soon, she'd fired all nineteen. Ten second passed, and that was enough. The Agency woman must have felt it: no more knives.

She dashed through the back door and up the stairs, followed by the other three agents.

Safiya turned and ran. But it was dark inside the store, and when she charged into one of the food aisles she slammed into the barista, who was fleeing from Jackson in the other direction. They both stumbled and fell. Safiya jumped up—

—but the Agency woman ran up to her, gun aimed straight at her face. The woman's gun arm was dripping blood where it had been slashed by Safiya's knife.

"Hands in the air, bitch," she said. Behind her came the other agents.

* * *

Juke stepped around Jackson's prone body and stormed into the store, shouting, "Front door is clear! Everybody, come out the front!"

From the second floor came a burst of noise—footsteps pounding, things crashing to the ground. He dashed up the stairs. Suddenly the lights blazed on. Frightened people were everywhere, trying to hide in the aisles while the lights exposed them. There were two agents with guns, a third over by the light switch—

—and then he saw Safiya, coming toward him down the middle of the floor. The Agency woman walked right behind her, grabbing Safiya with one arm while her other, bloody arm pointed a Ruby Ridge at Safiya's head.

"Put down your weapon, O'Keefe," she said.

Juke stood there , unable to move. He'd seen this same scenario in so many movies and networld shows, but now that he was facing it in real life he had no idea what to do.

"Just shoot her," Safiya said.

"You'll die, you dumb bitch." The Agency woman twisted Safiya's arm harder.

"Fuck you!" Safiya said, then yelled to Juke, "Help these people escape!"

The Agency woman pressed her gun into Safiya's temple. "Put your weapon down, O'Keefe."

Juke started to lay his gun down.

Meanwhile, hidden behind the grain bins at the left side of the room, Jeannie Bardach quietly opened up her backpack. She moved her son's old frog puppet out of the way and found her .22 Joe Hill underneath.

Jeannie had never shot it before. She'd never shot anything before. But now seemed like a good time to start.

She pointed the tiny gun and aimed at the nearest agent—the one standing next to a sack of potatoes with a huge .45 in his hand. She fired.

The agent went down.

One aisle over, Karolyn wanted to throw Safiya aside and race toward the gunshot. But the sudden crack had interrupted Juke just before he put his weapon down. Now his gun was aimed straight at her and Safiya, freezing her in place.

Then more gunshots exploded behind her.

Another agent, his .38 Patton drawn, was running from the other end of the store, firing at where he thought Jeannie was. His shots hit a bag of rice and a big plastic jug of corn oil, busting it open and spilling oil at Jeannie's feet.

She fired back.

He spotted her now—and this time, he took careful aim.

But Bobby Morelli was crouching behind a fifty-pound bag of coffee at the end of the aisle, and during his years of living homefree he'd done plenty of streetfighting. Now he lunged at the agent, driving him to the ground. The agent's gun went off, and immediately blood poured from his stomach. He'd shot himself. He screamed and dropped his gun.

In the chaos, Safiya twisted free from Karolyn and started running. Meanwhile the agent by the light switch—Adams—dashed out the back door into the street and was gone.

Karolyn was furious. She would never allow herself to be defeated by this bunch of two-bit Resistance thugs. She had the entire power of the Agency behind her. She had the Red Queen. Who were these idiots to defy her?

She pointed her gun at Safiya, who was running down the aisle trying to escape. She fired.

But just at that moment, Safiya slipped on the puddle of spilled oil and fell to the floor. The bullet went over her head.

Karolyn aimed at Safiya again—

—just as Juke aimed at Karolyn and fired. Karolyn fell to the floor, clutching her chest.

What the fuck?! she thought.

Juke shouted, "Everybody, go! Now!"

As Safiya, Cheyenne, and the New York Seventeen all ran out the door, Karolyn lay there with her hands to her chest. *Another suit ruined,* she thought. Her I*!* buzzed. She managed to take it out of her pocket and saw the red light indicating it was the Red Queen.

But Karolyn didn't have the strength to tap the screen. She dropped the I*!* on the floor, and her eyes closed.

* * *

The streets of the Lower East Side were packed with thousands of flarers, Dincs, Syncs, Fincs, agents, and just plain regular people returning home from bars and late movies. The Red Queen and the cops tried to sort out the chaos—but people kept pouring in by the second, dancing and drumming on every street corner. Safiya, Cheyenne, and the New York Seventeen, walking in groups of two or three, covered their features with hoodies, hats, and anti-pollution masks. By 12:30, they were all able to converge on the corner of Patriot and Houston.

Safiya directed everybody to the stolen cars. Since they couldn't use the Qilin, all nineteen of them would have to squeeze into just three vehicles; but it was doable, barely, since one of them was an SUV and one was a minivan.

Safiya supervised as Cheyenne and the New York Seventeen began piling into the vehicles. Then she looked up—and Juke, Haylee, and Diego were hurrying up the street toward her.

Safiya assumed Diego wanted to come with them to Canada. But what would Juke and his partner do?

She looked at Juke and felt unable to breathe all of a sudden. Would this be the last time she ever saw him?

She said, "Hi, Juke."

Juke looked back at her for a moment. Then he said, "We can ride in the trunks."

She'd been holding her breath so tightly she gasped. She felt warmth spreading all through her.

But she needed to stay focused. She turned to Haylee. "You're coming too?"

Haylee nodded. "We've kind of burned our bridges."

Safiya looked back at the vehicles, counting up the available spaces. "There's no trunk in the minivan."

Diego said, "Haylee and I can share a trunk. We're smaller than Juke."

Three minutes later everybody was in the vehicles, heading for Canada. They took back roads and agreed that if any law enforcement people pulled them over, they'd say they were on their way to an eleven-step meeting.

For ten hours nobody stopped them, until they made it to the electronic fence one hundred miles south of the Canadian border. This was the big test. What if something went wrong with Cheyenne's bio-alarm calculations? It would be unbearable to come this close to freedom and be captured here.

But they drove on through and the hundred miles piled up, one by one. They made it through the forests of northern New York without any syndie cops swooping down on them, and reached the border at last.

Freedom lay just ahead.

Several Canadian police officers stood guard at the border, wearing bulletproof vests and carrying weapons. "What's your business in Canada?" asked the lead officer, grim-faced.

"We're claiming asylum," Safiya said. "I'm transporting a group of fifty-one percenters escaping to Canada."

The officer's eyes narrowed. "Bullshit, those people never escape."

"We did this time," Jeannie Bardach said. She lifted her jacket sleeve to reveal her bandaged wrist. The others followed suit, showing the bandages where their chips had been removed.

The officers opened the gates, and the three vehicles drove onto Canadian soil. Jeannie, Bobby, Diane, Mychal, and all the others got out. The grim-faced guard, whose cousin was a fifty-one percenter down in Texas, began to weep.

The New York Seventeen kissed the cold ground and breathed in freedom at last.

Juke and Safiya stood in the background, watching. They looked up at the sky and saw something they hadn't seen in years.

The moon and stars were shining down.

They grabbed each other's hands at exactly the same moment.

VI

PART SIX

CANADA
THREE DAYS LATER

Chapter Sixty-Seven

9:15 am

Everyone

In a hotel room in downtown Toronto, Juke and Safiya lay in bed and watched the revolution—at least they hoped that's what it was, it sure felt like it!—playing out in networld, on their hotel room walls.

What an amazing three days it had been.

During the first fifteen hours, Haylee and the others put together a video and blasted it out to networld. The video had everything: Talia's murder, featuring Billingsley's dramatic confession; Bobby and Mychal's de-chipping footage, showing how easy it was; shots of the New York Seventeen in Canada, exulting in their newfound liberty; and Safiya delivering the passionate speech she'd been rehearsing in her mind for so long. "Today all the millions of slaves can break their chains and be free," she proclaimed, raising her arms high. "This is the beginning of the next American revolution!"

In the fifty hours since the video came out, it had received *five billion hits.*

Fifty-one percenters all across the country were freeing themselves and heading north or going underground. New flares were breaking out every day in hundreds of cities and small towns. Thirty and forty percenters everywhere were breaking their links and refusing to pay their P to the syndicates. From New York to L.A., Dincs were saying they would no longer jack people for nonpayment.

Right now, in Juke and Safiya's hotel room, the wall was showing scenes from a flare in Ogallala, Nebraska, of all places. The Ogallala cops had just released over six hundred nonviolent economic offenders from the city jail. The downtown was full of people drumming, singing, and hugging—and they'd been joined by the fifty-year-old chief of police and the seventy-year-old mayor.

Lying in bed, Juke watched the celebration and smiled.

He'd felt such a lightness these past three days. Maybe it was just from being with Safiya. But it seemed like there was a huge weight missing, that had been on his shoulders for so long he'd almost forgotten how much it hurt.

He could never fix the terrible mistake he'd made three years ago.

But maybe he deserved to be happy anyway.

He looked over at Safiya. She was watching the Ogallala flare too. But she was thinking about Talia and Rey, who hadn't lived to see this day, and a tear rolled down her cheek.

Juke put his arm around her. "I can't believe you pulled this off, Safiya."

"Well, I got a little help."

She kissed him fiercely, and they melted into each other's arms, just the way they remembered.

* * *

In the waiting room of a nearby doctor's office, Haylee sat with Diego. They had talked a lot during their many hours riding up to Canada in the trunk of a car. He was still recovering from Talia's death, and she was recovering from Harrison's, so they weren't getting romantic or anything…

But it sure was nice to have a friend as she went through her pregnancy.

The other good thing was, she didn't have to worry about paying for her baby anymore. In Canada, genetic enhancements were covered by the health care system.

Not only that, she had already heard from ten or twelve hot-shot Vancouver producers who wanted to turn the story of Talia's murder and Chocolate into a movie. Three of them were even flying into Toronto to meet her. It was looking like Haylee would get into the movie bizness after all. Haylee Navarro, star of the Resistance!

Haylee started to laugh.

"What's funny?" Diego said.

She didn't answer, just kept laughing, and Diego began laughing too.

It was the first time he'd laughed since Talia died.

* * *

Karolyn sat up straight in her hospital bed and smoothed her freshly washed hair. "I was honored to risk my life to preserve our freedoms. Make no mistake: we will defeat these violent radicals who attack innocent people and attempt to destroy our American way of life."

"Cut!" Raja said, as the Agency cameraman put down his I*!* "Nice job, Karolyn."

Raja and the cameraman spent a few minutes getting wide shots of Karolyn in her hospital bed, and then left. She lay back, gave herself another shot of morphine even though the pain in her chest was pretty close to gone, and smiled.

She hadn't been fired after all, like she'd expected, or reassigned to some faraway outpost where her career would wither and die. She was pretty sure Raja had pushed for that. But the Red Queen advised the National Director of the Agency that Karolyn would be a valuable spokesperson. She was the perfect national symbol: a poor girl from the rural South who embodied everything that was good about the syndicate system. Instead of making her a scapegoat, the Agency should make her a hero.

Karolyn felt herself drifting off in a lazy morphine cloud, dreaming about running the New York Division one day. But then a question she'd been meaning to ask rose up out of the haze. She reached for her I*!* and buzzed the Red Queen.

"Good afternoon, Karolyn. I trust you're feeling comfortable?"

Karolyn raised herself up on one elbow. "Do you think the Resistance will actually win? Will there be a revolution?"

The Red Queen analyzed this question. There were so many diverse factors to consider: money, power, fear, love, humanity's desire for freedom… When you put it all together, who would finally come out on top: the syndicates or the people?

"So what's your prediction?" Karolyn asked impatiently.

The Red Queen thought about it for a while longer, then finally gave up.

"I'd say it's fifty-fifty," said the Red Queen.

A Note from the Author

Several years ago, I went to see a talk by the TV network executive David Nevins, who said something that really struck me. According to Nevins, the best TV shows are the ones that speak to people's deepest fears.

As I walked home that night, I thought: what are my deepest fears? The very next morning, I began to write *51%*. The novel addresses my mounting alarm about privatization, the rise of billionaires and huge corporations, and the unraveling of our federal government. I used to think the world described in *51%* was thirty years away; now I think it's only twenty years.

Fortunately, that's enough time for us to save our country and our democracy as we know it. I see the message of *51%* as one of hope: people of goodwill, working together, can indeed make a difference. In every generation, some dangerous force has arisen to threaten us, and so far, every time, we've met the challenge.

Acknowledgments

Many thanks to everyone who helped me write this book, especially my beloved writing group The Oxnardians, starring Jonathan Beggs, may he rest in peace, Craig Buck, Linda Burrows, Jamie Diamond, Harley Jane Kozak, Bonnie MacBird, Andrew Rubin, Bob Shayne, and Patricia Smiley. Other writers who gave me valuable advice and encouragement are Philip de Blasi, John Henry Davis, William Fowler, Danny Greenspan, Alia Little, Byron Willinger, and my sons Jacob and Zack Witten.

I'm also grateful to my agent Josh Getzler, who has always believed in this novel, and Shawn Reilly Simmons, Deb Well, and everyone else at Level Best. It's been a joy working with these folks.

Thank you also to my TV/movie agent Paul Weitzman, Amanda Morgan Palmer and Rachel Slane at Madison Wells Media, Rob Golenberg, and my co-writer, Charlie Craig, for joining me in selling *51%* as a TV series. I have no idea what will happen, but I'm enjoying the ride.

Finally and most importantly, thank you to Nancy Seid, who is not only a great wife and girlfriend, but also a darn fierce editor.

About the Author

Matt Witten is a TV writer, novelist, playwright, and screenwriter who has written for many TV shows, including *House, Pretty Little Liars, Law & Order,* and *CSI: Miami.* His thriller *The Necklace* is an Amazon Editors' pick and has been published in seven languages and optioned for film by Leonardo DiCaprio. His novel *Killer Story* won a Foreword Indie award for best mystery. Matt wrote four amateur sleuth novels, including the Malice Domestic Award-winning *Breakfast at Madeline's,* and has been nominated for two Edgars and an Emmy.

AUTHOR WEBSITE:
  mattwittenwriter.com

SOCIAL MEDIA HANDLES:
  https://www.goodreads.com/author/show/206833.Matt_Witten
  https://www.instagram.com/mattwitten22/
  https://www.threads.net/@mattwitten22
  https://x.com/MattZWitten
  https://www.facebook.com/wittenmatt

https://www.linkedin.com/in/matt-witten-a83125186/
https://bsky.app/profile/mattwitten.bsky.social

Also by Matt Witten

Killer Story

The Necklace

The Killing Bee

Strange Bedfellows

Grand Delusion

Breakfast at Madeline's

www.ingramcontent.com/pod-product-compliance
Lightning Source LLC
Chambersburg PA
CBHW060516160726
47991CB00001B/56